THE OTHER OLIVIA

TAMARA M BAILEY

Improbable
PRESS

First published by Improbable Press in 2022

Improbable Press is an imprint of:
Clan Destine Press
www.clandestinepress.com.au
PO Box 121, Bittern Victoria 3918 Australia

National Library of Australia Cataloguing-In-Publication data:

Tamara M Bailey
The Other Olivia

978-0-645316-74-2 (pb)
978-1-922904-00-3 (eb)

Cover artwork by © Willsin Rowe
Layout & Typesetting by Dimitra Stathopoulos

Improbable Press
improbablepress.com

To Chris

Prologue

"Wait, let me zoom out—"

A blur of color, and the footage clears to show a young woman standing against a bright sky. Her hair is in a tufty black ponytail and her eyes are hidden by stylish sunglasses. A tattoo peeks out from beneath her board shorts, green on her dark brown skin. She shakes loose her limbs, and there's a flash of another tattoo on her shoulder blade beneath her bikini strap.

"How high did you say this was?" says the voice behind the camera, and the footage swivels down to show the long drop into the gorge. "Fuck me, look at that."

A thin waterfall gushes nearby. The forest around them is vivid green, the river below sapphire blue.

"Mmm, I've forgotten," says the limber woman. "Eighty feet? C'mon, let's do this. Got that phone ready?"

"It's ready," says the camera voice. The footage turns back to the woman, who already has her heels on the edge of the cliff, facing away from the drop. "Oh shit, Liv, your sunnies!"

Liv cackles and tosses her sunglasses to the ground. "That would've been disastrous."

"You know it doesn't count unless you do a flip, ay."

"Yeah, yeah," says Liv, who bounces a few times on the balls of her feet. "We gonna live forever, Kass?"

"We gonna live forever, Livvie."

And then, without a moment of fear or breath of hesitation, Olivia Sharp somersaults backwards off the cliff, plummeting to the waiting river below.

OUTSIDE

1

The mannequins looked like birdcages. They were made from golden wire, no limbs, no head – just shoulders and breasts and tapered waists. Olivia hardly noticed the delicate lingerie they sported. All she saw were the prisons.

"Not a lot of range for a fancy shmancy shop, ay?" Kass said, her thongs slapping on expensive tiles.

Olivia tore her exhausted gaze from the mannequins. "These are only a few samples. You're supposed to choose your own design. That's the point of 'custom-made.'"

"Just get your shit from Kmart like everyone else."

"I wanted something special."

"You didn't ask me here to help you choose undies, did you?" Kass said, scrunching up her nose. "No offense, but I have better things to do with my Saturday than picture you and Matt getting hot and heavy."

"No…no, I have to talk to you about something. Something important."

"You're not preggers?"

"No, I–"

Clarice, the designer, stuck her head around the curtain from the sewing room. "Just finishing up here, Mrs Alexan – oh." Her gaze fell on Kass, taking in the cut-off denim shorts, the tattoos against her suntanned skin, the skull-and-crossbones kerchief around her copper ponytail.

"This is my friend Kassandra," Olivia said.

"Sup," Kass said.

"Welcome, Kassandra." To Olivia, Clarice said, "I'll be a few more minutes."

"Thank you."

Clarice bustled behind the curtain again. She had handled Kass' appearance better than most people in Olivia's world. Olivia, at least, kept her tattoos hidden.

"So? News. Spill." Kass seemed crabby.

Olivia thumbed her wedding band and looked around the hushed shop, frightened to say the words out loud. Saying them would make them real, and she didn't want reality. Reality hurt.

The bell above the door tinkled as another woman walked in. "Sorry, babe, it took forever to find a park."

Kass' bad mood disappeared as she wrapped an arm around the woman's waist. Both of them were about the same height – as in, regular-sized. Olivia towered a head above them.

"Liv, you remember Bri?"

Olivia tried to smile. She vaguely recalled a mutual friend's wedding four months ago, where Kass and Briony had locked eyes over the cake and decided they were going home together. She hadn't realized they were still seeing each other.

Briony was in an olive-green pantsuit, vibrant against her pale complexion. She might've looked professional if not for the row of studs lining her ears and the tattoos peeking out beneath the collar. Her blonde hair was growing out from a pixie cut and had roots of dark brown.

"You all right?" she said in her lilting Yorkshire accent. She peered at Olivia, concerned. "You look a little peaky."

"Um, actually, I was hoping to speak to Kass in private for a second. If you don't mind."

"It's all good," Kass said. "Bri's my soulmate. Whatever you say to me will automatically filter to her anyway."

The pair grinned at each other. But when Kass turned back to Olivia, she pursed her lips, like a warning. What was going on with her today?

Olivia tried again. "It's sort of personal."

"Say no more." Briony held up her hands. "I'll wait outside."

"Don't bother." To Olivia, Kass said, "Selfish, much?

"I'm sorry?"

"I'm not going to come running at your beck and call just so you can shun my girlfriend."

"Er…" Briony said, at the same time Olivia said, *"What?"*

"You know the last time you texted me, Livvie?" Kass said. "Before Ginger's wedding. That was June. June! You can't be bothered with me unless it has something to do with *you.*"

"That's not true."

"It sure is. I gave up on you a long time ago, and you didn't even notice. You cut me out of your life after you married Matt, ay. I barely recognize you anymore. Your hair, your outfit."

Olivia's clothes were chosen by a personal stylist, her hair a freshly-colored double shot espresso with a foam melt. It sat in gentle curls around her face and tumbled down her back. She had never been prouder of it.

"I'm sorry," she said. "I didn't mean to cut you out. I've been busy–"

"Doing what? You don't even have a job."

Olivia flushed. "Matt said after the accident I didn't need to–"

"The accident was years ago. You're fine, get over it. Go talk to Starfish Steve and get your skydiving gig back. Take another trip to Machu Picchu. Hack off that fuckin' hair. As long as you do something to make you *you* again."

"Just because I've changed, doesn't mean it's not me."

"Maybe," Kass said. "But the Liv standing in front of me isn't my friend. And I don't want to deal with her shit anymore. Come on, Bri."

Olivia dug her manicured nails into her palms as Kass pulled Briony towards the door. It occurred to her that if Kass left, there would be no one else to tell. She could call her mum, but she didn't want to go down that road. Kass was – and always had been – the one Olivia confided in. The one she'd traveled half the world with, the one who cleaned up her vomit when she'd drunk half a bottle of tequila, the one who burnt her first boyfriend's love poems after he dumped her for being too independent.

She hadn't realized how hurt Kass had been by their estrangement. She should've made more of an effort. She should've noticed something was wrong as soon as Kass walked into the shop.

"Kass," she said as the bell tinkled over the door, "Matt's having an affair."

The words were blades, piercing Olivia's heart. They hurt more than the worst day of physical therapy. No, that was a lie.

But this wasn't: *Her husband was having an affair.*

A knot of disbelief had lingered in her stomach since last night. She was in a daze, a nightmare. This sort of thing happened in books and movies, or to people who already knew deep down their partner was scum. Amelie from the High Ts club complained endlessly about her husband Pete hitting on every woman in visual range. A few of the High Ts ladies were taking bets on when she might discover some lewd affair of his. No one would've even considered it happening to Olivia.

Kass paused by the door before turning back. "I'll kill him."

"You sure?" Briony said to Olivia. Her gray eyes were creased with concern.

"I overheard him talking to her on the phone last night." Olivia's breath caught, as if her body were reliving the moment. "I couldn't believe it, so I went into his emails while he was asleep and there were so many messages between them, going back at least six months… I spent all night reading about how much he loved her, how he couldn't wait to see her again, couldn't wait to get away from me–"

"I'll literally kill him."

"Are you going to confront him about it?" Briony said.

"I don't think so."

"Why the hell not?" Kass demanded.

"Thank you, Mrs Winning." Clarice stepped out from behind the curtain with her previous customer. "I'll be right with you, Mrs Alexander."

Olivia lifted her hand in acknowledgement, then dropped her voice as she said to Kass, "I don't want to throw away the last seven years. I can fix this."

"You don't need to fix it. Leave him."

"It's not that simple."

"Yes it is!"

"I just need to be more…more. I just need to be more."

Kass' jaw fell open.

"I need to put the effort in," Olivia said, gesturing to the mannequins. "Buy sexy lingerie, book romantic holidays, you know, remind him why he loves me. Then he'll forget all about Sarina."

A funny expression flickered across Briony's face. She looked surprised, as if the name meant something to her.

Before Olivia could ask, Kass said, "Have some self respect, ay. You can't give him any more than you already have. You changed your entire personality to suit him, and he still screwed you over."

Olivia's next words collapsed on her tongue. Kass scowled and shoved open the door. The bell jangled angrily as she stormed out. Briony shot Olivia a sympathetic glance before hurrying after her, leaving Olivia alone with the birdcages.

2

Wear something sexy underneath, okay?

Olivia kept hearing the words in her head, and Matt's low, warm chuckle as he said them. She hadn't even realized something was wrong with her marriage. And yet the more she thought about it, the more stunned she was that she had been so remiss. His late nights at the office. The increasing number of business trips. He went to the gym more, and had even changed the password on his phone. Anyone else would've laughed at her naivety, but how could she have believed her husband – doting, dependable Matt – was capable of such lies?

And that wasn't the only thing he was capable of. Matt's emails to Sarina consisted of dirty talk, pictures, sexy memories of their time together. Matt, who was as vanilla as they came, who Olivia could never envisage asking for shots of her tits, was doing just that with another woman.

Wear something sexy underneath, okay?

Olivia shuddered as the car pulled up outside her apartment block.

"Everything all right, Mrs Alexander?" said Leith.

"Everything's perfect. Thank you."

Leith held the door open for her, and she headed for the building. After she'd expressed her discomfort with driving, Matt had insisted on employing someone to do it for her. He was so attentive to her needs.

Had been.

No – still was. That was the problem. For the past half year, he'd been acting like the same old Matt. How could he look her in the eye and *lie* to her?

"Olivia Sharp?"

She turned. A caveman of a man approached. She appreciated the occasional manicured beard, but this guy clearly didn't own a pair of clippers.

"Er...hello?" she said.

He knew her maiden name. Was he someone from her traveling days? His scraggly hair was auburn, his skin the sun-soaked brown of an outdoorsman – just like hers used to be. A faint smell of alcohol drifted from his rumpled clothes. If he was someone from her past, she certainly didn't recognize him now.

"We need to talk," he said, voice low and urgent.

"Do I know you?"

"Equinoxx is about to ask you to sign something. You *can't sign it.*"

"The tech company?"

"It's a long story. I can explain, but not here." He glanced around. "They might already be watching you."

"O...kay..." Olivia's assessment of the man had escalated from 'alcoholic' to 'paranoid meth head.' "Sorry, how do you know my name?"

She would have to up the privacy settings on her social media.

"Listen." He advanced, and she stumbled backwards. "You can't sign that contract. Eidolon–"

"Oi!" Leith climbed back out of the car. "What are you doing?" He was five foot seven to this man's six foot six, but he was barrel chested, and moved aggressively.

The caveman swore under his breath. He slouched away, keeping his head down as if he didn't want to be noticed. Tough luck, at that height.

"Are you all right?" Leith said, joining Olivia.

She pressed a hand over her thrumming heart. "I think so."

They watched the man disappear up the tree-lined street, away from the riverfront.

"What did he say to you?"

"Nothing that made any sense. I think he was drunk. Or high."

"I should call the cops."

"That's not necessary."

Even so, Leith insisted on walking Olivia into the building. It was only when she swiped her phone for elevator access that he headed back to park the car in the garage.

As the doors slid closed, her distress from her encounter turned to distress for her impending confrontation with Matt. What was she going to say to him? They hadn't spoken this morning. Olivia had dragged herself to one of the guest bedrooms at five a.m. and slept until late. After spending the night reading those emails, she hadn't wanted to face her husband. Matt had gone to his rowing club brunch by the time she'd gotten up.

Her body was shaking as the elevator reached her apartment. She stepped into the open space. The marble tiles gleamed and the entrance table vase had a fresh, pungent bouquet – the housekeeper must've come while she was out.

She dropped her handbag in its drawer and wandered through, both dreading the moment when she'd come across Matt and wishing it would happen already. Every room she checked, her emotions swung. When she stuck her head into his empty office, she was angry, certain she would scream when she saw him. The theater brought her to near tears. The wide balcony, with its firepit and outdoor lounge suite, returned her to the determination she'd felt when talking to Kass. She'd try to be a better wife. She could do that, couldn't she?

She slid open the balcony door to listen for sounds of splashing from the plunge pool above. It was warm enough for Matt to be swimming.

But the pool was silent, as were the lower floors of the apartment.

What would happen if she actually confronted him? If she told him she'd read the emails, what would he do?

Confess he loved Sarina, probably. Ask for a separation. Olivia would have to move out of this beautiful place and go…where?

Her parents were in a camper van across the country. When they returned to Perth, they either house sat or rented for a month or two before hitting the road again. They were no safety net.

As for her friends… Asking help from Kass was clearly out of the question. There were the High Ts, but Olivia couldn't bring herself to beg accommodation with them. Having to face the wives and girlfriends of Matt's friends while her marriage fell into shambles…no. It would be humiliating. They were judgmental enough as it was.

So who did that leave? Who, in the past few years, had Olivia considered a friend?

No one.

She had turned to Matt with her problems She'd trusted his embrace, his self-assured voice, his comforting presence. Why had she needed anyone else?

She stared beyond Swan River to thick plumes of smoke billowing from bushfires a couple dozen kilometers outside Perth. It wasn't possible for her to stay here if they separated. Matt had bought the apartment as a wedding gift. They'd returned from their honeymoon, and instead of going back to his house in Peppermint Grove, he'd taken her here and told her it was theirs.

She couldn't bear the thought of living in this apartment day after day, knowing what it had cost her. And honestly, the place would go to waste. She didn't use most of the rooms She didn't swim in the pool, or go too far onto the balcony. Looking down at the road still made her feel ill.

But at the time, she'd been so delighted by the surprise that he hadn't had a chance to open the champagne before she'd pressed him against the pristine kitchen counter and unbuckled his belt. It was all for her, he'd said. He would provide her with whatever she desired, whatever made her happy. She'd felt like the luckiest person in the world that night. The sex had been incredible. They'd had sex again later, in the middle of the night, and then again during their morning shower. Matt had been an hour late for work. He'd said it was worth it.

Eventually, the sex dwindled to a few times a month. And, for the past year, it had been barely existent. Olivia hadn't been paying attention. She'd had social functions, beautician appointments, classes on various artsy activities. Occasionally, after a drunken night out, she'd try to seduce him as she slipped into bed, but he was always tired. He got up early. Green smoothies and meditation were part of his morning routine now. He didn't want to lose out on his required eight hours of sleep.

They had begun living separate lives. She should've been paying more attention. At least tried to join him during his morning jogs. The idea of getting out of bed that early had never appealed to her. Not when she could be lounging beneath the goose-down doona, waiting for the housekeeper to arrive and make her breakfast and mimosas.

And now he'd found someone else.

She closed the balcony door as the elevator slid open. Matt stepped inside, whistling. He saw her and smiled. "Hi, babe."

His face was angular, his black hair well past his ears, his fingers long and tapered and perfect for playing the piano…or her. She was used to seeing him in suits, so there was something delectable about him in his nice button-up top and casual pants.

"Hi," she said, breathless. "Where – where have you been?"

He tossed his keys into the drawer. "Had a few drinks with the boys. Where did you go this morning? You weren't in bed when I woke up."

So calm. So casual.

But then, he'd been that way for the past six months. He'd joked and laughed and said that he loved her for more than half a year. And all that time he'd been seeing someone behind her back.

Who was this person? This stranger who'd taken over her husband? Where was Matt, *her* Matt?

"Is everything all right?" He came over and tucked her hair behind her ear. "You look pale. Are you getting sick?"

There was a faint streak of makeup on his collar.

Those long fingers, had they just been playing Sarina? Had he been screwing some other woman while Olivia was getting fitted for custom lingerie to please him?

Bile burned her throat. She didn't want him touching her. She didn't want him anywhere near her.

Her phone buzzed in her pocket and she broke free gratefully. "I'm fine," she said, checking the message.

Hi, it's Briony. I'm so sorry about your husband. I know this is out of the blue, but can we meet up? Just you and me? I want to ask you something.

Olivia remembered the way Briony's expression changed when she heard Sarina's name. Did she have information about the affair? Did she know Sarina?

"Olivia?" Matt said, but Olivia was already heading for the elevator.

"Sorry," she muttered, texting Briony back. "I have somewhere to be."

To: jacobpwilcox@equinoxxtechnology.co
From: retrievalunit@basenxj451.com
Subject: Retrieval update

LEVEL FIVE CITIZEN (ARGENTINA POINT) SUCCESSFULLY
RETRIEVED
PREPARING FOR TRANSPORTATION TO AUSTRALIAN
BASE

EIDOLON

3

"Mummy, where's Daddy?"

Liv glanced at Bobbi, who was playing with a bead maze given to her by one of the policewomen. Even though Liv had tied Bobbi's hair up before leaving, black curls had escaped and bounced over her eyes.

"Mummy." Bobbi didn't look up from her game. "Mummy, when is Daddy home?"

A bubble of hurt sat in Liv's chest. "Soon, baby. Real soon." She returned her attention to the police officer. "Sorry, what was the question?"

She hadn't caught his name, and honestly, she didn't care. All that mattered was whether he could help her.

"Has your husband done anything like this before?" he said. Her phone was on the desk between them, open to a photo of Reef. "Left for a few days, maybe to cool down, maybe after a disagreement?" As he talked, he typed up the information from the missing persons report she'd completed at the front counter.

"No. And we're not married."

"You've written here that you last saw him two days ago. What took you so long to come to the police?"

"He said he would be back. He didn't explain where he was going – he just walked out with a bag."

"He said he would be back?"

"Yes, but…" Liv slid her phone off the desk and checked for new notifications. She hadn't let go of it since Reef disappeared. "Something was wrong. A man visited the house the day before he left."

"Who was the man?"

"An old friend, apparently."

"Did you catch his name?"

Liv shook her head. "He asked Reef to go with him – there was something he had to see. When Reef got back, he looked…different."

"What do you mean by that?"

Liv pictured Reef's expression. The bloodless complexion, the wide, dilated eyes. The way his hands shook as he poured himself a large glass of bourbon and downed it, gulp after gulp. Scared wasn't the right word.

"Haunted," Liv murmured. "He looked like ghosts were after him."

The officer lifted his eyebrows but continued typing. Liv stared at a crumb caught in the corner of his wispy moustache.

What had that stranger shown Reef to change him so dramatically?

"He's not answering my texts, and his phone's going straight to voicemail. I didn't know what else to do."

"You hadn't had a fight?"

"No, nothing like that."

In fact, the morning of Reef's disappearance, Kazzy had taken Bobbi to the zoo and Liv and Reef had seized their alone time to have raw, passionate sex. Afterwards, they'd sat naked in bed, finishing off the lemon gelato and talking about a potential fishing trip next weekend. Reef's brown eyes had sparkled with excitement at the idea of carving a little rod for Bobbi so she could pretend to fish, too.

"You haven't filled out his social media accounts."

Liv dragged her attention back to the officer, who was frowning at the report. "He doesn't have any."

"Strange for a guy in his thirties. Does he at least have the Ping Pals app?"

"He doesn't have a smart phone. Just one of those old ones."

"A burner phone?"

"Yes."

"Your man likes to live off the grid."

"I guess he's old-fashioned."

The officer grimaced. The crumb in his moustache quivered but didn't fall. "What about his friends and family? I notice you've left that part blank, too."

"Mummy, look. Look, Mummy. Boo." Bobbi was sliding a blue bead along the wire. "Boo."

"I see it, baby."

"Mummy, boo."

"Yes, it's blue. Very clever."

Bobbi beamed.

To the officer, Liv said, "I've contacted all our friends and they haven't seen him. His parents…I don't know. He doesn't talk about them."

"And you haven't filled out his banking details. Would I be correct in saying he doesn't have any?"

"He doesn't, no."

"Uh huh."

"It's easier – he's a handyman, he gets paid in cash…"

Liv trailed off. Was she was supposed to be telling the police this? Reef paid for everything – groceries, stuff for Bobbi – in cash, and she handled the online bills. Maybe he wasn't claiming all his income or something. Was she getting him into trouble by coming here?

The officer opened another window and typed something in. "Reef Davidson isn't coming up on the system." He typed something else. "Any system. Not even a driver's license. Does he have a car for his business?"

"We share one. He – uh – he took it with him when he left."

The officer lifted his eyebrow.

Liv shifted in her chair. "It's a 2004 Hilux. White, four-wheel drive. There's not many of them still around, right?"

"He didn't take the StarShine offer?"

"He likes to work with his hands. He wanted a car he could service himself."

The officer tsked. "It's not good for the environment."

"But it'll make it easy to find, won't it? If there aren't many left."

"On the contrary, without a GPS there's no way for us to track it." The officer opened a new window on his computer. "Is it under his name?"

"Yes. I mean…it's not under mine, so it must be in his. He uses it mostly for work."

"What's the registration number?" After Liv gave it to him, he said, "How have you been getting around without a car?"

"A friend has been staying with me. She lets me use hers."

"Good, good." The officer peered at his screen for a moment. His shoulders were stiffer than before.

Liv's mouth was dry. "Is it on the system?"

He swiveled his chair to face her fully and clasped his hands on the desk. "I'm afraid not."

She clenched her teeth against a growing headache.

"Miss Sharp, I need to know something about your partner. Anything. Where was he born? Where did he grow up? Where did he go to school? What was his childhood like? What were his parents like? Has he ever broken an arm, been to hospital? Has he ever travelled overseas?"

"I–"

She didn't know. She had never known those things. His past jobs were the only thing he talked about, but those weren't relevant – or welcome – at a police station.

Her fingertips were intimately familiar with every freckle on his tanned shoulders. He could build and fix basically anything. He had to use a calculator for his times tables. He kept his beard close-shaven by trimming it once a week, and always remembered to put the bins out on Sundays. Bobbi adored him, and he would do anything for her.

Liv knew the things about Reef that mattered. In their quiet moments together, they talked about the present, not the past. Reef was her anchor. When she was with him, the world felt solid and tactile and *real*.

He had mentioned his childhood two and a half years ago, in the hospital, while Liv had been nursing Bobbi mere hours after the birth. Reef had stroked Liv's hair and told her in a cracked, exhausted voice, that his parents hadn't been the type to bother with things like government records and official schooling. His own birth hadn't been registered, and it would make things complicated if his name was on Bobbi's birth certificate. So she had left the spot under FATHER blank. She hadn't realized he wasn't in the system at all.

She was curious to know more about him, of course she was, but it was a sore spot and she didn't like to hurt him by asking about it. Up until now, it hadn't been a pressing issue.

"Okay." The officer's voice was quiet. "We have to discuss the possibility that your partner isn't who he says he is."

The bubble of hurt swelled until it encompassed Liv's lungs and throat and stomach. "I know what it sounds like, but you have to believe that he would never, ever abandon us."

"How long have you been together?"

"Three-ish years."

"And how did you meet?"

"We—" Liv glanced at Bobbi. "It was a one-night stand. When I told him I was pregnant, he came around to help out a lot. We weren't exactly together at first. It just sort of…happened."

That was the briefest version. She figured the officer didn't need to know the whole story.

"So, all right, Reef's done the right thing by you," he said. "But what if this 'old friend' brought up something from his past? Something bad?"

"Mummy, cuddle?" Bobbi trotted over. Liv lifted her onto her lap and was overwhelmed with the smell of Play Doh and mango shampoo. Like Reef, Bobbi had a way of mooring Liv when she felt like she was drifting away.

"Tell me about the visitor," the officer said. Bobbi took Liv's sunglasses from the top of her head and put them on herself. "What did he look like? What kind of car did he drive?"

Bobbi stared around the room through the sunglasses.

"It was a StarShine. Sedan. Dark-colored. The man was in his sixties. He looked a bit like my dad – South Asian, maybe Indian or Sri Lankan. Short black hair with streaks of gray at the sides. He wore glasses and a suit. I didn't think Reef knew anyone who owned a suit."

A half-laugh, half-sob escaped her. Why hadn't she pressed Reef for the stranger's name? Why hadn't she tried harder to find out what was wrong? She had nothing of use to give the officer.

And he had nothing to give in return. All that time agonizing over whether to go to the police, and they didn't even know Reef existed. She thought again of him gulping down the bourbon.

Coming here had been a mistake. There wasn't time for bureaucracy. Every minute she spent filling out forms trying to prove Reef's existence was a minute wasted.

"Mummy," said Bobbi. "Hungry."

"Okay, baby." Liv gathered up her backpack with Bobbi's things in one hand, hefting Bobbi onto her hip with the other. "Thanks anyway," she said to the officer.

He rubbed his mouth, finally dislodging the crumb from his moustache. It dropped onto his collar and vanished. One moment it was there against the blue fabric, the next it was gone. Erased from existence.

Liv's grip on Bobbi tightened.

"Miss Sharp, I don't think you should leave. There are some serious questions we need to—"

"I can handle it."

"If you send through that picture of Reef—"

"I made it up."

20

"Excuse me?"

"There is no Reef Davidson." She grabbed the report from the desk. "It was a joke."

"I hardly think–"

"Sorry for wasting your time." Liv bustled out the office door with Bobbi and the backpack, shredding the report.

The officer called after her.

"Bye bye," said Bobbi, waving behind them.

Liv headed through the main area of the local station and shoved open the door with her shoulder. She moved fast, in case anyone tried to stop her.

If Reef had never fixed what his parents had done, if he had never put himself into the system, then she wasn't going to screw that up for him.

But he *was* in some sort of trouble. And since the police couldn't help, she would damn well get him out of it herself.

OUTSIDE

4

Briony folded and unfolded her linen napkin. No need to be nervous. This meeting had only taken four months to arrange. Only her job on the line. Only sheer luck she'd had the opportunity to do this.

The intel had been that insinuating herself into Kass' life was supposed to get her exactly where she needed to be.

The intel was wrong.

Damn the intel.

The one thing they'd gotten right was Sarina, but even that was different to what they'd expected.

Briony checked her phone again. Olivia was late, and the napkin may not survive.

She opened her emails to scroll aimlessly through. Reporting about Matt's affair to her boss had got a simple: **ACKNOWLEDGED**. Not a wordsmith, old Jacob P. Wilcox.

Her social media feeds were filled with bad news. Riots in the US, bushfires ravaging Australia, an eco-terrorist group threatening bombings...

Her fingers took her to Kass' website, almost of their own accord. She soaked in the stunning portrait of Kass at the top. Her eyelashes were thick and lined with black, her three freckles stark in a V-shape on her bronze nose. She was adorned with bracelets, rings and necklaces, and large gold hoops hung from her earlobes. Considering how much she was raking in, clients didn't seem to mind the sleeve tats. They cared that she could bridge the gap between the higher ups and the employees, that her consultancy services did what they promised. At least, that's what Briony understood about Kass' job. As long as it made Kass happy.

That, she thought with a sigh, was her problem. She shouldn't care whether Kass was happy or not.

She locked her phone as Olivia walked into the restaurant. Her eyes were slightly red. Briony gave her a warm smile, standing to welcome her.

Here went nothing.

"Liv, thank you for meeting me. I'm so sorry again about your husband."

"Olivia."

"Hmm?"

"Please call me Olivia. Kass is the only one who calls me Liv." Olivia thanked the maître d' as he tucked her into her chair. She waited until their sparkling water had been poured before saying, "What did you want to talk about?"

She was eager, that was good.

"I don't know if you know I'm a solicitor?" Briony dug into her briefcase and pulled out her StarShine tablet, which looked like a sheet of glass.

Olivia stared at her with something akin to horror.

Briony hesitated. "I'm not *that* scary."

"Is this about Matt? Is – is he divorcing me?"

"What? Oh, god no, nothing like that. I'm in corporate law." Briony laughed, more out of relief than anything. "I'm sorry. I didn't mean to frighten you."

Olivia pressed a hand to her heart. "Oh."

"Equinoxx have asked my firm to sort out a minor matter about the mapping—"

"Wait, *Equinoxx?*"

Olivia's surprise seemed disproportionate to the statement, but before Briony could ask, the waiter arrived.

"Order what you like," Briony said. "My bosses are paying."

She watched Olivia scan the menu. Something seemed off. Was it the Matt thing? Or was it the mention of Equinoxx? So much was riding on this meeting – if she didn't get the signature now, she didn't know what would happen. Mr Wilcox wouldn't be happy, that much was certain.

When the waiter left, Briony said, "You participated in the mapping four years ago, yeah?"

"What is this about?"

It wasn't Briony's imagination. Olivia was on edge.

"Practically nothing," Briony said airily, opening the contract on her tablet. **PROJECT EIDOLON** was stamped across the top. "A few clauses in the contract have been altered to suit adjustments to the project. I've been given the job of speaking to the people involved and getting signatures." She grinned, gesturing around her. "And enjoying a free lunch at the same time."

"What kind of adjustments?"

"Very minor. You'll retain the same rights you did before."

"Why me? Why not everyone who did the mapping?"

"The project adjustments only affect several individuals. You can imagine my surprise when your name popped up on the list." Briony passed Olivia the tablet. "Feel free to read through the contract. Oh, ta."

A waiter arrived with a martini for Olivia and iced tea for Briony. Olivia examined the glass sheet. "What is this?"

"StarShine tech. Nice, eh? Works just like a tablet."

"Have you met Nera Blake?"

"Not yet. But she comes to Australia a bit now they've got a hub a few hours' drive up north. I'm hoping one day...Cheers." Briony held up her iced tea, forcing proprietary onto Olivia. The more that martini went down, the easier this should be.

To her disappointment, Olivia only took the tiniest sip before her attention was back to the tablet. She was reading the contract much more carefully than Briony had hoped.

"What's changed between this one and the one I first signed for the mapping?"

"Just a few technical details."

The corner of Olivia's mouth twitched. "You know, for the first one, I didn't even read the terms and conditions. I just scrawled my name on the screen and let them scan my hand without questioning it."

Briony wished she would bloody do that now. Why was she being so careful this time?

"Even with all those opinion pieces and conspiracy theorists talking about personal rights and potential uses of the mapper's data," Olivia continued. "I didn't care. A lot of people didn't, considering the turnout for the mapping. Nera Blake's doing good things. I hope."

"She's doing brilliant things," Briony said, trying not to sound too enthusiastic. "Not just with StarShine, but with everything."

StarShine's mapping project was a massive undertaking which required the cooperation of tens of millions of people worldwide. Briony had still been in Leeds when Equinoxx had set up temporary labs all over the city. She, along with hundreds of other people, had waited hours in the humidity, the rain battering away outside, the closed marquees stinking of wet clothes. She'd shared a flask and played Jenga with a couple of Irish blokes while she waited.

When she'd finally been called in, an exhausted scientist briefed her about the project before she'd hopped into a machine that looked like an MRI scanner. It had taken twenty minutes to collect her data. Her knowledge of the physical world joined everyone else's, creating a crowd-sourced, self-correcting secondary world called Eidolon. Project Eidolon was supposed to change everything. It was a combination of a virtual reality and a mindscape. The possibilities were endless. Someone else might've used it to make money. Nera Blake was using it to save the world.

"Did you see that video of the French president crying after seeing Eidolon?" Briony said. "Nera showed a bunch of world leaders what it looks like inside so she could get their consent to change the program in her favor."

"Mmm, I saw it," Olivia said, still scrolling through the pages of the contract. She hadn't touched her drink again.

"Your contract doesn't even have all that stuff."

"Okay."

Olivia kept reading. Briony wanted to shake her.

"It's working, you know," Briony said. "Eidolon's doing everything Nera Blake claimed it would—"

"Hey, what's this bit? *The mapper agrees to release the rights of their mapped data – and any arising anomalies – to the company.* What anomalies?"

Bollocks.

"Right, the anomalies." Briony fixed her best breezy smile. "I asked Equinoxx about that too. It's just to cover them in case anything pops up in Eidolon that wasn't part of the original mapping process."

"Like what?"

"Well, mapping minds isn't an exact science. Memory is fallible. Your knowledge of the physical world goes into the system, yeah? But sometimes an anomaly will pop up. Maybe a person wrongly believes a cat lives in an isolated area where there's not a lot of collective data. The cat is coded into Eidolon, but they doesn't actually exist in this world. The cat's a brand new piece of data. Equinoxx are just covering themselves, because technically the person who mapped them created this anomaly."

"Oh, I see."

"Equinoxx needs to have rights to everything that appears in Eidolon, or they'll be stuck in legal battles forever."

"That sounds fair."

Thank the Lord. Briony gulped at her iced tea as she watched Olivia skim through the rest of the contract. She was looking appeased.

"So that's it," Briony said as Olivia reached the end. She handed her stylus across the table. "Sign, scan your hand, and enjoy the free lunch."

Olivia hesitated.

Breathe, Briony.

"What if I just promise not to sue?" Olivia said.

Long, slow inhalation.

"That's what the contract is. A promise."

Long, slow exhalation.

"I have nothing to lose by not signing it."

"You have nothing to lose by signing it, either," Briony said. "Nothing will change for you. This is about Equinoxx."

Olivia didn't answer.

"Look." Briony leaned forward. "Do me a favor. I'm not exactly an important member of the team. I want to look good for my bosses, and this is going to help my cause." After a beat, she added, "Maybe if I told Kass how much you helped me out, she'd be more open to talking to you again."

She was a dirty rotten swine for using Kass like that, but wasn't it the whole reason she was in this position? To lie and cheat and manipulate?

"What happened between me and Kass clearly won't be fixed with one small action," Olivia said.

"It's a start though, isn't it?"

Olivia frowned thoughtfully at the contract as the waiter returned with their meals. Briony used the distraction to shoot a message to Mr Wilcox. **What happens if Olivia refuses to sign?**

His reply came almost immediately.

We move to Plan B.

5

Aidan Smith climbed out of the car, his body groaning from
being cramped so many hours in the driver's seat. The task
had taken too long. They always did. He still saw the long stretch
of road and glint of the railway line whenever he closed his eyes.

The night was cool and black without the moon. The cottage
was set a hundred meters back from the road, among the marri
and gum trees. He picked his way through the darkness, only lifting
his gaze when warm illumination fell on his face. Valentina had
opened the front door. She stood over him like a vengeful angel
wrapped in a deep purple dressing gown.

"You missed dinner again," she said.

"I know."

"You could've called."

"I'm sorry."

She surveyed him critically. She was barring his way into the
house. "It's not me you should be apologizing to."

The lined brown skin of her face was creased tenfold in a scowl.
A breeze touched her cropped, gray-streaked hair, but besides the
slight movement, she could've been made of stone.

He swallowed at the dryness in his mouth. His throat ached for
a drink, for the burn of cheap vodka and the deep bliss of oblivion.

"Can I come in?" His voice rasped as he said it.

"This can't go on, Aidan."

He closed his eyes. The railway flashed in his mind, but he
ignored it. He could fall asleep where he stood. "Please."

"It isn't good enough."

"It wasn't just the one task. I had to see Olivia."

"The Equinoxx woman?" Valentina's voice had changed. Unlike Aidan's other job, Valentina approved of his new assignment.

But it was Olivia's fault he was so late in the first place. If it hadn't taken her until midday to return to her apartment, he could've scouted the railway line and come home hours ago.

"She's different to the other Olivia," he said. He thought of her long hair, her chic outfit, the haughty way she held herself. It stung all over again. Then, wincing, he remembered the alarm in her expression as he'd approached her. "I may have come across a little strong."

"You've forgotten how to have regular interactions."

"I think I managed to give her second thoughts about signing the contract."

Valentina's scowl faded, though the lines around her mouth remained. They were permanent, thanks to a lifetime of lips pursed from grief and too many difficult decisions. "That's a start."

The wind picked up, skittering through the bush. Aidan turned to survey the garden in the glow of the house light. The herb boxes needed to be weeded, the brick path to the house had to be repaved, the chicken run needed to be fixed. He had promised to help Valentina with the cottage if she let them move in, and that promise had slipped this year. In fact, he could pinpoint the exact date of his decrease in usefulness.

"Well, come on," Valentina said. "No use hanging around out here."

He exhaled in relief as she turned and headed back inside. How many more nights of forgiveness did he have left?

He followed her down the hall and slumped at the wobbly kitchen table. Books and dirty plates clanked against each other. Another thing he had meant to fix.

Valentina shuffled towards the kettle. She held up a mug in question, but he waved away the offer.

"I'm not surprised you came across a little strong, considering," she said. "Would it kill you to trim your beard, or at least get a haircut?"

With a groan, he rubbed his eyes with the heels of his palms. The need for a harder drink gripped him. "I don't have time for a haircut."

"You don't even have time to feed yourself, from the sounds of your stomach."

He didn't move.

"Eat."

He got up and opened the fridge. She never said it outright, but he suspected she knew about the stash of bottles in his room. She was always trying to send him to bed with a full stomach. It didn't help his nightly attempt at oblivion.

There was a leftover vegetable patty on a plate. Making an actual burger was too much effort at one in the morning, so he threw the patty in the microwave how it was.

"You know I don't have a choice in all this, right?" he said. "I'd be home for dinner if I could."

"You have a choice in everything you do, Aidan." She spooned out herbal tea from a tin. The stub of what remained of her left arm, just above the wrist, held her mug steady. "You could walk away from it if you really wanted."

Aiden watched the digital numbers count down. Valentina wasn't lying. He could drop the Equinoxx thing today and be free from that burden. No more hiding, no more secret meetings with Pravit, no more urgency in convincing Olivia Sharp – Alexander, *whatever* – that her signature would destroy lives.

But those lives…those were what he was doing this for in the first place. He'd gotten in too deep now. There was no turning back.

As for the other job, well. He could walk up to Forrest tomorrow and say he wouldn't participate in a single new assignment. Problem was, that came with a price too high to pay.

The microwaved beeped, and he threw the patty between two slices of bread, downing it in a few desperate bites. When *had* he last eaten?

Valentina poured her tea. "Get some rest."

"I know, I know, I'm going to bed in a second." His eyes

narrowed when he caught sight of the open math book on the table, the page only half-finished. "Is Sophie asleep?"

"As far as I know."

Aidan had learned over the past three years to trust his instincts. He checked down the hallway. Sophie's door was closed, but there was a tell-tale blue light shining underneath.

"Sophie." He knocked.

No answer.

"Sophie, I'm coming in."

He waited a beat then opened up. She was on her bed, her head crunched against the headboard with her neck at an angle that seemed impossible to his mid-thirties body. The laptop was perched on her chest.

Unsurprisingly, she didn't acknowledge him.

"It's late," he said.

A grunt. She didn't look up from her screen.

He tried again. "You have lessons tomorrow."

"I'll survive."

He thought about pressing it, but what was the point? She'd have the same old argument ready for him.

I'm practically an adult; it's not like you're ever around anyway; stop trying to be Dad; I might as well go back to my real home; I hate you; I hate you; I hate you—

They had liked each other once, before Forrest had returned and the assignments had started. Now, the respect between him and his half-sister was shattered, maybe permanently.

The vodka in his room was calling to him. He had learned to look forward to it from the moment he woke each morning. It drowned out Sophie's spiteful words. It dulled his guilt. And it blinded him to the blood on his hands; the blood that had spilled because of Forrest, which, no matter how hard Aidan scrubbed, had forever stained his skin.

He shut the door on Sophie and headed for his bedroom, where oblivion lay waiting for him at the bottom of a bottle.

To: jacobpwilcox@equinoxxtechnology.co
From: retrievalunit@basenxj451.com
Subject: Retrieval update

LEVEL FIVE CITIZEN (CANADA POINT) SUCCESSFULLY
RETRIEVED
PREPARING FOR TRANSPORTATION TO AUSTRALIAN
BASE

EIDOLON

6

Liv's knee thudded against the punching bag. "Ow. Shit."

She veered around the bag and put down the washing basket. Rain pattered on the patio roof as she hung out the many, many tiny clothes. No one had warned her how much washing one small child could accumulate.

She was halfway through when her phone, balanced on a damp sock on top of the pile, started flashing. Her heart sprang painfully to attention. But it was only her mother, and Liv wasn't ready to have that conversation. If her parents knew about Reef's disappearance, they'd come rushing home, and Liv was certain they'd only make it halfway across the country in their little camper van before she'd have to call them to say not to worry because Reef had come back and everything was fine.

At least, she'd been certain of that scenario a few days ago.

She glanced towards the work shed. On Sundays, the door should be rolled open, with Reef inside, building something, fixing something, working on the car. It shouldn't be closed, locked, and empty.

Liv turned away. She couldn't stand it. She couldn't handle not doing anything.

She left the rest of the clothes in the basket and opened the patio cabinet to grab her inner wraps and boxing gloves. The rain grew heavier as she strapped them on.

"Dammit, Reef," she said under her breath, hitting the bag with each word. "Where – the – hell – are – you?"

At first, she was just pounding out her frustration. But then she fell into her usual rhythm, jab-cross-knee-kick, building up a sweat, building up a scream, because Reef was gone and she was scared.

What if he never came back? What if something terrible had happened? What if Bobbi had to grow up without her father, and Liv had to navigate this world alone?

Her rhythm turned sloppy, until it was just straight punching, *wham, wham, wham, wham*–

"Bad time?"

She spun, gasping, her eyes burning with unshed tears. Kazzy had opened the sliding door, laptop in hand. The smell of baking pizza wafted onto the patio with her.

Liv swiped sweat from her forehead and unstrapped her gloves. "No, it's fine."

"I got good news, and maybe real good news. The good news is, lunch is ready. The maybe real good news is…" Kazzy held up her laptop to show a traffic cam snapshot of a man driving a StarShine sedan. "Is this the old mate who talked to Reef?"

"Yes! Yes, that's him!"

Kazzy handed her a slip of paper. "Name, address, phone number. You're welcome."

"How did you…?"

"Don't ask, I won't have to lie."

A proper sob ripped through Liv's lungs. She grabbed her phone from the washing basket and dialed the number. The name scrawled in Kazzy's handwriting said he was Pravit Arya.

Pravit Arya.

Her single clue to Reef's disappearance.

Kazzy leaned next to her to hear over the rain. Their heads touched, and Liv was reminded of their pre-teen years of co-conspiring, calling their crushes or playing pranks on their friends, giggling and silly and blissfully ignorant of what was happening in the world around them.

Pravit Arya's line rang. And rang.

The sprint of Liv's heartbeat turned to a furious pounding. "Who doesn't answer their phone these days?"

"Maybe he's in the loo."

The line continued to ring.

"He doesn't even have a voicemail."

"It's all good, ay," Kazzy said. "Keep trying while you eat. If he's still not answering, go see him in person."

Liv reluctantly disconnected the call. "I want to head straight there."

"Fuck no. You're sweaty and stinky and you haven't eaten all day."

"I want to find Reef."

"I know. But what if Pravit doesn't want to help? Sounds like he and Reef have got dirt. You need to be ready to wring info."

"I could just punch it out of him."

"That's the hangry talking. Come. Eat. Shower."

Kazzy ushered Liv inside and finished hanging out the washing while Liv crammed down a couple slices of pizza. She kept calling Pravit Arya's number. Why wasn't this asshole answering his phone?

As she finished her last mouthful, Bobbi padded out from her bedroom, one fist rubbing her eyes, the other clinging to Mr Piggy.

"Hi baby," Liv said. "Did you have a nice nap?"

Bobbi stared at her crankily. It always took her a few minutes to wake up.

Kazzy came back inside with the empty laundry basket. "Well, well, look who's joined the land of the living. You hungry, chickadee? Aunny Kazzy will make you lunch."

Liv left Kazzy to feed Bobbi and had a quick shower. She

visualized what she would say to Pravit as she pulled on jeans and a clean tee shirt. When he'd picked up Reef last week, he'd seemed polite but somber. There was no reason to think he would get violent if she confronted him. But Kazzy was right – there was a chance he wouldn't be willing to tell her what he'd shown Reef. Liv was determined not to leave his house until she had answers.

She tied her short black hair into a ponytail and checked her phone. Besides the one voicemail from her mother, there were no new notifications.

When she returned to the living room, Bobbi was watching television and chewing on a pizza slice while Kazzy washed the dishes in the adjoining kitchen.

"Better?" Kass said.

"Yes, yes, you're always right, all hail Kassandra White."

"Fuckin' A."

"I'll be back soon."

"Watch yourself," Kazzy said. "Call me and keep me on speaker while you talk to him."

"I can't tie up the line. What if Reef tries to call?"

Kazzy pursed her lips before saying, "At least text me when you get there."

"Mummy, where's Daddy?"

Liv kissed the top of Bobbi's head. "He'll be home soon. I'm just going out for a bit. Aunny Kazzy will look after you."

"Yup."

"I love you."

"Yup." Bobbi's attention was back on the screen. Small miracles.

Liv blew a two-fingered kiss to Kazzy as she moved down the hall. "You're my angel."

"Oh, wait." Kass put a wet dish in the draining tray. "Pravit works for Equinoxx."

Liv stilled. "What?"

"Might be a coincidence, ay. A lot of people work for Equinoxx. But I thought you should know."

"Was he part of the mapping?"

"Dunno."

Liv continued down the hall, her mind spinning. If Equinoxx had something to do with Reef's disappearance, then she had been looking at it all wrong. Maybe Reef hadn't left of his own volition. Maybe someone had *made* him leave.

She got into Kazzy's StarShine and headed south, following her phone's GPS. The car's automatic wipers swished dutifully the whole way. Her back ached a little. She should've stretched properly after her assault on the punching bag. It was a faint reminder of her accident.

According to Kazzy's info, Pravit lived on the south side of the river, in one of the swankier suburbs. Liv pulled up outside the address and stared up at the multi-storey limestone building. Other cars had parked along the curb and across the street. Biodegradable streamers hung from Pravit's letterbox.

Liv texted Kazzy that she'd arrived, then hurried through the rain to the front door. Pravit answered the bell almost immediately. He was wearing a My Little Pony party hat and a broad smile. "Hello, hello, come in."

There was the sound of laughing children and chatting adults from further in the house.

"I'm not here for the party," Liv said.

"Oh? Beg your pardon. I don't know all my daughter's friends. Between her mothers' group and work colleagues–"

"Where's Reef?"

Pravit's smile fell. "Sorry?"

"Reef. My partner. Where is he?"

"Reef? Reef Davidson? I wouldn't have any idea. I haven't spoken to him in years."

"Don't lie to me. You saw him four days ago."

Pravit searched her face. "I'm sorry, I don't even know who you are."

"What are you talking about? We met when you came over. You took Reef somewhere, he came back completely freaked out and now he's gone. What did you show him? Where did he go?"

Liv's voice lifted, partly out of frustration, but also out of panic, because Pravit looked genuinely baffled.

"You're certain it was me?" he said.

"Yes! One hundred percent. You were wearing a pinstriped gray suit and one of those tie pin thingys. You had different glasses and your hair...your hair was shorter..."

Liv trailed off, unsure how Pravit's hair had grown several inches in a few days. She might've started to doubt herself if not for the fact that Pravit straightened, his face flashing with realization.

"What?" Liv said.

A woman's voice trilled from inside. "Pravit? Where are you?"

"Just a minute, my love," Pravit called back, then he stepped onto the porch, closing the door gently behind him. He peered up at Liv through his spectacles. "The man you saw wasn't me, it was a visitor."

"A what?"

"I'm sorry. I can't help you."

"Don't give me that bullshit. Reef is *missing.*"

"Be that as it may, I'm not the one who has your answers."

"Then who does? Where do I have to go? Who was that visitor?" Liv took a desperate stab as Pravit opened the door to step back inside. "Does this have something to do with Equinoxx?"

"I imagine so."

"Did Reef find out what they did to us?"

Pravit lifted his eyebrows.

"We've both had medical issues since the mapping. Our brains...something went wrong. We suffer from hallucinations, derealizations, anxiety. But the doctors haven't diagnosed us and nothing came up on the MRI. Equinoxx isn't taking responsibility for it."

Pravit's gaze shifted to her phone, which remained clutched in her hand. "Yet you use StarShine technology. You know that's Equinoxx, right?"

"It's hard to avoid. And you're changing the subject."

"What is your name?"

Liv was thrown by his gentle tone. It took her a moment to switch gears. "Er – Liv. Olivia."

"Olivia," Pravit said, kindly. "Let me be clear. *I* cannot help you." He stared at her, unblinking.

Liv understood. "But Equinoxx can?"

A slight nod.

"Okay." Liv let out a breath. "Okay, I can work with that."

It wasn't an answer. But at least it was something.

OUTSIDE

7

The car was a StarShine, powered by solar batteries, and fully automated. Olivia sat behind the empty driver's seat, clinging to the door handle as if for her life. When she'd received a text from Briony that a car would pick her up, Olivia hadn't realized what exactly that entailed. The StarShine slowed at stop signs and kept a careful distance behind the traffic in front, and it might've been a better driver than Leith, but all she could think was that a single glitch could kill her.

When it reached the open stretch of Indian Ocean Drive and set its speed to a hundred and ten, she almost had a nervous breakdown. She couldn't shut her eyes. Not being able to see her potential death was worse than gasping every time the car overtook a slow-moving caravan. Brown paddocks and squat, native shrubs sped past.

Was this worth the chance to meet Nera Blake? Maybe. Olivia couldn't believe the world's most successful inventor would take time out of her busy schedule to meet *her*. Olivia had agreed because the mystery intrigued her. Yesterday, a caveman stranger warns her not to sign an Equinoxx contract, and mere hours later Briony produces that very contract. Now the face of Equinoxx, the owner and inventor Nera Blake was offering to meet Olivia – for what? A small amendment to her rights?

Why was her signature so important to Equinoxx? Olivia was as keen for an answer as she was to get out of the apartment. At least it was something else to think about besides those damn emails. Her need to see more of Matt and Sarina's conversations, to read everything, to know everything, felt like a perverse addiction.

She'd slept in the spare bedroom again last night. The worst thing was, Matt acted upset and kept bugging her about what was wrong. He couldn't seem to take "I don't want to talk about it," as an answer. Was he paranoid she'd discovered the affair? Or was he genuinely worried?

It had been a long time since Olivia had left the city – maybe not since the accident. Huge windmills lined the eastern horizon as they headed north of Perth. Rows and rows of them – she almost forgot to be scared for a moment as she stared at their enormous white blades.

After the wind turbines, the dry paddocks to the west petered out into native bush again. A stretch of blackened tree husks lined the road from the bushfires. The post-apocalyptic scenery lasted a long while, too long, before at last the bushland returned. Now multiple signs interspersed the trees, warning that beyond them was private property and to keep out, with the Equinoxx logo stamped on each. The tight knot in Olivia's chest eased at the hope that she was almost at her destination.

It was another twenty minutes before the car finally turned west off the main road. More private property signs sprang up between the native bush, stating that only Equinoxx employees were allowed past this point. There were two black boxes on either side of the road that flashed a red light as the car passed between them. Then, when the car slowed around a curve, the landscape changed. Olivia had to lean across the backseat to see, because while the bushland remained on her right, the left held something extraordinary.

Sparkling structures grew from the ground like crystal trees – or perhaps more like mushrooms, as they were bulbous at the top. They were a good ten feet tall, with a purplish shine. It was a whole forest of them. Kilometer after kilometer, and there was no end in sight. In the distance was a large metal frame, sort of a cross between a mobile phone tower and an electrical transmission tower. It soared high above the glinting canopy, with a large wire at the top in the shape of a spider's web.

The ocean came into view. Finally, the sprawling crystal forest ended at a stretch of sand dunes bordering a river mouth. A two-storey building sat among the trees. It had an open window plan and a mottled green roof that matched the native flora. On top was the same spider web shape as the metal tower.

The StarShine car passed a parking lot next to the beach filled with other StarShine cars and large buses with the same solar panels, then up to the entrance of the building. When the door opened by itself, she scrambled out, grateful to no longer be at the mercy of a machine. The door closed and the car drove away.

Olivia slung her handbag over her shoulder and wiped her sweaty palms on her tailored jeans. She'd rather walk home than go back in a StarShine car. Her high heels clapped on the pavement as she climbed the ramp to the automated doors, which whooshed open at her approach. The lobby had gold-and-blue checkered tiles. In places the tiles had been dug up to make room for native plants – banksia, wattle, kangaroo paw and many she didn't know the names of.

Staff bustled past, shooting her curious looks. They were all wearing black polo shirts with the Equinoxx insignia above the heart. Some shirts had a red stripe like a sash across the chest.

At the reception desk a freckled redhead in his twenties, with goatee and eyeliner, beamed as Olivia approached.

"Hello, Olivia," he said, like they'd known each other for years. "Welcome to Equinoxx. Thank you so much for coming. I'm Killian. Would you mind checking in before we start?"

Olivia used a stylus to input her details onto a thin piece of glass like Briony's tablet. She also scanned her handprint.

"And there's a non-disclosure agreement I need you to sign."

This contract was easy enough to follow. Olivia couldn't tell anyone Equinoxx's corporate secrets, but so what? Who did she have left to talk to?

"What are those crystal trees outside?" she said as she passed the tablet back.

Killian's smile widened. "You'll find out. Nera will give you the whole tour."

"Olivia, thanks for coming in."

Olivia turned at the cheerful American accent. The Black woman who strolled over looked like she belonged in a hipster café. She was in her thirties, with corkscrew curls, a knitted infinity scarf and jeans with dirt patches on the knees as if she'd been gardening. She practically slapped her palm into Olivia's for the handshake.

"Nera Blake. Pleasure."

Olivia could only gape, starstruck. Nera Blake's smile was easy, her demeanor casual. She felt so…ordinary.

"How did you like the ride?" Nera asked. Her dark eyes shone with a keenness that made it impossible to disappoint her.

"Amazing," Olivia heard herself say. "Your work is incredible."

"Well, thank you very much." Nera seemed gleeful, as if Olivia's opinion was worth something. Olivia doubted that was the case. It wasn't as if she were an important figure in the scientific community.

"How long have you been in Australia?" Olivia said.

"I come and go." Nera strolled forward, and Olivia followed. "I like to check up on things. Be involved, monitor progress, chat to the employees, make sure everyone's happy. And meet people like you," she said, shooting Olivia a warm look. "It's because of volunteers like you that we were able to create an entire world. So tell me about yourself. What do you do for a living? What are your aspirations? If you could change anything about your life, what would it be?"

Olivia's mind jumped unwillingly to Matt's affair. She suppressed a shudder. "I don't know. I live quietly. Nothing to write a biography about."

"You travel?" Nera was too enthusiastic for the little Olivia had to offer. Why did she care about Olivia's life and aspirations?

"I used to."

"Where have you been?"

"Um…I went to Nepal. Hawaii. Germany. I lived in the north of Sweden for a year."

"That's fantastic! I love Sweden!"

Nera seemed oblivious to the awed looks thrown her way by the people around them. She was like a celebrity in this place. A geeky, over-excited celebrity.

Olivia didn't want to talk about her travels. They were another lifetime. A different person.

"What's happening with Project Eidolon?"

Nera laughed good-naturedly. "Everyone always asks me that. Let me give you the tour first."

Olivia had expected Equinoxx to be impressive in appearance, but it turned out to be more than that. The building had a second outer layer called 'intelligent skin', keeping the interior hot or cool without the use of heaters or air conditioning. The windows were made of solar panels. Nera and her team had designed a photovoltaic system that was years ahead of the current technology and was how everything – including the StarShine cars – could be powered without being connected to the grid. Olivia had seen fleeting headlines about it on social media, but she hadn't realized what it meant.

The cafeteria's entire menu was free from animal cruelty, most of the food grown on farmland near the property. A delicious-smelling meal similar to spaghetti bolognaise turned out to be vegetable mince, and for dessert there were protein packs created by one of Nera's other companies. Nera let Olivia have a try. It was sweet and chewy, and completely synthetic.

"Saves water because it's not made from crops, and saves us having to source food from factory farms," Nera said. "Healthy, and fills you up."

"But it's actually tasty," Olivia said.

"I know. We're currently giving most of our stock to international aid and rescue organizations, but it'll be on the market next year."

"Where's the profit in that?"

"Who cares?" Nera said, charging onwards. "We're trying to save the world, here."

They were indeed. Equinoxx's logo was *Taking the world back*. Olivia had read once that Nera had blatantly stated in an article that she was taking the world back from the one-percenters, who hoarded their wealth to the detriment of the planet. It had made her some powerful enemies. And other energy companies, like SInation, were years behind her innovative creations.

"We use a cyclic water system," Nera said after showing Olivia the sewerage treatment plant, a wetlands zone with wildlife and native trees. It didn't even smell bad. "We barely use the river water, though my aim is to get the numbers down to zero. I want to create a lifestyle that's not only self-sustaining, but contributes to the wellness of the local environment."

They returned indoors and headed back to the lobby.

"So," Nera said, "the lawyers are telling me you'd like to know what anomalies have arisen from your mapping."

"Surely I'm not the only one questioning it?"

Nera gave a wry smile. "You'd be surprised how many people signed that consent without even reading it. Terms and conditions can be a killer if you're not careful. But don't worry. We're just trying to make sure Project Eidolon isn't slowed down by constant legal battles. I hate legal battles."

"Isn't that what Briony is for?"

"Sorry?"

"Briony McKinney. The lawyer you sent to get me to sign the consent form? She happens to be a friend of mine."

Sort of.

"I don't have much to do with the lawyers, thankfully," Nera said. "You know, I could've brought back a dozen species from near extinction and stopped the ice caps from melting if it weren't for the goddamn legalities. People are up in arms about their personal rights when the entire planet is dying."

"I don't mean to slow down your work," Olivia said. "I just want to be sure."

Nera turned to face her. Her expression had changed. There was something secretive, inviting, in her smile. She moved closer, and Olivia felt a hiccough of air rush into her lungs.

"All right then," Nera said quietly. "Do you want to see?"

"See what?"

"Eidolon." Nera's excitement was palpable. "Do you want to see Eidolon?"

8

Nera led Olivia to a broad glass elevator at the back of the lobby. Signs plastered the walls on either side, stating in large, angry letters that only authorized personnel were permitted past this point.

Nera scanned her handprint and the door slid open. As soon as Olivia stepped in after her, the glass around them turned red and there was a metallic sound like a lock clicking into place. A sharp male voice said, *Unauthorized person detected.*

"Nera Blake, override," Nera said cheerfully. "Olivia Alexander, visitor." The red glow disappeared. Whatever had locked unlocked again.

They reached a sub-level floor and the door slid open. Olivia's eyes took a moment to adjust. The place was dim, with flashing lights on various technical equipment, but the first thing that caught her attention was the vegetation. Lush plants flourished beneath glowing blue. They climbed up support pillars and crept along the ceiling, kept damp by mist sprayers. A sweet, lily-like fragrance lingered in the air, sparking a whimsical springtime atmosphere.

Between the foresty pillars were rows and rows of what looked like thrones. There were at least seventy in the room. Each throne had a person sitting on it and a person standing beside it.

The people standing typed notes into glass tablets as they watched a monitor, which showed images of places around the world – busy streets, lakeside picnics, hotel rooms, rainforests. The people sitting on the thrones had a tiny silver device shaped like a spider attached to their temple. They appeared asleep.

"Wow," Olivia said, the word whooshing from her. "This is… wow."

Nera gestured to the monitors. "You're looking at Eidolon. The people with the transmitters on their heads are currently visitors inside the world. The people monitoring their progress are called anchors."

Olivia moved closer to a monitor showing a street crammed with pedestrians, bicycles, and cars. The anchor moved aside to let her see properly.

"This is Shijou Street in Kyoto, Japan," said the anchor without looking away from the screen. "Touma's collecting data. We're doing weather at the moment – temperature, humidity, wind speed. Earlier he was counting pedestrians and cars, and checking the physical surroundings like buildings, alleyways, drains."

It looked like regular footage from someone filming in Japan. People bustled past with shopping bags and fast food. Every now and then, Olivia, Nera, and the anchor watched through Touma's eyes as he glanced down to type things into his tablet. And yet Touma's physical body was currently sitting on the throne beside them.

"You're telling me that's not real?" Olivia said. "What we're looking at right now is virtual?"

"Half-virtual," Nera corrected. "A complex, secondary world that is self-sustaining, with limited external programming abilities. Viewing the screens through visitors like Touma is the only way to monitor it from the outside. Shall we take a tour?"

Olivia glanced at her, startled. "A tour?"

"Of Eidolon," Nera said. "I told you I'd show you." She half-jumped in excitement as she turned to head down the row. "Let's find a free station."

Olivia followed her in a daze.

"Ah, perfect," Nera said as a man who reminded Olivia of her father strode up to them. He, like everyone else, was wearing a polo shirt. It seemed only the people with the red stripes were allowed in the sub-level lab. Names had been stitched into the fabric in a thread that showed up when they were beneath the blue lights. This man's shirt had *Pravit* sewn onto it.

"Pravit Arya, meet Olivia Alexander. Pravit is our regional director."

Pravit bobbed his head to Olivia in acknowledgement.

"Can you find us a couple of stations?" Nera said. "I'd like to show our guest what we've been up to."

"This way," Pravit said, and led them down the row to two empty thrones.

"Take a seat, Olivia. Pravit, will you anchor?"

Olivia climbed onto the throne. Pravit started flipping switches attached to her system.

"Where do you want to go?" Nera asked. "Choose somewhere in the world you haven't been before."

"Shouldn't I choose somewhere I *have* been? To see how similar it is?"

"Absolutely not. Once you've been in Eidolon, you can claim you've been there in the real world. Saves you a flight."

"Is it safe?"

"Of course it's safe," Nera said, settling onto the second empty throne as if she were on a deck chair at the beach. "I have seventy-five of the brightest minds visiting Eidolon in this very lab, and thirty other labs all over the world. The entire secondary world is contained in server plantations like the one you passed on your way in. You know those structures that looked like crystals? There's a whole forest of them across the inarable parts of the outback. They're completely solar powered, no human maintenance required, and will probably last longer than the planet, especially at the rate we're going. That spider web antenna you would've seen in the middle of the plantation is the way in and out of Eidolon. It transmits a signal, sort of like radio waves, but my own special frequency that no one else can tap into." Pravit attached the silver spider to her temple. "I promise, there's nothing to be afraid of. Now. Where would you like to go?"

Olivia watched as Pravit came to her with a second silver spider. "Um…I don't know."

"Where's somewhere you've always wanted to go? It could be a mountain. A forest. A city. We could stroll along bustling New York if you like—"

Olivia's entire body spasmed involuntarily. Adrenaline exploded through her – not the good kind, but the painful, frenetic kind seeped in terror. The underground lab, with its multitudes of plants and misting rain, was suddenly hot and airless. She jerked away from Pravit, who had been about to place the silver spider on her temple.

"What's wrong?" he said in alarm.

Nera jumped off her throne and rushed to Olivia's station. "Pravit, will you get some water?"

Olivia couldn't breathe. She put her head between her knees, gasping.

"Olivia, what's wrong?"

Without looking up, Olivia jerked her hand in a short wave to show she was okay. And she would be.

She would be.

She would be.

She clung to the edge of the throne, waiting for the panic to subside. "S-sorry."

"Don't be sorry. What do you need?"

"A minute. I'm fine." She forced her breaths to slow. "I. Am. Fine."

Nera lay a comforting hand on her arm.

It took some time before Olivia's heart stopped pounding. Pravit returned with a glass of water, and Olivia sipped it obligingly.

"Sorry," she said again. This time, her voice sounded normal.

"We don't have to go into Eidolon," Nera said.

Olivia shook her head. "I'll be okay."

"Are you sure?"

Olivia didn't answer right away. First, she had to talk herself through the anxiety.

Eidolon was not real. There were no risks involved. It was just like virtual reality.

Almost.

She glanced at the monitor on the station across from them. The visitor to Eidolon was currently crossing a road, with cars and mopeds zooming back and forth in a disorganized crush. It looked like India.

"Can we die in there?" she said.

"No," Nera said. "Don't get me wrong, it *seems* real. And pain feels like pain. But everything that happens to you in Eidolon is just a mental experience. We're avatars in a game, that's all. When you return here, you'll be in the same shape as when you left."

"So if I were to, say, fall off a cliff…"

"Pravit would stop the program and bring you back. You might feel a little stunned, but only for a few moments. We've never had any injuries from the NTD, even in an emergency extraction."

"NTD?"

"Sorry, the Neuro-Transit Device."

"The same thing you used when you mapped us?"

"Not exactly. That's the Neuro-Relay Device. The NTD actually sends you to Eidolon."

Olivia looked again at the screens around her. All these people were in the mindscape right now. And they were fine.

"We don't have to do this," Nera reminded her.

"No, I'm all right." And she was – her adrenaline was fading, her breathing less constricted. Pravit took her empty glass. "I don't think I'd mind traveling again if it was as safe as Eidolon."

"Are you absolutely sure?"

"Yes." Olivia laughed awkwardly. "What happened just then…it wasn't from anything to do with this. I sort of have, um, trauma."

"What triggered it?" Nera said. "How can I prevent it from happening again?"

"It's fine. I have it under control. I'm so sorry."

"Please don't ever apologize for that. But maybe we shouldn't go in."

"No, I want to. Really."

Nera searched Olivia's gaze. "Okay," she said after a moment. "Only if you're sure." She returned to her throne. "Where do you want to go?"

"Just Perth will do. Elizabeth Quay."

"You don't want to see anywhere else?"

"No. Not right now."

"Okay." Nera signaled to Pravit, who placed the silver spider on Olivia's temple.

Olivia glimpsed a red light at the top of her eyesight, and there was a faint tingling sensation over her third eye.

"Does it hurt?" Even as she asked it, she realized how frightened she sounded.

What a coward she'd become.

"You won't feel a thing," Nera said, before there was a slight humming and the red light turned silver.

Olivia closed her eyes against the glare, and when she opened them again, she was standing beside Swan River.

"What...?"

It was like she'd been transported. A few people gazed at her curiously as they passed, but they continued around her on their way to lunch, or back to the office.

She caught snatches of warm sun on her skin between cool gusts that smelled of the river. The pavement was hard beneath her shoes. When she rubbed the sleeve of her blouse between her thumb and forefinger, she could feel the fine fibers of the material.

"Holy shit," she said.

She cupped her mouth as the enormity of what she was experiencing began to sink in. Her breath was hot against her hands. It was real. It was so, so real.

Nera stood beside her.

"It's okay," Nera said as tears fell down Olivia's cheeks. "Everyone reacts like this. I had one technician sobbing in the mountains in Idaho – it took ten minutes and a goat to calm him down."

Olivia pulled her hands away from her face. "Nera," she croaked. "This is incredible. What you've done..."

"It wasn't just me. Thousands of scientists helped bring this place into existence, not to mention everyone who volunteered to do the mapping." Nera gave a one-shouldered shrug. "And there are still glitches to work out."

"Glitches." A bubble of laughter fell from Olivia's lips. She spun on the spot, taking it all in. The sky, the towering buildings, the swirl of birds above them, the noise, the smells, the sounds–

"You've created a *world*." She hadn't comprehended what that meant until now.

"I'm glad you like it," Nera said.

This woman wasn't even forty, and she had done the unthinkable. Forget the Equinoxx building. This was phenomenal.

"Would you like a look around?" Nera said.

She offered an arm, which Olivia took, and they strolled along the riverfront. As they crossed the quay's suspension bridge, Olivia realized something. "It's the same. The same as what it looks like now, I mean. But it didn't look like this when we did the mapping. There have been changes in the past few years."

"Eidolon isn't static. The people here act as they would in the real world."

Olivia surveyed the crowd. There were elderly folk, and bike riders, and kids playing in the water feature.

"They're the simulations," she said, remembering reading about them when Eidolon was first announced. They were the reason for much of the backlash against the project.

"We call them citizens," Nera said. "Mapped into the world with everything else. And no, despite what many of the public were worried about, we're not going to be using them for explicit purposes."

Olivia remembered the alarmists blogging about it in near hysteria. Equinoxx would use their copies for pornography, or testing, or surveillance. People would be able to pay to have sex with whoever they wanted. The government could spy on them.

"So can you program the citizens?" she asked. "Make them do what you want?"

"Yes, but there are strict legal parameters in the first release form you signed. We aren't allowed to reprogram anyone without the original mapper's explicit permission." Nera smiled at a father and daughter on the footpath, who both smiled back. There was a fondness in Nera's expression as she watched them pass. Olivia couldn't blame her; Nera had created them, after all. The woman was practically a god.

"The citizens are just to keep Eidolon as parallel as possible to our world," Nera continued. "Although we've made some changes. Governments in here have granted us funding to explore different energy options, release products, develop biodegradable plastics, all that sort of thing. We're monitoring the impact the reduced fossil fuel usage is having on the planet. Look at the cars. Almost all StarShine."

Olivia watched the vehicles on the street hum past. "So everything else is the same?"

"Not exactly. The citizens in here have different levels. When you mapped this world, an imprint of yourself remained in the program. This imprint would be just like you, because your own mind put it there. They're called a level three citizen. But you also mapped imprints of the people you knew, and that's not the same. Humans are complex – it's not as simple as making a copy."

"Why not?"

They stopped in the shade of a pop-up bar. "Say you had a brother who didn't do the mapping. His citizen would be based on how you, and everyone else who did the mapping, construct him in your heads. But those views would conflict, because no one sees him in quite the same way. The citizens of people who never did the mapping aren't quality copies. They're only level two."

That would be Kass, who hadn't joined Olivia the day she did the mapping. Kass' work didn't lend itself to sharing – she must be living as a level two citizen somewhere.

"What are level one citizens?" Olivia said.

"People who were mapped in, but no one who did the mapping knew them very well, so there's very little data on them. And babies."

"The people in here can have babies?"

"Yes, but they're nowhere near as sophisticated as our level two and three citizens, because the program is creating them using random data. They grow like normal humans, but they're glitchy and unpredictable. One of the more frustrating aspects of Eidolon, unfortunately."

Nera ordered a scotch for herself, and Olivia a sparkling shiraz. The bartender seemed real enough. He had a brief chat to Nera about the weather and the best wines of the year.

"Are you a level three citizen?" Olivia said to him.

He winced visibly.

"Simulations are self-aware," Nera said. "But that doesn't mean they like thinking about it."

The bartender slid Olivia's drink across the counter. "Sort of like if someone were to wander over and remind you of the inevitability of death. No one wants that ruining their day."

"It's better that way," Nera said. "If they reacted as simulations rather than people, knowing the world isn't real, they might behave differently and our data could end up compromised."

"How would they behave differently?" Olivia said.

"I'm not sure, and that's the problem. Maybe they'd be more reckless. Try harder to clean up the world. Or try less hard. Who knows? The point is, I want to keep the data as reliable as possible."

The bartender grinned. "That being said, you're still Nera Blake, and drinks are obviously on the house."

Nera laughed and thanked him. She clinked her scotch glass against Olivia's flute. It made a delightful ringing sound. Olivia sniffed the bouquet then sipped, relishing in the sharp taste and bubbles fizzing across her tongue. Sunlight reflected off the shiraz and cast glittering rubies across the bar's counter.

"Amazing," she said. "This place is amazing."

Nera smiled over the rim of her glass. Olivia liked the way she held Nera's attention. Nera had this way of making her feel important, as if Olivia was worth every second of her precious time. Matt hadn't made Olivia feel like that for months.

Wait…Matt hadn't done the mapping. If the copy of him in

here came mostly from her mind, maybe his citizen self might not have had the affair. She'd never believed him capable of cheating. Eidolon's version of Matt was probably as loyal as she'd always believed.

She put her glass on the counter. "Do you think I could meet myself?"

"I'm not sure." Nera glanced at the clock on the bar wall. "We can only enter this world through location coordinates. It's not easy tracking down an individual."

"I live over there," Olivia said, pointing across the river.

"You do in the real world, but not in Eidolon. I checked before you arrived."

"I don't live in my apartment?" Olivia frowned. Maybe she and Matt had decided to move somewhere different here.

What else had changed in her simulated life? Had she and Kass still drifted apart? Was she still friends with the High Ts? Did she still drink mimosas on Monday mornings? Had her wedding day, which had occurred after the mapping, gone as perfectly as the one in the real world? What kind of life did she live with Matt?

Curiosity burned in her. "There has to be a way to find myself. Social media? A phone call? Do mobiles work here?"

"Everything works the same as the real world. I could–"

Olivia didn't hear what Nera was about to say. When she blinked again, she was back in the lab with the blue lights. The transition from standing to sitting made her feel dizzier than the other way around.

"Sorry," Pravit said. "Are you all right?"

The lab was abuzz with noise. Technicians were standing around, muttering, cursing. All the monitors were black.

"Dammit." Nera jumped off her throne. "Who's the culprit this time?"

"Sounds like it's Francoise," Pravit said.

Olivia rubbed her forehead, which was tingling. They weren't talking sense.

Something small and white fluttered near her eye. It was a piece of paper, something she hadn't expected to see in this otherwise-green lab. It seemed to have come right out of her palm. She picked it up and squinted at the message scrawled inside, but it was too hard to read in the soft lighting. Someone must have put it in her hand while she was in Eidolon. Pravit?

"What happened?" she said, folding the paper into her fist. She looked at Pravit, but his attention was on the switches at the throne.

"One of the signal towers somewhere in the world went down," Nera said. "Which means the whole system goes down." At Olivia's expression, she added, "Don't worry. Eidolon will still hum away without us. We just don't have access to it right now."

"Francoise is our signal tower in the Congo," Pravit said. "It keeps getting hit by lightning."

"Why did we put it in the Congo, Pravit? Why?"

"The system should be back online in an hour or two."

"I don't have an hour or two." Nera sounded cranky. She checked her phone. "And what do you know, Wilcox wants to meet with us."

"I'm sure it's just about Francoise."

"Probably." Nera shoved her phone in her pocket and glared at the black monitors.

"Um," Olivia said. "Technical issues aside, that was incredible."

Nera's sour mood softened. She clasped Olivia's hand. "Thank you for visiting. It was lovely meeting you. I'm sorry to have to rush off like this. If you wait here, I'll get Killian to escort you out."

"Thank you for…" Olivia gestured to the throne. Any words to describe her experience seemed inadequate.

"You're very welcome." Nera gave her that warm smile once more. "Come on, Pravit, our doom awaits."

The two of them hurried away. Olivia waited until they were out of sight before moving beneath the nearest blue light and squinting again at the small piece of paper. The lettering was handwritten, too difficult to see. If only she had a bit more light…

She pulled out her phone and switched on the flashlight.

Across the room, the elevator opened. Killian, the redhead from the welcome desk, moved towards her. He had a glass tablet with him.

The contract.

Olivia would be expected to sign it, but she still didn't know what the anomaly was. Was it mere coincidence that a signal tower went down when she was supposed to find out? Or did Nera Blake orchestrate this whole thing just to keep Olivia from finding out the truth?

Surely that sounded paranoid?

She shone her light on the piece of paper. This time, the writing was clear.

DO <u>NOT</u> SIGN CONTRACT

Olivia shoved the paper in her pocket as Killian approached. Maybe, just maybe, she should be a little paranoid.

9

If there was a way to harness Nera's excess energy and use it as a resource, the world would be saved. At least until she died. Nera wasn't yet at the point where she considered herself above the common failing of death. She was a god, yes. A god of so many lives.

But not immortal.

"Must you pace?" The words were punctuated with a long-suffering sigh.

"Yes, Jake. I must. I must pace."

Her investor, business partner, confidante, her intellectual equal – Jacob P. Wilcox to the world, Mr Wilcox to his employees, Jake to Nera – sat on the other side of the screen, waiting at his desk with utmost serenity. Despite his exhaustion, he still managed to look a little like George Clooney. Never a bad thing in the business world. People had confidence in him.

Nera was too fidgety to be trusted by the older generation. Even when she was supposed to be drawing up new plans, *especially* when she was supposed to be drawing up new plans, she needed to move. As if her body was trying to keep up with the lightning speed of her brain. She tossed and turned in her sleep, too, from the tangled state of her sheets every morning. Her muscles refused to relax.

It didn't help that guilt poisoned her breath, dogged her footsteps. Sure, she was revolutionizing energy, doing everything she could to bring this world back from the brink. But being here –

breathing, moving, existing – damaged this planet. Everything she threw away, every plane trip she had to take, every drop of water that couldn't be recycled. She had seen the coal pits, the dumps, the Great Pacific Garbage Patch. She was doing so much and yet it wasn't enough.

She kept pacing.

Jake knew Nera's habits and anxieties, and didn't comment again. It was late in Equinoxx's California headquarters. His weariness would've been the only reason he'd mentioned Nera's restlessness in the first place.

"It's a nice office."

Nera glanced around. It was the regional director's office, and was decorated similarly to how she had done her own. It had a native garden in the center, recyclable light fixtures hanging from the ceiling in old milk bottles, carpet grass that Nera had developed for offices that felt *so good* beneath bare feet, and a collection of bouncy balls. The bouncy balls were made of a lab-designed fungi – completely biodegradable, of course – and were excellent for someone like her who needed an outlet for nervous energy. The glass-spex screen took up the entire exterior wall, which was normally a window, only now it projected Jake's image.

"Francoise will be up and running again in no time," Pravit said, bent over the tabletop, typing and dragging his fingers along the glass screen of the desk.

Nera liked Pravit. Competent, calm, rational. She was glad she'd made him regional director. She wanted the Australian hub to be in good hands. That hot, vast outback was a goldmine of geothermal energy, something her competitors had yet to efficiently harness.

"Thank you, Mr Arya, that will be all," Jake said.

Pravit used his handprint to log off the tabletop and excused himself. It was only when the door closed behind him that Nera said, "I'm having second thoughts."

"You mean ninth thoughts."

"Jake. I don't want to do this."

"It's the only way."

"But is it?"

"Do I need to bring up the financials again?"

"God, no. Don't threaten me with financials."

Jake didn't smile. Nera didn't either. They had this conversation like a careful dance, each and every time.

"I don't know if I did enough," Nera said. "That power outage ruined our trip."

Pravit had helped her set up a whole story for the anomaly – a small grove with a little creek, right in the heart of the Darling Ranges. Nera had planned and practiced the narrative, about how it must've been in Olivia's subconscious when she did the mapping, maybe something she'd misremembered as a child. It was supposed to be magical.

Nera had felt slimy with each rehearsal, and was secretly grateful she hadn't had to lie at all. But then, maybe that small saving grace meant one large failure.

"You did what you could," Jake said. "Really, it's my plant who messed up. We paid her a healthy sum to get that signature, and she failed."

"You're talking about Briony McKinney, the lawyer?"

Jake's eyebrows lifted.

"Olivia mentioned her," Nera said, trying not to sound sulky. "You could've told me you'd used a plant."

"Plausible deniability, Nera. Every secret I keep is to protect you."

Nera knew that. Jake got his hands dirty to keep hers clean. He was the reason this company was still – barely – afloat. She had tried so hard to ensure Equinoxx was fair and equitable in every aspect of the business, and her integrity was killing them.

Jake's gaze slid over Nera's shoulder as someone knocked on the door. "Come in."

Killian entered. Nera's body tensed, almost involuntarily. She did *not* like Killian. He was Jake's sister's nephew's cousin's son or something, and he was good at his job. But Nera had caught him in this office last year. He claimed he was replacing a lost stylus. Only the screensaver for the tabletop was off – he said he'd knocked it on his way past. Did she believe him? She wasn't sure, and that was the problem.

A lot of people wanted to ruin Equinoxx. Oil companies, mining corporations, politicians, rival entrepreneurs. There was a fine line between being careful and being paranoid, and Nera wasn't sure whether she was crossing that line by being suspicious of Jake's own relatives.

"I'm sorry, Nera," Killian said. "Mr Wilcox. She didn't sign. And she wants us to email a statement of any anomalies that have arisen in Eidolon directly from her mapping."

Nera's heart sank at the same time her hopes lifted. It was impossible how badly she both wanted this and didn't want it at the same time. Maybe, just maybe, they could find another way.

"Thank you, Killian," Jake said.

"Close the door behind you," Nera said, and Killian gave her an indulgent smile before obliging.

"We're running out of time," Jake said once they were alone again. "We have to have the anomalies prepped and delivered by the new year. The companies involved have deadlines of their own."

"Have I mentioned how much I hate this?" Nera picked up a bouncy ball and thumped it against the carpet grass.

"If we don't get that anomaly, we risk the entire agreement."

"We already have two. Isn't that enough?"

"Two won't get us out of the red. Even selling all six barely covers us. Project Eidolon is sucking funds from every pocket. Unless we start utilizing its financial aspects–"

"I told you not to threaten me with financials."

"You're failing to see the consequences of not getting the money. How will we show the population we can stop climate change if we can't run Eidolon long enough to prove it?"

Nera hurled the ball against the wall. "Then what are you going to do? Take the anomaly without the right permissions? If we get caught doing anything against the contract, it will sink the whole project anyway."

"I have a backup plan."

"Of course you do."

There was a time when Nera thought she might be in love with Jake, despite the fact he was a rich white guy twenty-six years her senior. But she'd come to realize their relationship was so much more complex than love. They were two pieces of flint in a world full of kindling, able to spark flames and set humanity alight with hope…as long as they worked together.

It was Jake who'd come up with the idea to use the Eidolon anomalies as their source of funds. It was Jake who'd ensured they kept their legal rights in the gray area. Equinoxx and all of Nera's companies would continue perpetually because of Jacob P. Wilcox.

"Do you trust me?"

Nera turned away from the screen. It was easier if she wasn't looking at him.

"Nera. I can deal with Olivia Alexander."

Sometimes she hated his dirty hands.

"We're taking the world back," he said, quoting the Equinoxx slogan.

Nera shut her eyes and replied with the little-known addition – the one their legal team had advised them to leave out.

"Whatever it takes."

To: gtuyangxha483917@landofnod.com
From: jacobpwilcox@equinoxxtechnology.co
Subject: Job

OLIVIA ALEXANDER
CHEATING HUSBAND – SUICIDE APPROPRIATE
DEPLOY SLEEPER ASAP

10

Olivia didn't know how much longer she could live like this. How many nights could she spend in the spare room, ignoring Matt's pleas to talk? She had to make a decision. Act like nothing was happening and patiently wait for the affair to be over? Or confront him and lose everything?

She hated to admit it, but she missed him. The first thing she'd wanted to do, after being driven home by that hell-car, was tell him about Equinoxx. The building, the thrones, meeting Nera Blake. And the dreamscape. How could she keep all of it to herself? How could she not share her day with the one person she trusted most?

Had trusted.

Olivia tossed and turned all night, her thoughts full of Eidolon, the mysterious anomaly, Matt, Sarina. When she heard Matt leave at seven, she got up too, restless. Maybe she'd exercise. She couldn't remember the last time she exercised.

Swimming was out of the question. The pool was right up against the balcony and she couldn't handle heights. Not any more. Going for a run seemed a bit much, especially considering the sky was gray and there was a slim chance of rain. A nice, quiet yoga session might be the way to go.

She set up the TV in the theatre. A YouTube ad played, featuring a smiling, sixty-year-old man wearing a hat with corks hanging from the brim.

"*G'day*," he said. "*The name's Forrest, and I'm here to offer you a newer, greener way of living. At Symbiosis—*"

Olivia hit the skip ad button, and the preppy yoga instructor had just started talking about centering the core when her phone buzzed. She paused the video to check the message. It was from an unknown number.

Get out.

A shiver rushed through her. Who would send her something like that?

Oh god…Sarina?

Or maybe it was a prank? A wrong number?

A stalker?

She decided to ignore it when another text buzzed through.

My informant warned me Equinoxx has a contract on your life. Run.

Olivia laughed through the fluttering of her heart. Someone was playing a joke on her. Despite knowing better than to feed the trolls – or the psychopaths – she typed back:

Who is this?

We talked on Saturday.

The caveman. Anger replaced the fear.

How did you get my number?

The apartment elevator dinged before she received an answer, and she rushed out of the theatre, half-expecting the shaggy man to walk in. But it was only the housekeeper bustling through with a bag of groceries. He looked as surprised to see her as she did him.

"Sorry," he said. "I was told you're usually sleeping at this time."

"You aren't Pat."

"No, Pat's sick. I'm Winken. I'm filling in." He had an American accent and twin silver streaks in his black hair that were so symmetrical they had to be dyed.

And his name was…Winken?

Olivia forced out a heavy breath. Just because she had a new housekeeper with a weird name, didn't mean he was an assassin.

An *assassin*.

Ridiculous.

He held up the bag of groceries. "You want your usual scrambled eggs?"

"Sure. Thanks. And coffee."

"Milk, one sugar." When he smiled, he flashed two gold teeth. "I have strict instructions."

She laughed because it was the polite thing to do, but she couldn't dispel her nerves. "Want me to show you where everything is?"

"I'm at home in a kitchen, Mrs Alexander. You just relax."

That was supposed to be her plan, but she didn't feel like doing yoga anymore. She could have a shower and get ready for the day. Or...

She glanced at Matt's office door. The addiction was irresistible. She wanted to see more of those emails. She *needed* to.

She ducked into the office and closed the door, as if she were doing something dirty. Waiting while the laptop powered up felt like an eternity. She fell into Matt's chair and watched his email account update. A dozen new work messages, along with one from Sarina, received eight minutes ago. It had a lot of silly gushing and heart emojis. Olivia scrolled down to see what Matt had sent earlier this morning.

She's still acting weird, it said. *I really think she knows. Part of me hopes she does, because every time I'm with her, I think of the next time I can be with you. I love you, my darling. I can't wait to see you tonight.*

Olivia stared at the message for a long, long time. She couldn't bring herself to close it.

Tonight.

Fucking *tonight*.

She didn't realize she was shaking until she heard the chair rattling beneath her.

What, exactly, did they have planned for tonight? And what cover story was he going to use this time?

She reached for her phone. Her mind had gone to Kass because Kass was always the first person she called in a crisis.

Her phone screen switched on when she picked it up. She'd received messages while she'd been staring at the email. All five were from the shaggy man.

7.41: They're going to kill you.

7.42: I don't know exactly what they're planning, but I know it's happening soon.

7.45: Are you there?

7.51: Olivia, for god's sake, at least let me know you got my message.

7.54: I'm nearby. I'm going to check on you.

A chill seized her. She thought again of Winken in her kitchen.

It wasn't real. It couldn't be real. The caveman was completely delusional.

Why would they kill me for a lousy signature?

She set down her phone and rubbed her temples. She had enough to deal with without this absurd claim.

Her phone buzzed.

If you die, it's enough of a legal gray area that they have a better chance of securing the rights of everything you mapped.

Are you sure?

YES

And then, several seconds later:

THEY'VE DONE IT BEFORE

She let out a shuddering breath and checked over her shoulder to make sure the office door was still closed.

My usual housekeeper is sick and someone called Winken has replaced her. I don't know who he is.

There was an agonizing silence before a new message came through.

Have you eaten the food?

Not yet

Come up with an excuse not to eat. Don't say anything to make him suspicious. I'll be there in a few minutes.

This couldn't be happening. She couldn't have a cheating husband *and* a global corporation trying to kill her. Her life wasn't drama anymore. It was mimosas and sleep ins and safe, creative classes like pottery or life drawing.

Someone knocked on the office door. A surprised yelp escaped her.

"Sorry," said Winken. "Your breakfast is ready. Would you like it out on the balcony? It's humid out there, but it hasn't started raining."

The balcony? Oh hell no.

"Leave it on the dining table," she said. Her voice sounded funny. She couldn't quite catch her breath. "I'll be done in a second. I'm just finishing an email."

"No problem, Mrs Alexander."

She stared at Matt's laptop, wondering whether to email him through his own account. But how ludicrous would it sound? *Help, I think the housekeeper's trying to kill me.*

Not only would she come across as paranoid, but he'd know she'd gotten into his account, and they'd have to talk about Sarina. She wasn't ready to deal with that.

She drummed her fingers nervously, wondering how long she could get away with hiding in here.

Too soon, Winken knocked again. "Your breakfast is getting cold, Mrs Alexander."

Were housekeepers always this pushy?

Paranoia had gripped her now. The office wasn't secure enough. What she needed was a locked room, and there was only one of them in the apartment. She exhaled slowly, gathering the courage to get up and open the door. Winken was standing in the hallway. Waiting.

Jesus.

"I'm going to have a quick shower." She gestured to her workout gear, even though she'd barely done two minutes of yoga. "Won't be long."

He smiled and nodded. "I'll pour the coffee."

It was difficult not to sprint to the *en suite*. She forced her pace to remain at a relaxed stroll. When she got to the bathroom, she locked the door and turned on the shower without getting in.

"God," she moaned, sinking onto the toilet seat. The stress was too much. How long would she have to wait for the shaggy man?

She dropped her head in her hands. Her empty hands.

Her phone was still in Matt's office.

She jerked her head up again. "Shit," she hissed to herself. "Fuck fuck fuck. Oh shit. Oh god."

What if Winken took it? What if he saw the message before the shaggy man arrived? If he was really, actually here to kill her, he wouldn't care about subtlety once he realized she knew. He'd just kill her outright.

"Ohhh my god."

She got up and rested her head against the door. She had to go out again. Soon. *Now.*

Get it done, Livvie.

Her body refused to follow her commands.

"It's okay," she told herself, as she always did during an anxiety attack. "I'm fine. I. Am. Fine."

Except her anxiety attacks were usually about normal things. In those circumstances, she was able to convince herself she'd be safe as long as she was careful.

She was starting to feel lightheaded.

"I'm probably overreacting," she whispered, eyes squeezed shut. "He knows what I have for breakfast. He knows how I like my coffee. He *must've* talked to Pat. It's going to be fine. I'm safe. I'm definitely safe."

Get it done, Livvie!

At last, she slipped out of the *en suite* and shut the door behind her without making a sound. Winken was in the kitchen, washing up. His back was to her.

She steadied her nerves and crept down the hall, returning to Matt's office. Her phone was still there. She pounced on it, praying for a new text.

Nothing.

"Shit," she whispered, perching on the desk.

Where the hell was the shaggy man?

Her thigh must've nudged the wireless mouse, because the laptop woke up again. The note-taking app was open, with a pink sticky on the screen. Weird – it hadn't been there before. She leaned down to read what was written.

I know about Sarina, you bastard. How could you do this to me? I hope the guilt eats you alive. I hope you see my body every time you close your eyes.

Olivia stared blankly at the message. She hadn't written this, but it looked like it was from her. It was what she'd *wanted* to email him, sure, except for the part where she hoped he saw her body when he closed his eyes. She wasn't that vain. And it was a weird way to phrase–

Body.

Body.

It wasn't a scathing divorce demand.

It was a suicide note.

"Oh my god," she moaned softly. "Oh my god, oh my god."

The shaggy man was telling the truth. Equinoxx were going to kill her, and their hit man was in her apartment.

"Oh my god. Oh my god."

She fumbled with her phone to send the shaggy man a message for help. Her fingers tripped over the keys.

Stay calm, came his immediate reply. Then, not long after, **I'm outside your building. Pull yourself together. Don't make him suspicious.**

She tucked the phone in the waistband of her yoga pants and pressed her sweaty palms to her eyes. Help had come. She was *not* going to die.

A sharp buzzer echoed through the apartment.

"Delivery for Olivia."

Perhaps the most beautiful words that had ever been spoken. She held back a sob of relief.

She heard Winken say she was in the shower.

"No, not yet," she said, walking a little too quickly into the main living area. "I've been fussing about, sorry."

Winken turned to the bedroom, where there was clearly the sound of running water.

"I put bleach in the shower recess earlier," Olivia said with a smoothness she didn't know she had. "Just rinsing it out." She shot him a smile that wobbled a bit. "Back in two shakes."

She got into the elevator. It seemed to take forever for the doors to close. Even when she was descending, she kept imagining the elevator would stop and head back up.

It was only when the lobby sign dinged that she allowed relief to flood through her. The shaggy man was waiting at the exit. She raced across the lobby and threw herself into his arms. He grunted in surprise.

"He was going to kill me," she said between dry sobs. "He was going to *kill me*."

The shaggy man pried her off him. "Come on," he said, glancing at the elevator as it closed again and made its ascent. "We need to get out of here. Now."

EIDOLON

11

For the third time in a minute, Liv checked her phone. The route to the Equinoxx hub was up on StarShine Maps. In the corner was a bunch of data – air quality, global temperature averages, carbon emissions. Liv didn't pay much attention to the numbers, but at least they were green. Her immediate problem was her GPS tracking dot, which was blinking a happy purple in the same spot.

Around her, the café bustled with early morning commuters grabbing a coffee or quick breakfast. Their cars waited outside, plugged into charging stations. The clouds and rain of the past few days meant the vehicular photovoltaic systems needed a boost.

Liv watched a blue sedan drive away as a black van rolled in. She had wanted to rush off to the Equinoxx hub yesterday afternoon, but it was several hundred kilometers north and Kazzy had wisely pointed out they'd be closed on a Sunday. So Liv had waited the whole night, restless and frustrated and terrified. Who was this 'visitor,' this man who wasn't Pravit? What had he shown Reef about Equinoxx? And, more importantly, what had

Equinoxx done when they'd discovered Reef knew…whatever it was he knew?

She wanted answers. Now.

Except she hadn't realized Kazzy's car needed charging, so she was stuck waiting an extra thirty-five minutes just off Wanneroo Road, which would lead her to the long drive north.

"Mummy, juice?"

"Please."

"Peas."

Liv passed Bobbi her cup. She'd gone back and forth about whether to take her daughter on this trip. Eventually she'd decided Bobbi was already missing one parent, and couldn't bear the thought of her asking where Mummy was too.

Bobbi used a spoon to scoop her juice. Red light shimmered on the window beside them, reflected from her little sparkly shoes. The car's charging station showed it was 76% done.

Liv drummed her fingers on the table. 76% might've been enough, if not for the fact Equinoxx was so far away. Liv wanted to be prepared. She was going to confront those people face-to-face. No calls, no appointments, no way for them to evade her.

A man in a leather jacket entered the café, supporting a hobbling, frizzy-haired woman. A warm breeze followed them in, though it was still early.

"Mummy, we see Daddy?"

"I hope so," Liv said, dragging her attention away from the doors.

"I miss Daddy."

"Me too, baby."

Bobbi pretended to feed Mr Piggy part of her half-chewed breakfast. The croissant had been a bad idea – there were pastry flakes all over the table, all over Bobbi's dress and all over Liv. If Liv had thought about it for two seconds, she would've gotten something different.

The man led the frizzy-haired woman to the next table over. She eased into a chair with a pained expression.

"Wait here, darlin'," the man said, in a Southern US drawl. "I'll get you a coffee."

"And a croissant," the woman said in the same accent, eying Bobbi's. She grinned at Liv. Liv gave a strained smile in return.

The car was 79% charged.

"Mummy, Bobbi cat?"

"I'm using the phone right now."

"Bobbi cat. Cat!"

Liv switched her map to the camera and turned on the cat filter. Bobbi stared at herself, now overlaid with the ears and nose of a cat.

"Bobbi cat!" she said, pleased.

Liv took her phone back. "Finish your food. No more for Mr Piggy. All for Bobbi."

The man waited in the queue as the woman leaned gingerly to one side to check her pockets. She sniffled. "Sorry to be a bother, honey, but would you mind grabbing me a serviette?" She pointed to the counter, where there were utensils and a pile of serviettes.

Liv got up, batting flakes from her tank top. Maybe they should just leave. She was terrible at sitting around doing nothing.

Her phone dinged with a work notification. She shoved it into her jeans pocket without checking. She'd been calling in sick since Reef went missing, and honestly, she didn't care what her boss thought. There were plenty of other employees to serve pies to the public. Liv had been meaning to contact her old skydiving job for months now. She grabbed a couple of serviettes and made the decision that when – *when* – she got Reef back, she would talk to Starfish Steve.

"Mummy!"

Liv turned to find the frizzy-haired woman grabbing Bobbi from her chair. Mr Piggy fell to the floor. The woman ran for the automatic doors with Bobbi in her arms, her hobble gone.

Liv moved before her brain had caught up. She sprinted halfway across the café before someone yanked her back. The man with the leather jacket had grabbed her wrist.

"Help!" The word ripped from Liv as a shriek. Outside, the

woman bundled Bobbi into the back of the newly-arrived black van. Bobbi was screaming.

"My baby!"

Customers stared at her, agape. Useless.

Liv spun to the man and smashed her fist into his nose. He reeled back with a yelp. She took advantage of his surprise to slam her knee into his crotch. As soon as he let go, she raced for the automatic doors. The woman was climbing into the van. She shut the door and the van started to move.

"No no no!"

The people at the charging stations were *just standing there*.

"Stop it! Stop the car, stop it!"

She wasn't going to make it. The van was moving, and she wasn't going to catch up–

A dirty Hilux screeched into the station, swerving in front of the van to block its path. Someone jumped out.

"Reef!"

Hope was effervescence in her veins. Reef wrenched open the van's door and dragged the woman out by her frizzy hair. Liv reached the back. She fumbled with the handle, almost sobbing in relief when it clicked open. Bobbi's screams were near deafening.

Liv hauled her out and wrapped her arms around her small, quaking body. "It's all right, baby, it's all right. Mummy's got you." The scent of mango shampoo engulfed her. "Shhh, shhh. Mummy's here."

"Liv!" Reef's panicked voice cut over Bobbi's wails.

The man with the leather jacket was running towards them, blood streaming down his face.

"In the car," Reef said. "Go!"

Liv rushed with Bobbi to the passenger side of the Hilux. There was no time for the car seat – she climbed in with Bobbi on her lap. Reef threw himself into the driver's side and gunned the engine before he'd even closed the door. Liv pulled her seatbelt across herself and Bobbi.

The frizzy-haired woman lunged in front of them. Her body hit the bonnet with a violent thud. Liv sucked in a horrified breath.

Reef accelerated. The woman toppled off the bonnet and the car jolted as they ran over her.

Liv's curse was lost beneath Bobbi's screams. She checked the side mirror to see how the woman had fared. The body lay on the road…and then vanished. Just gone. Like the crumb on the officer's collar, one moment the woman was there, the next she wasn't.

Reef turned a sharp corner, careening into traffic.

"Reef," Liv said weakly.

"I didn't get rid of the other one," Reef said. "But I don't think it matters. They'll just keep coming."

"Reef."

"Wait." He swerved between cars. Horns blared. They sailed through a red light and barely missed a bus.

"Oh god," Liv said, clinging to Bobbi tighter. Bobbi hadn't stopped screaming.

"Hang on, I have to lose them."

Liv shut her eyes, reliving the woman hitting the bonnet. "She disappeared. She *disappeared.*"

"I know, Liv." Reef turned sharply onto Wanneroo Road, forcing cars to slam on their brakes. At least now they were heading north, opposite peak hour traffic. Reef pushed the car well past the speed limit. They shot forward. Bobbi started to sob.

"Turn off your phone."

Liv glanced at him.

"They'll track you," he said. "Turn it off."

Liv wriggled her phone from her pocket, ignoring the painful throb in her knuckles from when she'd punched the man. She switched the phone off and chucked it in the back.

Reef continued to check the rear view mirror.

"Who are they?" Liv said.

"I'll explain when we're safe."

Liv jiggled Bobbi on her lap. "Shhh, baby, it's okay. Look who's here. It's Daddy. Daddy's back."

"Dad-dy," she blubbered.

"Hello, Bob-Bob." Reef's voice was extra cheery. "Did you miss me?"

"Uh…huh," she said through saliva and tears.

He reached across to tousle her hair. "I missed you too. So much."

"Can we stop somewhere and put her in the car seat?"

"Not yet." He checked the rear-view mirror again.

"It's too dangerous–"

"I'd rather be dead than let them catch us."

"Oh, Jesus."

"I'm sorry."

"Is it Equinoxx? Did you find out what they did to us?"

A shiver passed through him.

"Were they the ones…the people who tried to take Bobbi?"

"Sort of. I promise I'll tell you everything." His gaze fell to Bobbi, who was hiccupping and staring at him with wide, wet eyes. "Later."

Wanneroo Road turned into Indian Ocean Drive, giving them a smooth and spacious path, with bushland on either side. Reef continued to drive north until the traffic became non-existent. He pulled off onto a dirt track.

"We can put her in the car seat now." He got out, coming around to Liv's side to pick up Bobbi. "How's my little Bob-Bob?" He kissed her a dozen times on the head and face and was rewarded with a watery giggle.

"Daddy, look at my shoes."

"They're very sparkly. Let me guess. Aunny Kazzy bought them for you?"

"Red."

"They are red, good girl."

"Red!"

Liv listened to the buckles click on the car seat behind her. She stared straight ahead at the bush. Her door stayed open.

"I thought they were going to take her away," she said quietly.

Reef closed the back door. "Me too."

"They almost did." Liv blinked back tears.

"I'm sorry. I should've come home sooner."

"Where were you? I thought…" She swallowed. "I didn't know whether I was going to see you again."

He leaned in and kissed her, hard. His mouth was hot and rough and achingly familiar. She ran her fingers through his overgrown beard.

He felt like home.

"Come here." He pulled her out of the car and wrapped his arms around her. His mouth found hers again.

Bobbi sang out from inside the car, but Liv needed this moment. She needed to feel Reef's living, breathing body. His heart beat strong and steady beneath her palm.

"Where did you go?" she said, drawing away. "What happened?"

He lifted her hand to kiss her fingertips and knuckles. His eyes closed and pleasure crossed his face. Or perhaps it was pain – there was something about the way his brow creased that confused her.

"You feel so real," he said hoarsely. For the first time, she noticed the bags under his eyes.

"When's the last time you slept?"

"I don't remember." He kissed along the inside of her wrist. "I've been trying to prepare…We have a safe house, at least for now. Somewhere we can hide Bobbi."

"From who? Who wants her?"

He didn't answer.

She gently tugged her hand from his grip. "Reef. I need to know what's going on."

With what looked like great effort, he opened his eyes. He started to speak, but was cut off by a cry.

"Mummy!" Liv turned. Bobbi was kicking her arms and legs in the car seat. Liv opened the back door as Bobbi yelled, "Mr Piggy, Mr Piggy!"

Liv had a dreadful flashback of Mr Piggy toppling to the ground as the frizzy-haired woman snatched Bobbi.

"Oh no, he's still at the café."

"We can't go back," Reef said.

"I know, but–"

Bobbi's wails grew louder. Considering how much she'd already screamed, Liv had been sure she'd tired herself out.

"I'm sorry, Bob-Bob," Reef said, moving to kiss Bobbi on the forehead. "Mr Piggy's gone on an adventure. He'll come back later."

"Puh-Puh-Piggy," Bobbi sobbed.

Liv's heart broke. She stroked Bobbi's hair as Reef double-checked the car seat buckles.

"We have to get to the safe house," he said. "It's a few hours from here. When we're there, I'll tell you everything."

"You mean what Equinoxx did to us?"

Rather than answer, he closed Bobbi's door and started for the driver's side. Liv hurried to stop him. "Oh no you don't. You're exhausted. I'll drive, you direct."

"I–"

"If we want to make it there alive, I'm driving. Understood?"

He nodded.

Liv opened the driver's door, then paused, chest tight. "It's tumors, isn't it?"

"Huh?"

"What Equinoxx did to us. It's tumors, or brain damage, or something like that."

Reef touched her arm and said softly, "There's nothing wrong with us."

"But the hallucinations. The derealizations. Reef, that woman you ran over *disappeared*."

"I promise you, Livvie. We're not sick."

The tightness in Liv's chest eased somewhat. "Then…?"

"Just let us get to the safe house first. We shouldn't be out in the open."

"We're definitely not dying?"

"We're definitely not dying."

"And Bobbi's okay?"

"Bobbi's fine," he said, even as Bobbi continued to blubber in her car seat. "Normal. Perfect."

Liv dared a breath of relief.

But then, if they weren't affected by the mapping and Bobbi was okay, what the hell was going on?

OUTSIDE

To: jacobpwilcox@equinoxxtechnology.co
From: retrievalunit@basenxj451.com
Subject: Retrieval update

LEVEL FIVE CITIZEN (AUSTRALIAN POINT)
UNSUCCESSFULLY RETRIEVED
INTERFERENCE BY (FATHER?)
CONTACT RETRIEVAL TEAM IMMEDIATELY

12

The shaggy man was talking, but Olivia couldn't concentrate on what he was saying. She clung to her seatbelt as he sped onto the freeway, without much space between his Ute and the next car. She should've gotten into the backseat. Normally, she would have.

But this wasn't a 'normally' situation. *Someone had tried to kill her.*

"Olivia." The man snapped his fingers in front of her face. "Olivia! Are you hurt?"

"Huh?"

"Did that guy hurt you?"

"No." She cringed as the car in front of them braked, causing them to careen up to the tailgate. "Can you please slow down?"

"What? Why?"

"Please."

The man obliged, smiling wryly. "A hit man comes into your house to murder you, and you're worried about a car ride?"

"Imagine if I escaped a hit man, only to get killed by your reckless driving."

"Reckless? I'm driving normally."

"Who are you? Do you work for Equinoxx?"

He snorted.

"Okay, then how are you involved in this?"

"I'm Aidan. An old friend of mine, Pravit Arya, got me involved."

Olivia's hands ached. She loosened her stranglehold on the seatbelt. "I met Pravit."

"He told me." Aidan shot her a sideways glance. "I hear Nera Blake took you to Eidolon. That's big."

"Was it Pravit who left the note in my hand?"

"Yes, and he thanks you for not signing the contract."

She had so many questions. Where to even start?

Someone had tried to kill her.

Why? What could she have possibly mapped into the mindscape that Equinoxx wanted so badly?

"Why is this happening to me?" she said at last.

"Pure bad luck," Aidan said. "Have you ever had a near-death experience?"

"You mean besides just then?"

"I mean, as in, your heart stopped and you were resuscitated?"

"Why do you ask?"

"You wanted to know why this is happening. Pravit has a theory I want to test out. So have you?"

"Had a near-death experience?" Olivia gazed out the window. "Yes."

"What happened?"

"I got hit by a car."

She felt them slow. Aidan had taken his foot off the accelerator. Vehicles zoomed around them as they eased to well under the speed limit. Olivia exhaled gratefully.

"What does it have to do with Equinoxx?" she said.

"You know about the different levels of citizens in Eidolon, right?"

"Uh, I guess? Level one is people who had done the mapping—"

"Other way around. Level one citizens are the glitchy ones. The program only has limited data of their personalities. That includes citizens born inside Eidolon."

"Right. Then level two were the good friends or relatives of people who had done the mapping."

"Level three are people who did the mapping."

"Did you do the mapping?"

"Unfortunately," Aidan said, his hands tightening on the steering wheel. "Pravit asked me to participate years ago. I had insider information that he wasn't sure they could get anywhere else."

"Like what?"

"Just…various corporations and places that aren't easily accessed."

"My best friend is like you. Her specialty is secrets." In fact, Olivia still didn't know what Kass really did for a job. The business consultancy was a front for something much more dubious. They'd made a game of it over the years. Olivia's guesses had ranged from bank thief to Bond-style villain. She added, "But she didn't do the mapping because she's smarter with her insider information."

"My point is," Aidan said, annoyed, "I did a favor for a friend, and it bit me in the ass."

"So your simulation is a level three citizen."

"No, actually. Neither is yours. Some of the simulations glitched when they were programmed in. They're classified as a level four – a completely unexpected consequence of the mapping. That's why I asked you about the near-death experience. Pravit suspects it's happening to the simulations of people who've been resuscitated."

"What's a level four citizen like?" Olivia pictured some horrifically warped version of herself roaming the streets of Eidolon like a bloodthirsty monster.

"They're unprogrammable, completely independent and have no idea they're a simulation. They think they're the real version of themselves, and that Eidolon is the real world."

"Whoa."

"Yeah."

Olivia tried to imagine it. Somewhere in Eidolon, there was another her walking around, living her own life without any idea she was in a mindscape. "Wait, are you sure *we're* not the fake ones?"

"You visited Eidolon yesterday."

"What if it was a world inside a world? Eido-ception?" Olivia pinched herself, as if that would make a difference.

"Eidolon was created to study the effects of renewable energy. Look around. Does our world look any better to you?"

Considering there was a slight haze in the air from the bushfires, no. No, the world didn't look any better.

"So the copy of me is what Equinoxx is after?"

"No. You would still retain the rights to your simulation, even though she's level four. The first contract you signed is ironclad about that. But what she produced…no one in this world technically has those rights."

"What she produced?"

"Your simulation had a baby. And not a level one, either. She's a fully formed, perfectly functioning, unprogrammable citizen. A level five."

"I had a *baby?*"

"Her name is Bobbi. She's two and a half. She's one of the few level five citizens in Eidolon, and Equinoxx wants full rights to her."

"Why?"

"So they can sell her."

"What! How? To who?"

"Pharmacies," Aidan said, and something strange happened in his voice – a rough, choking sound that bordered on rage. "Level five citizens are the perfect candidates for human testing. They react just like us without being technically human. Pharmaceutical companies are willing to pay incomprehensible amounts to get their hands on them."

"Oh…god."

Olivia thought of the bartender who'd poured her a sparkling shiraz in Elizabeth Quay. The people walking past, laughing, talking, feeling as alive as anyone in the real world. Then she imagined what it would be like to take a child – a child who had no idea she was computer generated – and *do things* to her.

"Oh god," she said again. "How? How could anyone think that's okay?"

"Equinoxx is fast falling into bankruptcy. If they do this, with everything clear and legal, no one can stop them from profiting off the sales, and they can keep Eidolon running."

"Surely a court would rule against human testing? If a simulation thinks they're human–"

"And there lies the gray area. Are they human? Or are they just a computer program? That question is what will keep the case in courts for years, maybe decades. In the meantime, the human testing can continue unimpeded and Equinoxx will have time to get definitive proof that their renewable technology can affect global temperatures. That's all they need, really. Enough time to show it works."

Olivia sat in stunned silence as Aidan turned east.

"There has to be another way to get funding," she said finally.

"Maybe, but this way will give them a mountain of money, fast. They want the rights to your daughter, and to them your signature – or your death – is worth trillions of dollars."

"Oh." Everything was starting to feel fuzzy.

"I'm sorry," Aidan said. "It's a lot."

"It...is." Olivia stared at her hands. "But in the end, they *are* just simulations. Right? And I'm a living, breathing person. Maybe I should sign the contract–"

"No."

"I don't want to die for a computer program!"

Even as she said it, it felt wrong.

"Don't make any decisions yet. At least until you see her for yourself. Meet Bobbi, and then tell me you're willing to let them hurt her."

"Shouldn't we call the police?"

"Pravit's gathering evidence to whistleblow. He's intercepting memos and orders from the top level. We have to sit tight until he's got enough to stop Equinoxx in its tracks."

"Sit tight? Did you miss the part where someone tried to kill me?"

"You'll be safe at my place."

"For how long? When is Pravit planning to come forward? And – shit – what about my husband? What if the hit man goes after him?"

"He won't."

"Matt's signature is worth as much as mine, surely." Olivia fumbled to grab her phone from her yoga pants.

"Why?"

"Why do you think? The father's signature is just as important, isn't it?"

Aidan reached to stop her calling. "Matt's not Bobbi's father. You're not with him in Eidolon."

It was like a hornet's sting, right through the heart. Their simulations weren't together? Why? What happened? Not Sarina. Please, not Sarina there too.

"There's no father listed on the birth certificate," Aidan continued. "You're the only one who can grant Bobbi's rights to Equinoxx."

"No father listed? What was she, a bloody immaculate inception?"

"It's complicated."

"How is it complicated?"

"There are elements involved—"

"What elements?"

Aidan was silent for a while. His knuckles were white on the steering wheel. "I'm not technically in the system."

"What system? Equinoxx?"

"No, the government."

"But what does that have to do with anything?"

He looked at her, exasperated. And sort of uneasily. Like he was uncomfortable? It was hard to tell under all that shaggy beard and – *holy shit*.

"You're the father."

He turned his gaze back to the road.

Olivia gaped at him. "You're Bobbi's father."

"My simulation is, yes."

"We...?"

"Are together in Eidolon. Have been for years."

"You...and me?" Olivia shook her head. "That doesn't make any sense. I was engaged to Matt when I did the mapping. Why would we have broken up?"

"Different circumstances led to different outcomes, I guess."

"But it feels like my simulation isn't acting at all like me. I thought our minds were duplicated into the system."

Aidan gave a one-shouldered shrug. "A lot can happen in four years. I hardly recognize myself, either."

"You've met your simulation?"

"Pravit needed me to convince the simulation that he's in Eidolon. He didn't take it well."

"I imagine that's a hard conversation to have."

"You're going to have to do it too."

Olivia grimaced. She didn't know how she felt about this other version of her. Although, she was intrigued at the thought of seeing herself as a mother. Having children had never been at the forefront of her mind.

"Both our simulations need to be told the truth so they can protect Bobbi," Aidan said. "Pravit's worried Equinoxx is going to go after her, if they haven't already."

"How are they going to stop Equinoxx when Equinoxx has full control over the mindscape?"

"Equinoxx can't reprogram any citizens without consent, which means the only thing our simulations really have to worry about is the visitors – the people from our world going in."

"But they can just pop in and grab Bobbi whenever."

"Visitors can only enter the world by locations, not people. If the other versions of us stay hidden, it'll be difficult to find them."

"So they have to stay hidden until…when? Pravit whistleblows? Why don't we just put all this up on social media right now? I don't mean to sound like a broken record here, but *someone tried to kill me*. I should at least be able to tweet about it."

Neither of them laughed at this…not-absurdity.

"Equinoxx have the resources to cover up their actions; maybe hide the level five citizens altogether. The mindscape is an unknown variable to everybody except their scientists. If people start investigating now, they won't know what to look for. Pravit needs to gather enough information to be ready and actionable as soon as it's out. In the meantime, we can't blow his cover. So no, you can't tweet about it. And no, you can't tell anyone else what's going on."

Olivia, who had her messages open, closed them again. "What am I supposed to tell Matt?"

"Nothing. You need to disappear, at least for now. If he doesn't know what's going on, then he's safe from Equinoxx."

Olivia swallowed at the marble that had appeared in her throat. She didn't want to disappear. She wanted to go home.

And what about her parents? They would be frantic.

As if reading her mind, Aidan said, "It's better everyone thinks you're missing than knows you're dead. Switch off your phone – we don't want anyone tracking you."

Olivia turned off her phone. "It's lucky my best friend doesn't care about me anymore."

"Why?"

"Because if anyone would be able to track me down, it's her."

13

This was not supposed to be happening. Briony pressed more buttons on the coffee machine, but it kept blinking an error message. Something about descaling?

Bloody piece of junk. It was always beeping about one thing or another. More water, more beans, clean out grounds tray, do this, do that. Sounded like bloody Wilcox. Bloody Wilcox and his bloody orders.

"Shit," she whispered, and banged on the side of the machine. Why wouldn't it just make a coffee?

"What's taking so long?" Kass padded in with her empty cup. "You kill the machine or something?"

Briony turned to her, guilty. If Kass had heard her hitting the machine, she didn't say anything.

"Sorry, love. It needs a descaling or a manicure or something."

Kass laughed and put her cup in the sink. "That's all right. I could probably lay off the caffeine for a bit." She checked the clock hopefully. "Suppose it's too early for a wine?"

Briony laughed, but it was loud and giggly, and Kass looked at her strangely. Briony worried it would turn into tears.

Bloody Wilcox.

"Listen," Briony said. The kitchen window was open; the smell of the neighbor's roses was tangled in the October sunshine. "We have to talk."

Kass' brow creased.

Oh Lord. Briony would never see those three freckles again, set in a V-shape on Kass' nose. She would never again make Kass toss back her head and cackle-laugh. There would be no more nights cuddled up on Kass' couch, sharing a bottle of wine, crammed beneath a blanket as they made jokes about the terrible plot of Emmerdale, and while Kass claimed the soapie was ridiculous, Briony knew she was hooked.

Kass probably wouldn't keep watching Emmerdale after Briony was gone.

Bloody, bloody Wilcox.

He should've known better than to send a non-spy to do a spy's job. Briony was the lowest tier in her legal firm. She was chosen because she was young and outgoing and into women, and she'd said yes because she needed the money. But she'd give every cent back if it meant she could stay with Kass without having to confess their relationship was a lie.

"What's the matter?" Kass said.

Briony didn't want to do this. She wanted to sit in the sun and smell the roses and debate the merits of having a wine at eleven in the morning.

Assignment is over. Extract yourself.

Mr Wilcox's text was like a black hole in her phone.

"Babe," Kass said. "What is it?"

The doorbell chimed, a sweet, pealing sound that rang across the marble tiles. Kass searched Briony's face a moment longer before leaving to answer it.

Briony sagged, relieved for the reprieve, but the silence didn't last.

"What the fuck are you doing here?"

Briony hurried to the door, unsure what had caused the bite in Kass' voice. Her nostrils were swamped with cologne before she saw the man on the porch.

"I'm looking for Olivia," he said.

Ah. The infamous Matt. While Briony had never met him in person, she'd heard enough ranting from Kass over the past few days to feel like she knew him.

He was in a dark blue suit. His brown hair curled at the nape of his neck and there was a soul patch on his chin. A diluted attempt at being cool. If Briony hadn't already hated him from Kass' tirades, she would now.

"She's not here." Kass moved to close the door. Matt stuck his polished shoe on the threshold to stop her.

"I dropped home to talk to her, but she's gone."

"Maybe she went shopping."

"Her handbag and wallet are still in the drawer."

"Then maybe she went for a walk."

"She's not answering her phone."

"There might be a reason for that."

"What's that supposed to mean?"

Kass drew herself up to her full height. Even shorter than him, and in her trackpants and singlet top, she looked formidable. "I think you should leave."

"If you have something to say to me, why don't you just say it?"

It was a trap; Briony recognized it immediately. Matt suspected Olivia knew about the affair, and he wanted confirmation from Kass. Briony willed Kass not to answer.

But Kass was Kass, and there was no stopping that tsunami.

"Do you remember what I told you on your wedding day? If you ever hurt Liv I would stitch up your eyes and mouth and throw your thrashing body into the river."

"It was an odd pep talk," Matt said with a wry smile.

"So who the hell is Sarina?"

Matt's smile died.

"Bri," Kass said coldly, without taking her glare from him, "get my sewing kit."

Briony's phone buzzed.

"I think there's been a misunderstanding," Matt said. "Where did you hear about Sarina? She's just a work colleague—"

"You fucking *liar*!"

"Listen to me. Olivia wouldn't leave her purse behind. She never called for her driver. If she didn't come here, I don't know where else she would've gone—"

Briony slipped her phone out of her pocket to check the message. It was from Mr Wilcox.

Change of situation. Hold position. Inform me immediately if Kass hears from Olivia.

What the hell? Was Olivia really missing?

"She's finally come to her senses and left you," Kass was saying to Matt. "I'm giving you one warning. Leave now, because I'm starting to feel murdery."

"I just wanted—"

"Murdery!"

Matt jumped back as Kass slammed the door. She stalked down the hall, breathing bull-like through her nose.

Briony glanced at the message again to make sure she hadn't made a mistake. Did this mean Equinoxx hadn't gotten Olivia's signature, even after her visit to the hub? How had *Nera Blake* not managed to talk Olivia into signing?

And, maybe the scariest thought of all, did Mr Wilcox have something to do with Olivia's disappearance?

14

Considering his appearance and the lingering scent of alcohol, Olivia had been expecting Aidan's house to be old and grimy and, well, much like Kass' childhood home. Curtains stained with cigarette smoke, a rusted screen door, possibly a mangy mutt in the concrete backyard.

Instead, Aidan took her to a cottage in the Darling Ranges. It was tucked in a shady valley, down a long driveway. He parked next to a beat-up Camry. Bees delighted among the bursting bottlebrush, frangipanis, agapanthus, and lavender, and wisteria spilled over the gutters. Native vegetation stretched on all sides, with no sign of where the property ended. They climbed the steps to a porch filled with succulents in clay pots. He opened the door. The interior smelled floral and woody. Rugs covered the floorboards, old ones, like her grandmother used to have.

To their left were squashy couches facing a fireplace, but Aiden led her straight through to the kitchen, where an older woman and a teenage girl sat at table covered in books. The girl's thick eyebrows flew up beneath her curly brown fringe. "Who's she?"

"Sophie, Olivia. Olivia, my sister Sophie."

"Sister?" Olivia would've more easily believed Aidan was the girl's father.

"Half-sister," Sophie said.

"This is Valentina," Aidan said, and the older woman nodded in acknowledgement. Her earrings, longer than her cropped hair, jangled from the movement. She looked less surprised at Olivia's presence. Sophie was still agog, as if she'd never seen another human before.

Valentina hauled herself out of her chair. Beneath her loose red tunic, her left arm ended in a stump at the wrist. "I'll make a cup of tea."

"Maybe water first," Aidan said as his phone rang. "She's had a shock."

Olivia shivered, remembering Winken. Aidan headed down the corridor to answer his phone.

"I have so many questions," Sophie said to Olivia. "Firstly, who the eff are you?"

"Manners, Sophie," Valentina said.

Olivia tried to catch part of Aidan's conversation down the hall.

"–to the safe house? We'll head there in a few hours then–"

"So you're, like, Aidan's girlfriend?" Sophie said.

"Uh, no, I…"

"Here." Valentina passed Olivia a large glass of water.

"–yeah, she's here. No, but they were damn close–"

"Drink," Valentina said.

Olivia's fingers tightened around the glass. If Aidan hadn't warned her about the assassin, she would be dead right now.

She would be *dead*.

Her breath drew in, ragged and sharp. She was acutely aware of the air on her skin, her tongue in her mouth. The muscles in her calves. Her eyelids, blinking. Her flesh, still warm. Her heart, pulsing and pulsing and pulsing…

The world was getting static-y–

"Drink," Valentina said again, louder.

Olivia obeyed, fighting off the dizziness as she gulped the water down. She set the empty glass on the table and said, "Got anything stronger?"

"Tea."

"Stronger than tea?"

Jaw tense, Valentina flicked the kettle on.

"That was Pravit," Aidan said, returning. "Equinoxx made a

move on Bobbi. Guess they assumed you'd be out of the picture by now."

Olivia wrapped her arms around herself.

Aidan continued. "We'll need you to go to Eidolon in a few hours, once our other selves have made it to the safe house. Liv's going to need a bit of convincing, if the experience with my simulation is anything to go by."

"Are you talking about the tech company?" Sophie said.

"Why don't you go for a walk?" Aidan said.

"No way. What's going on? What's Equinoxx got to do with us? Who's Pravit? And Bobbi? What simulation are you talking about?"

"Sophie. Walk. Now."

Sophie opened her mouth to argue, but Valentina said, "It may do well, for the time being. Perhaps dig up some potatoes for dinner?"

Throwing a death glare at Aidan, Sophie thumped her textbook closed and stalked away, muttering to herself. She slammed the door on her way out.

"Teenagers," Aidan said to Olivia, although privately Olivia thought Sophie had a right to be angry.

"Why don't you tell her the truth?"

"I don't want to put her in danger."

Valentina pulled a promising-looking brown bottle from beneath the sink, adding the amber liquid to Olivia's tea. Olivia accepted it gratefully and let it set her stomach alight.

"She should probably know to watch out for assassins," she said, wiping her mouth.

"Sophie doesn't leave the property. As long as we don't lead anyone here, she'll be safe."

Olivia eyed the textbooks cluttering the table. "She doesn't go to school?"

"Valentina teaches her."

"But she meets up with friends? Goes shopping? Hangs around McDonald's with a bunch of local kids?"

Valentina snorted. "You'd never catch Sophie at McDonald's."

"She leaves sometimes, though, right?" Olivia looked between Valentina and Aidan. Valentina turned to Aidan.

"She has online friends," Aidan said at last.

"*Jesus.*" Olivia sank into a chair.

"Sophie is hidden here for protection," Aidan said.

"From whom?"

"People you don't need to worry about. It's called a safe house for a reason."

Olivia massaged her temples, staring wide-eyed at nothing. She needed another swig of that amber drink.

"I'll pick you up supplies from the shops," Aidan said. "Clothes, toothbrush, that sort of thing. We don't have another bedroom, but you can share with Sophie."

"Maybe I should go to a hotel."

"You'll need ID, or at least a credit card. Equinoxx could track you."

The tea was starting to slosh in Olivia's stomach. These people were complete strangers, with what sounded like their own rather alarming problems.

She pulled out her phone. "I need to talk to my husband."

"Olivia, please. We've already discussed this."

"I know, but he'll call the police if I've gone missing, and they'll check the security camera from the lobby. They'll see you. They'll put your face all over social media. Considering you and Sophie are trying to stay hidden, I doubt that's what you want."

Aidan gave her an exasperated glance.

"I'm just telling you what will happen."

"All right, fine," he said, sitting across from her. "What are you going to say to him?"

"That I'm in danger and I'm in hiding."

"He'll still call the police."

"I'll ask him not to."

"If he knows you're in danger, he'll likely call the police, even if you tell him not to."

"Do you have a relative or a friend who might need your

assistance?" Valentina said. She was making another cup of tea. "You could tell him you've rushed off to help them with something. Maybe a friend's been through a breakup and needs you to stay for a little while."

Olivia grimaced. She'd already come to the realization that Matt was all she had. "I don't think that will work."

"Is there anything else you can say to him?" Aidan said. "Come on, Olivia, we're all at risk here."

Her fingers hovered over the screen. Yes, actually. There was one thing she could say. A biting cold spread through her chest as she began to type out the message.

"What are you writing?" Aidan said.

She ignored him. This was hard enough without having to explain it. Her throat was tight as she deleted and edited and deleted again. She didn't want to press send. She really, really didn't want to press send.

"Olivia?"

She held up the phone for Aidan to see.

I know about Sarina. I need some time alone. Please don't contact me for now.

"Perfect," Aidan said. "That'll keep him off our backs."

"Is this real?" Valentina said.

Olivia swallowed hard and nodded. Valentina gripped her shoulder comfortingly.

"Oh," Aidan said, and at least had the grace to look awkward. After a silence, he got to his feet. "I'll fetch those supplies then. Tell Sophie to finish her geography, would you, Valentina? I'll be back before it's time to go to the shed."

"The shed?" Olivia said.

"Our way into Eidolon." His gaze flickered to her phone. "Make sure that's turned off once the text is sent."

She glanced down at the message. Then, after Aidan had gone and Valentina had poured her another cup of that amber liquid – straight this time – she counted to three and pressed send.

15

The shed in question was literally a shed. It wasn't on Aidan's property – they'd had to drive about twenty minutes, climb over a fence and crunch through bushland to get there – but it was still a brick building the size of a double garage, with a roller door and the smell of engine oil. It was behind a house that had broken windows and graffiti on the walls.

The shed's windows were intact, but blacked out. There was the same spider web antenna on the roof as the one Olivia had seen at Equinoxx.

She slowed as they approached it. Aidan glanced back at her questioningly.

"It's just occurred to me that you could be a serial killer," she said. "And this is your killing room."

"Really?"

"I'm in the middle of nowhere with a complete stranger. No one else knows I'm here. I'd say I have the right to be on edge."

"Did you forget the part where I saved your life?"

"Maybe you were only saving me so you could have me for yourself."

Aidan gestured to her outfit. "Why would I have bought you a new wardrobe if I was planning to kill you?"

The clothes Aidan had returned with weren't exactly fashionable. They were more for working in the garden or lounging around the house. He'd underestimated her size – she was too tall for normal outfits – and it looked like the packet of underwear had come from a supermarket.

She'd had to wear them, though. It turned out that almost being assassinated made a person sweaty and gross, and after her shower she'd needed a fresh change of clothes. It had occurred to her as she was pulling on a tank top that Aidan probably bought Sophie's clothes too. The poor girl. No wonder she was so angry.

"The thing with your sister freaks me out," Olivia admitted. "How she's not allowed to leave the house. It feels like you're keeping her prisoner."

Aidan considered her. After a long silence, he said, "Sophie grew up in a cult."

"*What?*"

"Her mother asked me to take her away."

"Holy shit."

"She turns eighteen next year. By then, she should be safe from them. Legally, I mean."

"Were you in the cult too?"

"Look, I promise that Sophie's not a prisoner, and I'm not a serial killer. Okay?"

"That sounds like something a serial killer would say." Aidan sighed, but Olivia waved a dismissive hand. "All right, fine, I'll trust you for now. I guess I'd take you over Winken."

"I feel so validated." Aidan went around the side, and not long after came the hum of a generator. When he returned, he opened the roller door to reveal a setup of computers and a monitor and throne like the one in Equinoxx's lab.

"Where did you get all this?" Olivia said, moving to the throne.

"Pravit managed to get his hands on it when they upgraded the equipment." Aidan held up a silver crown. "These are the old versions of the NTDs. Nera Blake thought they looked too gaudy, so they changed the design–"

"To look like little spiders. I remember."

Aidan fired up the computers.

Olivia twisted her fingers, eying the throne. "Is it safe?"

"It's the same as the ones at Equinoxx."

"Even though it's an older version?"

"I've used it. It's fine." He switched on the monitor. "I'm going to send you to their safe house in Eidolon. My simulation should be expecting you, but it'll be up to you to convince your other self that she's not real."

"How am I supposed to do that?"

"Your presence should do most of the work. And my simulation will be there to help."

"It feels cruel."

"I agree," Aidan said. "But Liv needs to know, so she can protect Bobbi. Take a seat."

Olivia climbed onto the throne. "Have you met her? The other me?"

"I saw her through Pravit's monitor. He went to Eidolon to tell my simulation what's going on, and he briefly met Liv and Bobbi."

"Is she..." Olivia trailed off as Aidan placed the crown over her head. "What's she like?"

He concentrated a little too hard on adjusting the crown. "Different," was his eventual response, then he returned to the computer and said, "Get ready."

She closed her eyes. Shapes popped up in her vision. Valentina had made her play Tetris for the hour or so Aidan was shopping for supplies. Apparently, it helped with trauma. Olivia didn't know how to feel about the fact Valentina had known that off the cuff.

Cults and safe houses and secret sisters. Who *were* these people?

There was no red or silver light this time – when Olivia opened her eyes, she was standing somewhere else.

It was a small beach house with blue walls and sandy floors. Through the window was the ocean and a bright sky. She doubted she'd ever get used to how real this secondary world felt.

She smelled cooking garlic and onions, and turned to find a man standing at the kitchen stovetop. He was tall with chestnut-brown hair. A red tea towel was slung over one broad shoulder.

When he saw her, he stilled. A range of emotions crossed his exhausted features. "I barely recognized you."

"I'm Olivia," Olivia said tentatively. "From outside?"

There was the slightest flinch before the man returned his attention to the pan. "Yes, I know. Thank you for coming. Liv hasn't taken the news well. To be fair, I didn't expect her to."

"You're Aidan?"

Was this what Aidan looked like if he trimmed his beard and took care of himself? Maybe she could understand why her simulation jumped into bed with him, after all.

"Reef," he said.

"What?"

"My real name is Reef. My other self changed his name after going into hiding."

"Oh."

Well, at least this version of him was…freer with information.

He opened a can of something called Cheat Meat and tipped it in the pan.

Olivia crinkled her nose. "What are you cooking?"

"Synthesized beef." He grinned at her expression. "It's not as bad as it looks."

She remembered the dessert she'd tried at Equinoxx. "Nera Blake's invention?"

"Of course. Stops the need for so much cattle. Less methane, more trees. Although they're experimenting with their own version of silvopasture too – combining forest, agriculture, and grazing in the same space."

"Huh." Olivia wandered over and peered into the pan. She could feel the steam on her face and the heat of Aidan's body beside her.

Reef's body.

She peeked up to find his attention fixed on her.

"What?" she said.

"Sorry. It's just…you're so different."

"Different how?"

The back door opened.

"Stamp the sand off your feet," said a woman's voice. "That's it. Stamp stamp stamp."

"Mummy, where's Daddy? I show him my shell."

A little girl in a pink swimsuit ran into the house, but she stopped when she saw Olivia. Her black curls sprang around her face. Her wide brown eyes took in Olivia's appearance.

"Mummy," she cried, and Olivia's heart lurched in panic, but the girl ran back to the woman coming in and dove against her legs.

The woman stared at Olivia.

"It's all right," Reef said gently. "Liv, this is Olivia. Olivia, this is Liv and our daughter Bobbi."

Olivia gulped. It wasn't like looking in a mirror, not at all. Liv's short, tufty hair was scraped back into a ponytail. She was in boardies and a bikini top. Her hips were wider, there was muscle definition in her arms, and her complexion was several shades darker than Olivia's.

All her tattoos were visible.

"You're kidding," Liv said after a silence. "You think this is the real version of me?"

Olivia looked down at the horrible clothes Aidan had picked out. "I'm usually much more fashionable," she said.

Liv gave a strangled laugh. "Oh my god." She hefted Bobbi onto her hip. "Reef, Pravit is screwing with you."

"Was he screwing with me when those people tried to take Bobbi?"

"I don't know what that was, but I know we're not *computer simulations*. I mean, come on." She gave Olivia the once-over. "This is just, I don't know, an Equinoxx robot or something."

"A robot?" Olivia said.

"It's more believable than this world not being real. Than Bobbi and Reef and I not being real. Go stick your hand on that pan and tell me this is a simulation."

"I don't want to do that."

Liv smirked, as if she had won.

"Nera Blake took me to Eidolon before," Olivia said. "She explained I could feel pain while I'm in here, and honestly, I think I've felt enough pain to last me a lifetime."

Liv's smirk faltered. Olivia turned her gaze to Bobbi, who was clinging to Liv's neck.

"Was it worse?" Olivia whispered. "The birth? Was it worse than the accident?"

Liv looked to Reef. Olivia had the feeling they were silently communicating, but she couldn't tell what either were thinking.

"No," Liv said at last. "No, the accident was worse."

"Oh."

"You know about the accident?"

"I *lived* the accident. And the fallout. I flat-lined for fourteen seconds. I had bones from my hip put into my spine. The pain was so bad it felt like I was concreted to the bed. And the damn rehabilitation, where the physio, the core workouts, the hydro in the hot pool – it was all excruciating. I know. Believe me. I still feel an ache when I lift heavy objects, or when the weather's bad. I still wake up with pins and needles in my feet."

Liv's eyes were wet, even as she gritted her teeth. "They must've taken my memories when I did the mapping."

"It doesn't explain the derealizations," Reef said, switching the stovetop off. "Or the hallucinations. They're not delusions, Liv, they're glitches in Eidolon."

"I'm so sorry," Olivia said, because it looked like Liv was about to have a breakdown. "I'll do whatever I can to help."

Bobbi, who had obviously grown bored of being shy, wiggled to be let down. Liv set her on the floor, and she toddled over to Reef. "Daddy, look at my shell. Daddy! Look!"

He crouched down to examine the blue shell she held out. "That's amazing."

"Hungry."

"Lucky I've cooked for you."

"I don't want that."

"You don't even know what it is."

"I want banna."

"A banana? Hmm, let me see what I can do." Reef stood and opened the pantry. It was crammed with cans. To Olivia, he said, "We've stocked enough for a few months. Pravit says it should be over by the end of the year."

"Did he?" Olivia could feel Liv's stare on her. "I hope so. I don't like the idea of being stuck in a stranger's house for more than a few months. I mean…no offense, I know you're not a stranger here, but you are in my world. And no one knows where I am, not my parents, not even Matt."

"Matt?" Olivia turned to find her simulated self staring at her in shock. "You're still with Matt?"

"Daddy," Bobbi said, "I want banna!"

"I'm sorry, Bob-Bob, I don't think we have any bananas."

"Banna! BANNA!"

"What's wrong with Matt?" Even as Olivia said it, she thought of Sarina. Had he left Liv for Sarina in this world?

Before Liv could answer, Bobbi opened her mouth and let out a deafening scream. Everyone winced.

"She's tired," Liv said. "She hasn't had her nap today."

"There's no point talking right now," Reef said to Olivia over the wails and stomping feet. "You might as well go. You've done what you came to do."

"But I–" Olivia looked desperately to Liv. She still had so many questions. And Liv must've needed more, after everything she'd discovered.

But Liv was calmly moving to the floor next to Bobbi, holding out her arms for a cuddle as Bobbi screamed, and the next time Olivia blinked, she was back in the gloom, the air stifling, the smell of bushfire smoke lingering in her nose. The silence settled as thick as the dust in the shed.

"You okay?" Aidan said.

"Holy crap." Olivia pulled the crown off her head. "That was me. Me as a mum. I'm a *mum.*"

"I know."

"That was my daughter. That's what my daughter looks like."

"Do you see why you can't sign the contract?"

"Yes, obviously. That little girl…how could anyone want to hurt her?" She turned to the monitor, but of course it was black. "It's so surreal."

"How do you think your other self must feel?"

"I can't even imagine." Olivia examined the crown, thinking again of Bobbi. "Can I go back?"

"Maybe not now," Aidan said. "You've just disappeared into thin air. I think Liv's going to need some time."

"Do you think she's going to be okay?"

Aidan began powering down the machine. "She has to be. If she wants to protect Bobbi. She has to be."

To: jacobpwilcox@equinoxxtechnology.co
From: retrievalunit@basenxj451.com
Subject: Retrieval update

Eidolon police confirm OS tried to file a missing person report for partner, likely father of LEVEL FIVE CITIZEN (Australian point). Name of Reef Davidson. NO CITIZEN DATA FOUND. Suggest search Outside.

EIDOLON

16

After all the screaming, the whoosh of the ocean sounded too lovely, too peaceful. Liv hugged her legs, sitting on the wooden steps of the back porch as she gazed at the sandy path down to the beach.

The door creaked and Reef's heavy footsteps thumped behind her.

"Can I join you?"

Liv gestured to the empty spot on the step. She didn't look over as he sat down.

"She's finally asleep," he said. "Terrible timing. We're going to be up all night."

"I doubt I'll be sleeping, anyway."

She flinched as Reef touched her shoulder. He drew away. "Sorry."

"It's not you. It's…everything." Her fingers trailed the bumpy wood beneath her, warmed from the sun. Tiny grains of sand rolled against her fingerpads. "It feels the same."

"But not always," Reef said. "We've both had moments where we've been out of it, like we didn't really exist in the world."

Liv drew a shaky breath. "So how do we get back to the real world?"

"We don't."

"But–"

"We don't belong in the real world."

"We don't belong *here!*"

"There is no getting out, Liv. And I know exactly how you're feeling – that claustrophobic, horrified panic – because I went through it less than a week ago." He took her hand and kissed the inside of her wrist. "We're more than a simulation. You, me, Bobbi. We have to be, otherwise Equinoxx wouldn't be hunting us. That's what's getting me through. Our world might not be real, but we are. All I care about is that you and Bobbi are safe."

"How are we going to be safe, if Equinoxx is after us? This whole world belongs to them–" Horror gripped her throat, stealing her words.

They were in a *simulation*.

The sun, partway through its descent in the sky, wasn't real. The air she was breathing wasn't real. She had watched another version of herself vanish right before her eyes.

"Equinoxx created it, but they don't have complete control," Reef said. "The whole point was for this world to be self-sustaining. They can't just make citizens of Eidolon do what they say, not without permission from their counterparts."

"Reef?"

"Yeah?"

"Who are you?"

His brow furrowed.

"Who are you?" Liv said again. "Where were you born? Where did you grow up? Why have you never told me about your past?"

"It's complicated."

"That's what I told the police officer when you went missing, and you know what? Now it sounds like you're a plant, put here by Equinoxx to make me comply."

"That's not how this works, Liv."

"How do I know that? I don't know anything." She could hear her voice lifting in fright, but couldn't snatch control. "Who are you? Why was I drawn to you? Why did you sleep with me that night? Are Equinoxx just breeding children in this place–?"

"Stop, stop, stop. It's nothing like that."

Liv found herself rocking in her spot, her wrenching gasps sharp in her ears. Reef wrapped his arms around her.

"I'm so sorry," he said. "I'll tell you anything you want to know."

"I need to get out."

"We can't get out."

"That other woman, that other Olivia, she's not me. She can't be the real me. We should switch places. She should come in, and we can go out."

"It doesn't work that way."

"Why not?"

"Because it doesn't."

Liv's chest wracked with a dry sob. "She looked so delicate. So afraid. Like a porcelain doll. She'll do just fine in a computer world."

"She did seem a little fragile, didn't she?" Reef gave a wry smile. "But she's stronger than she looks. She has to be, if she's you. And that's good, because we're relying on her to keep Equinoxx from coming after Bobbi."

"That's it? We're just going to hole up here until *she* fixes the problem?"

"Pravit and my other self will help too."

"Three people against a global corporation?"

"Pravit has been amazing. He's been intercepting memos, collecting data–"

"Reef, it's not enough. They're going to take Bobbi away, and there's nothing we can do to stop them."

"We're not completely helpless. Let me show you."

He held out a hand, and together, they got up. They went around the side of the house to a locked steel toolbox. The padlock was heavy duty. Reef took a key from his pocket. His gaze was grave.

"Liv," he said. "Are you willing to kill to protect Bobbi?"

Liv thought about the moment when the woman at the charging station took Bobbi. There was terror, but also fury. Someone had tried to kidnap her daughter, and now Liv knew it was for human testing, the fury was surpassed by an inferno of rage.

"Yes. I am."

"Okay. Hopefully, you won't actually have to kill anyone, because the people coming after us will be visitors, not citizens. It's impossible to kill outsiders. But it's good to know you won't hesitate."

"Who cares, anyway? Everyone here is just a computer simulation."

"Some aren't. Some are like us. And we can't go thinking that about the people here. This is their world as much as ours. They live and die like we do. Just because they know they're simulations doesn't mean they don't have emotions."

"How can you be so calm and reflective?"

"I'm not. I'm just quoting what Pravit told me while we were prepping the house."

"Oh."

"He said it would take time to get used to everything."

No kidding. Maybe later Liv would find space in her mind to care about the citizens of Eidolon, but right now, she had other problems.

"If we can't kill the visitors, how do we stop them?"

Reef slid the key into the padlock. "Hurting them will send them back to the real world, and they'll remain stunned long enough for us to escape. Like when I ran over the woman trying to take Bobbi. Equinoxx extracted her because she was too injured."

As grim as the conversation was, it felt good to talk about it. Liv needed something to cling to, something to do. If she could focus on the immediate crisis, she didn't have to think about the bigger picture. About what it all really meant.

"Tell me you've got something in that box that'll hurt them," she said.

"Yes," Reef said, opening the lid. "I believe I do."

OUTSIDE

To: jacobpwilcox@equinoxxtechnology.co
From: retrievalunit@basenxj451.com
Subject: Retrieval update

LEVEL FIVE CITIZEN (U.S. POINT #1) SUCCESSFULLY
RETRIEVED
PREPARING FOR TRANSPORTATION TO
AUSTRALIAN BASE

17

Olivia staggered out of Sophie's room well past a respectable waking hour to find Sophie and Valentina at the dining table again. This time, instead of geography books, Sophie's laptop was open to what looked like a page on the Russian revolution.

"Good morning," said Valentina, getting up. "I'll make you a cuppa."

"You don't have to–" Olivia cut off as Valentina flicked the kettle on. "Er, thanks." To Sophie, she whispered, "Is there any coffee in this place?"

Sophie shook her head. Olivia slumped onto a chair.

"How did you sleep?" Valentina said, which Olivia thought was unnecessary considering she must look a mess. Not only was Sophie's mattress lumpier than she was used to, but her brain wouldn't shut off.

"Let's just say, it's lucky I didn't have my phone last night."

It had been Olivia's idea to pass along her phone before she went to bed. She'd realized that if she lay there in the dark, she'd be tempted to turn her phone on to see Matt's reply to her message. Would he deny it? Apologize? Send a long email explaining himself?

When she'd finally drifted off, instead of Matt, she dreamed of Winken stalking her through Equinoxx's crystal forest.

"Where's Aidan?"

Valentina started making preparations for breakfast. "Left before dawn. Without fixing my chicken run, I might add."

"Why go so early?"

Sophie lightly drummed her fingers along the keyboard. Her gaze was on the screen, but she didn't seem to be reading. "He comes and goes at all hours."

"To help Pravit for Equinoxx?"

"I don't know about Equinoxx. Or Pravit. Or anything," Sophie added under her breath.

Valenina cracked an egg into the pan.

"He just wants to keep you safe," Olivia said.

Sophie scoffed, and Olivia couldn't help feeling sorry for her. Trapped in here, with danger all around, no one telling her anything. Olivia would've hated it too.

She gazed around the adjoining living room, appreciating the aesthetics of the quaint cottage. It was colorful and cozy, very Insta-friendly. While there were no photographs, there was a fancy display cabinet that held cheap knickknacks – feathers and glossy stones, friendship bracelets, a plastic ring, a lock of hair tied in a dirty ribbon. It looked like the collection of a young child.

"Gifts," said Valentina as Olivia stared at it.

"From who?"

"From precious people. Your breakfast is ready."

Olivia ate her eggs on toast while the other two talked revolutions. Aidan hadn't joined them for dinner. He'd gone to bed early – for the early departure, Olivia realized.

She felt useless. How could she help when she barely understood what was going on?

After gulping down her tea, she had a shower and changed into her freshly washed yoga gear. It was better than anything Aidan had bought her.

"Why don't you go for a walk?" Valentina said as Olivia returned to the kitchen. "It'll be good for you to get some sunshine, after your shock from yesterday."

"Is it safe?"

"If you stay on the property, you'll be fine. In fact, Sophie, why don't you show her the river?"

Sophie glanced up from her work. "Me?"

"If she's going to be staying with us a while, it'd be nice to introduce her to the area."

Sophie didn't need any more convincing. She closed her laptop and jumped to her feet. "Let me get my shoes on."

"Are you sure?" Olivia said to Valentina.

"She knows the rules."

Olivia shivered. It had been all right going out when Aidan was here. He knew what he was doing. If Winken attacked them while they were alone on the property, Olivia would be completely useless at protecting herself and Sophie. She could almost smell the shampoo, feel the steam, from that moment she'd been trapped in her bathroom with Winken harassing her about breakfast, her phone in the office, her paranoia turning to full blown panic–

"I'm ready," Sophie said, charging to the front door. "See ya, Val."

Valentina ushered Olivia outside. "You'll be fine."

"I–"

"Sunshine. Fresh air. Enjoy." Valentina shut the door on her.

Sophie was already heading down the uneven brick path. She seemed sprightly considering she'd been bundled up in a sleeping bag on the floor all night.

Olivia controlled her breathing like her therapist had taught her. They were only going for a walk around the property. No one knew they were here. Olivia hadn't turned on her phone since sending that message to Matt, and there was no possible way for Equinoxx to connect her to this place.

It would be fine. It would all be fine.

"Come on," Sophie called, veering into the bush.

Olivia stepped off the porch. One foot in front of the other. There was a time when even that had been impossible. A time when she had thought she would never enjoy the simplicity of a stroll again.

Every now and then, after she'd relearned how to walk, she reminded herself of this.

"Watch for spider webs," Sophie said cheerfully. "And snakes."

"Right."

Olivia crunched more gingerly through the undergrowth. There was a worn track that they followed, and when it weaved a few more times, the house was no longer in view.

"The river isn't far. I'll show you the house Aidan built me."

"Aidan built you a house?"

"Uh huh. He's pretty good with that stuff. He was doing a carpentry course and everything at one point." Sophie glanced over her shoulder. "So who are you?"

"Um. I don't think I can tell you."

"Can I at least know your last name?"

"You want to look me up."

Sophie grinned guiltily. "Busted."

"I don't think that's a good idea," Olivia said. "The people who are after me might be watching who visits my social media page. You, er, know there are people after me?"

"I figured as much. Something about Equinoxx and simulations?"

"Sort of."

"I looked up Equinoxx last night," Sophie said. "They have this project called Eidolon, a VR thing–"

"It's so much more than that. But I'm not supposed to talk about it."

"Yeah, yeah."

"I'm sorry," Olivia said. "I know it must suck for you. If it makes you feel any better, I barely understand anything myself."

Rather than reply, Sophie stomped further into the forest. Olivia had to pick up her pace to follow.

Valentina was right. It felt good outside. The air was warm, and the wind must've swung direction, because the haziness from the bushfires had gone. Magpies hopped along the ground; small things rustled in the bushes. It reminded her of hiking in the jungles of South America, or through the Swedish mountains. While the dry Australian bush was nothing like those places, it was the feeling of being in the wilderness, away from cafés and traffic lights and beeping electronics. Of losing herself among nature.

When was the last time she'd done this? It couldn't have been before the accident…could it?

She caught up to Sophie, who was on her phone, typing away. She stood by a little wooden house next to a dry riverbed. This was no half-hearted attempt at a cubby, either. It had windows, and even a working door.

"Wow," Olivia said, peeking inside. "Aidan really built this for you?"

"When he liked me, yeah."

Olivia snorted. "He still likes you."

There were dusty cushions with the stuffing coming out, drawings on the walls and a little table and bench made of the same wood as the house. Everything was covered in spider webs.

"I suppose you're too old for a cubby house now," Olivia said, ducking back of out of it. "But it's really lovely. Maybe you could clean it out and come down here when you need some space."

"Mmm." Sophie tucked her phone into her back pocket.

"Your brother must be talented. You said he was doing a carpentry course?"

"For a bit. He quit at the beginning of the year."

"Why?"

Sophie shrugged and headed down to the dry track covered with leaves. "This is the river Val wanted me to show you. It's more impressive in the winter. Up that way is a sort of waterfall. Aidan and I used to jump off the rocks into the pool when it had rained enough."

"How high?"

"No idea."

"Can we see it?"

It had been a long time since she'd done cliff jumping, and she was content to never do it again. Still, she was curious.

Sophie led her further up the river. The trees grew tightly in this area – they had to break spindly branches and fight through more spider webs to get there. When they reached the rocks, everything was completely dry. Olivia judged the jump to be less than ten feet. Nothing. Easy.

Yet even the thought of climbing up there had her legs weakening.

"Well," said Sophie. "That's it." Then, after a silence, she added, "I suppose we'd better head back. I'm supposed to be doing lessons right now." She sounded completely depressed, as if all the enthusiasm from before had been sapped out during the walk.

As they headed back through the thick forest, she checked her phone again. Surely the signal out here would be patchy. What was she so desperate to see that couldn't wait until they were back at the house?

"Does your brother own all this land?" Olivia said.

"This is Valentina's property."

"Is she a relative of yours?"

"No. She's a friend of Aidan's. They met when Aidan was with Sea Shepherd, I think. Something about him saving her life?"

"I'm sorry, backtrack. Aidan was with Sea Shepherd?"

"He's been with a bunch of environmental groups."

"He saved whales and stuff?"

"I guess. He doesn't talk about it much."

This was so far removed from everything Olivia had imagined about Aidan. She'd assumed, after her initial reaction of 'caveman,' that his life was much like Kass' had been growing up. A bogan smoking pot on the weekends and racing souped-up cars after midnight.

How could she have been so wrong?

They passed the little house. Olivia eyed it with new appreciation. "He should start a business making cubby and tree houses. I bet there's a market there."

"I think he was about to start a business last year. Not tree houses, but building stuff. He registered it and everything."

"Really? Wait, how can he register for a business? He told me he's not in the system. Aidan's not even his real name."

"You know about that?"

"I…" Olivia hesitated, thinking of Reef in Eidolon. "It's a long story, but yeah."

"Valentina hooked him up with fake IDs. He and I had to change our names after I left…"

"The cult?"

"How much do you know?"

"Just that he's hiding you from them."

"That's it?" Sophie looked disappointed. "Then I shouldn't tell you anything else."

"Did they…hurt you?"

"What? No, definitely not. I don't even know exactly why we had to leave. Aidan came and got me from my mum's place one night. She told me to never come back."

"That's awful."

"Mmm."

Olivia couldn't tell how Sophie felt about it. The kid was good at keeping her face expressionless. "How long since you've seen her?"

"Five years. Every time I ask Aidan why I can't go back, he says it's too dangerous, but he won't tell me anything else."

Again, Olivia's opinion of Aidan swung. She couldn't figure out whether she trusted him or not. Why did he keep so many secrets?

"It wasn't so bad at first," Sophie continued. "Aidan introduced me to, you know, the rest of the world. The internet. TV. Do you know I'd never seen a TV show before then? I watched a *lot* of stuff when I first got out. And I know I can't have a social life, but I have a lot of friends online. I can use a fake name." Something changed in her voice. "I had a vlog for a while, where I showed my face. I wanted to talk to people about all the horrible things that are happening. There are videos of factory farms, where they cut the chicken's beak off without anesthetic or anything. It's awful. I had a whole plan to get activists together and start petitions and stuff. It was only a small channel, so I didn't think it would matter much. But…somehow, Aidan found it."

"Uh oh. Was he mad?"

"You have no idea." Sophie laughed shakily. "He took away my tablet at first, but I guess Valentina must've talked to him, because he gave it back after about a week. But it didn't matter. He's never forgiven me."

"I'm sure he has."

"Oh yeah? It happened in January, and since then, he hasn't spent any time with me. We used to play board games and go hiking. Now he disappears at weird hours. I barely see him, and when I do, he's always angry."

"Maybe that doesn't have anything to do with you. There's this Equinoxx thing – my thing – that he's dealing with. He must be pretty stressed out about that."

"I don't think that's it. He hates me."

"He doesn't hate you, Sophie. You're his sister."

"It doesn't matter. He didn't even know I existed until my mum called him. Now he regrets taking me in."

"I doubt–"

"Why else would he be gone so much? He gave up his activism, his work, his whole life for me. He never started his business. He quit the course around the same time he found my vlog. He must've realized it was too risky to be out in the open so much." She swiped her eyes with the back of her hand. "He *hates* me, Olivia. What other explanation is there?"

18

Aidan reached the first gate of what he liked to call cult camp. It was a good two-hour drive south, on farmland adjacent to a state forest. Here, on the dirt track running through semi-green paddocks and fringed with trees, was his personal hell.

There was no lock on the gate, just a metal hook, easily removed. He tried to ignore the habitual chills that always seized the back of his neck once he'd gotten onto the property.

As soon as he'd driven past the first rise, out of view of the road, the second gate appeared. This one had a happy sign requesting everyone leave their cars here. Racks of bikes were provided instead, glinting in the heat.

Aidan gave the bikes the finger and continued driving all the way to the camp. Goats strolled out of his path in a disinterested way as he veered between elongated white buildings with thatched roofs. Dust from his tires billowed towards washing on the line. He ignored the frowns as he jumped out of his car and headed towards what was the original farmstead. Indigo paused in the middle of weeding the lavender patch. She met Aidan's eye and looked hurriedly away.

Aidan had mixed feelings about Indigo. It entirely depended on what her motivations were behind begging him to take Sophie. Because from where he was standing, she'd completely screwed him over.

"Hey, Reef," called a shirtless, blond boy carrying a bucket full of yabbies from the dam. "Welcome back."

Aidan bit back a retort. The kid was only Sophie's age. He wasn't deserving of Aidan's wrath.

The screen door of the farmhouse swung open. Forrest stepped out wearing his ridiculous hat with corks hanging from the brim. His gray moustache seemed to have doubled in size, almost as bushy as his sideburns. Here was the man who deserved to have the shit beaten out of him.

"G'day, Reef," he said. "What have I told you about the car, mate?"

"That while she was a beauty in her day, she's now held together by rust and hope."

Forrest gestured to the rainwater tanks and large solar panels created by StarShine. "We're trying to make a difference here."

"Yes, because one person riding a bike three hundred meters is going to repair the ozone layer."

"The exercise would do you good. Maybe get rid of those love handles." Forrest clasped a hand on Aidan's shoulder. Despite his broad smile, his grip was claw-like. People had come out of the houses, along with several children. They were all staring at Aidan. "Come inside, then. Wipe your feet."

Aidan followed him into the farmstead and was instantly hit with woody, homely smells.

"Want a cuppa?"

"Let's just get this over with."

"Always in a rush," Forrest said, leading him into the home office. "Stop and smell the wattle. Did you know our residences are booked solid until next year? Everyone wants to stay, to feel what it's like to live in nature."

Aidan shot a glance at the computer and printer setup. Nature, right.

"We've had a slew of new Symbiotes sign up, too," Forrest continued happily. He sat at his desk and woke the computer. "Money's flowing in like never before. People are finally realizing this world isn't going to survive much longer unless we take action. Now, where is that...ah." He fumbled with a pencil tin, pulling out a USB in the shape of a wooden clothes peg. Then he plugged it into his computer.

Aidan rolled his eyes. "I thought you would've been ready by now."

"I had to get Sweetpea to encrypt it," Forrest said. "She's only just finished. Now just let me copy…"

"I can wait in the car."

"Nonsense. We're going to make a difference, Reef. You and me, together. Right?"

"Sure."

Forrest unplugged the USB, still smiling as he offered it up. "For the good of the planet. Or, at least, for the good of paying the rent."

Aidan snatched it from him. "You know why I'm doing this, Forrest."

"I do indeed, mate. I do indeed."

His laughter followed Aidan out the door.

EIDOLON

19

Liv's body was sweaty and achy in a delicious way. Running along the beach worked muscles she didn't normally get to tone. Her legs and abs felt particularly cranky, but not in a bad way, not like after physical therapy. She had kept her core strong, kept her posture correct. She'd done everything right over the years to build her fitness again.

And yet - the adrenaline, the pulse, the sweat – none of it was real.

She headed for the steps to the back porch, passing a ladder leading up to the roof. Whenever she started to panic about her 'simulation situation,' she switched her focus, the same way she did when her mind brought up the endlessness of death. No point worrying about that now; there were things to do.

She stepped inside to find Reef holding a remote control and switching channels on a working television.

"Oh my god," she said, shutting the door. "You fixed the aerial."

"I fixed the aerial." He stopped his channel surfing on a kids' station. Bobbi, who had been watching the screen curiously, was now fully entranced. Reef tossed the remote on the couch and turned triumphantly to Liv.

"Truly, you are the hottest man alive," she said. "C'mere and have a sweaty hug."

She wrapped her arms around his neck. He pulled her in, close. The sounds of the television were a joy to hear. Now they could have snatches of peace, a chance to catch their breath.

Bobbi had been taken out of her routine, her familiar environment, and she wasn't handling it well. She cried for Mr Piggy, she asked for Aunny Kazzy. She wanted to go to the shops – 'Sops! Sops!' – as she had become accustomed to the sounds and sights of the local shopping center and her regular babycinos.

They couldn't use anything with a SIM card, so there had been no way to hold her attention for long.

Until this moment.

"I'm so attracted to you right now," Liv said, nuzzling Reef's jawline as the high-pitched sounds of a cartoon pierced the shack. "You are one hundred percent getting lucky tonight."

"Why not now? I mean, you're already hot and sweaty–"

Liv giggled as Reef's hand crept up her shirt.

"Mummy, look."

Liv glanced at the screen. "Yes, baby, I see. Giraffe."

Reef kissed along Liv's neck.

"Don't tease me," she murmured.

"But that's half the fun."

"Bobbi cat!"

"Mmhmm."

"Miaow! Mrow Mrow Mrow. Prrrr!"

Reef grinned against Liv's neck. "What's she on about?"

"She's obsessed with that filter on my ph–" Liv cut off and spun around.

Bobbi had Liv's phone. It was on, the camera was on, the filter was up. Bobbi's little cat face stared out from the screen.

"Oh *shit.*"

Liv lunged across the room and snatched the phone from Bobbi's hands. Bobbi screamed.

"Oh shit, oh shit—"

"Turn it off."

"I am! Shit shit shit—" The phone seemed to take an eternity to power down. "I don't know how she did that, she's never turned on my phone before."

Reef went to soothe Bobbi, but she was still screaming and reaching for the phone. "Bobbi cat! Bobbi cat!"

"Are they going to find us? Was that long enough for them to track the signal?"

"I don't know."

"Reef, do we have to leave?"

"I don't know!"

"Do we have anywhere else to go?"

"I just – I need a moment to think. Bob-Bob, shhh, shhh."

Liv grabbed the car keys from the counter. "We should go."

"No, wait. Even if they caught our location, we still have a few hours before they get here."

"The outsiders?"

"Yeah."

"But can't they show up wherever they want in Eidolon?"

"They'd be without weapons, without transport vehicles, without backup. If they're coming after us, they'll have to do it the long way around, which means we have time. Have a shower, pack a bag, and I'll try to think what to do."

"Are you sure?"

"Yes, we'll be okay, at least for now."

Liv dashed into the bedroom and peeled off her sweaty gear. She soaped herself down, lamenting having to leave. She didn't want to be out in the world, running for her life. And how would Bobbi cope?

She knew Reef must've hated being in this place. He had finally told Liv everything about his past, including his time here, in his parents' holiday home. Things had happened to him in this beach house – horrific, traumatic things. But, despite the dark memories, the shack was secure and isolated and perfect for what they needed. Where else could they go?

When she was clean and changed, she headed back out into the lounge room. Reef had done the desperate dirty trick of giving Bobbi ice cream to settle her down, for which Liv was eternally grateful. He looked calmer than before.

"I've been thinking," he said, "I'm almost certain the phone wasn't on long enough for them to catch our location."

Tendrils of hope unfurled in her. "You reckon we can stay?"

"It would be a risk. A big one."

"It would also be a risk to be on the road."

"And we'd lose touch with Pravit. If we left, he wouldn't have any way to contact us and keep us up to date with what's happening in the outside world."

Liv sat down at the table opposite him and Bobbi. "But what if you're wrong, and they did catch our location?"

"We could pack up the car, prepare to leave, and wait at the turnoff from the main road. If they come, I'll take them down, and we'll get out of here. If no one shows up by sunset, we should be safe."

Liv let out a long breath. She watched ice cream dribble down Bobbi's chin.

"What do you think?" Reef said.

"I think we have supplies, running water, gas bottles, plenty of generator fuel, and a working television. It's worth a try."

"All right," Reef said. "Let's start packing up."

They spent the next hour cramming as much as they could into the car. When Liv couldn't take the suspense anymore, Reef opened the steel box from the side of the house and pulled out the shotgun he'd acquired from a local farmer.

Liv had practiced with it a few times, but while her aim was good, the recoil was a bitch and she hated using it. She strapped Bobbi into the backseat.

"Mummy, where we going?"

"Just a little outing." Liv kissed the top of her head and climbed in the driver's seat. There was a fair distance between the shack and the main road, with only a dirt track to follow. She parked out of sight, behind the trees by the main road. Reef waited on the other side of the track with the shotgun.

With every car that passed, Liv tensed, willing it not to slow down. Car after car whooshed by, with no sign of anyone noticing them.

Bobbi got bored quickly and started acting up. They should've stayed longer in the shack. Liv regretted her haste as she unbuckled Bobbi's car seat to let her wander around. It was risky, but she couldn't leave Bobbi strapped in.

She watched Bobbi inspect sticks and leaves on the side of the road. Sunset seemed years away.

"Liv." Reef's voice was tense.

Liv glanced over to find a car slowing with its indicator on. It was a rumbling, lurid green HQ Monaro rather than the expected StarShine, and in the back of her mind she vaguely thought she knew it. Reef lifted the shotgun as Liv bundled Bobbi back into the car, swearing to herself.

They would have to leave, dammit, and they still hadn't decided where to go—

"Liv? Where the shit have ya been?"

Liv whipped around to find the Monaro stopped on the track. "Kazzy?"

Kazzy jumped out of the car. "I thought youse were dead, ay."

Liv wrenched her into a hug. She stank of cigarettes, which went to show how stressed she was, considering she'd quit ten years ago.

"I'm so glad to see you! How did you find us?"

"Had Ping Pals open for days, obvs. Almost had a heart attack when it dinged. Borrowed my brother's car, in case this is like some conspiracy thing. Is it a conspiracy thing?"

Ping Pals. How could Liv have forgotten? She was pretty sure it only worked if the phones had been synced before, which meant at least Equinoxx wouldn't have gotten the notification.

"Liv, bring her over." Reef had come around the front of the Monaro with the shotgun.

"What? No!"

"Holy shit," Kazzy said when she turned. "What the fuck, Reef?"

The shotgun was pointed at the ground, but it was still monstrously there.

"Bring her over," Reef said again. "The other side of the track, where Bobbi can't see."

"You can't be serious," Liv said.

"She's a simulation. She can be reprogrammed."

"Only if her outside self consents!"

"We don't know what's going on outside. She might've already signed the contract."

"I haven't been reprogrammed," Kazzy said, lifting her hands to pacify them. "I don't know what's going on. Last I heard, you were heading off to find Reef, then there's footage of people trying to take Bobbi in a charging station all over the net, the coppers are knocking at my door, people in suits are looking for you—"

"Outsiders," Liv said. "Visitors, from Equinoxx."

"No shit? Why are they looking for you?"

"They're trying to take Bobbi," Reef said. "Which is why we have to get rid of you."

"Reef!" Liv cried.

"I'm sorry. I don't want to do this. But it's too big of a risk. Even if she's not reprogrammed now, she could be at any moment. She could turn on us."

"Kazzy would never sign the contract. She's too smart for that – she was smart enough not to do the mapping in the first place. Please, Reef! She could help us. We'd have someone else on our side."

"Aunny Kazzy!" They all glanced in the car, where Bobbi was strapped in. She waved through the window. "Hi, Aunny Kazzy!"

"Hi, chickadee." Kazzy's voice was breathless. She looked desperately to Liv. "I, uh, brought something. If I can get it?" With her gaze fixed on Reef, she edged to the Monaro.

Reef lifted the shotgun. Liv choked a cry.

Cringing, Kazzy brought something out from the front seat. "I thought she might be missing it." She held up Mr Piggy.

Bobbi screamed in delight.

"Shit," Reef said.

Liv burst into tears. At last, the stress of the past week, from the moment Reef walked out on her, came flooding through. She couldn't handle this anymore. It was too much, everything was too much. If she lost Kazzy, she didn't think she would survive.

"Reef," she croaked, but he must've already realized what she was going to say, because with a look of reluctant resignation, he lowered the shotgun.

"Okay," he muttered. "Goddammit. I just hope you're right about the Kazzy on the outside."

OUTSIDE

To: jacobpwilcox@equinoxxtechnology.co
From: retrievalunit@basenxj451.com
Subject: Retrieval update

LEVEL FIVE CITIZEN (U.S. POINT #2)
SUCCESSFULLY RETRIEVED
PREPARING FOR TRANSPORTATION TO
AUSTRALIAN BASE

20

Aidan returned before dinner. Olivia, who had been playing a game of Scrabble with Valentina, stood up from the couch.

"Hi," she said tentatively. "How are you?"

"Fine." He dumped his backpack at the front door. To Valentina, he said, "Did Sophie get her work done?"

He seemed irritable. What the hell had he been up to all day?

"Every bit of it," Valentina said.

"Good. I'm having a shower."

Olivia exchanged a glance with Valentina and hurried after him as he stomped down the hall.

"You were gone a long time."

"So?"

"So, um. Was it about Equinoxx?"

He stopped at the bathroom door. "I have things besides Equinoxx to deal with."

"I understand that. But the longer it takes to stop Equinoxx, the longer I have to stay here. In your way. Asking you annoying questions." Olivia tried for a playful smile.

Aidan didn't smile back. "Pravit wants to meet me later tonight at the shed. Apparently, something happened in Eidolon. Nothing bad, I don't think. But he wants to talk to our other selves about it."

"Oh." Olivia hesitated. "Can I come with you?"

She couldn't deny her intense curiosity to see her parallel self again. This time it would only be on the monitor, but maybe that would be easier. She could stare as much as she liked, at herself, at her daughter…at the strangely-hot version of Aidan.

"If you want," Aidan said. He didn't sound like he cared either way.

He walked into the bathroom and closed the door in her face.

"Sometimes, I think, he has very bad days," Valentina said, approaching. She rapped on the bathroom door. "Aidan."

The shower turned on.

"Aidan," Valentina said again.

He groaned. "What?"

"You need to fix the chicken run. I don't want a fox getting my girls."

"Fine."

Olivia followed Valentina to the kitchen. The oven was on, emitting heat and an aroma of baking vegetables.

"Why does he have bad days?"

"You'll have to ask him. Cup of tea?"

"I'll take a wine?"

"We don't have any."

Olivia exhaled noisily. "From what Sophie says, I doubt he'll answer any of my questions. What are these 'other things?' Nothing could be more important than Equinoxx, right?"

Valentina grabbed a mug from the cupboard. Olivia waited, assuming she was formulating an answer, but no answer was forthcoming. Instead, she called out, "Sophie, come and set the table."

Olivia really needed that wine. A wine, her wallet, and Leith to drive her home.

Sophie's bedroom door opened. She drifted out, shoving her phone in her pocket. "Can we watch a movie tonight?"

"Sure," Valentina said. "We can find a nice one, just the two of us. I think your brother and Olivia are going out."

"On, like, a date?"

"You know I'm married, right?" Olivia said, holding up her left hand.

"I was only kidding. As if anyone in this house can get a date." Sophie eyed Olivia's rings. "Am I allowed to ask?"

Olivia looked to Valentina, who shrugged. "I guess so. His name is Matt."

"How did you meet? Was it romantic?"

"She watches a lot of TV," Valentina said to Olivia as she passed Sophie a handful of cutlery.

"He ran me over with his car," Olivia said.

"*What.*"

"It was totally my fault. He was going the speed limit. I stepped out on the road without looking. I can't remember what I was thinking or doing at the time, but I'd always been a little careless about, well, everything. I used to think I was invincible."

"Were you hurt?"

"I broke my back, among other things."

"Holy crap!"

"The recovery took years. And Matt stayed by my side throughout. At first it was guilt, but it turned into love." Her voice softened. Matt had been her angel.

"Nyaww, that is so sweet," Sophie cooed. "I wish someone would run me over with their car. I should go stand out on the road for a bit."

"You don't want to do that."

"If it's the only way I can talk to someone, maybe I do."

"You talk to plenty of people," Valentina said.

Sophie grinned guiltily and said in a low voice, "Val takes me out to different shopping centers and markets when Aidan goes away."

"Really?" Olivia said, glancing at Valentina. "Is that safe?"

"We go to places far from here, and Val's license plates are fake, so no one could ever track us. Don't tell Aidan. He'd lose his shit."

Olivia zipped her lips.

"But it sucks that you have to be away from your husband," Sophie continued. "You don't even get to message him, do you?"

"Yeah," Olivia said. "It's frustrating."

146

Her fingers itched to get her hands back on her phone, to see what Matt had replied to her text. Had her disappearance made him realize how much he loved her? They had been through so much together. Surely he would at least want to talk, and Olivia had so much to say. And yell. Probably while crying.

She needed a cathartic release, and being stuck here was like letting poison fester in a wound.

Hopefully Pravit's news tonight would be about how much progress he'd made. The sooner this was over, the sooner Olivia could talk to Matt without fear that an assassin was going to come after her.

An assassin, she thought bitterly, who was not only going to murder her, but expose details of Matt's affair for the world to see…

"Huh," she said aloud.

Sophie and Valentina turned to her.

How did Winken know about the affair? It wasn't like Olivia had blabbed about it. The only people she'd told were Kass and–

"Briony," she whispered.

"What's wrong?" Sophie said.

Briony was the one who had tried to get Olivia to sign Equinoxx's contract. She'd been in on it from the start. She was probably a plant, trying to get close to Olivia.

And Kass was right in the middle of it.

"Oh my god. Val, I need my phone."

"You know you can't turn it on."

"I need a way to contact – Sophie. Give me your phone."

Sophie looked startled.

"I think my friend is in danger," Olivia said. "Please. Let me have your phone."

From down the hall, the shower turned off.

"Aidan doesn't think it's safe for you to contact anyone," Valentina said.

"I have to warn her!"

"You can't make calls from Sophie's phone."

"I know how to block my details," Sophie said eagerly. She pulled out her phone and played around with the settings.

Olivia willed her to hurry. The bathroom door opened; Aidan's heavy footsteps headed further down the hall, to his bedroom.

Sophie opened the keypad. "What's her number?"

"I have no idea. Look her up. Kassandra White, business consultant. She has a website."

It was a fake website, but at least the number was real. Sophie clicked on it. Olivia's heart lurched as the line connected. This was her last chance to remain fully hidden, to keep Sophie safe.

But she couldn't let Kass get hurt. Never, ever.

The phone rang once. Twice. Three times, four–

"Kassandra White." Her voice was smooth and professional, missing its regular cadence.

"Kass, it's me, don't hang up."

Her tone switched immediately. "Liv?"

"I don't have time to explain, but you need to be very careful. I think Briony isn't who she says she is."

"What?"

There was movement down the hall. Aidan would be out any moment. Olivia edged into the living room, as far back as she could go. She was well aware Sophie was listening intently.

"Briony is a spy," she whispered. "She's a plant, put near you to get to me. She was trying to convince me to sign a contract, but I didn't, and now people are after me."

"The fuck? Are you high?"

Olivia hadn't had time to plan this call. How was she supposed to convince Kass she was telling the truth?

"Ask her about Ginger," she said desperately. "You met at the wedding, right? I bet Briony doesn't even know her. She slipped in among the guests and seduced you."

"You've lost it, ay."

"Please Kass. My life is in danger, and yours might be too. I'm risking everything by calling you."

"You've snapped. Get help. Call your therapist. While you're at it, tell Matt to stay the fuck away from me. He came around looking for you, and I almost made good on my promise to stitch up his eyes and mouth and toss him in the river."

Olivia's breath caught. "Matt was looking for me?"

"He *denied* the affair, that fucker. Next time I see him, I'm cutting off his dick."

"Kass, listen–"

Aidan's bedroom door opened.

"Be careful," Olivia whispered urgently as his footsteps headed closer. "Do your thing, look into Briony, find out how she's connected to Equinoxx–"

"Wait, Equinoxx?"

Olivia hung up and tossed the phone on the couch as Aidan appeared.

"Ready for dinner?" Valentina said, while Sophie hurried to get cups and asked a little too cheerfully if Aidan wanted a drink.

He didn't seem to notice they were acting strangely. He slumped at the table, dragging a hand through his wet beard, staring at nothing.

Olivia's relief at not being caught was smothered by worry. There sat a man who carried the weight of something big. Was it about Equinoxx, or did it have to do with this mysterious other job?

And what could be more concerning than Equinoxx?

Wine, she concluded. Sometime soon, they were definitely going to need wine.

21

"Who was that?" Briony said as Kass returned, shoving her phone in her pocket.

"No one," Kass muttered. "Drink?"

Briony held out her empty wine glass – or rather, wine plastic. The patio around them was heavy with smoke – both weed and cigarette – and crammed with people. Kass' family and friends were loud and brash and dropped the c-word every second sentence, but they had welcomed Briony without suspicion or hesitation, for which Briony was eternally grateful. It was nice to be part of a decent family dynamic. When Briony had left Leeds, the last thing her mum had done was lock herself in the bathroom and scream that Briony was an ungrateful bitch who was ruining her life.

Kass' brother was over at the carport, showing his friends the newest additions to his ostentatious car. Every cent he earned driving a forklift at Woolies went towards that thing. Apparently, Kass used to race him on the streets back when they were in their early twenties.

Briony loved how Kass was a series of contradictions. Who lived in a mansion in South Perth and consulted for multi-million-dollar businesses while wearing thongs and swearing like a sailor? Kass had flourished in the corporate world while staying exactly who she was. And occasionally she'd drop comments like that time she got bitten by a turtle while swimming in the Great Barrier Reef, or getting sick from a parasite while trekking through Borneo. It surprised Briony every time. She would've asked for more, but Kass didn't like to talk about her travels, because they always involved Olivia.

Briony sipped her wine.

Where the hell was Olivia, anyway? Why had she disappeared? What had bloody Wilcox done? And why was he bugging her about getting a signature from Kass now? What did Kass have to do with anything?

"It's cold," Kass' sister complained. "Mum, turn on the heater."

"Fuck's sake, get a blanket," was the reply. "We're not made of money."

Kass got up and fiddled with the patio heater. "I'll buy you lot a new gas bottle, all right? Jesus."

When she returned to her seat, she got out her phone again. She seemed grumpier than before.

"You okay?" Briony said. She was starting to suspect something was up with that phone call. It had been a blocked number, and it was too late for business.

Could Olivia have made contact?

"Who rang?" she tried again. "Telemarketer? I know how cranky you get—"

Kass switched off her phone. "It was Ginger. She wants to catch up this weekend. You free?"

Ginger. The bride from the wedding Briony had crashed.

"I think so," Briony said. "I'll have to check my calendar. I might have a work thing."

Kass gulped at her drink. "How d'you know her again? You told me at the wedding, but…"

"I was on her rowing team. Just for a year. It was when we went to Sydney for the regatta."

"Oh yeah. Cool."

Briony had done more research than was necessary when she'd first been assigned the job. She'd seen how much Equinoxx had first deposited in her bank account and realized she was going to have to live up to some very high expectations. She hadn't anticipated still needing her cover story four months later.

"You still row?" Kass said.

"Who has the time?"

"Fair enough. Hey, Mik, chuck us a ciggie."

Her sister Mikayla shoved a pack with a lighter across the table. "When you start smoking again?"

"Very recently." Kass flicked the striker and dragged in a mouthful.

Briony had no idea when Kass had started up again. As far as she knew, Kass hadn't smoked in a decade.

"You sure you're okay?"

"Sugar and spice, babe." Kass exhaled, rubbing her eyebrow with her ring finger as if she had a headache. White cloud billowed around them.

"Do you want to go home?"

"No." When she looked at Briony again, she smiled a proper smile. "It's just...talking to Ginger made me realize how lucky it is me and you met. It's like fate, ay. We don't exactly travel in the same circles. We never would've crossed paths if it wasn't for Ginge."

Briony took her free hand and laced their fingers together. Kass gave her a reassuring squeeze.

"You know I'd do anything for you, Bri."

"I know. Me too."

"So I got thinking, that contract you asked me to sign. The one for Equinoxx. I shouldn't have dismissed it so quick. If it helps you move up in the world, I should be fully behind you."

Was this really happening? Was Briony finally going to give bloody Wilcox what he wanted?

"Thanks," she said, keeping her voice as even as she could. "That'd be great. I've been a bit under the pump trying to get all these signatures."

"No worries. If you say it's good, it's good. I trust you."

"Glad to hear it," Briony said with what she hoped was a casual laugh.

Thank the Lord. At least Wilcox wouldn't consider her a complete failure.

Kass let go of her hand to pick up her wine glass. Briony texted through the good news, while Kass finished the rest of her drink in one large gulp.

22

Aidan said very little during dinner, and his silence continued on the car ride to the shed. Olivia noticed gratefully that he drove under the speed limit again.

"I'm sorry you had such a bad day," she said.

He grunted in reply.

"Is there anything I can do?"

"No."

"You're letting me stay with you, even though I can't pay for anything or help out. I feel like I owe you."

"The best thing you can do is keep quiet."

"Oh." She dropped her gaze to her lap. It was beginning to dawn on her how useless she had become. At everything.

"I wasn't telling you to shut up." Aidan said. "I meant stay quiet about our location, and about Equinoxx. What matters most is keeping Sophie and Val safe."

Olivia's chest burned with guilt. But she hadn't told Kass anything, really. And she'd called from a blocked number. Besides, just because Kass was a professional when it came to secrets, didn't mean she'd bother finding Olivia. Somehow, they were no longer friends, and Olivia hadn't even realized.

"You know, Sophie isn't in Eidolon," Aidan said. "I didn't know she existed when I did the mapping."

"That's kind of sad."

"Yeah, I suppose so."

He didn't sound convinced. Olivia snuck a peek at him. His expression was unreadable in the glow of the dash.

"Sophie thinks you hate her."

"Teenagers," he muttered.

"I don't think this is hormones. She says you regret taking her in."

There was no exasperated rebuttal, as she'd been expecting.

"My life is…less easy with her in it," he said carefully.

"Aidan. That poor girl. She's so alone, without a parental figure to love her–"

"I never said that. I just – look, consider what my life is like in Eidolon. I have a job, a home, a family."

"Sophie and Valentina are your family."

"Valentina is two breaths away from kicking me out. And these days, I can't even look Sophie in the eye."

"Is this about those videos she put up? Because–"

"It's not because of what *she's* done, it's because of what *I've* done."

Olivia hesitated. "What have you done?"

"Nothing. Never mind."

He had closed up again. A conversation with him felt like picking her way through inscrutable terrain – she never knew when her clear path would hit a cliff face.

"How am I supposed to trust you with Equinoxx stuff if you keep so much from me?" she said.

"What I'm talking about isn't Equinoxx stuff. I promise. Look, I've already told you plenty of my issues. You must know by now my life is falling apart. More than yours, even."

"An assassin is trying to kill me."

"It's not a competition."

"You *just* tried to outdo me."

"I have no memory of that."

He parked outside the property, next to a silver Prius.

"That's his son-in-law's car," Aidan said. "Pravit's StarShine's GPS would track him here, otherwise."

They crunched through bushland with torches. Pravit was waiting for them, the shed lit up by the generator. A dark jacket was zipped to his chin to keep out the crisp air.

"Evening," he said, shaking Aidan's hand. He turned to Olivia, clasping her hand too. His grip was warm and rough, and again she was reminded of her father. Her heart curdled in her chest. How frantic were her parents right now? Had Matt told them what had happened?

"Please know, Olivia, that you have my deepest apologies," Pravit said. "Equinoxx is in dire financial straits and are doing desperate, terrible things for a worthy cause. I know it doesn't excuse them, but I'm trying my best to make up for it. Come, let's get out of the cold."

Olivia and Aidan followed him inside. It wasn't much warmer in the shed, but at least it had the illusion of heat with the lights and computer humming.

"Is everything okay in Eidolon?"

"Thankfully, yes, but there was a close call today and I want to check on your simulations."

Pravit sat on the throne and put on the crown while Aidan started the program. Coordinates had already been put in.

"Ready when you are," Pravit said.

He closed his eyes. The monitor, which had been black moments ago, flared to life. Olivia recognized the beach house where she'd met herself, its blue walls glowing under the soft light. As Pravit moved his head, their vision moved with it. They were seeing Eidolon through his eyes.

"Pravit." Aidan's – no, Reef's – voice came through the screen, sounding relieved. There he was, tidying a pile of toys in the living room with Liv.

Olivia still couldn't believe that woman was her. She looked like Olivia's past self, only older, like the person she might've been if she hadn't dolled herself up under Matt's influence and money.

"Is everything okay?" Reef said. "Did Equinoxx…?"

"We caught the signal for mere seconds. Not long enough to get a reading on your location. What happened?"

"Bobbi got hold of Liv's phone. It couldn't have been for long – we switched it off as soon as we realized."

In another room somewhere came the sound of Bobbi loudly singing nonsense words. Olivia hoped they'd get another chance to see her.

Pravit turned his attention to Liv. "We haven't officially met."

"I suppose not," she said warily.

"Pravit."

"Liv."

They shook hands, Liv still looking doubtful. At least she wasn't in denial, or angry like before.

"You've settled in nicely," Pravit said. "I'm glad that little blip didn't cause any problems"

Liv and Reef glanced at each other.

"Well…" said Reef.

"It depends what you mean by problems," said Liv.

"Mummy!" Bobbi thundered out in cozy pajamas, her hair wet, her arm clinging to a stuffed pig. She slowed when she saw Pravit. "Who that?"

"C'mere, ya rugrat, I haven't finished with you."

A freckle-nosed woman appeared from the hallway, brandishing a hairbrush.

"Kass?" Olivia whispered.

Kass caught sight of Pravit and grabbed Bobbi, picking her up protectively. "Who are you?"

"This is Pravit, the guy who's helping us," Liv said.

Pravit looked at Reef. "What's going on?"

"She found us with Ping Pals," Reef said. "I'm sorry, I didn't know what to do."

"We need her help," Liv said.

Bobbi buried her face in Kass' neck. The two seemed familiar with each other, as if Kass were a common presence in Bobbi's life.

"This won't work," Pravit said. "Equinoxx knows you're close. They'll be trying to get Kassandra's consent in the real world to reprogram her here, if they haven't done so already."

Liv set her jaw. "Kass would never sign."

"The Kass here wouldn't. But you saw how different your other self was. Maybe the outside Kassandra doesn't care as much about signing consent forms."

"Just tell her not to," Kass said.

"Aunny Kazzy, play with me?"

"In a minute, chickadee. Look, just tell my other self what's going on. I can be an asset, you know."

"Perhaps not," Pravit said, and he sounded apologetic. "From what I understand, you and Olivia aren't close in the other world. Equinoxx tried to send someone to insinuate themselves into Olivia's life, to gain her trust, but they did it through Kass and were unsuccessful."

He knew about Briony.

Olivia shut her eyes. Of course he did. He was intercepting messages within Equinoxx.

She should've waited. She shouldn't have hastily called Kass, perhaps giving away too much. All Aidan had asked was for her to stay quiet, and she hadn't done that.

On the monitor, Kass rounded on Liv. "What crap is this? We're not friends anymore?"

"Apparently, my other self is still with Matt," Liv said. "Maybe staying with him was enough to separate us."

Kass pretended to gag. Bobbi tried to copy the sound and beamed when she got a laugh out of Kass.

"Tell the other Olivia he's a waste of time," Kass said. "Look at what she's missing." She jiggled Bobbi. "Still with Matt, honestly. If I wasn't holding your daughter, I'd smack you over the head."

"It's not me!" Liv said.

"Then get the other Olivia in here and I'll smack her instead."

"Smack!" Bobbi said.

"Exactly, chickadee."

"But you'll talk to the other Kassandra," Reef said to Pravit. "Right? To warn her about Equinoxx?"

Olivia cringed. She'd mentioned Equinoxx on the phone to Kass this evening. If Kass brought it up with Briony, things could get messy.

Then again, Kass never missed a trick. She was smart enough to double check things. Sure, she'd jump out of a plane for a thrill, but when it came to money and security, she was always vigilant. Hopefully, her love for Briony wouldn't leave her off-guard.

"I'll do what I can, but the more people I bring into this, the harder it's going to get," Pravit said.

"You don't have a choice," Kass said. "I know where this lot are now. You can't risk me being reprogrammed. I'd rather die than give them up."

There was a beat of silence as everyone absorbed this, then Bobbi said, "Aunny Kazzy, play with me! Aunny Kazzy!"

Kass took the stuffed pig from Bobbi's grip and wiggled it in Bobbi's face. "Rar rar rar."

"Oink!"

"Yeah, that's what I said, oink."

"Is the other Olivia okay?" Reef said while Kass and Bobbi snorted at each other.

Olivia experienced a flicker of gratitude that he asked about her.

"She's staying with your other self."

"Where?"

"I've made sure not to know their exact location, but they're with an old friend of yours. Someone from your past, I believe. Someone who owes you their life."

Reef clapped a hand to his forehead. "Of course. Why didn't I think of her?"

"Who?" Liv said.

"A friend. Another place we can go if we have to escape here. I'll tell you later." To Pravit, he said, "Thank you. She didn't even occur to me."

"You need to get Kazzy on board so she doesn't sign the contract," Liv said. "Tell my other self to get her best friend back. And ditch Matt while she's at it."

"Olivia can hear you just fine. She's watching and listening to our conversation."

"She is?"

"We have ways to view Eidolon through visitors' eyes."

"Good." Liv raised her voice. "Olivia. Get your shit together. You're the one with the real life, and you're wasting it."

"Your life is no less real than hers," Pravit said gently.

"Yeah, right."

"I wouldn't be putting so much time and energy into protecting your family if I didn't believe that. Eidolon isn't just a computer world. It's a mindscape. Even Nera Blake doesn't know the extent of its possibilities. I've spent more time in this world than anyone, and I can tell you that every citizen at every level has thoughts and feelings and dreams and fears. Selling Bobbi for human testing is as unspeakable as doing the same to a child from our world."

Liv and Reef were quiet. Liv looked begrudging, and a little confused.

"Your lives aren't nothing," Pravit said. "Why do you think we're trying to save you?"

Reef wrapped an arm around Liv's waist. "Thank you."

"I should go," Pravit said. "Stay safe."

"You too, Pravit."

Kass, who had migrated to the kitchen to make Bobbi a hot chocolate, waved with her spoon. "See ya."

"Bye bye!" Bobbi said.

In his place by the computer, Aidan flicked switches, and the monitor went dark. Pravit opened his eyes, lifting the crown from his brow.

"Well," he said, "it seems we have a problem."

"Are we really going to bring someone else into this?" Aidan said.

"We don't have a choice. All our efforts will be for nothing if Equinoxx gets consent to reprogram Kassandra."

"I'll talk to her," Olivia said.

Pravit and Aidan turned to her.

"Neither of you can," Olivia pointed out. "Pravit can't be seen with her, and Aidan looks like a caveman. No offence."

"Some taken."

"You terrified me when we first met."

"You didn't sign the contract, did you?"

"Kass won't trust you."

"You can't go out in the open," Pravit said. "There are still people looking for you."

"I'll wear a wig or a hat or something. I'll go to the city, turn my phone on, and text her to meet me somewhere away from her place."

"Can't you just call her?" Pravit said.

"Doing this over a phone call isn't going to work. Trust me."

"Turning your phone on will give away your location," Aidan said, exasperated.

"I'll only have it on for a minute or so, to send the message. If Equinoxx weren't able to pinpoint the others' location inside Eidolon, they're not going to find me in this world. Besides, if you come along, I should be fine. We can go tomorrow morning."

"No, we can't. I have a meeting tomorrow morning."

Pravit shot him a curious glance, but Olivia didn't bother to ask. It was hit or miss with Aidan, and she suspected this time would be a miss.

"Tomorrow afternoon, then."

"I don't know how long this meeting will last."

Olivia groaned. "We can't waste time. We don't know whether Kass is going to sign that contract."

And what if she had ruined it? What if her phone call to Kass had only driven her further away? Maybe Kass would trust Briony *more* because Olivia had seemingly turned against her. It would be just like Kass to do something reckless because of a grudge.

"Wait until the day after tomorrow," Aidan said. At Olivia's frown, he added, "If our Kass hasn't signed the contract these past few days, she's unlikely to sign it now."

"We can't be sure of that."

"Look, Equinoxx would only want to reprogram Kass if Liv tries to get in touch with her. They don't know that Kass is with our other selves yet. We have time."

But they didn't, that was the problem. Olivia had already called Kass, had already started that snowball of a potential disaster.

She should confess what she'd done. Explain to Aidan that she'd betrayed him, that she'd used *Sophie's phone* to do it…

No. She couldn't. Aidan would never forgive her for risking exposure.

She would solve this problem on her own.

To: jacobpwilcox@equinoxxtechnology.co
From: lakebroadsideprivateinvestigations@lakebroadside.
com
Subject: Reef Davidson

Dear Mr Wilcox,
We regret to inform you there is no record of a Reef Davidson
in the Perth metropolitan area. Should you wish for us to
expand our search, please contact us at your convenience.
Invoice is attached.

Regards,
Steven Saulsbury
Lake Broadside Private Investigators

23

The crystal forest was especially magnificent in the moonlight. Nera wandered between the large purple structures, occasionally stopping to run her fingers along the artificial walls. Information from Eidolon flowed at her fingertips, down beneath the earth, sparking to other crystal trees, storing and changing and – annoyingly – glitching. The lines of data glowed softly, like an electronic pulse underneath the crystal.

Her beautiful world, her beautiful people were right here, beneath her hands.

Breath clouded before her, steaming in the cold night air. This was the one place her mind finally quieted. Sometimes she just wanted to walk through her forest and keep walking, forever and ever.

She could probably do that in the Australian outback. She had so many plans for that place, to nurture those vast spaces. If only the government would let her, if only they would all *let her*...

But that's what Eidolon was for. To prove that she could do all the things she promised, that they could clean up this planet and stop the devastating effects of humanity's existence.

She patted a crystal tree as she passed it. In her experience, there were three reasons people denied climate change. One, they were lazy; two, they were scared. Hearing the facts and stats was alarming, so when some sneering politician or scientist came out and said it was a load of crap, people found it easier and less terrifying to believe them. No hard work required, nothing to be fought for.

The third reason was from those who benefitted from letting the world burn. Fossil fuel companies had hefty wallets, and in a coal-reliant country like Australia, governments didn't hide how much they loved those sooty riches, regardless of what it meant for the future of the children currently playing around them.

The children.

Nera's icy fingers curled beneath her sleeves.

God forgive her.

The *children*.

"Contemplating your righteous fight for justice?"

Nera spun to find a Clooney-esque figure strolling towards her. "Jake? What are you doing here?"

"I spend a day and half on a plane, and that's the hello I get?"

"Sorry." Nera hurried toward her partner for a brief hug. There was a slight undertone of sweat beneath his earthy cologne. His suit was crinkled – had he come straight here after landing? "It's great to see you in person."

"It's great to see you too."

"How did you find me out here?"

Jake tapped the pocket of her jeans. "Your phone can be your worst enemy when you're trying to hide."

"I wasn't trying to hide."

"Then what are you doing out here?"

"Basking in the splendor of my genius."

"Atta girl." Jake's smile was strained. It could've been jetlag, but Nera suspected more. They'd agreed to keep their travel to necessities only, until they'd figured out how to keep emissions down on flights.

So if Jake was here, it was likely something had gone wrong with this backup plan of his.

Really, really wrong.

"Jake…"

"Plausible deniability, Nera. Don't ask."

"Please tell me you have everything under control."

He clasped her shoulder. "It's going to be fine."

"That doesn't sound like you have everything under control."

They started back towards the hub. The intelligent skin of the building gave it a dim glow, like a beacon calling them home.

"I'm concerned," Jake said, shoving his hands in his suit pockets. "I think perhaps we have a mole."

"Why do you say that?"

"Olivia Alexander not only refused to sign the contract, but evaded our...other methods of solving the problem. She's acting as if she knows what's going on. I think someone's been taking a peek at my personal correspondence and warning her in advance of my moves."

Nera needed a bouncy ball. She didn't know what moves Jake was talking about, but she was sure they weren't good.

"Who has the ability to hack into my emails?" Jake said.

Nera exhaled another cloud of steam. "You won't want to hear it."

"Tell me."

"Killian. From the front desk, he has access to all kinds of things."

"Fah." Jake waved the thought away. "My sister wouldn't have recommended him if she thought he wasn't one hundred percent on board with the company."

"He's a distant relative. Strong bonds are hardly forged with diluted blood."

"He cares more about what new eyeliner is on the market than what we're doing to keep Equinoxx afloat. Besides, if he screws us over, he's out of a job."

He wouldn't need a job if he'd been paid off by a mining company. Nera thought again of how she'd found the redhead in the regional director's office last year.

"How bad is it going to get if your 'backup plan' becomes public?" she said.

Jake didn't answer.

"Jake, if Project Eidolon goes under, we'll never be able to prove that our energy solutions work. We won't get the investments to run them in reality, we won't be able to implement our designs globally and we won't lower emissions in time."

"Exactly," Jake said. "Which is why we need the funds to keep it running. Without being able to sell the anomalies, we're screwed anyway."

"But—"

"We know for a fact that selling the anomalies will save the project. What we don't know is who this mole is working for, what their agenda is and whether we can flush them out before they do any lasting damage. Rectifying the situation with Olivia Alexander is a higher priority than worrying about some mole that may not even exist."

"But you said—"

"I said I *think* there's a mole, not that there is one. Besides, I have my own suspicions about who it might be. Just keep your eyes peeled and let me know if you notice anything amiss. All right?"

Nera pursed her lips. When it had first come online, Project Eidolon had been a tranquil lake; pure, uncorrupted. Now, each questionable action she and Jake took was a drop of poison spreading further and further across the surface, polluting everything in its path.

Humans, she thought bitterly as they climbed the stairs to the hub. *We ruin everything.*

24

The bus station attached to the Galleria wasn't as crowded as Olivia had hoped. It was the middle of the day – there were no school kids, no commuters. She was surrounded by seniors and people with babies.

She pulled the brim of Sophie's hat lower over her face, standing as casually as she could at the stop right in the center. The station had a roof but no walls, and buses arrived and left along different lanes around her.

There was a chance this could be a total bust. The negotiations she'd made with Valentina and Sophie, the terrifying drive here, the risk of being out in the open – it could lead to nothing. She didn't know whether Kass had believed her babbling attempt to explain about Briony, and she couldn't be sure Kass would come now.

Olivia turned her phone over in her hand. It was off now, but she'd had to turn it on to contact Kass. The dings of incoming messages had been a balm for her addicted soul…briefly. Her parents were worried about her – she'd sent them a text to tell them she was taking some time away from the world. All they seemed to know was that she and Matt had had a fight. He hadn't told them the truth, probably not wanting to air their dirty laundry.

Clarice had messaged saying Olivia's custom lingerie was ready. That delicate, beautiful set Olivia had spent ages designing to win her husband back was waiting to be picked up. At the moment, all she wanted was underwear that didn't come from a rolled-up six-pack. If she had her wallet, she'd be in the Galleria finding something that was at least displayed on a hanger.

She gazed down the pathway to the shopping center. Stealing a few things had already crossed her mind, but she couldn't risk attracting attention. If she got caught, Winken might find her. She knew enough to keep her head down.

Which was why she had turned her phone off again as soon as she'd texted Kass.

Because Matt had answered her message. Olivia was still reeling from his response. She wanted to call him, scream at him, sob and threaten.

She thumbed her wedding band, hating that she was cut off from the world.

"Nice hat." A redhead woman in a business suit joined her at the bus stop.

"Ha. Nice wig."

"The fuck we doing here?"

Olivia took a moment to allow the relief to flood her body. Despite everything, despite how they'd left things, Kass had come through for her. Kass always came through for her.

"I'm in trouble."

"Yeah, I got that, after your phone call. And I figured you hadn't suddenly decided to talk in code for funsies."

Olivia grinned. She didn't know whether Equinoxx could intercept her texts, so she'd sent two words to Kass: **Kissing virginity**.

At this very bus stop, some twenty years ago, Henry Chen had kissed Olivia goodbye after they'd seen a movie together. Kass had been standing right next to them at the time. As soon as Henry left, Kass and Olivia jumped up and down, squealing in the proper way of teenage girls. Kass had claimed Henry had taken Olivia's kissing virginity, and they'd laughed about it ever since.

"Did you look into Briony?"

"Yep." Kass didn't meet Olivia's eye. "I checked her financials. Some very nice lump sums from Equinoxx landed in her account. The first one was right before Ginger's wedding."

"I'm so sorry."

"Always check the financials, Livvie. It's the first thing they tell you in spy school."

"I didn't know for sure whether I was right, but…"

"Yeah, whatever. Fuck her."

"You didn't tell her I contacted you?"

"Nah. I pretended I was going to sign her shitty contract, then picked a fight and told her we were done."

"You always got the best marks in drama."

"The tears were real."

Olivia bit her lip.

Kass sucked a breath through her nose and said, "So what the fuck is going on?"

"Let's walk. There are too many cameras here."

They headed out of the station, following footpaths next to bustling roads and weaving to suburban areas. All the while, Olivia talked. About Eidolon, about Winken, about Aidan and Sophie and Valentina. Kass stopped her once – "Need to take these fucking heels off" – but otherwise let her speak without interruption.

They stopped at the edge of a park. Kass shielded her eyes against the sun and said, "We've been through some crazy shit, Livvie, but this is *bananas.*"

"Sorry. I didn't mean to get you involved."

"Nah. Sounds like you need me." Kass regarded her. "You really drove down the hill? Yourself?"

"I went about forty ks an hour and stopped for at least a minute at every intersection, but yes. I did."

"This is big, Liv. You haven't driven since–"

"The accident. Yeah. But I had to see you. I could never forgive myself if you got hurt because of me."

"Aw, shit." Kass looked away, blinking rapidly.

"Is there somewhere safe you could hole up? I'm worried Equinoxx will turn their attention to you now your simulation is with mine."

"Let 'em come. I'll fuck that Winken guy up."

"He's a *paid assassin.*"

"You've forgotten my mad skills with a pocket knife."

"No, I haven't," Olivia said. "Last time you tried to get rough with your pocket knife you needed thirteen stitches in the ER."

Kass held up her hand, where a small scar glistened between her thumb and pointer. "Yeah, but the other guy was wrecked, ay."

They started back towards the Galleria, keeping to a lazy pace. Kass was used to being barefoot and didn't seem to mind the heat of the pavement. Her heels hung from the crook of her fingers.

"You're gonna need to defend yourself too, you know," Kass said. "Don't suppose you've been keeping fit?"

"No," Olivia said moodily. "But you should see my other self. She has some sweet guns."

"Nice."

"She has a lot of things, actually. A tan. A kid."

"A husband who doesn't cheat on her."

It was only when they reached a set of traffic lights and Kass slipped her heels back on that Olivia said, "I texted him, you know. To keep him from calling the police about my disappearance. I told him I knew about Sarina."

"What did he say?"

"Okay."

"Okay?"

"No apology. No explanation. No asking if I was all right. He cheated on me for over six months, and his response to my finding out was 'Okay.'"

"Darl, the man's a cu–"

"Fine, he's a cheater. And Briony's a plant. We all have our issues."

Kass sniffed but didn't push it. The Galleria came into view.

"Want me to buy you some shit?" Kass said as they passed the bus station. "I got cash, so your assassin mate isn't going to find me."

"What kind of shit?"

"A burner phone? Maybe some different clothes?" She looked

Olivia up and down. "Call me nuts, but I reckon you didn't choose that pair of knee-length shorts for yourself."

Olivia couldn't decide whether to laugh or cry. "Kassandra White, I love you."

"I know," Kass said. "Don't you forget it."

25

Olivia had been gone for hours. She was expecting a berating from Aidan when she returned in Valentina's rusted Camry, but the car port was empty.

Valentina and Sophie came out to the porch as Olivia made her way to the cottage.

"Everything go smoothly?" Valentina said.

"Sure did." Olivia held up her bags. "She even bought me stuff. With cash."

"Does she have somewhere safe to go?"

"She'll be fine. Trust me, Kass can look after herself." Olivia climbed the steps. "Where's Aidan?"

"Who knows?" Sophie muttered, her gaze fixed on her phone as she typed away.

"He messaged to say he wouldn't be home until tomorrow," Valentina said.

"Equinoxx stuff?"

Sophie and Valentina shrugged.

Olivia couldn't help feeling a little disappointed. Kass had thrown in a bottle of wine among the purchases, and Olivia had been looking forward to sharing it with him, maybe loosen him up a bit.

But on the bright side, more for her.

"At least I could do one job for him," she said cheerfully. Anything felt possible now she was in proper clothes. An A-line dress was a million times better than shorts. And she had cute heels to match.

Sophie and Valentina followed her into the house.

"What job was that?" Sophie said as they walked down the hall. Valentina sighed. "Sophie."

"You might as well tell me. I pick up bits and pieces all the time. And I listen when you think I'm asleep."

Olivia dumped her bags on Sophie's bed and eyed the girl thoughtfully. "My best friend got caught up in the Equinoxx thing."

"But what is the Equinoxx thing? I don't understand – aren't they the good guys? They're trying to save the world."

"They are," Olivia said, glancing at Valentina. "But there's more to it than that."

Sophie looked between them, waiting. Olivia hesitated. The kid was old enough to know, surely. She'd obviously been through some stuff herself, and it was awful being stuck here–

"Fine," Sophie said. "Don't tell me. I have my secrets too." She spun on her heel and stalked away. The front door slammed behind her.

"I think we should tell her," Olivia said.

"We'll talk to Aidan when he gets back." Valentina rubbed her mouth with her hand. "I'm worried about these 'secrets' she's talking about, though. Have you noticed how often she's on her phone?"

"That's not unusual."

"She acts excited when she gets messages. Sometimes giddy."

"She might have met someone online." Olivia started unpacking her new outfits. She had a small amount of wardrobe and drawer space next to Sophie's stuff. The clothes Aidan had brought her were unceremoniously dumped on the bed. "I wouldn't be too concerned, since she's not allowed to meet anyone in person."

"For now," Valentina said. "But Aidan can't keep her locked away forever. If he doesn't let her rejoin the world soon, I'm afraid she'll take matters into her own hands, and she's young and naive. She could get hurt out there."

"Have you talked to Aidan?"

"He's terrified her people will snatch her back and turn her to their side."

"I think she's smarter than that. She's been exposed to enough of the world to know better, right?"

"Unfortunately, her morals align more with them than we're comfortable with."

Olivia grabbed the wine bottle and they headed into the kitchen. "Who are these people, anyway?"

"People who are very good at convincing others. Aidan and Sophie's father…he's bad news."

Was there ever any good news?

Olivia checked the clock. It was close enough to five for her to justify cracking open the bottle. "Drink?"

"No, thank you."

She got herself a wine glass, thinking of Kass' advice. "I don't suppose there's a running track or something nearby? I need to get fit again. You know. To run away from people."

Valentina didn't smile; after all it was true.

"There's gym equipment in my shed. Weights, a treadmill, that sort of thing. Aidan bought them for Sophie a few years ago but she hasn't used them in a while." Valentina paused. "Aidan could show you some self-defense moves, too. He used to teach Sophie… back when they were speaking to each other."

"Huh. That sounds useful."

Olivia sniffed her wine, too lost in thought to appreciate the nose. This was going to work. She would get her fitness back and learn how to fend off an attacker, shedding this feeling of helplessness. The secret burner phone from Kass was sitting in her shopping bags – they were going to keep in contact and investigate Equinoxx themselves.

Olivia was taking the wheel on this situation. Sure, she might only go forty ks an hour at first, but it was time she got back in the damn driver's seat.

And that meant, starting tomorrow, she'd have to betray Aidan's trust.

26

The constant pounding on Briony's front door didn't help with her hangover.

She staggered out of bed, crookedly buttoned up a long flannel shirt, and only had pants on.

Underpants. Underpants, for these wacky Australians who laughed when she called them pants. In fact, there'd been a well funny miscommunication when she'd first moved here and was talking to a group of cute boys in the pub when–

Who was knocking so hard?

She swung open the door to find a man she could only describe as a silver fox on her porch.

"Ms McKinney," he said, exasperated.

She blinked through her haze.

He gestured to her state of undress. "What the hell are you doing?"

His American accent registered in her brain.

Mr Wilcox.

Mr Jacob P. bloody Wilcox was standing at her front door, and she was in her pants.

"Oh shit," she said.

"Get changed," he said like a tired teacher. "I'll wait here."

"Er…sure."

She didn't know whether to close the door or leave it ajar. She started to half close it, panicked, and slammed it shut the rest of the way.

"*Shit.*" She turned to look at the state of her lounge room. "Shit. Fuck. Bollocks."

With a pounding head, she scurried into the kitchen, downed a pint glass of water then rummaged through the piles of laundry on the couch to find something suitable to wear. A pack of painkillers was unearthed in the debris. She swallowed four of them.

What was Mr bloody Wilcox of bollocking Equinoxx doing in Australia? Was he here to fire her personally? Had anyone fucked up as badly as she had in the history of humanity?

He could've at least *texted* first.

She stuck her head under the cold water of the shower for several seconds and slicked back her hair. The mirror still reflected puffy eyes and red splotches on her pale cheeks, but it would have to do.

With some semblance of decorum, she re-opened the front door.

"Mr Wilcox," she said. "So good of you to drop by."

He smiled wryly. "What's going on?"

"I don't know what you mean."

"Kassandra White." He moved past her, into the house. She cringed as she noticed a G-string on top of the washing pile. "What happened?"

"I wish I knew." She was proud to hear her voice didn't waver. "Do you er…want a cuppa?"

"I want to know why you didn't get her signature."

"I was going to. She agreed and everything. But we drove home and she said she wanted to read the contract while she was sober, and when she came around the next day, we had this massive argument that seemed to come from nowhere and she broke up with me."

Briony swayed in place. She wanted to vomit, and not all of it was from the hangover. What had she done to turn Kass so vehemently against her? Kass was saying something about Briony not respecting her family, how she looked down on them, acting like she was superior – the ranting was hard to follow.

"Then fix it," Mr Wilcox said.

"I've been trying. I've called her a bunch of times and left her messages, but she's not getting back to me. I don't even know if her phone is on."

Briony's mouth was dry again. It was important, very important, that Mr Wilcox not realize her broken voice wasn't just from all the drinks last night.

She had done that thing they did in movies; the thing the plant isn't supposed to do. She had fallen in love with the target.

"Maybe she'll cool off in a few days," Briony said quietly.

She could feel Mr Wilcox's stare pounding at her skull along with her headache.

"Are you sure you didn't tip her off?" Mr Wilcox said.

"I'm positive. I've been really careful."

"You didn't start to feel sorry for her? Perhaps...get in a little too deep?"

Briony massaged her temples. Hair of the dog, that's what she needed.

"Has she heard from Olivia?" Mr Wilcox said.

"Not that I know of. What's happening with her? Is she really missing?"

"It seems that way." His gaze wandered around her lounge room and adjoining kitchen. "The thing is, Ms McKinney, I think someone tipped her off. An insider's told her there's more to the contract than what appears on the surface."

"It wasn't me," Briony said in alarm.

"Considering how much I paid you to secure those signatures, you've given me very little in return. In fact, you've given me nothing."

His heavy cologne wasn't helping her nausea.

"I'll think of something," she mumbled.

"Good," he said. "Be creative. Fast. We only have until the new year to have everything wrapped up. I'd like Kassandra's signature before the end of October."

"I'll do my best."

"That's not good enough. I need you to understand the delicate position you're in. Those signatures will make or break Equinoxx."

"What?"

"Why do you think I paid you so much to get them? Everything Nera Blake and I worked for, every government and legal restriction we fought against to make our goals a reality, will have been for nothing."

Briony managed not to gape at him, instead keeping her face professionally calm.

"So please," he said. "Get Kassandra's signature. Whatever it takes."

27

It was important Olivia win this fight. She stared Valentina down, refusing to budge. The lines around Valentina's mouth deepened.

"Didn't you take a big enough risk yesterday?"

"This isn't a risk," Olivia said.

"You should wait for Aidan to return."

"The sooner I get there, the better."

Valentina hesitated. "I don't think—"

"Check this out!" Sophie bustled into the kitchen with her laptop. Her eyes were wide, but there was glee in her features.

"Hang on," Valentina said. To Olivia, she said, "I don't think you should take anyone else to the shed."

"What shed?" Sophie asked.

"Kass is already up to her neck in this. There's no point keeping her away. Besides, she's a useful ally. And my best friend."

"What's going on?"

"I know Aidan's used to doing everything on his own, but he doesn't have to anymore. Kass can help. *I* can help. The others deserve to know as soon as possible that their Kass won't be compromised."

"What if our Kass is followed?"

"She's good at evasion. Trust me. It's part of her job."

"And what job is that, exactly?"

Sophie cleared her throat loudly and banged her laptop on the table. "There was a *terrorist attack* in Western Australia!"

Olivia and Valentina turned.

"What are you talking about?" Valentina said.

"Look at this."

They crammed around the laptop to see the news article. A train had derailed, broken and sideways off the tracks. Black dust from its carriages blanketed the earth. There was a close-up of part of the track that had been blown away in an explosion.

"Apparently," Sophie said, "the bomb exploded when the train was halfway across it."

"Was anyone hurt?" Olivia said.

"The driver's in hospital with minor injuries, but it was a coal train, so there were no passengers."

Valentia exhaled heavily.

"The media are saying it's the Guardians again. You know the group that spiked all those trees at the beginning of the year?" Sophie ran her fingers lovingly across the screen. "They are *so* cool."

"They killed someone," Valentina said sharply.

"So what? The company was logging an old growth forest."

"A man doing his job is not the enemy."

"Didn't Nazis say they were just doing their job?"

"Sophie!" Valentina's voice lifted. "Bombing and murder aren't answers."

"Why not? The government isn't listening to protests. Why shouldn't we start getting violent?"

"*We?*"

"Yes, we! Us. The next generation. The people who'll have to live in the mess you left."

"Is that what you want to do, girl? Go around killing everyone? How many workers will you have to murder before the mining stops?"

"Then we'll cut off the head of the corporation instead."

"What *we?*" Valentina roared.

"Uh, hey." Olivia held out her hands between them. "Let's just…let's all take a breath. Why don't we sit down and talk about it over a cup of tea?"

"There's no point," Sophie said, nostrils flaring. "No one listens to me, anyway." She shot a glare at Olivia. "And I don't care what your problem is with Equinoxx, they're the only big company fighting to save us. They might even be our last hope. So you should just let them do whatever it is they're doing and shut up."

She stalked back into her room. The slam of her door echoed through the house.

"Woah." Olivia'd forgotten how mean teenagers were.

Valentina filled up the kettle. "We should take away her devices."

"I don't think that's a good idea."

"What she said just now is exactly the kind of thinking Aidan's been trying to keep her from."

"Don't isolate her. You'll only make an enemy of her."

"This whole situation is impossible," Valentina said. "She should be in school, with peers. Then perhaps she'd have other things to concentrate on."

"Or maybe she'd be just as passionate. You can't know for sure."

"I'm worried." Valentina flicked on the kettle with the stump of her arm. "Legally, she'll be out of reach from her family when she turns eighteen, but she might end up going back to them anyway."

"Does the cult think along the same lines as her?"

"Very much so. Oh, Aidan will be heartbroken. He's tried so hard."

"And sacrificed so much," Olivia murmured. She picked up the laptop. "Let me talk to her."

Valentina sighed. "Good luck."

Olivia headed down the hall and knocked gently on the bedroom door. When no answer was forthcoming, she opened up. Sophie was curled on her sleeping bag, typing at her phone. She glowered without looking up. "I get no privacy in this place."

"I know. I'm sorry. I would offer to sleep on the couch, but after the accident, my back—"

"Whatever. It doesn't matter."

"Of course it matters." Olivia closed the door behind her and sank down onto the bed with the laptop. "I think you're really brave for living like this, hidden away from the world, keeping safe while stuck in a house filled with secrets. It's enough to drive anyone nuts."

Sophie snorted in agreement.

"I used to be brave, too. A long time ago." She opened YouTube. "Want to see?"

It was enough to pique Sophie's interest. She climbed up onto the mattress next to Olivia and they sat side by side against the wall as the video loaded.

Kass' voice echoed out from the speakers. "*Wait, let me zoom out—*"

"Is that you?" Sophie said as a young version of Olivia came into focus.

"*How high did you say this was? Fuck me, look at that.*"

"What are you going to do?" Sophie said as the camera panned to the waterfall plummeting into the gorge below.

"*Mmm, I've forgotten. Eighty feet?*"

"You're not going to jump?"

"*Oh shit, Livvie, your sunnies!*"

"You are *not* going to jump!"

"*You know it doesn't count unless you do a flip, ay.*"

"Oh my god. Oh my – GOD! You just jumped off that cliff!" Sophie's shouts joined Kass' whooping. "You're still falling! Oh my god!"

"Got in a double flip before I hit the water." Olivia said it proudly, but she felt as if she were speaking about an old friend rather than herself. That Liv, the one in the video, didn't feel like her anymore.

"Oh wow," Sophie said as the Liv from the video resurfaced below and floated casually on her back. "Wow wow wow. Why didn't you show me this before? My little jump at the river must be nothing to you."

"I'm a coward these days. I wouldn't go anywhere near the edge, even for your jump."

"How come?"

"The accident made me afraid, I guess." Olivia was already searching for another of her videos. "I have some skydiving footage, and I did BASE jumping for a while."

"What's that?"

"Where you jump from buildings and stuff with a parachute. Let me see if I can find them."

Sophie shifted closer, keenly. Olivia felt just as keen. Watching the footage was like watching herself in Eidolon, a version of her that was capable and powerful and unafraid – it was almost addictive.

"Hey," she said as a video played of her and Starfish Steve doing a skydiving routine. "Do you think you could help me get fit again?"

Sophie glanced at her curiously.

"I hear you have gym equipment in the shed. I need a workout buddy. And I'll pay you."

"You don't have your wallet."

"Not with money." Olivia glanced out the window. "How about I teach you to drive?"

"Seriously?"

"What do you say?"

"But...Aidan would never agree."

"Aidan doesn't have to know."

Sophie's jaw dropped.

"It's a life skill," Olivia said, "and one day you'll need to know how to do it. Besides, who better to teach you than the most cautious and terrified driver in the world?"

Sophie was practically vibrating. "Can we go for a drive now?"

"Not yet," Olivia said, passing the laptop to her. "Right now, I need the car for something important. Assuming I can convince Valentina to let me go."

28

The problem was the coordinates.

Kass and Olivia had figured out the generator, how to turn the system on, and how to start the Eidolon program. It was all waiting...but Olivia didn't know the coordinates to the beach house.

"It's piss easy to use," Kass said, sitting at the computer. "For the basic people, ay. Maybe there's a place with – aha. Past entries." Her fingers flew across the keys. "Gotta say, I'm looking forward to this. Seeing you like you're supposed to be."

"Ouch."

"I'm serious. This level-whatever Livvie sounds like my gal."

"Level four," Olivia said. "Level one citizens are the people who were mapped in but there's limited data on them, including babies born there. Level two were mapped in by close friends and family."

"Like me."

"Yep. Level three are people who mapped themselves in."

"Then level four are the ones who aren't supposed to exist, right? The ones who don't know they're a simulation."

"Exactly. And level five are like Bobbi. Born in Eidolon, completely independent." Olivia hesitated as Kass' fingers hovered over the keyboard. "Do you know how to extract me?"

"I'll figure it out."

Maybe they should've waited for Aidan.

"If you trust me to belay, you can trust me with this," Kass said.

After another beat, Olivia sat on the chair and set the crown on her head. The whole reason she was doing this without Aidan was so he wouldn't hear the conversation she had planned.

Valentina had been more obliging after Olivia had subdued Sophie, and had promised not to tell Aidan. But she'd called out dire warnings as Olivia left, about how the more people were involved, the more danger they'd be in. Olivia was showing Kass their most important asset. If Equinoxx found out they had a station, they would lose their way into Eidolon. But Olivia trusted Kass more than anyone.

She thumbed her wedding band, thinking it wasn't that long ago that she would've trusted Matt with this secret.

Before she could contemplate it further, the beach house appeared. It was a little messier than before – there was a blanket and pillow strewn over the couch and toys across the floor. The air was heavy with heat.

"Oh," she said. "It worked. Good job, Kass."

Footsteps thundered behind her as Bobbi raced into the living room, completely naked except for floaties on her arms. "Mummy, beach!" She slowed to a stop when she saw Olivia.

"All right, all right, we're coming."

"Wait, ya rascal, you need sunsc–"

Liv and Kass came out in swimsuits and sarongs, with towels slung over their shoulders. They stopped when they saw Olivia.

"Who–" Kass started, then said, "Liv, is that you?"

"That's me," Liv said, eying Olivia warily. "From the outside world."

"What the hell happened?"

"Oi," Olivia said, then caught herself when she realized how rough her voice sounded. Hanging around Kass again was starting to rub off on her.

"I told you," Liv muttered. "She stayed with Matt." To Olivia, she said, "What are you doing here?"

"Mummy, beach!"

"In a minute."

Bobbi ran to the back door and reached for the doorknob just as it opened.

"Hey, Bob-Bob." Reef walked in, wearing board shorts and nothing else. He scooped Bobbi up. She squealed in delight. "Ready for a swim?" His gaze landed on Olivia. "Oh. Hi. Is everything okay?"

While concern laced his voice, there was a warmness to it that was missing from Kass and Liv.

"Everything's fine," Olivia said. "That's what I've come to tell you. I've spoken to Kass – to my Kass – and she knows what's going on. She won't sign any Equinoxx forms. You're safe."

"Huh," said Kass. "You still call me Kass on the outside?"

"She's Kazzy here," Reef said. "Aunny Kazzy."

"Aunny Kazzy!" Bobbi echoed gleefully.

"What's this I hear about us not being friends anymore?" Kass – Kazzy – said to Olivia.

"She's with me right now, watching on the monitor. Um, if you want to say hi?"

"Sup, me," Kass said, waving at no one. "Is she any different?"

"Not really."

Kazzy looked from Olivia to Liv. "Can't say the same for you two."

"You think that's bad," Reef said. "Wait until you meet my other self."

"Daddy, beach!"

Reef put Bobbi down and picked up the esky waiting by the door. "All right, chicken, let's go."

"We're going for a swim if you want to come," Kazzy said to Olivia.

She sounded like she was joking, but Olivia said, "Okay," and Liv looked at her curiously.

They picked up supplies and headed down the little path to the ocean. It was a scorcher of a day. Olivia squinted into the brightness. "I thought Eidolon was supposed to be doing something about the climate."

"It's not going to happen right away," Liv said. "Besides, it's still W.A."

"Right."

Kazzy jabbed a beach umbrella into the sand while Bobbi sprinted to the water with Reef in tow. Liv opened the esky and sat down on a towel with a beer. "Want one?"

Olivia took it. "If I get drunk in Eidolon, do you think I'll feel the effects in the real world?"

"Guess you could find out."

Kazzy slipped off her sarong and sunglasses. "I'm going for a swim before I melt." To Liv, she said, "Be nice."

Olivia watched her run to join Reef and Bobbi. "Why am I getting the distinct feeling you hate me?"

"Can't imagine." Liv sipped her beer, her gaze on the water.

"Is it because I'm still with Matt?"

"Hey, it's your life. You do what you want."

Olivia cracked open her bottle. When was the last time she'd had a beer?

"Are you doing okay here?"

"We're surviving," Liv said. "How about you? Getting everything you need on Equinoxx?"

"I think so. Pravit's doing most of the work. My big job is to… stay put." It came out sulkier than she'd intended.

"That seems to be all of our jobs," Liv said.

Bobbi shrieked as Kazzy lifted her into the air and swooped her over the waves. Reef was chest deep in the water.

"Doesn't seem like too bad a place," Olivia said. "And at least you're with your family. I haven't been able to contact mine."

"But you're staying with Reef."

"I'm staying with Aidan, and he's not my family."

"Right." Liv's attention slid to Olivia's wedding band. Olivia hadn't even realized she was playing with it.

"I have to ask…" Funny how nervous she felt. This place wasn't the same as hers. Just because it happened in a simulation, didn't mean it would happen in Olivia's world. "Why did you and Matt break up?"

"Forget about him."

"He's my *husband*."

Liv sighed and gulped her beer again. Olivia sniffed hers before taking a sip. Nice on a hot day. She kicked off her heels and buried her toes in the sand. Would she ever get used to how real everything felt?

"Is Reef listening right now?" Liv said.

"You mean Aidan? No, it's just Kass watching the monitor."

There was a pause, then following another sip of beer, Liv said, "I started to experience strange things after the mapping. Hallucinations. Derealizations. I thought something had happened to my brain. Turns out, the hallucinations were glitches in the program, and the derealizations weren't a case of me feeling disconnected from the world, but my brain trying to tell me the world was wrong." She pulled at the sticker of her bottle. "It's not as bad anymore. Now I know what's causing it, I don't freak out as much. But it was bad then. Nothing felt real, including Matt. I started to drift from him. And then, a few months after the mapping, Equinoxx hosted a party for everyone who'd volunteered. I went by myself, as something to do. That's where I met Reef."

"He doesn't strike me as the kind to go to a corporate-hosted party."

"I found out recently that Pravit asked him to go. This wasn't so much about the mappers, but about the level four citizens. Equinoxx had caught on by that stage that something was happening with some of the simulations. They were trying to get us all together, to study us in groups. They wanted to figure out why we weren't reacting to their pings. We're not part of their program. We're sort of…independent residents."

"Did they say something to you at the party?"

"Not at all. They were just watching us, from what I understand. But they would've seen how Reef and I gravitated towards each other. Reef was the first person I'd come across since the mapping that felt real to me. We talked, and I kept wanting to touch him, to be near him."

"So the only reason you were drawn to each other was because you were both glitches?"

"At first, yes." Liv took another swig. "We got drunk and slept together that night."

"Wait…you cheated on Matt?"

"It was so good to be with someone who felt tangible—"

"You cheated on Matt!" Olivia couldn't decide whether to laugh or sob.

"I told Matt everything."

"Straight away? You just…told him?"

"He was devastated. Said he could never trust me again. I tried to reconcile, but he wasn't interested. So I got a job at a pie shop, found a crappy unit and rented on my own. Until I found out I was pregnant, anyway. I still had Reef's number, so I called him."

"How did he take it?"

Liv smiled over the lip of her beer as she watched her family play in the waves. "The first thing he did was come around with crackers and fizzy water. Then he took me to doctor's appointments. Repainted the nursery. Made a cradle by hand. Fixed stuff around the house when I needed it. I kept inviting him over for coffee, for dinner, for breakfast. It was only a few months before we decided to move in together. We hated being apart."

"Because you're both the same. You're both blips in the system."

"No. At least, it's not just that. Matt made me feel safe after the accident, but he was coddling me. I wasn't able to step out in the world while he kept me in bubble wrap. I never had the chance to overcome my fears. When we broke up, I had to find the courage to drive again, to take care of myself, to face the world. Being with Reef is…freeing. It's his personality. He lives fearlessly, and taught me to do it too. When we went skydiving—"

"You've been skydiving again?"

Liv grinned. "Starfish Steve almost cried when I rocked up at Aussie Adventures last year."

"Holy shit."

Olivia had never imagined a world where she could go skydiving again.

Liv clapped a hand over Olivia's knee. "I don't blame you for still being with Matt. I just think you're with him because it's safer. Because you feel obligated, after all he did for you after. And, honestly, I think he stayed with me out of guilt rather than love."

Olivia's throat was tight.

That's it. That's what it was. That's why, even though Olivia had done everything right, Matt had found someone else. He didn't love her. He felt guilty for hitting her with his car.

The sob came from nowhere. Tears streamed, as if she'd been smacked in the face.

"I'm sorry," Liv said. "I didn't mean—"

"He's h-having an affair."

"That *fucker.*"

"It's been going on for six months."

"What a piece of shit! After the guilt trip he laid on me for a one-night stand. I swear to God, if I get a chance, I'm going to slap him."

Olivia couldn't answer. The sobs wracked at her lungs as Liv patted her on the back.

"Hey," Kazzy said, running up. "You right?"

"She's going to be fine," Liv said.

"How much beer did you give her?"

"Turns out, Matt's a piece of shit."

"Flat on my back with surprise, I am."

Olivia cried harder. Or maybe she was laughing. She couldn't tell anymore. The beer sloshed unpleasantly in her stomach.

"On the bright side," Kazzy said, squeezing out her hair, "at least you've got a sweet backup."

"Reef reckons he's different in the other world," Liv said.

Olivia dried her face with the edge of a towel. "He's right. Aidan's not like Reef."

"Chuck us a beer."

Liv passed Kazzy a bottle and Kazzy sat down between them, not bothering to dry herself. They watched Reef skim Bobbi through the waves. Bobbi's pink floaties were dazzling against the blue.

"He's a good egg," Kazzy said.

"I love him so much," Liv said. "I can't imagine life without him. You're missing out, you know. Especially on the sex."

Kazzy choke-laughed on her beer. "As if you two are getting any with a toddler around."

"You know this morning, when we asked you to watch Bobbi so we could go for a run?"

"Huh. That explains all the sand."

"Outdoors?" Olivia said to Liv. "Really?"

Liv grinned. "I won't spoil you on any more details. You can find out for yourself."

"I'm not hooking up with Aidan. I'm still married, and...I dunno. Something's wrong with him. He's moody and depressed and mean to his sister. He's not your Reef."

"Gotta be honest with you, that hurts."

"It's not my fault."

"No, I mean it hurts to hear Reef is suffering in your world." Liv dusted sand from her toes. "This sister of his. She's changed everything for him, hasn't she?"

"It sounds like it, yeah."

There was a silence, where they listened to the whoosh of the waves and the shrieking laughter of Bobbi.

"You told me you have nothing to do," Liv said. She met Olivia's gaze. "Well, I'm giving you a job. Take care of him."

"I'm not a babysitter. Besides, he's barely at home."

"Get him to open up to you. No, don't argue. He is the love of my life, and there's nothing I can do to help him from here. *You* need to do it."

"You're really bossy."

"Noticed that, have you?" Kazzy said.

"You can help him," Liv said. "I know for a fact he's got a weakness for me. You. Whatever."

"I suppose all our lives sort of rely on him keeping it together," Olivia said. "I could probably talk to him. A bit."

"Olivia Rachel Sharp, get your shit together. Dump your cheating husband, talk to Reef, and get a haircut while you're at it, because long hair is a pain in the ass. Jesus," Liv said, as Kazzy clinked the necks of their bottles together in approval, "do I have to do everything around here?"

To: jacobpwilcox@equinoxxtechnology.co
From: retrievalunit@basenxj451.com
Subject: Retrieval update

LEVEL FIVE CITIZEN (CHINA POINT) SUCCESSFULLY
RETRIEVED
PREPARING FOR TRANSPORTATION TO AUSTRALIAN
BASE

29

Olivia woke to distant screaming. She fumbled to throw off her blanket as Sophie leaped out of her sleeping bag and thundered from the room. Valentina's footsteps thumped down the corridor. Olivia's bleary mind translated the sound.

The chickens.

The chickens were screaming.

She scrambled out of bed to follow th e others. A security light illuminated the garden bordering the house. Valentina's dressing gown flapped behind her as she ran to the henhouse.

Sophie made it there first. She shrieked and turned away, her hands cupping her nose and mouth.

"Damn you!" Valentina cried at the disappearing swish of a fox's tail. "Damn you, damn you!"

She hurried into the enclosure. There was a broken board where the fox had gotten in. A dead chicken lay beside it, as if the fox had tried to drag it out but couldn't get it through the hole.

Olivia passed Sophie, moving as near as she dared. Another dead chicken was inside.

Valentina made a soft crooning noise as she crouched by the third and final creature, which was splayed, alive but bleeding in the dirt. Tears stained her face.

Still, when she stepped out to fetch a shovel, her expression was hard. Olivia only just realized what she was doing in time, and spun away before the spade came down.

"My girls," Valentina whispered. "My poor, poor girls."

Sophie was shaking. Olivia moved to her, but they were drenched in headlights as a vehicle rolled into the car port.

Aidan was home.

"You!" Valentina practically roared as he got out of the car. "You promised me you'd fix the run. You promised!"

"What happened?" His voice was rough; exhausted.

"What do you think?" Valentina stormed forward with the shovel – for a second, Olivia thought she was going to hit him with it. At the last moment, she tossed it away and poked him in the chest. "You're out. Pack up your things, and leave."

"Val–" Sophie started.

"You can stay," Valentina said without turning to her. "But your brother is out. That was his last chance. He hasn't been helping around the house like he promised. He's been gone for *two days* without explanation. I'm done, Aidan. My debt to you is paid. Pack up your bags, be gone before morning."

Olivia couldn't see much of his face, since his back was to the security lights, but from what she could tell he didn't look surprised. He looked resigned.

Valentina pulled her dressing gown tighter to herself and stalked back to the house.

There was a moment where Sophie and Aidan stared at each other. Olivia held her breath, hoping one of them would speak. But then Sophie shook her head, and followed Valentina back into the house. She didn't look at Aidan as she passed.

Aidan remained still until the front door closed. Then he picked up the shovel and headed out to the fringe of the forest, where he started to dig.

Olivia moved towards him. "What are you doing?"

"What does it look like?" Every word, every movement, seemed as if it were a great effort.

"Have you slept since you left?"

The reply was a soft scoff.

"Go to bed."

"Apparently, I don't have one anymore."

"I'm sure Valentina's just upset. She'll change her mind in the morning."

The security light switched off. Aidan kept digging. Olivia's eyes adjusted to the moonlight. She hugged herself. She could feel the night's chill as the shock wore off.

"Where have you been?" she said gently.

"Nowhere."

"Aidan."

"Just let me dig these graves, all right?"

"I want to help," Olivia said.

He paused, leaning on the spade. "There's another one in the shed."

She picked her way through the darkness. The security light came on again when she was close enough. The shed had a light too. Gym equipment was stacked in the corner. She eyed it before finding the shovel.

When she returned, Aidan had started on the second grave. She didn't say anything, just broke earth. Almost immediately, her hands felt the burn. They were soft and delicate, unused to labor. She should've gotten gloves.

But she didn't want to leave Aidan again, so she thrust the blade down and hefted as much dirt as she was able.

Neither of them spoke for the duration of the task. When the graves were ready, Aidan left and carried the chickens over one by one. He dropped them in, and Olivia scattered dirt on their small bodies.

"I'll talk to Valentina," she said when the last hole was filled. Her hands were aching. His hands were covered in blood.

"Don't bother," he said.

"We need you here."

"You're better off without me."

He turned and walked towards the house. Olivia dropped the shovel to hurry after him. "That's not true. You're the only one who can help me against Equinoxx."

"Pravit can do it."

"Aidan, stop. I went to see Kass without you."

It was a last-ditch attempt – she hadn't expected a response – but he turned.

"We met at the Galleria. She bought me stuff." In what she hoped was a joking voice, she added, "Didn't you notice my new clothes?"

He sighed heavily.

"I also met Kass at the shed today. She was my anchor while I went to Eidolon."

"You showed her the shed?"

"You have nothing to worry about when it comes to Kass. I'm more concerned about Valentina's car. I didn't think much of it at the time, but maybe it wasn't a good idea for me to drive it."

"We have spare license plates," he said. "I can change them before I go."

He didn't even sound mad. He sounded…empty. Like he didn't care about anything anymore.

"Please don't leave," she whispered.

"I don't have a choice."

"You shouldn't be driving right now. Let me talk to Valentina."

"I–"

"*Please.*"

"Fine," he muttered. He headed for the tap on the side of the house.

Olivia put the shovels away. It seemed best to keep Valentina as happy as possible. Aidan was crouched by the tap when she returned, trying to scrub the blood from his hands. He had his back to her, but his shoulders were shaking.

Olivia hesitated. Imagined Liv urging her, *begging* her, to go over to him.

But he was so determined to push her away, and they were practically strangers. Even Reef didn't know what was going on in this world. What was *she* supposed to do?

Olivia lingered a moment longer before continuing into the house. Valentina was at the kitchen table with a steaming cup of tea. Down the hall, Sophie's door was closed.

"I'm sorry about your chickens," Olivia said.

No answer.

"Aidan dug their graves."

Valentina sipped her tea. She looked straight ahead, her eyes red but dry.

"I don't think he should leave," Olivia said. "He seems to be… in a bad place."

"He's been in a bad place for a while."

"He's in a worse place tonight. It feels like he's at the end of his tether."

"I asked him to fix the chicken run. Over and over, I asked him. The deal was, he stays here, he works for it. He was supposed to help me. Now my girls are dead."

"Valentina." Olivia pulled up a chair. "Let me make this perfectly clear. Your chickens are dead, and I'm so sorry. But something is wrong with Aidan. I'm really scared that if you make him leave tonight, he's not going to survive until morning. Either he's going to fall asleep at the wheel or…"

"Or what?" Valentina and Olivia turned to find Sophie standing at her bedroom door. She was still shivering, her gaze on Olivia. "Or *what?*"

Olivia pursed her lips. She hadn't wanted to have this conversation with Aidan's little sister here.

"I just think," she said carefully, "we should look out for each other. Something he said to me just now, about us being better off with him gone–"

"We *are* better off with him gone," Sophie said. "Whenever he's here, he just hides in his room. He only comes out to tell me off."

Olivia shifted her appeal back to Valentina. "Val, please. I don't think we should take what he said lightly."

The front door opened. Aidan entered. In the stark light of the house, Olivia could see what a mess he was. Had he showered, or even eaten, since he'd left? And despite the scrubbing, there was still a streak of blood on his wrist.

"Aidan," Olivia said. "If Val lets you stay, you'll help around the house, right? You won't leave anymore?"

"I'm supposed to be laying low," he muttered. "So no, I won't go anywhere."

Sophie rolled her eyes and went back into her bedroom, shutting her door behind her.

"And you'll help around the house?" Olivia said.

"I guess I'll have nothing else to do." He swayed slightly. He was half-dead on his feet.

"Go to bed," Olivia said.

He didn't argue. His footsteps were slow and heavy, all the way to his door. The lock clicked.

"All right," Valentina said, finally turning to Olivia. "I'll let him stay. On one condition."

"You'll have to talk to him about that."

"Not a condition for him. A condition for you."

"Me? What can I do?"

"Find out what he's hiding in his room."

Olivia gave her a blank look.

"That door stays locked. When he's here, when he's not here – it's always locked. He's keeping something from me."

"Is it about his other job?"

"No," Valentina said. "He doesn't bring home his other work. Which means he has another secret. I want to know what he's hiding in my house. You agree to find that out for me, I'll let him stay."

EIDOLON

30

A month and a half. That was how long the food lasted.

Liv nibbled her lip, staring at the eight cans left. Reef had taken them out of the pantry to highlight the importance of their dwindling supplies. The morning sun streamed in, bright and hot and angry.

"What do we do?" Reef said to Pravit, who had arrived a few minutes before. Liv wasn't sure she'd ever get used to people popping in and out of existence. She didn't like the reminder that the world wasn't real, and, more importantly, that she couldn't leave it.

"I had enough to last until the new year, like you told me," Reef said, "but we hadn't taken into account an extra mouth to feed."

Kazzy, who was on the couch with Bobbi, looked up from the TV. She and Liv exchanged a glance.

Pravit rubbed his chin. "This is a problem."

"We need more food, Pravit. Or…" Reef trailed off. "Is there a chance you can whistleblow now? Surely you've gathered enough evidence by this stage. Why not expose Equinoxx today?"

"I can't," Pravit said. "I'm sorry. There's something important that happens after the new year. It's what I'm waiting on."

"What's going to happen?" Reef said.

At the same time, Liv said, "We won't last until the new year."

"I can see that." Pravit eyed their eight precious cans, a combination of synthesized meats and vegetables. Even if they rationed, it wouldn't take them to January, which was almost a full month away.

"Why can't you expose them now?" Reef said.

"There's a vital piece of the puzzle missing. I understand your plight, but this is worth the risk."

"More than the risk we'll have to take to get extra supplies?" Liv said.

Pravit turned his kind gaze to her. Again, she was reminded of her father. Homesickness flared up, the ache becoming sharper, more refined. She missed talking to her family. She missed her home. Her friends. Not the pie shop so much, but she'd been planning to quit that job, anyway.

She wanted to go back into the world. Even if it was a lesser, glitchy world, it was still somewhere other than this beach house. Shopping centers, charging stations, department stores, airports. She wanted to buy Bobbi some new clothes. She wanted to plan a trip. Dammit, she'd happily take the simple pleasure of sitting at a coffee shop, watching Bobbi drink a babycino. She'd be able to handle being a simulation if she were allowed to sink back into regular life.

"I'll go."

They turned to Kazzy, who was extracting herself from Bobbi's cuddle to stand up.

"We can't risk—" Reef started, but Kazzy said, "It's my fault you're out of food, ay. There's a mini charging station about thirty ks down the road. I can get more."

"They might not have enough," Liv said. "We're going to need, like, forty more cans."

"But a supermarket's too risky," Reef said. He gestured to the TV, which was currently playing for a transfixed Bobbi. "Your face has been all over the place, almost as much as ours."

The news had made it sound like they were missing and in trouble, rather than fugitives, but it wouldn't matter. People would approach them, talk about them, report seeing them.

And Equinoxx would come.

Reef turned back to Pravit. "Are you sure you can't whistleblow now?"

"I know it's difficult. I need you to hold on for a little longer. I'm sorry."

Reef stared Pravit down, hard. What was he thinking? Liv had relied heavily on Pravit's intel, his protection – they all had – but there was something about this interaction that worried her.

Was it possible Pravit wasn't here to help them, after all? Did he have his own agenda, perhaps his own arrangement with a pharmaceutical company...or something worse? What if he was working against Equinoxx, but for his own gains?

"You can trust me," Pravit said, unwavering under Reef's scrutiny. "We all have to make difficult choices. This is one of them. I need until the new year. I'm sorry."

"Then I'll get us food," Kazzy said. "Later tonight. It'll be fine, Livvie. I'll park in the bush down the road, away from any cameras. Smash a window, grab as many cans as I can, skedaddle before the coppers bat an eyelid."

"But you'll be bringing police to this area. If they do a sweep, they might find the track leading here."

"Then I'll go to the charging station further south. It's what? Eighty ks? And it's bigger, too. Got a café, hardware store, Chinese restaurant. Might be able to snag some prawn crackers. I love me some prawn crackers."

Bobbi looked up from her show. She was chewing on Mr Piggy's tail. "Aunny Kazzy love pawn cakkas?"

"I'll grab some for you too." Kazzy mussed her curls and grinned at Liv. "It'll be easy. I promise."

Liv looked to Reef. Now it wasn't just the lack of food that was worrying her – it was Pravit, too. She didn't know Pravit, not as well as Reef did. What if he had changed in the last four years, like her other self? What if he was no longer a person Reef could trust?

"Pravit," she said. "Is the other Reef with you right now?"

"He's my anchor, yes."

"Do you think we could talk to him?"

Pravit hesitated. Liv's pulse quickened. Why would he be uncertain about letting them talk to someone else? Since their trip to the beach with the other Olivia, they hadn't seen another visitor for the past month and a half...except Pravit.

"I'm not hiding anything," Pravit said. "It's just...he mentioned to me that he doesn't want to see you."

Reef frowned. "Why not? He's spoken to me."

"I don't think you're where the problem lies." Pravit's gaze flickered to Liv.

"Me?" she said, bristling. "What did I do? Why doesn't he want to see me?"

"It's not that he doesn't want to see you. It's that he doesn't want *you* to see *him.*"

"Why not? Bobbi, not so close to the screen, please. Pravit, why doesn't the other Reef want to see me?"

In the silence that followed, she remembered what Reef had mentioned, about his other self looking a mess, like he didn't take care of himself. And the other Olivia had said he was depressed and moody. Had she done *anything* these past weeks to help him?

"Is he okay?" Liv said quietly.

"Honestly?" Pravit said. "I don't know."

"Can he hear us?"

"Yes, he's watching through my eyes."

"Then excuse me while I do this." Liv clasped her hands on Pravit's shoulders and met his gaze. "Reef, honey, listen to me. It's going to be all right. Come here. I want to talk to you."

"I'll have a chat with him," Pravit said.

"He can meet Bobbi," Liv said. "Properly, I mean. Doesn't he want to say hello to his daughter?" She hadn't meant to sound as hurt as she did.

She'd wondered about the other Reef over the weeks, but it hadn't been at the forefront of her mind. Now it was.

Why hadn't he ever come to see Bobbi?

"I'll ask if he wants to visit," Pravit said. "But I have to leave so he can use the NTD. If he agrees, he'll be here soon."

Liv released Pravit's shoulders, and he disappeared, erased from existence like some perverse magic trick. She watched the empty space. Any minute now, the other Reef would appear. He'd be different to her Reef, but he would still be Reef.

She wanted to check on him. She wanted him to know everything would be fine, that when her other self figured out her shit, they'd be deliriously happy together.

And she wanted to ask whether Pravit could be trusted. Because while she didn't know Pravit, she knew Reef absolutely, and she was certain that no matter what form he came in, he would do anything to keep his daughter safe.

Kazzy returned to the couch to sit by Bobbi, who had started to complain that she was hungry. Liv glanced briefly at their last eight cans of food. Reef, her Reef, moved to wrap an arm around her waist.

They waited.

The other Reef never came.

OUTSIDE

31

"Get on your knees."

"My god, Aidan, at least buy me dinner first."

Aidan let out a long-suffering sigh. Olivia grinned and dropped to the blue gym mat, feeling as childish as when she and Kass attended self-defense classes together in their late teens.

Aidan moved behind her. He bent down and said, "Someone's tying your hands behind you. What's your move?"

"Slam my head into their nose."

"Good, okay. So they're reeling backwards. Then what?"

"Get up and kick them in the nuts?"

"No," Aidan said. "Run, Olivia."

"Oh yeah."

"Always run. Your first move should be to get out of danger. Why do you think I've been asking you to spend so much time on the treadmill?" Olivia opened her mouth, but he spoke before she could. "That doesn't need an answer."

She flashed him a cheeky smile. He didn't return it.

"Say you try to slam your head into their nose, but they avoid it. What would you do then?"

"I could use their weight against them. Flip them over my shoulder."

He grasped her wrists behind her back. "Show me."

It took her a few tries, and a lot of guidance from Aidan, but she managed to roll her body in a way that sent him over her and onto the mat. Her back gave an unhappy throb. She had to be careful. She was still rebuilding her core strength.

"Good," he said, "now you–"

Olivia swung herself onto him. She straddled his chest, her knees pinning his shoulders and biceps. "This?"

"No," he said, exasperated. *"Run."*

"Oh yeah."

She lingered in her spot. It was nice having the advantage over him for once. Very rarely in these seven weeks of training did she feel like she had any control. She knew she wasn't going to be a pro fighter overnight, but they had worked hard every single day, and she wanted something to show for it.

Her fitness, at least, was wildly improving. Even after all these years, her body remembered how to build muscle, how to maintain a steady running pace – once she'd recovered from the first few disastrous sessions, anyway.

"Olivia," Aidan said, the vibrations of his voice rolling through his chest and along her thighs.

"Huh?"

"Can you get off?"

"Right." She climbed to her feet and flapped her gym shirt for air. She was still sweaty from her earlier workout with Sophie. "Is it time for a shower yet?"

"Go," he said. "I have to start lunch, anyway."

She left him to pack away the mat and equipment, and headed back towards the house. The garden was weeded and neat. The windowsills had a fresh coat of paint. She passed a ladder, where Aidan had been clearing the gutters. He had made good on his promise to help around the house.

Olivia, however, had made no progress on her own promise. She walked inside and stared down the hallway. That damn door at the end had eluded her.

She'd tried catching him off-guard, checking it every now and then to see if he'd forgotten to lock it when he went out to do Equinoxx stuff, like this morning. But it was no good – he was too careful, not just with the lock, but with the key too. She hadn't been able to get her hands on it.

She'd examined his bedroom window from outside. Even if she could pry off the fly screen, it would still be difficult to jimmy open the window itself. She'd even watched a YouTube video on how to pick locks. They made it look easy, but she'd yet to master it.

Valentina continued to remind her that Aidan was only allowed to stay on the condition she find out what he was hiding. So sure, she'd tried a little flirting. She wasn't above playing dirty. But it didn't matter – nothing was getting through to him. She tried not to take it personally. Despite working around the house, despite training her how to fight, Aidan still spent a lot of time in his room. He hadn't cut his hair or trimmed his beard. She'd yet to see him smile. Whatever was wrong with him hadn't disappeared just because he was taking time off this mysterious work of his.

She tried his door handle, more out of habit than hope. Finding it locked, she went to the bathroom and freed her hair from its long plait. The gentle curls and cappuccino colors were gone. This household didn't exactly have the right products to maintain her hairstyle; the ends were getting knotty and gross.

As she undressed, she heard Aidan enter the house. She held her breath, hoping…

Yes. He was going into his bedroom.

She knocked on the bathroom window three times, turned on the shower and wrapped a towel around herself. It wasn't long before–

"Aidan! Aidan, come quick, Val's fallen over!"

Olivia pressed her forehead against the bathroom door.

Please leave it open, please leave it open, please leave it open.

She could hear Aidan's footsteps down the hall.

"By the lemon tree," Sophie said breathlessly. "I think she's hurt her ankle…" Her voice grew fainter as they rushed out of the house together.

Olivia switched off the shower and ducked out of the bathroom. A welcome sight greeted her at the end of the corridor. She almost whooped in triumph.

He'd left his door ajar.

Seven long weeks, and she'd finally done it. A small win in the scheme of things, but it was nice to have succeeded at *something*.

She kept her towel on and hurried into his bedroom. Who knew how long Sophie and Valentina could delay him?

The room was bare except for a bed, dresser, and nightstand. The bed was unmade. There was a staleness to the air.

She started with the nightstand. The top drawer had spare charger cords, pens…and an open box of condoms.

Her body seized up. Sweat slicked her palms.

Was Aidan sleeping with someone? When? Where? He wouldn't be bringing anyone to the house – he must be keeping a packet or two in his wallet.

Maybe that's where he'd been going. Maybe he didn't have another job at all. Maybe he hooked up at bars, heading home with strangers, unable to stay in this house when his relationships with Sophie and Valentina were so fraught.

Her fingers drifted over the box. She could check the use-by date. That might give her some clue as to–

As to *what?*

What, exactly, did she want to find out?

She gripped the knot of her towel, forcing herself to breathe evenly. What was she doing? This wasn't Matt. Her body had reacted out of instinct, feeling the sting of betrayal even though Aidan didn't owe her loyalty. Just because they were together in Eidolon, didn't mean anything here. It wasn't her business.

It felt like trauma. Her rational thought had been overtaken, triggered by something else.

Damn Matt to the fiery pits of hell. How long would she carry this pain?

Still shaking, she shut the drawer. Aidan could be back at any moment, and she was supposed to be finding out what he was hiding.

The middle drawer had a strange assortment of old gumnuts with eyes drawn onto them. Among them was a cutting from a newspaper. It was a family photo with parents and three children, all boys. There was no caption included, nothing written on the back. It was folded many times.

The final drawer was empty except for a single wooden peg. She picked it up, examining it curiously. As she shifted, her knee knocked something under the bed, causing it to clink. She lowered her head.

There was a cardboard box hidden under the mattress. She dragged it out to find–

"Oh, Aidan," she breathed. She rocked back on her heels as she took in what she was seeing.

The box was filled to the brim with empty vodka bottles. It was hard to tell how many – fifteen? Twenty? It explained the faint smell of alcohol she'd noticed when they first met. There was still another full bottle beneath the bed.

The sound of talking caught her attention. She glanced out the window to find Aidan carrying Valentina towards the house. "Shit."

She shoved the box back under the bed and closed the last drawer, scrambling out of the room. She remembered to leave the door ajar before diving back into the bathroom and switching the shower back on.

It was only when she was taking off her towel that she realized she still had the wooden peg in her hand. She buried it at the back of the cupboard to be retrieved later. A quick duck beneath the spray was enough to make it look like she'd been in the whole time. She exited the bathroom, back in her towel, and remarked innocently on poor Valentina's ankle.

"It's fine," Valentina said, her foot propped on a pillow on the couch. "Ice and rest will do the trick."

Sophie, who was sitting beside her, patted her shoulder then winked at Olivia.

Olivia returned to her bedroom to change. Aidan had already locked his door again. When she came out, he was in the kitchen starting lunch. She settled herself on the couch with Sophie and Valentina and whispered beneath the boiling kettle, "I found a few things. I'm not sure which one you were after."

They leaned forward. Sophie had only agreed to help with the plan on the condition that she was told what was going on. Surprisingly, Valentina had consented. If Olivia had known earlier that including Sophie was a possibility, she would've done it weeks ago.

"I found this weird wooden peg. It was the only thing in his bottom drawer. I accidentally took it out with me, though. I'll have to figure out how to get it back before he notices."

Valentina's brow furrowed. "No, that's not what I was looking for."

"There was also a photo from a newspaper of a family. I didn't recognize any of them. It looks worn. Would either of you know what that's about?"

Sophie shrugged. Valentina said nothing.

"Some gumnuts with eyes drawn on them?"

"He still has those?" Sophie said. "I made them years ago, when we first moved here. They were my little gumnut village."

"I remember that," Valentina said. "They had whole lives and dramas and everything."

"Pepper Gum was always getting teased by Crystal Gum. Crystal Gum was the mean one. And Laska Gum didn't say a word until one day she started speaking and never stopped."

"Er," said Olivia, "weren't you, like, twelve when you moved here?"

"Yeah, but...I was lonely." Sophie stole a glance at Aidan. "I can't believe he kept them."

"They're not why he's locking his door," Valentina said.

Olivia hesitated. "He has alcohol in there."

"Ah."

"That might be the reason for the lock. Maybe it has nothing to do with some dark secret–"

"No, Olivia, that *is* the secret. That's what I suspected. I don't allow alcohol in this house."

"What about when I bought wine?"

"You were a guest, and it felt impolite to say anything."

"What about the drink you poured in my tea when I first arrived?"

"I use that as a cleaning product."

"Oh."

"So what are you going to do?" Sophie said. "Are you going to kick him out?"

Olivia was relieved to hear she didn't sound as eager to get rid of her brother as she used to be.

Valentina turned her steely gaze to Olivia. "You handle it."

"Me?"

"Make sure he gets rid of it."

"But I'm not even supposed to know it exists."

"Figure out a way."

"But I–"

"No arguments," Valentina said, and then she said something that Olivia hadn't heard from anyone since before the accident. "You can do this, Olivia. I have complete faith in you."

32

"What do you reckon?" Olivia said as Sophie examined the wooden peg.

"It's a weird thing for my brother to have in his nightstand."

"And it was the only thing in that drawer. It has to be something, right?"

There was a scraping from outside. Aidan was nearby, clearing gutters.

Sophie gasped. "Oh, I know!" She tugged at the sides of the peg. "I saw this Buzzfeed article on weird shapes for – aha."

The end popped off, revealing a USB underneath.

"You're a genius," Olivia said.

"Thank you."

"Let's see what's on it."

Sophie grabbed her laptop and settled on the mattress. She plugged the USB in, then hesitated. "What if it's porn?"

"The internet is filled with porn. He doesn't need to save it to a USB. Give the laptop here." Olivia made herself comfortable against the wall beside Sophie. They often sat together like this now, binging shows together.

"What if it's *his* porn?" Sophie said. "What if the reason he's been going away all the time is because he's a porn star?"

"Relax, would you? If he were really getting laid that often, he wouldn't be as grumpy as he is." Olivia opened the folder. There were a bunch of documents with names like CDX7438952.doc and PCTT5015088.pdf.

She opened the PDF, but it was nonsense text grayed out with a pop-up box asking for a password.

Olivia tried SOPHIE and Sophie's birthday. Then she tried Aidan's birthday. Then Valentina's name.

"No good," she said, closing it. She opened another document. Same problem – nonsense text, password protected.

The laptop dinged with a message from one of the open tabs in the browser.

"Ignore that," Sophie said.

"Are you sure?" Olivia watched the browser icon blink patiently. "You can check it. I won't look."

"No thanks. Try this document here."

Olivia did as she was told. The browser dinged again. Sophie said nothing.

Olivia's fingers itched to click on the blinking icon. She felt that familiar build up of panic – that someone was hiding something from her, that there were secrets, too many secrets – and forced herself to take in a few long, deep breaths.

"It's no good," Sophie said. "We're not going to be able to get in."

"Maybe my friend can help. Can I open the browser? I'll make a fake email account and send the documents to her."

Sophie took the laptop back. She was careful to hide the screen as she closed a bunch of tabs.

"Is this the friend you called when you first got here?" she said casually. "The one who you went to see in Val's car?"

"That's her."

"Do you think Equinoxx is watching her emails?"

"I think she's smart enough to hide stuff from them."

Sophie's fingers tapped away as she created a new email account.

"Is she safe?"

"She can look after herself."

Olivia sent the documents to Kass and made a mental note to text her with the burner phone later to let her know what was going on. Sophie probably knew about the burner phone – it was hard to keep things hidden when they practically lived on top of each other – but Olivia didn't want to explicitly have it out in the open. She wasn't sure how Aidan would feel about her taking a risk that might lead someone to Sophie, even if she'd never given Kass their address.

There was the thump of footsteps on the roof as Aidan walked above them.

Did she feel guilty about invading his privacy? Yes, absolutely.

At the same time, she was sick of secrets. The irresistible need dogged her to uncover everything, to sit there like she had with Matt's emails, reading and reading, unable to look away. She wanted answers. Truth. From everyone, and everything.

"What do you reckon is in there?" Sophie said as Olivia unplugged the USB.

"I have no idea. Hopefully, we'll find out soon."

She was regaining control. It felt good, really good.

And she'd thought of a way to do what Valentina asked, too – a way to get rid of Aidan's alcohol. It even tied in with what Liv had asked her to do. When she'd first noticed how depressed Aidan was, she'd concluded that they needed to share a bottle of wine so he would open up a bit. Well, wine wasn't available. But that bottle of vodka would do the trick.

33

"Can we talk?"

Aidan dried the last of the cutlery and turned to Olivia. "Sure."

"Somewhere private?"

Sophie and Valentina were setting up a game of Scrabble in the living room. Valentina had done a good job of play-acting her sore ankle. She happily bossed them around from the couch.

Olivia hoped Aidan would lead her to his bedroom, but as if she would be that lucky. Dropping the wooden peg back into his dresser was going to take as much cunning and ingenuity as it had taken to get it out in the first place.

Instead, they headed outside, towards the shed. The night was balmy, the sky clear. Valentina's new chickens roosted securely in their rebuilt hen house.

Aidan switched on the shed light and pulled up the bench press for Olivia to sit on, while he settled on a storage box. "If this is about when you'll be able to go home, I'm sorry, I still don't know. Pravit's waiting on something. I'm not sure what, but he seems adamant that he'll be able to whistleblow after the new year."

"It's not about that," Olivia said. "Although I'm glad to hear this might be over soon. Not that I don't appreciate what you've done for me—"

"It's fine, I understand. What did you want to talk about?"

"Sophie," Olivia said. "I think she's hiding something from you."

"I'm sure she's hiding a lot of things from me."

"Yes, but I think she's talking to someone online. Like a crush."

Aidan shrugged. "What can I do? Forbid her from talking to anyone at all?"

"Well, there's another thing. Last week I walked into the bedroom and she had her phone up to her ear, as if she'd called someone. She tried to hide it, but…"

Aidan frowned.

"I suppose she could've just been listening to a video," Olivia said uncertainly. "But maybe you should talk to her."

"As if she'd tell me anything."

"You could try."

"She's eighteen next year. We don't have long until she's making her own choices, anyway."

"You know, I've been wondering about that," Olivia said. "Sophie's in the system, right? That's how her parents can take her back. How come she's registered and you're not?"

"My father was more inclined to let Sophie's mother have her way, at least at first. She was rich, and he wanted her family's land for his cult."

This was the most Aidan had ever talked about his past. Olivia wondered how far she could push it. "Do you think he only married her for her money?"

"Absolutely."

"And she fell for it?"

"My father can be convincing when it comes to talking about 'the cause.'"

"What cause?"

"Protecting the environment."

"But…isn't that a good thing?"

"He doesn't care about the environment," Aidan said. "He's like anyone who uses religion to control people: manipulative, conniving, and a complete psychopath underneath."

"Really?"

"Why do you think I risked everything to get Sophie out of there?"

Maybe it was the stillness of the night, or the liminal space of a fluorescent-lit shed, but this conversation was freaking Olivia out. She imagined Aidan's dad – an older, perhaps even hairier version of him – stalking them in the darkness.

She shivered.

Aidan's expression closed up, and she felt herself bump into that cliff face again. "We should go back inside."

"Wait," she said, cursing herself. She shouldn't have reacted like that. Aidan was being vulnerable with her – she should've leaned into it. She still had a job to do. "There's one other thing I want to talk to you about."

He sighed and sank back on the box.

"It's about Matt," she said.

He waited.

"Remember how I texted him when I first got here, telling him that I knew about Sarina? Well, I never told you that I saw his reply."

"You switched on your phone?"

"When I met Kass at the Galleria. He sent me a message back."

"Okay…"

"Funny you should say that," Olivia said. "Because that was his answer. 'Okay.'"

"It's a pretty big conversation to have. I'm sure he didn't want to start it over text."

"Aidan, I read the emails. He's been seeing her behind my back for months. He told her that he loved her, that he wanted to be with her instead of me."

She dragged in a ragged breath. Despite the fact that this was supposed to be part of her plan, no acting was required. Every time she thought about it – *Wear something sexy underneath, okay?* – pain fizzed in her chest.

"I told you that I took Kass to the shed," she said, "but I didn't tell you that Liv and I had a conversation about Matt while I was in Eidolon. She said he and I were together for the wrong reasons; out of guilt and obligation, not love. She said he was wrong for me, and I guess he already knew that, because he found someone else."

She dropped her head in her hands.

"I've made a decision," she said. "When this Equinoxx thing is done and I can go home, I'm going to leave him. There's no chance for reconciliation. It's over."

It's over.

She heard the words out loud and they seemed to reverberate through time, splitting her life into BEFORE and AFTER.

Her marriage was over.

"Oh god," she said. "Fuck." She swiped her cheeks. "This sucks."

Aidan looked uncomfortable and lost, like he needed to be told what to do.

Perfect.

"You know," she said through tears. "I'd kill for a drink right now."

To: jacobpwilcox@equinoxxtechnology.co
From: retrievalunit@basenxj451.com
Subject: Retrieval update

TARGET KW ACQUIRED
REQUIRE BACKUP FOR INTERROGATION PURPOSES

EIDOLON

34

"She should've been back by now."

"Give her a little longer." Reef checked the clock on the wall. "She would've had to scope out the station, figure out the best way to break in."

Liv had taken into account the fact that the charging station was eighty kilometers away. She had factored in the need for Kazzy to pull over as other cars went past. She'd even thought about the prawn crackers Kazzy wanted to pick up.

Kazzy had taken too long. Something had gone wrong.

"I need to get her." She spoke quietly. Bobbi was sleeping, and the walls in this place were thin.

"You can't go out there," Reef said.

"What if she's been caught?"

"Your other self said she won't be reprogrammed. No consent form, no betrayal."

"There's other ways to get someone to talk." What if Equinoxx had caught Kazzy? What if they were hurting her? They weren't against selling children to pharmaceutical companies – they wouldn't stop at torturing a person for information. "We can't leave her high and dry."

"Liv–"

"You said yourself that we should treat simulations as real people. That's my Kassandra out there, mapped by me. I can't let anything happen to her."

"What if you get caught? Are you willing to risk Bobbi's life? Would Kazzy even want you to?"

"Kazzy gave up everything to find us. She's out there because she volunteered to get more food."

Reef reached across the table and gripped Liv's hand. "I know how much you love her. But I can't lose you."

"You won't," she said, squeezing his fingers.

He met her gaze, and held it. She didn't look away.

"All right." He sounded resigned as he released her hand. "I'll go."

"No. You stay here and take care of Bobbi. Because," she said over his rising protests, "she'll need your protection if anyone comes looking."

"Dammit, Liv. I hate this."

She grabbed the Hilux keys. They had been idling the engine on occasion to keep the battery going, prepared for a fast getaway. It had enough fuel to get her to the charging station. There would be an old petrol pump there. She'd fill up if she needed.

"Take the gun," Reef said.

She hesitated. She still wasn't comfortable with it, and that damn recoil–

"Take it," Reef said again. "I'll feel better if you had it."

"What if you need it?"

"You're the one going out there."

Reluctantly, Liv followed Reef outside to the steel box. She packed the shotgun into the car and stared down the dirt track, hoping for any sign of Kazzy's Monaro.

"You don't have to do this," Reef said.

Liv wrapped her arms around him. His embrace was warm and solid. Her anchor in this world. Him, and Bobbi.

Her gaze flickered towards the beach house. She would be home before Bobbi woke up.

"If Kazzy isn't there, I'll come straight back," she said. "If she's been caught by the cops, I'll take care of it."

"And if she's been caught by Equinoxx?"

She drew away. "I'll take care of that, too."

"If there are too many people, or if they're armed…"

"I'll be smart."

"You'd better." Reef brushed a stray strand of hair from her face. "Bobbi and I will be waiting."

He kissed her, and then she was in the car and driving away, well before she felt ready. It was as if she was leaving her heart behind. Her family, so precious, so vulnerable. It nearly broke her to go.

But she had to fetch Kazzy. Liv couldn't explain to Reef, or even herself, her reasons. It wasn't sentimentality, and it wasn't compassion, not exactly. She and Kazzy were bound, like sisters. They took care of each other, whether it be in high school, traveling the world, or after the accident. They had each other's backs. Even in Eidolon.

Liv switched her lights off and pulled over every time another vehicle approached. She listened for the rumble of the Monaro, but it was only ever StarShines and trucks. There were a lot of trucks out here.

It seemed to take forever to get to her destination. She parked a hundred meters away to stay out of sight, and found the empty Monaro nearby.

Liv got out the shotgun. There were four rounds loaded. If Reef was right, and the visitors needed a few minutes after being extracted from Eidolon to regain their bearings once they'd been injured, one shot per person was all she needed. Hopefully, there were less than four in there. Hopefully, her aim would be true.

She walked towards the station, pulse thundering in her ears. The building itself was a large semicircle, with all the shops connected inside. The lights were off everywhere except for the café in the charging station. There was only one car parked in the lot, a StarShine. Liv kept to the shadows, moving against the bricks until she could peer through the window. Kazzy was there. She was sitting on a wooden café chair, one wrist handcuffed to the chair's arm. She looked uninjured. Even bored.

Liv recognized the two other people inside – the man and frizzy-haired woman who had tried to take Bobbi. Liv's grip tightened on the shotgun.

The frizzy-haired woman kept checking her phone. They'd obviously been waiting a while. It would've been at least two hours, considering the time that had passed.

Liv stepped away from the light and moved along the front of the adjoining shops. All the windows were intact.

The back was a different story. There was splintered glass, where Kazzy would've broken in. A security light flashed outside, but there was no sign of the cops. Surely they would've come by now?

But maybe they had. Maybe that's how Kazzy was handcuffed to the chair. They must've called someone from Equinoxx after recognizing her.

Liv slipped through the broken window and found herself in the kitchen for the Chinese restaurant. It smelled so good. After eating canned food for weeks, she was ravenous for a proper meal.

Ignoring her growling stomach, she headed to the doorway and paused. The building was open plan, with each section blending into the next. There were other food shops, a hardware store, and the charging station's café. Only a few lights were on, allowing Liv to remain in shadows at the threshold.

She watched the frizzy-haired woman help herself to a slice of cake from the display case.

"Really?" the man said.

"Hey, how can you pass up all the taste and none of the calories?" The woman didn't seem particularly choked up about the fact that she was kidnapping babies for human testing.

Liv was going to shoot her in the face.

"You planning on sharing?" Kazzy said, her eyes on the cake.

"What did I say about running that mouth? You want me to interrogate you myself?"

"We wouldn't be very good at it," the man said. "Might accidentally kill her before we get any information."

"But it would be worth it to shut her up."

"That it would."

Liv needed to get closer. She didn't want to shoot from this far away and risk hitting Kazzy. But as soon as she stepped out, they'd see the movement, even in the darkness.

She was going to have to draw them to her.

She headed back into the kitchen and grabbed a handful of serving spoons, allowing them to clatter to the floor.

From the café, the frizzy-haired woman yelped. "What was that?"

"The interrogator? Maybe he ended up in the wrong area."

"Or is it someone coming to rescue whatshername here?"

"They said neither would risk it."

"Then go check."

"You check!"

There was silence. They were probably working out a plan of attack. Liv aimed the shotgun to the door. Her shoulder was already hurting in anticipation.

She strained her ears, trying to catch signs of movement. They were too quiet.

A light flashed through the doorway, suddenly, blinding her. She fired, the sound a roar in her ears and echoing around the kitchen. Her body took the impact of the recoil.

The frizzy-haired woman shrieked from a distance. The man was swearing, closer, although all sound was muted after the discharge. He must've been the one to shine the light at her. And she'd missed him.

One shot down.

She blinked away the spots and pumped the gun before chasing the sound of footsteps. She aimed for the man's back as he ran, thinking again of how Bobbi had been bundled into the back of the van, screaming.

She fired.

The man flew forward, blood spraying from his body. He vanished before he hit the ground.

Two shots down.

"Holy mother of God!" The frizzy-haired woman had a meat tenderizer from one of the other kitchens. She was halfway across the building, in the hardware section, hiding behind a supporting pillar.

Liv took aim. The shot hit the pillar. Pieces flew everywhere. The woman curled in a ball on the floor, shielding her frizzy hair.

Three shots down.

Liv's shoulder was aching. She lowered the gun and strode forward. The woman scrambled away on her hands and knees, still clutching the meat tenderizer. She reached a shelf of gardening equipment and cowered against a pile of hoses. "Please," she said.

Liv lifted the gun. "Come after my daughter again, bitch." But before she could pull the trigger, someone grabbed the gun from behind and flung it away.

She spun around to find a man in a suit. His black hair had gray streaks on either side, and when he smiled, he flashed two gold teeth.

The frizzy-haired woman laughed behind her. "Oh, you are so fucked."

There was a clattering sound, of what Liv figured was the meat tenderizer dropping as the woman was extracted.

"My," said the man, looking Liv up and down. "You're not like the other one."

He moved to snatch her arm but she whipped away, stooping to grab the meat tenderizer. She swung it as she rose. It hit his face with a disgusting crunch, and he went down.

Liv let the meat tenderizer go and sprinted to Kazzy, who was tugging at the handcuff holding her to the chair. "Where's the key?"

"The counter."

Liv snatched the key and fumbled with the lock.

"No," Kazzy whispered, staring behind her.

Liv glanced back. Her stomach swooped. The gold-toothed man was getting up. His face was mangled and bloodied, and *he was getting up*.

Liv realized too late that she should've grabbed the shotgun. That she should've kept the meat tenderizer. Shit, there was a whole hardware store back there and she hadn't thought to pick up a single thing.

The handcuffs unlocked and Kazzy sprang to her feet. They ran for the automatic doors...which didn't open.

Kazzy scrabbled around the frame. "There should be a switch somewhere—"

The gold-toothed man selected a small garden fork and ambled towards them. Outside, a slow-moving truck rumbled past. Liv's hands were slicked with sweat. The man didn't seem at all phased by his injury. And why would he have gone for a small weapon when there was a shotgun right there?

He grinned a lopsided, bloodied, nightmarish grin. Kazzy couldn't get the door open. Liv ran back to the café corner, around the counter with the espresso machine. No weapons, just cutlery, cups, useless items.

The gold-toothed man came for her in that relaxed saunter. She hurled cup after cup at him. He dodged each one, calmly, capably, the garden fork tucked in his hand.

"Where's the anomaly, Olivia?" he crooned. "Where's your little baby?"

Liv ran out of cups and began to throw teaspoons. Kazzy found the switch for the automatic doors. They whooshed open as another truck rumbled past, faster than the last one.

"Run!" Liv yelled to her, but of course Kazzy didn't run. She grabbed the chair she'd been handcuffed to and lifted it high to bring slamming down towards the man's back.

Without taking his eyes from Liv, he sidestepped out of the way. The chair hit the floor where he'd been standing, two of its legs snapping off. He turned to Kazzy and grabbed her tank top, yanking her towards him.

"Oh, fuck," she said as he scooped the garden fork towards her torso, and Liv burbled a plea, stumbling forward–

There was an explosion. A blast that rang through the building, leaving Liv's already-damaged ears pounding and her fumbling to comprehend what she was seeing.

The gold-toothed man had a hole in his head. Pink and red and gray covered the floor and tables in front of him. Kazzy tugged herself from his grip as his body fell forward.

Behind him was Pravit with the shotgun. "Run!" he shouted, and then he was gone, vanished from the world. The shotgun clattered to the ground.

Kazzy snatched it up. "Go, go, go!"

Liv didn't need any more encouragement. The gold-toothed man's body disappeared as they passed him and sprinted out the door.

"Un-fucking-believable!" came a cry from behind them, a familiar Southern US drawl. The frizzy-haired woman had returned, and the shotgun had no rounds left.

Liv and Kazzy raced up the road towards the cars. Kazzy's Monaro was first, so that's the one they got into. Liv found herself in the driver's seat.

"Keys!"

Kazzy grabbed the keys from behind the sun visor and Liv gunned the engine. It growled to life.

"Fuck fuck fuck," she said as she saw the frizzy-haired woman run for the StarShine parked at the charging station. "I can't lead her to Bobbi."

"Then drive south!"

Liv was already pulling onto the road. The Monaro shot past the charging station just as the StarShine screeched out. It was right on their tail.

Liv changed gears. She had overcome her fear of driving for the most part, but only when she was careful, and within the speed limit. The Monaro had already passed a hundred ks an hour.

Kazzy twisted in her seat to see, the shotgun in her lap. "She's too close. Go faster."

The speedometer crept up. Liv felt a familiar twisting sensation in her chest. She was about to have a panic attack.

"Liv, we have to lose her."

Liv's breaths were coming in short and sharp. She wanted to slow down, pull over. She wanted to get out of the car.

"Oh no you don't." Kazzy punched at the touchscreen on the dash. "Remember street racing with my bro? Remember those sweet burnouts we did at the back of KFC? Fuckin' *A*."

Nicki Minaj blasted from the stereo. Liv could barely hear – the world sounded underwater after the gunshots – but she could feel the bass thrumming in her seat.

She changed gears again, pushing them up to one-hundred and eighty. The Monaro hummed lovingly in her care. It turned out, as well as remembering the pain of the accident, her body remembered the thrill of a souped-up car.

Kazzy whooped and pulled on her seatbelt. "Atta girl!"

The StarShine was starting to pull back, but there were trucks up ahead, including the slow-moving one from before. The one behind it was shifting into the right lane to overtake the other. Liv saw the gap.

If she got through that gap, the StarShine would be stuck behind the trucks long enough for them to get away.

If she got through that gap.

She pushed them faster. Two hundred. Two-twenty.

"We gonna live forever, Kazzy?"

"We're gonna live forever, Livvie."

Liv floored it.

This was going to be close.

OUTSIDE

35

Nera pressed down on the earth, setting the sapling into place. The little banksia had hardy leaves and would one day grow exquisite flowers. It was what Nera loved about the arid parts of Australia – plants grew strong while retaining their beauty. They were trying so hard to survive the increasing bushfires.

She set a slow-release nutrient bubble in place next to the stem and gazed across the patch where she had planted five other saplings this evening. Or rather, this morning. It must be close to dawn by now. She could feel it, even if the sky had yet to lighten.

This was the problem with checking her phone before bed. Maybe she would've had a proper night's sleep if she hadn't seen SInation's announcement out of the US.

After several hours of tossing and turning, she'd come here, because here at least she felt like she was doing something good. Whenever she stressed about her impact on the planet, or the data, or the people who stood in her way purely so they could get rich, she went outside and planted trees.

She stood, swiping the sweat from her brow with the back of her dirty hand. She had sacrificed some of the land around Equinoxx for the crystal forest – it seemed only fair that she repair the rest.

The trek back to the hub passed through the parking lot, and she spotted Jake's car. She slowed, frowning. He had definitely left earlier that evening. What was he doing back, and at this hour?

She went inside, having to clean her palm on her jeans before the monitor accepted her handprint.

The lobby was empty. Nera lingered for a moment at the front desk, wondering whether Killian had anything to do with SInation's announcement. Jake hadn't mentioned the mole again since their initial conversation, but he hadn't gone back to the US yet, either. Was he ever going to investigate this distant relative of his? Surely he'd have to now.

She dug out her phone and pinged his. He was on the higher level, in the DreamView lab. What was he doing there?

Nera headed upstairs. She'd wanted to talk to him anyway. She would've messaged him as soon as she'd seen what SInation had done, but figured he deserved a good night's sleep. Maybe that's what he was doing in the lab – recording his dreams. Nera had done it on occasion out of curiosity. It was bizarre to see the images that formed in her mind while she slept. They were hazy and hectic and nonsensical from an outsider's point of view. As restless as her mind always was.

She tried the door to the lab and found it locked. Her ID pass overrode it. Jake was inside, standing rather than hooked up to the DreamView machine. He looked hastily dressed, as if he had been called away from his motel at short notice. It was strange to see him in a sweater and track pants rather than a suit.

"Nera," he said, his eyebrows flying up. "What are you doing here?"

There was another man next to him, someone she didn't recognize. He had twin silver streaks in his black hair.

And Pravit. Pravit Arya, her regional director, was hooked up to the DreamView machine. *Strapped* to the DreamView machine.

"What's going on?" Nera said.

"You should leave." Jake moved towards her, trying to usher her to the door. "This doesn't concern you."

Nera held her ground. "What are you doing to Pravit?"

"We're not hurting him. We just need answers. He's the mole."

"What?" Nera looked to Pravit, astonished.

"He interfered with a vital assignment in Eidolon. His anchor pulled him out, but too late. He allowed a source that would've led us to an anomaly get away."

Pravit met Nera's gaze. His jaw was set, his expression determined. Even so, a bead of sweat trickled down his bruised face.

"Let him up," Nera said.

"We haven't questioned him yet," Jake said. "The DreamView machine will allow us to see his answers, even if he doesn't tell us—"

"Let him up." Nera pushed past and began unstrapping Pravit's wrists. "Christ, Jake."

Out of the corner of her eye, she noticed the stranger move towards her. Jake shook his head and the stranger stopped.

Nera helped Pravit sit up. "Are you all right?"

Someone had hit him in the face. This sixty-year-old man, so gentle, so clever, and someone had *hit him in the face.*

"Nera," he said. His hands were shaking. "Please know, I am loyal to Equinoxx, until the end."

"Have you been passing information to SInation?"

"Never. I would never do that."

"What information?" Jake said.

Nera turned to him. "You must've been too busy hurting our employees to see the news. SInation just announced a large-scale evaporative energy generator."

"Since when have they been working with evaporative energy?" Jake demanded.

"And their patent looks eerily familiar. In fact, it's almost identical to the one we've been experimenting with *in Eidolon.*"

"But that's impossible," Pravit said. "They couldn't be harvesting data from Eidolon. We're the only ones with access to it."

Jake curled his lip. "Unless someone's been feeding them information."

"No." Pravit dug into his pocket. He pulled out a yellow mint tin, which rattled in his shaking hands. "I told you, I'm loyal to Equinoxx. I believe you're doing good work. Vital work. I would never turn against you."

"I'd beg to differ," said the stranger, with an odd smile. Nera caught a flash of gold in his mouth.

Pravit popped a mint in his mouth. "Nera, I need you to stop hunting the children."

"That's not really – I mean, Jake's sort of in charge of–"

He took her hands. "They are *real*. You can't do this to them."

"They're a simulation, Mr Arya," Jake said. "I know they seem human, but they're just coding."

Pravit kept his attention on Nera. "You and I know that's not true."

"You see? He *is* against us." To the stranger, Jake said, "Strap him back in the machine. We'll find out what else he's done, and who he's working with."

"You want to know how much I believe it?" Pravit said to Nera. His eyes shone with tears. His entire body trembled. "You want to know what I would do to protect those children?"

Foam bubbled from his mouth. Nera jumped back with a cry. Pravit fell onto the machine, his body convulsing.

"Shit," Jake growled, shoving Nera out of the way and running for him.

"It's no good," said the stranger, calmly. He gave a soft scoff and walked from the room.

Nera fumbled for her phone. "I'm calling an ambulance."

"We're too far away for emergency services." Jake shook Pravit's shoulders. "Tell me who you're working with!"

Nera couldn't tear her gaze away, not when Pravit gagged, not when he defecated, not when his body slumped, dead on the DreamView machine.

Jake slammed his hand on the machine next to Pravit's head. "Fuck! You fucker! For a bunch of coding? No! Fuck off!"

And Nera, with the earth under her fingernails and on the knees of her jeans, said nothing at all.

36

Olivia squinted one eye then the other, trying to get a good view of the board. It brought back memories of her and Kass – pubs, drinks, guys crowded around them.

Best. Nights. Ever.

Her dart went flying and missed the board completely.

"I thought you said you were good at this."

"I am *excellent* at this. Just gotta recalibrate." She loosened her shoulders. "It's been a while."

"Clearly."

She ignored Aidan's jabs and concentrated on getting her next dart towards the board. She could do this. She was going to beat him, and make him grovel at her feet.

A smile played at her lips. That sounded like her twenty-year-old self talking. An old friend, returning.

The dart hit the outer edge of the board.

"Oof," Aidan said. "At least you didn't impale the shed this time."

Olivia threw her last dart and it hit the twenty. "Ha." She turned to Aidan, arms outstretched as if she had hit the bullseye. Then she picked up her mug and poured another generous shot of vodka. The bottle was well on its way to being empty. She was going to get rid of it tonight, just like Valentina wanted.

Aidan got up to collect her darts. He was more stable on his feet than she was right now. She wasn't happy that he didn't seem to be affected, but it was unsurprising. If the box under his bed was anything to go by, he could hold his drink.

"Hey," she said as he chalked up her score. "I'm not that far behind. I can still beat you."

He was slow to work the numbers out. She watched how carefully he concentrated and realized his math was terrible. Possibly being homeschooled by a psychopath didn't lend itself to academic achievements.

He stepped to the line and took aim.

"Are you going to hit the middle?" she said, standing next to him. "Is that where you're going to hit?"

His dart went left, just missing the double ring.

"You're cheating," he said.

"I'm cheering you on. Aidan. Aidan, are you trying to hit the red circle? Aidan."

"You're as annoying as Sophie, d'you know that?"

"Aidan. Aidan, try to hit the – ooo, good shot. Aidan, throw the last dart." He nudged her away and she giggled. "Aidan. Hit the middle. Hit the – aww, too bad."

"I'm starting to see why you think you're good at this," he said as she stood in front of him. "You spend all your time trying to put off the competition."

"No, I actually have very good aim. *Really.*"

He planted his hands on her hips to move her away. His touch was hot; it sent warm ripples up her sides. She hurried after him, keen to feel that heat again. When he picked up the chalk, she splayed herself across the blackboard. "You don't need to put your score in."

"Move."

"I already know the number. You lost. Sorry."

"Does that mean I've won?"

"I don't know what you're talking about."

"Move." His warm hands were on her again, pushing her away, and there was a soft sound coming from his lips – he was *laughing.*

"Aidan," she breathed. "Is this possible? Are you...are you enjoying yourself? Quick, stop that immediately."

"Move, so I can see how thoroughly I beat you."

"Isn't it lucky I found this dartboard? Imagine if we didn't get to experience the joy of you laughing and me winning all in one night."

"I'm beginning to think you've never won a game of darts in your life."

Out of instinct more than forethought, she lay her hands over his, keeping them in place. There was a moment of stillness before he shifted forward. He was mere inches from pushing her up against the blackboard. His breath was hot and vodka-laden like her own.

Her smirk died.

Sure, she may have fantasized slightly during their self-defense classes, when his tall, masculine figure had her wrists locked to the wall, or pinned to the gym mat.

But this wasn't vague fantasies. Heavy desire flooded her as Aidan pressed against her body. How long had it been since she'd last gotten laid? Way too long.

This was the way into his bedroom, to return that USB, but the thought only dimly registered in the back of her mind. She wanted to be in that bed, with him on top of her. Liv's words resonated: *You're missing out, you know. Especially on the sex.*

Olivia thought of Reef, shirtless in the surf, and attached that image to the man in front of her. The same guy, the same body, the same...everything.

A sound escaped with her next exhale. Aidan heard it for what it was and dipped his mouth to hers.

She wrenched her head back. It banged against the blackboard and she laughed, trying to hide the combination of awkwardness and pain.

Oh god, what had just happened?

Aidan moved away, looking as confused as she felt. Something had replaced the desire flowing through her.

Terror.

She was *terrified*.

"Let's trim that beard!" Her words were too bright, too cheerful.

"What?" Aidan said.

"Come on, we should tidy you up. No time like the present!" She half-skipped over to the bottle of vodka and picked it up. "It'll be fun!"

She wanted to stop. The humiliation was raw. But her mouth wouldn't close, and her voice flooded out, sounding as ridiculous as a teenager's.

She was scared of Aidan.

Of trusting him, of letting him in – emotionally and physically. She was scared because he was an unknown entity; new; unexpected. Just because they were together in Eidolon didn't mean she knew who he was here.

Damn it, she didn't know how to take risks anymore.

He searched her face. Then his expression softened, as if he understood. "Okay," he said gently. "I was thinking of getting a haircut, anyway."

She kept up her chipper smile, swigging straight from the bottle as they headed towards the house. A hint of dawn touched the sky. Aidan didn't seem mad or even frustrated at the situation, for which she was eternally grateful. There had been similar times with other men…petulant, sulking men. This was a refreshing change.

She tried her best to be quiet as they slipped into the house, but furniture seemed to be everywhere, and she couldn't stop giggling. Aidan shut the bathroom door behind them. Olivia dug in the cupboard for the beard clippers. She dusted it off and plugged it in. "So…how does it work?"

"Oh no," he said, grabbing it off her.

"I can do it!"

"Something tells me that you can't."

"Trust me. I'm an expert."

He switched it on. "Like you're an expert at darts?"

"Let me try. Please?"

When she pouted and held out her hand, he passed it over with great reluctance. "I have a terrible feeling about this."

"How short do you want it? Like Reef's? I mean…you know. Reef in Eidolon."

"What do you think?"

She met his gaze. He really did have such pretty brown eyes.

"I like Reef's look," she said.

"All right."

She brought the clippers to his beard, and he caught her wrist, guiding her before she even started.

"Can I ask you," she said tentatively, "how, um, how did you get away from your father?"

He didn't answer. She wondered whether she'd hit the cliff face before the conversation had even begun, but after some time, he said, "I escaped after my mum died. I went to Pravit. He and Mum were friends from high school. He hunted down her parents and I stayed with them."

"How old were you?"

"Fourteen."

"Jeez."

"It didn't work out with my grandparents, though. They were incredibly strict – which is why she left them in the first place – and I hadn't had a proper upbringing before that. We…didn't get along. I'd never been to school before, never had a curfew. I ended up running away from them soon after."

"Where did you go?"

"Various safe houses. I found a sort of vigilante group. They were hell-bent on bringing down a makeup company that was using animals for testing, and that's how I got into activism."

"Did your psycho dad ever find you?"

Another silence. This time, she waited, curving the clippers up the side of his face.

"I never told you about my near-death experience," he said. "It happened at the beach house our Eidolon selves are staying."

"Was this when your dad found you?"

"This was before I ran away. My family was there for a holiday and I'd broken a cupboard door by hanging off it. Mum tried to hide it, but Dad found out. The last thing I saw was him smiling calmly before he took a pillow and smothered me until I suffocated."

Olivia pulled the clippers back.

"My mum revived me," Aidan said, "but…" He stopped, momentarily. "She had a bad heart. Everything must've been too much for her…she went into cardiac arrest after I was resuscitated. Dad didn't call an ambulance. He said she deserved it. She died right there, in front of me."

"Aidan–"

"I'm telling you this because I need you to understand how important it is that I keep him away from Sophie."

"I understand, Aidan. *Jesus*. I can't even imagine…" Aidan dodged as Olivia waved her hand, forgetting the clippers were still going. "Whoops, sorry!"

He pried them from her hand. "Let me finish this, all right?"

She moved away, giving him access to the mirror so he could trim his beard until it was as short as Reef's. He concentrated on the job, perhaps a little too hard.

"You've come a long way," she said as he evened up the sides. "Considering what you've been through. I think it's amazing."

"Maybe what my simulation has done is amazing. He's built a life for himself."

"So have you."

"No," he said, and he spoke so firmly, it didn't sound like modesty. "I'm not the same as my version in Eidolon."

He switched the clippers off and knocked them against the sink to get rid of the hair. The effect of the trim was incredible. He'd been working out over the past few weeks in the shed gym with Sophie and Olivia – his biceps now bulged beneath his T-shirt.

"You sure look like Reef now."

"It doesn't matter how I look. I've done things he hasn't."

"Like what?"

Rather than answer, he picked up the vodka bottle and took a long swig.

"What have you done, Aidan?"

"Enough," he said, swiping the back of his hand against his mouth. "Enough to know I don't deserve what he has."

He looked at her, and she realized what he was talking about. *Her.*

Had she been in his mind all along? Had he contemplated the idea of them, together?

But that was obvious – she'd also considered it. How could she not, after seeing them in Eidolon, after talking to Liv? She'd just assumed he wasn't interested, since he'd never brought it up, or even reacted to her flirting.

Except tonight he had. Tonight, after she'd told him that she was leaving Matt.

Oh no.

Where was her brain? She was married, and he'd respected that. Just like he'd respected her decision to back away from the kiss earlier. Just like he'd respected her fear of cars.

He'd been keeping a distance from her because his morals were...well, they were better than Matt's.

Was it true, then? Had she really found a better man in Eidolon?

She wondered this as she watched him down the rest of the vodka in several long gulps. He set the bottle on the counter, but misjudged, and it fell into the bath, shattering.

"Shit," he said.

"Leave it. We'll clean it up tomorrow."

"I should–" He moved to pick up the pieces but she tugged him back.

"Leave it," she said again. "It's okay, Aidan."

"Val will see–"

"Val knows."

"What?"

"Shh. We're not finished here."

She picked up a brush and fussed with his hair. When he tried to squirm free, she grabbed his shirt to hold him still. He was less steady than before. The alcohol had finally started to hit.

"I was going to give you a haircut," she said, "but I dunno, it looks all right as it is."

It was shoulder-length, and when she ran her fingers through it, combing it back, she appreciated the rugged style it gave him.

She untied her own hair, letting it tumble down, and used her hair band to tie his back. He had to bend forward slightly to give her access. She was tall, but not that tall.

It hadn't escaped her notice that he was holding his breath. They were incredibly close again, his mouth kissing distance from the crook of her neck. Her spaghetti straps meant a lot of bare skin – every inch of her neck and shoulder tingled in anticipation.

If she weren't such a coward now, and if he weren't under the inexplicable impression that he didn't deserve her, maybe, right now, right this very second, they could be–

Aidan's phone buzzed.

He stilled. She pulled away. "Who's sending you a message at this time?"

There was an expression of dread as he pulled his phone from his pocket, but when he saw the screen, relief flooded his features.

Olivia watched him read the message. The relief disappeared. The more he read, the paler his complexion grew.

"Aidan?"

"No," he choked.

"Aidan, what–"

He leaned back against the wall, his breaths shallow and uneven. "Oh Jesus."

"What's wrong? Aidan, please. You're scaring me."

He tried to speak, but gave up and shoved the phone at her. Then he walked out of the bathroom.

She checked the message. It was an email from Pravit.

Eidolon's Kassandra has been taken by the retrieval team. Interrogators have been sent to force her to give up Bobbi's location. I may have to expose my position to save her.

Attached are all the documents I've collected so far against Equinoxx. I wish I had more time to explain, but you'll have to do the rest from now on. Because, I'm so sorry, Aidan, but if you've received this scheduled message, I've been caught. I won't give up your daughter to Equinoxx. I'll be using the Exit Strategy rather than let them question me.

Tell my family I love them, so very much.

Stay strong. Save Bobbi.

Your friend,

Pravit.

37

Olivia found Aidan on the porch steps with his face buried in his hands. Moths fluttered around the security light, casting flickering shadows. Olivia sat beside him.

"We don't know for sure that—"

"Don't." His breaths were broken. "Please."

"But—"

"If Pravit was caught by Equinoxx, he's dead. He had a plan in place to ensure they didn't get information from him."

"The Exit Strategy?"

He nodded. She didn't dare imagine what that might entail.

With a wince, he dragged his hands down his face and stared into the darkness. "We have to go to the shed."

"What?"

"We have to warn the others. Put another plan into place." He stood, wavering slightly.

Olivia jumped to her feet. "We just finished a bottle of vodka."

"It doesn't matter."

"Yes it does!"

Aidan headed into the house. When he grabbed his keys, Olivia snatched them off him. "You can't drive."

"I have to. The others might not even know Kass is caught."

"What use are we if we're dead from a car crash?"

"It's dawn. No one else will be about." When he reached for the keys, she darted back.

"You might pass out halfway there," she said.

"I'm *fine.*"

"S'going on out here?" Sophie said, staggering blearily out of her room. "S'there an emergency? Whoa, what happened to your beard?"

Olivia gasped. "Sophie! Sophie can drive us."

"Sophie can't drive," Aidan said.

"Yes she can. I've been teaching her."

"You what?"

"I'll apologize later." Olivia tossed Aidan's car keys aside and grabbed Val's instead. "Sophie, honey, we need you to take us somewhere. Both of us have had too much to drink."

Sophie stopped mid-yawn to stare at her.

"Don't ask, it was a whole thing. Can you drive us?"

Sophie peeked hesitantly at Aidan. "We've only ever driven around the block before."

"I know," Olivia said, "but no one will be on the road, and it's only about twenty minutes away. We'll be right there with you."

She thought she'd get more pushback from Aidan, or at least an angry comment about letting Sophie drive. But the news of Pravit's death must've shaken him deeply – he said nothing as Sophie pulled on her runners beneath her pajamas and led them to the car port.

He hovered near the passenger seat. "Do you want me to…?"

"No, it's okay," Olivia said, climbing in. "I've gotten used to it over the weeks. She's a careful driver, especially since I'm the one teaching her."

"Where are we going?" Sophie said.

"We'll direct you."

"Is this about Equinoxx?"

"Yes. Something bad's happened. Aidan's friend has died."

Sophie, who had just started the engine, twisted in her seat to look at Aidan in the back. "Oh my god."

"Yeah," Olivia said. Her stomach churned uncomfortably as she thought of Pravit, who reminded her so much of her father. She'd had too much to drink to fully comprehend what that meant. Or maybe it was just the enormity of it. Someone had *died.*

"Are you okay?" Sophie said to Aidan.

"Not really." Olivia had a moment of surprise at hearing an honest answer before Aidan added, "But can we go? The others might be in trouble."

Sophie switched on the headlights and checked the mirrors then carefully began reversing out.

"Take your time," Olivia said. "That's it."

"So…how long has this been going on?" Aidan said.

"I promised to be Olivia's gym buddy if she taught me to drive. We take Val's car out when you go grocery shopping."

"Or when you went to the shed," Olivia added.

"Is that where we're going now? This mysterious shed?"

"Yeah. I guess you'll see what's been going on."

"She doesn't have to come in," Aidan said.

Sophie scowled, but Olivia said, "Maybe she should. If we don't have Pravit anymore, we're going to need all the help we can get."

"I'm not putting Sophie in any more danger."

"I can take care of myself."

"Don't be naive," Aidan snapped.

"I'm driving you now, aren't I? You clearly need me."

"It's not happening, Sophie."

"Why not? Why can't I help? I'm not a kid."

"Neither was Pravit, and he's still dead."

Sophie fell silent. Olivia watched the road, biting her lip.

"I'm not getting you involved," Aidan said. "So drop it."

Sophie said nothing, though her jaw was tense, and an angry tear rolled down her cheek. No one spoke for the rest of the ride except to direct her. Olivia understood why Aidan didn't want to make her a part of their fight against Equinoxx. Just the memory of Winken in her apartment was enough to freak her out. But, like it or not, Sophie was already tangled up in this. They could at least tell her what was going on.

Olivia dreaded the moment when they'd reach the property, and they'd have to leave her in the car.

Except it didn't end up being an issue. When they arrived, another car was already parked, waiting.

"What the…?" Olivia said, as Sophie pulled up on the side of the road.

"Don't stop," Aidan said in alarm.

"No." Olivia unbuckled her seatbelt and opened the door. "It's Kass. What's she doing here?"

Kass climbed carefully out of her car. "Livvie?"

"What are you doing here? How did you find me?"

"Didn't you get my text?"

"I haven't had time to check my phone. We're here for…" She glanced at the car behind her. "Something else. What's wrong?"

Aidan got out. Kass' body seemed to seize up at his appearance.

"Kass," Olivia said. "What is it?"

"I have a problem, Livvie. Really big." Kass didn't take her gaze from Aidan. "I need your help."

"What can we do?" Olivia said.

"It's personal. I just need you."

Olivia checked on Aidan again. She couldn't leave him.

"Olivia," Kass said, and Olivia almost recoiled at her full name coming from Kass' mouth. When had Kass last called her Olivia?

Never. She had never called her Olivia, not even in the hospital after the accident.

"Come with me," Kass said, finally tearing her attention from Aidan, her gaze instead boring into Olivia. It was like she was trying to tell her something, but Olivia couldn't figure out what it was. "This is the most important thing I will ever ask you to do. Please."

Olivia's throat closed up. Sophie was still behind the wheel, her face ghostly in the lights of the dash.

Aidan took an unsteady step towards them. "You can't go. I need you to be my anchor."

"Sophie can do it."

"I don't want to get her involved."

"Maybe you don't have a choice." Olivia's resolve was hardening, even as she spoke. This was something she could do, something big, to help both Aidan and Sophie. The two of them had to learn to trust each other.

"I'm going with Kass," Olivia said. "She needs me, and you have your sister."

Aidan looked briefly at Kass. He had a tentative sort of expression. Almost... fear. But that couldn't be right. Why would Aidan be afraid of Kass?

Olivia walked to Kass' car.

"We'll contact you when we're finished," she said, opening the passenger door. "Stay safe, okay? Both of you."

Aidan didn't answer.

Kass practically fell into the driver's seat and started the engine before Olivia had finished putting on her seatbelt.

"What's this about?" Olivia said as they screeched into the night. She was going to have a heart attack if Kass didn't slow down.

"You asked me to decrypt those files."

Olivia shut her eyes. Sneaking into Aidan's room felt like a lifetime ago. The USB was still tucked in her jeans, waiting for her to return it to his dresser.

"It was bad?" she said.

"Shit yes it was bad. It was plans and information on the coal train that got blown up."

"What?"

"Olivia," Kass said, the whites of her eyes gleaming in the dashboard light, "the dude's a motherfucking terrorist."

38

Aidan had a choice to make. A big choice. A painful, dangerous, lifetime's-worth-of-regret choice.

His head hurt. He needed to take a shower. Go to sleep. His face felt strange, exposed without the bushy beard. The alcohol in his blood warped his senses.

He had a choice to make.

He had two choices to make.

The first was more pressing, even as he stood in the darkness, staring after the car that had taken Olivia away. He needed to turn away.

He needed to turn *around*.

"Aidan?" Sophie said behind him. Her voice was small.

"Fuck," he whispered.

"Why did Olivia leave?"

"Fuck," he said again.

He turned around. Sophie stood in the headlights of Val's car, looking young in her pajamas. Like the wide-eyed child he'd picked up five years ago.

He was a monster for dragging her into this. But he thought of Bobbi, even younger, even more vulnerable, and knew he would do whatever he had to do to save his daughter.

"I don't know," he said to Sophie. "That was Kass, Olivia's friend. Maybe she's realized how dangerous the Equinoxx thing has gotten."

Sophie didn't look like she believed him. He didn't believe it, either. Olivia had mentioned that Kass was good with secrets —

had she discovered his? If she had, he was completely screwed. But with Pravit dead, maybe he was screwed anyway. These may be his final few actions as a free man. He had to make them count.

"I need you to help me," he said. "Without Olivia, you're the only one who can."

First choice, made. Sophie's mouth pursed, and he could tell curiosity was battling with fear. Her desire to throw herself into dangerous situations for the greater good was going to get her killed if he wasn't careful.

"Come with me," he said. "I'll show you the shed."

He switched off the car and together they picked their way through the bush, using their phone flashlights. On the way, he told her about Equinoxx. He explained how Pravit had asked him to volunteer for the mapping mere months before he'd found out about Sophie. About how mid-way through this year, Pravit asked for help again. About the glitch that had caused his and Olivia's simulations to become level four citizens. About Bobbi. About Equinoxx's unspeakable plans to stay in the black.

Sophie listened with less questions than he'd expected. Olivia's mysterious departure had clearly unnerved her.

He switched on the generator as he talked, and powered up the system inside the shed.

"Is that what was on the USB?" Sophie said as he set the coordinates for the beach house.

He turned to her. She was staring at the throne rather than looking at him.

"What USB?" he said, already dreading the answer.

"The peg one in your room. Olivia found it and sent the files to Kass."

And there it was. His secret had been exposed. He thought of Kass' wide, frantic eyes as she'd pleaded with Olivia to go with her. She knew what he'd done. What he was. And she'd tell Olivia.

A brief memory of earlier that night flashed through his mind, of Olivia pressed up against his body, her hands in his hair, his mouth achingly close to her neck. Any potential of that vanished in an instant.

As it should. His hands were too dirty for homely pleasures. He should've known better than to even dream.

"Yeah, that was all Equinoxx stuff," he said. Sophie still didn't know what he had done, and he was going to delay that inevitable moment for as long as possible. "Some of the more dangerous information. Maybe Kass thought it was too much for Olivia to handle."

"I dunno. Have you seen those videos of Olivia jumping off cliffs? She can probably handle Equinoxx."

Aidan thought again of Pravit, who had been so very clever and capable. It didn't matter how competent any of them were. If they survived this, it would come down to luck alone.

He couldn't think of Pravit right now. It was like an anvil of hurt every time it hit his brain.

Pravit, his friend, and, honestly, his safety net in this whole Equinoxx business, was gone. There was no one left to help them. And if Olivia didn't come back, he was on his own.

His second choice loomed, but he didn't have to make it yet.

He connected the NTD. "Let me show you how to extract me once I'm in there."

Sophie listened carefully, repeating his instructions until he was confident she could get him out safely. She watched with wide eyes as he sat on the throne and put on the crown.

"Okay," he said. "When you're ready."

The beach shack blinked before him. It was lit up – his other self sat at the kitchen table, facing the door, his fingers laced as if in prayer. He stood at Aidan's appearance.

"Pravit's dead," Aidan said.

Reef's jaw tightened reflexively. It took him a moment to swallow, and another moment to speak. His voice was sleeping-baby soft. "And Liv?"

"Liv?"

"You haven't heard where she is?"

"I don't know anything about what Liv's doing. Pravit sent me an email with what he'd gathered so far against Equinoxx. He said your Kass had been captured and he may have to expose his position to save her. He also said he'd be using the Exit Strategy—" Aidan cut off. He needed to catch his breath before he could say, "Liv's missing?"

"She went to get Kazzy. She took the car. The gun."

Aidan nodded to the phone that was sitting on the dining table. "That yours?"

"Yeah."

"Burner?"

"Always."

"Then switch it on," Aidan said. "See if they've messaged you."

"I will, when I can't take anymore. But it might bring hell down on us. Equinoxx can track locations of phones pinging off their towers."

"But they don't have your number, right?"

"They've already got their eyes on this area. If a new signal appears in the middle of the bush, they'll find us. And without a car or a gun, Bobbi and I are sitting ducks."

Aidan glanced out the window at the lightening sky. "You think they'll get your location out of Liv or Kazzy?"

"Liv's the strongest person I know, but I think Equinoxx has ways to get what they want." A spark of hope flared in Reef's expression. "It doesn't matter though, right? Because Pravit's sent you what you need. You can go public. Stop Equinoxx now."

"I don't know what Pravit was waiting for," Aidan said. "There must be some piece of evidence that will fall into place after the new year—"

"Surely there's enough with what you have. If Pravit's been collating data since they first decided to steal children, he'll have memos, emails, documents. That's enough to stop Equinoxx."

"What if it's not? What if the court throws it out, and Equinoxx is free to do whatever they want with Bobbi? Let me at least go through the documents and see if I can find what Pravit was waiting for."

"And what do I do in the meantime?"

"I know you're sick of hearing it, but wait a little longer. I promise I'll figure something out."

Reef gave a tight smile. "Easy for you to say."

"Nothing about this is easy."

"You're right about that." There was a pause, then Reef said gently, "Do you want to see her?"

Hope buoyed Aidan's chest at the same time fear clouded it. "I should…she's sleeping so…"

"She's dead to the world when she's asleep. Come on."

Aidan had seen her through Pravit's eyes, through the monitor. He was almost afraid to see her in person, as if his very presence would endanger her.

Still, he couldn't stop his feet as Reef led him to the nursery and opened the door. Light seeped through the crack onto Bobbi's sleeping form. Her mouth was slightly open, curls askew around her face. Her little chest rose and fell in a soothing rhythm.

Aidan's hands ached to pick her up, to hold her against him. It was a strange desire – he hadn't had a lot to do with small children, and he couldn't tell whether it was some echo phenomenon from Eidolon, or whether the mere knowledge that this was his daughter was enough to invoke a paternal response.

Reef closed the door, not quite all the way. It seemed a cruelly short time to see Bobbi. Aidan felt like he'd gotten barely a taste of his family, just enough to make him desperate for more.

"At least you've cleaned up," Reef said, giving Aidan the once over. Aidan frowned.

"How are you going to survive this if you can't take care of yourself? And why won't you let Liv see you?"

"She might think differently about you if she ever clapped eyes on me. The potential–"

"To be thoroughly messed up? Yeah, she figured that out without seeing you. She's worried. And honestly, I am too. If you aren't in the right headspace to go up against Equinoxx–"

"I am," Aidan said. He gazed towards Bobbi's door. "I have to be."

"Yeah, you do. We all do. Promise me you'll do whatever it takes to bring them down."

"I will. Stay safe, all right? Sophie, can you extract me?"

When he blinked again, he was back in the shed.

"Holy crap," Sophie said from the computer. "Was that really your daughter?"

He pulled off the crown and got out his phone. "Yeah, it was."

The second decision, the one that was looming, had been made. A quick search on Olivia's social media and he found Kass' website for some sort of consultancy business. Her number was listed on the contacts page.

Please ask Olivia to call me, he texted. **Tell her I'll explain everything.**

EIDOLON

39

Liv didn't know where to go. She had memorized the woman Valentina's address after Reef realized that could be their backup safe house, but without her phone, she didn't know how to get there.

Charging stations might still have paper road maps. She'd never thought to check. That would require breaking into somewhere again, though, and neither she nor Kazzy were keen.

They'd taken winding, unsealed tracks off the main road after losing the StarShine car, then slept an hour in the car, down a small dirt path in the bush. Kazzy had claimed they were wired enough to keep going, but then came their biggest problem – a dwindling supply of fuel. They were going to need to find a petrol station, soon. And the only way they were going to find it, and Valentina's house, was by switching on one of their phones.

Liv turned hers over in her hand. She was desperate to call or message Reef, tell him they were okay. He must be worried sick, and without a car or the gun, he would be antsy. Liv had wanted to go back, but Kazzy pointed out there would probably be vehicles stationed along the road now. Visitors to Eidolon, lying in wait. The Monaro and the Hilux had been parked facing south, which highlighted the fact they'd come from the north. Equinoxx would figure it out. They'd be ready.

"If I check Valentina's address on Maps," Liv said, "will anyone be able to track it?"

Kazzy pressed her lips together.

"Then let's hope they have road maps in the charging station," Liv said.

"Let's hope there's a charging station close enough for us to make it."

Liv's finger hovered over her phone's power button. As soon as she switched it on, that was it. They were found.

But at least they were in the opposite direction to Reef and Bobbi. Equinoxx would turn their attention away from the beach house. Liv was willing to take that risk.

She switched on her phone. It took a long time to power up. She felt the urgency with every passing second, as she swiped her thumbprint, as the phone searched for a signal, as Maps loaded, as it scanned for nearby charging stations.

"Shit," Kazzy said. "The next one with a petrol pump is too far. We don't have enough fuel for that."

"Then what do we do?"

"First things first. I need to piss."

While Kazzy got out of the car, Liv sent a text to Reef. If he got desperate enough to turn on his phone, she wanted him to know they were all right.

Except…they weren't all right. Not really. They were in the middle of the bush with no food, no water, no fuel, and no idea where to go.

"I've thought of a plan," Kazzy announced as she returned. Her eyes were on the shotgun, which she'd put in the backseat. "But you're probably not going to like it."

OUTSIDE

To: jacobpwilcox@equinoxxtechnology.co
From: retrievalunit@basenxj451.com
Subject: Incident Report

Name of reporting officer: EPOC889573
Time of incident: 10:05hrs
Location: Mooliabeenee Rd
Event summary: Probable activity of targets OS and KW.
Report: Terrence and Tanya Miller called local police at 10:07hrs, having found a green HQ Monaro on the side of the road with flashing hazard lights. While checking the abandoned car, they were held at gunpoint from behind and forced to place their hands on the top of the Monaro. Neither got a look at their assailants, but identified both as female. Assailants told them to remain facing the Monaro for two minutes, then drove away with the Miller car. The Millers' wallets and phones were left on the side of the road. Millers claim no loss of other possessions except a picnic basket and expensive bottle of champagne. OS SIM card was briefly pinged at same location.

Completed Equinoxx actions: Monaro searched by local police. Nothing found. BOLO put out for a white '97 Land Cruiser, number plates TOML415. All sightings to be reported directly to Equinoxx POC. OS and KW photos to be posted on news sites, assuming cooperation of state police.

Recommended future Equinoxx actions: Place scout avatars at points highlighted on map provided. Inform local police in a fifty-kilometer radius.

40

It was strange being back in the elevator to her apartment. Olivia hadn't been here for almost two months. She didn't have her digital passkey, but she knew the backup code, and the elevator rose unhindered.

She stared at her reflection in the mirrored walls. Her eyes were tired, her hair limp. She didn't look like the version of her that was married to Matt, but she didn't look like the version in Eidolon, either.

The last time she had been in this elevator, it had been escaping Winken. She had leaped into Aidan's arms without a moment's thought that perhaps he was as dangerous as the assassin.

She'd looked more into the attack on the train line. A group called the Guardians was claiming credit. Olivia vaguely remembered they had caused the death of a logger earlier in the year. Sophie and Valentina had been talking about it. From their conversation, Olivia had pieced together that Sophie had no idea what dark deeds her brother had been doing, but Valentina knew, and probably didn't approve.

But disapproving wasn't enough. Why hadn't she turned Aidan in to the police? Did he have something on her? Some blackmail or threat? Olivia would've ratted him out immediately if it weren't for Equinoxx. She couldn't reveal herself, or Winken would come.

And without Pravit...

She squeezed her eyes shut. Reef and Liv needed Aidan. *Bobbi* needed Aidan.

How could he do this to all of them? And yet, even after all the betrayals, even after Kass had proved who Aidan really was, a tiny part of Olivia still wanted to believe in him. She flinched away from the thought. The man had *blown up a train*.

But all it took was a memory of his stressed, exhausted face during the past seven weeks – him crouched at the garden tap, shoulders shaking as he washed chicken blood from his hands, the box of vodka bottles under his bed – and she was third-guessing her judgement. He had told her he couldn't look Sophie in the eye after what he'd done. He'd said he didn't deserve the life that Reef had. That didn't sound like a fanatical eco-terrorist. It sounded like he was acting against his will.

She curled her fingers into fists, as if physically stopping herself from reaching for Kass' phone, even though it was with Kass, who was waiting outside for signs of trouble.

He had texted Kass, asking Olivia to call him.

She *wanted* to call him.

The elevator doors slid open at her apartment. Immediately she felt it: this wasn't home anymore. There were new flowers on the entrance table, but their scent was sickly, mingling with the lemon of cleaning products. The place was so sterile, so big. Why did they need all this space for just the two of them?

She stole upstairs, aware that Matt was at work but still feeling like an intruder. It was risky, being in the open with Winken about. But she and Kass had spent the night in a hotel, talking over how they could escape Equinoxx without Aidan, and this was a solid start. Kass could hook her up with fake IDs, credit cards, whatever she needed. Olivia just had to have the cash on hand. And while Kass was rich, cash in a hurry was something Olivia could do better.

The safe in her bedroom was locked by a code; her thumbprint still opened it. Emergency funds sat inside – tens of thousands of dollars' worth. She stuffed it all into a backpack, feeling only a twinge of guilt. Matt wouldn't miss it. In fact, he'd probably never realize it was gone.

She stood, strapping on the backpack, when there was a feminine giggle from down the hall.

Olivia froze. Her body made the connections before her brain did, adrenaline flooding her system.

"You hungry?" said Matt's voice.

"Famished. How could I not be, after all that exercise?" Too soon they were there, walking into the room in swimsuits and towels, their bodies glistening with pool water.

Matt stopped abruptly. "Olivia!"

The woman was model-beautiful, long dark hair, brown skin – Matt clearly had a type.

Sarina paused, hovering behind Matt. Her hands tightened around the knot in her towel. She looked very awkward.

"You cunt," Olivia said.

Sarina winced as Matt said, "Now, Olivia–"

"You actual cunt. I thought the affair was the worst thing you could ever do to me, but to bring her *here?*"

"You – this – it's the first time…now look." Matt seemed to have grasped his use of language again. "You've been gone almost two months. I've searched everywhere, left dozens of messages, emails, voicemails–"

"And then what? Declared me gone and rushed to the next woman?"

"We need to talk about this."

"I think my current view–" she gestured to the two of them "– says plenty. We made vows, Matt. Does that mean nothing to you?"

"I wasn't happy," Matt said quietly.

"Well, you missed a few million steps by jumping to an affair. Did you try communicating? Or marriage counselling? What about sexual experimentation?"

Sarina shifted her weight. She was dripping pool water on the carpet. They both were.

"That's fair," Matt said. "You're right. I should've tried all that first. I don't know what I was thinking." He paused, regarding her. "Are you okay? You look a little…"

"Now that you mention it, yeah, I've had a shitty past few weeks."

"Staying with Kass, I imagine, considering you've brought the language home with you."

Matt didn't sound like a husband. He sounded like a father. She'd been in a protective, paternal bubble. No wonder she'd become a useless sponge. This is what the other Olivia had been trying to tell her.

She pulled off her wedding rings. They felt like they were strangling her finger, anyway. After dropping them on the dresser, she pushed past them and headed downstairs.

"Olivia!" Matt called after her as she jabbed the button for the elevator. "We need to talk about this."

"I've got more important things to do."

The elevator opened and she rode it down with a bizarrely similar feeling to the one she used to have drifting 10,000 feet over the countryside strapped to a parachute.

It was only when the elevator stopped at the lobby and the doors opened to reveal a smiling Winken did she realize exactly what she had risked by coming here. Had he been watching *Matt* this whole time, thinking she'd crawl back to him? Had she really come across as that pathetic?

Winken stepped inside and stood against her. She felt something in his jacket pocket press against her waist.

"Going down?"

To: jacobpwilcox@equinoxxtechnology.co
From: retrievalunit@basenxj451.com
Subject: Incident Report

Name of reporting officer: EPOC889573
Time of incident: 12:08hrs
Location: Private property off Beekeeper Nature Reserve
Event summary: Sighting of **level five citizen.**

Report: Scouts received comms of phone pinging from tower along stretch of Indian Ocean Drive. A search uncovered a dirt track headed west, which led to a beach house. When scouts got out to investigate, they were ambushed by assumed father of level five citizen and injured to the point of necessary extraction from Eidolon. Father then stole the scouts' car, which was later tracked to charging station of original incident. It was abandoned, though station's security footage shows Hilux that had been left north of the scene the night prior was filled up with petrol and taken. Footage shows level five citizen is with father.

Completed Equinoxx actions: Forensic evidence of car and beach house forthcoming, to be sent directly to Equinoxx POC.

Recommended future Equinoxx actions: URGENT appointment of every available team member to the area, both north and south. Stop and search required of every passing vehicle under the authority of cooperating local police.

To: jacobpwilcox@equinoxxtechnology.co
From: lakebroadsideprivateinvestigations@lakebroadside.
com
Subject: Reef Davidson

Dear Mr Wilcox,
The beach property ownership documents you requested
are below. They are under the name FORREST DAVIDSON,
whose date of birth suggests this could potentially be REEF
DAVIDSON'S father. If you agree for us to continue our
investigation, we will attempt to contact FORREST DAVIDSON
for more information.

Current invoice is attached.

Regards,
Steven Saulsbury
Lake Broadside Private Investigators

41

Winken nudged Olivia out of the elevator. She stumbled into the underground garage. It was humid and gloomy. The roller door to the street was closed. The pedestrian door beside it had been propped ajar with a pipe by some careless resident. Olivia stared at the gap longingly.

"Not going to happen." Winken pressed harder against her waist. "This way."

"I don't have access to my car. My driver—"

"Don't fret. We don't need access to your car. Come along, now."

"Don't kill me."

"I wish I could say it's nothing personal, but your virtual self gave me quite the knock. This way."

"There are security cameras—"

"It's all taken care of, Mrs Alexander. Stop here."

They were at the end of the lot, as far away from the door as possible. Winken kept the weapon in his jacket pocket trained on her as he used his free, gloved hand to pull a small silver gun from his holster.

"Here's the pistol you bought to kill your cheating husband," Winken said. "But when confronted with him, you found you couldn't do it. You loved him too much. So you came down here and put a bullet in your brain."

"Please—"

"On your knees."

"Please. Please."

"I'm afraid pleas don't work on me. Neither does bribery."

"But I *can* pay you," Olivia said through broken breaths. "I have access to my husband's account–"

"You couldn't possibly offer me more than what Equinoxx is paying. Besides, I've been looking forward to this. Now on your knees."

Olivia could've refused. It was unlikely that Winken would shoot her in a way that looked like something other than suicide.

Unlikely. Not impossible.

She dropped to her knees and Winken let go of the weapon in his pocket to force the silver pistol into her hand. She tried to make her grip loose, but he squeezed her fingers around it, still dexterous in his gloves.

A hot tear spilled down her cheek. How many breaths did she have left? Five? Six?

Winken leaned over her from behind and she moved out of instinct. Her head slammed back, catching him in the nose. He reeled away, but not far enough – his grip remained over her hand on the pistol. It fired, loud and hot across her, hitting the far wall. She screamed.

He forced the barrel towards her. She used his weight to roll him over her shoulder. He landed on his back. She twisted his wrist to try to get the pistol away, but his grip was too strong.

She heard Aidan's voice in her head – *RUN, Olivia!* – and surrendered the gun, running towards the door.

She heard Winken give chase.

Her fingers found the door handle, and she had to stop to yank it open. She expected to feel herself being dragged back, an explosion, a bullet in her side, but she burst out into the sunlight, free. She sprinted up the slope and almost broke into tears when she saw Kass idling out the front.

"Did I hear a fucking *gunshot?*"

Olivia flung herself into the passenger seat. "Drive, drive, drive!" She wrenched the door shut and sank down below the window, cramming herself in the footwell. Kass' tires squealed as they pulled out onto the road. Another car honked, and there was a second squeal of tires. But there was no crunch, no jolt. Kass zoomed away.

"So he was home, then? Tell me you shot the cheating motherfucker."

Olivia couldn't answer at first. She was shaking, hard. "W-Winken."

"Oh shit, the assassin? You got away from the assassin?"

Olivia nodded.

"That's – my – Livvie!" Kass slammed the horn to punctuate every word. "You hurt?"

Olivia shook her head, then stopped to check that she hadn't actually gotten shot. Her body was zinging – she might have missed a graze. But, besides the throbbing reminder of her spinal injury, she was unhurt.

She had escaped Winken. Again.

"I thought I was going to piss myself."

Kass burst out laughing. Olivia laughed too, although it had a tremor to it. Her backpack was still slung around her body, so at least she had gotten something out of the trip. She climbed up into the passenger seat and pulled on her seatbelt.

"Matt was home," she said. "With Sarina."

"Are you shitting me? Do I need to turn this car around and make pulp outta him?"

"We're never, ever going back there."

"All right. But you say the word, and I'll take care of him. I can hurt him in ways he'll never see coming."

"Maybe later," Olivia said. "Can I borrow your phone?"

Kass used her thighs to steer the wheel as she lifted her entire butt off the seat and dug into her back pocket. "Sure thing. What for?"

"I'm going to call Aidan. I don't think he's doing this stuff of his own volition."

Kass harrumphed.

"He's been protecting me," Olivia said. "He sacrificed so much to take in his sister. And he's risking everything for people who are supposed to be simulations. He values life, Kass. The actions of the Guardians don't match that. Something doesn't add up, and if he can give me a decent explanation, then I'm going back."

"All right," Kass said, tossing the phone.

Olivia found the message that Aidan had sent and hit the call button. The phone had barely begun to ring before he picked up.

"Olivia?"

Something happened to her body when she heard his voice. It was like a balm spreading through the adrenaline, melting away her fears. She realized that some time over the past two months, she'd come to associate him with safety.

She put the phone on speaker. "I thought I should let you explain."

"I'm really glad you called."

Kass slapped a hand over her heart with a sarcastic dreamy face.

"Can you meet me somewhere?" Aidan said.

Kass shook her head.

"I'd feel safer if we did this over the phone."

"You know I can't risk that."

"Winken attacked me today. I don't think I can handle another confrontation."

"The assassin? Are you hurt?"

Kass gave Olivia a sappy look and mouthed, *Awwwww.*

"I used your training," Olivia said. "It saved my life."

Kass dropped her silly face.

Olivia continued. "I've never been that scared before. He was going to make me shoot myself—" She stopped, hiccupping.

"I'm not going to hurt you," Aidan said gently.

"I know."

There was a beat of silence.

"Olivia," he said at last, "Sophie's father found us."

"What? When?"

"At the beginning of the year. I can explain if you'll let me. Just please come home. And know that everything I've done, I've done to protect Sophie."

Olivia let out a long exhale. Of course this was about his sister. What else could've been behind Aidan's uncharacteristic behavior?

"All right, I'll come back," she said, looking at Kass. "But this time, I won't be alone."

To: jacobpwilcox@equinoxxtechnology.co
From: retrievalunit@basenxj451.com
Subject: Retrieval update

Discussion with Forrest Davidson in Eidolon produced no
results, as he claims not to have seen his son in twenty years.
Recommend interviewing Forrest Davidson on the Outside.

42

Olivia had forgotten Aidan's new look. He was waiting out the front as the car eased up the dirt driveway, the close shave of his beard tidied since last night, his hair pulled back in her hair band. A black cord sat around his neck beneath a blue collared shirt she'd never seen before. He looked good. And when his attention fell on her, her hormones partied in a way they hadn't since she was a teenager.

"You," Kass said as she jumped out of the car, "had better start talking. And if I don't like what I hear, there will be consequences."

"All right, but away from the house. Sophie's working inside." His gaze returned to Olivia. "Are you okay?"

"Yes."

The three of them took the path towards the river, where Olivia had walked with Sophie many times since arriving. She watched for spider webs and snakes. It was slightly cooler in the shade, but the air was still uncomfortably damp.

"That YouTube channel Sophie created," Aidan said. "Her dad found it and tracked her here."

"When you say her dad, isn't he yours too?"

"Unfortunately, yes."

"How would he have tracked her here?" Kass said.

"I don't know, but he showed up on our doorstep in January, threatening to take her back. He said he'd accuse me of kidnapping her. Unless…"

"Unless?" Olivia said.

"I have a certain skill set. Things I picked up during my activism years."

"Explosives."

"I never hurt anyone," Aidan said. "We were freeing animals—"

"You don't have to explain yourself. After the videos Sophie's shown me over the past two months, I understand why people go to extremes in those cases."

Kass was walking behind them, listening. They passed the cubby house. Aidan didn't give it a second glance.

"I was offered a choice," he said. "Do Forrest's dirty work, or give Sophie back."

"So your dad's behind the Guardians?"

"Since the beginning, yeah. I only started recently—"

"Did you kill that guy?" Kass said. "The logger?"

Aidan stopped. Olivia turned to him.

"I'd spiked a bunch of trees in an old growth forest, to make them useless as timber. But I put up signs. You're supposed to put up signs warning the loggers, otherwise they'll fell them without realizing, and then everyone loses. The forest is wiped out, but the wood can't be used."

Olivia noticed how erratic his breathing had become. "What happened?" she said.

"That sonofabitch filmed me spiking the trees as collateral if I ever turned on him. Then he took down the signs after I'd gone. He didn't want to save the forest. It's not about activism for him. It's about control."

He turned away from Olivia and kept walking. She and Kass had to hurry to keep up with him.

"Someone *died*," Kass said.

"Yes. His name was Todd Sturgeon. Father of three. He created a little comic series on the side about a superhero called Hotdog Boy. It was for his kids, but he put it online and it got a few followers. He and his wife were mid-way through building an extension on their house when the spike killed him. He had taken a shift at the mill to cover for a friend."

Olivia remembered the newspaper photograph in Aidan's dresser, of the family with three boys. He was torturing himself.

"It wasn't your fault," she said, stunned that he would even think of taking responsibility. "Your father was the one who took the signs down."

"And I'm the one who spiked the trees. I send the family cash anonymously every month, but I don't think it's enough. I hear they're struggling a bit."

"Aidan, you can't do this to yourself."

"Nothing will make it all right again."

"Expose your old man," Kass said. "Take him down."

"If I do that, he'll release the footage of me spiking the trees. I'll go to jail, and Sophie will end up right back at cult camp."

"The fuck is cult camp?" Kass said.

"Have you ever seen those YouTube videos about Symbiosis? It's set up to look like a sanctuary where everyone grows their own vegetables and milks their own cows—"

"I've seen the beginning of them, but I always hit skip as soon as I can," Olivia said. She put on the voice. "*G'day. The name's Forrest, and I'm here to offer you a newer, greener way of living.*"

"That's him," Aidan said grimly.

"That's your dad?"

"And Sophie's."

"He's running the Guardians?"

"He gets trusted people inside Symbiosis to do the work for him. He's been at it for years, but now he has me, he's able to make a bigger impact."

"Like the train."

"He wanted me to detonate as soon as it passed over so it would kill the driver. He was livid when I didn't do it. He threatened to take Sophie away. That was the same night the chickens died."

"Oh Aidan." Olivia remembered how exhausted he'd looked that day, how he'd broken down while washing blood from his hands. How he'd told her that they were better off without him. She should've gone to him that night, talked to him.

They reached the dry riverbed and paused, as if their way had been blocked.

"I don't know how to get out," he said, voice cracking. "I don't even know if I can. He's corrupted everything I am. I don't recognize myself anymore."

"You look like Reef to me," Olivia said.

He smiled bitterly.

"I'm still stuck on the bit where he tracked you from a YouTube video," Kass said. "You not protecting your tech?"

Aidan shrugged. "I thought I had. Maybe it was something in the footage he recognized, I don't know. It doesn't matter now."

Sophie had told Olivia that her brother had changed since finding her channel. She thought he was angry because she'd put herself online, but it wasn't that at all.

"Do you think he got your location the old-fashioned way?" Olivia said. "By just asking? She's been talking to someone secretly for as long as I've been living here. What if it's not a romantic interest? What if Forrest contacted her through the YouTube channel and they've been communicating ever since?"

Aidan dragged a hand down his face. "If that's true, then he's already gotten into her head, and I've lost her. He can be very persuasive when he wants to be."

"It would explain her more radical viewpoints," Olivia said.

"Left field idea, here," Kass said, "but have you considered, like, telling your sister the truth?"

"I don't want her to know what I've done."

"I'm more worried that she's going to be inspired rather than horrified," Olivia murmured.

She gazed at the rocks Sophie had pointed out on their first visit. She had stared at them every time she came here, hoping to one day build up the nerve to climb them. Now probably wasn't the time to try.

Aidan sank down on a fallen log. "It's not like I don't already have enough on my plate. Pravit's left me instructions on how to intercept memos to Jacob Wilcox, but I don't know how to help from here. Both our simulations are on the run. I think they're trying to get to Valentina's house in Eidolon, which means there's nothing I can do until they reach her. And I can't make sense of Pravit's dossier. I don't know why he was waiting until the new year. I would go public now, but I don't have an official identity, so anything coming from me has no weight–"

"I'll do it," Olivia said. "Just tell me what to click."

Kass sat next to Aidan. "I'll take a squiz at those documents. Follow the money, is usually the answer."

"Kass'll figure out what to do," Olivia said.

"I hope so." Aidan dropped his forehead into his palm. "Look, I know it's not a priority, but Pravit's been declared missing. Equinoxx have done something with his body. He died protecting us, here and in Eidolon. I want him found. His family deserve closure."

"How can we find him?" Olivia said. "Besides calling the police, I don't see a way for us getting anywhere near Equinoxx."

There was a silence. Then Kass groaned. "Well, fuck. I might know a way in."

To: jacobpwilcox@equinoxxtechnology.co
From: lakebroadsideprivateinvestigations@lakebroadside.
com
Subject: Reef Davidson

Dear Mr Wilcox,
Forrest Davidson claims he has unfinished business with
Reef (who, according to him, is living under the name AIDAN
SMITH) but will be in contact with us again shortly. Please
wait for an update.

Current invoice is attached.

Regards,
Steven Saulsbury
Lake Broadside Private Investigators

43

Briony wrenched masking tape over the box more violently than necessary. There was still so much to pack and the house was already full of boxes. Maybe she should just toss everything. Eliminate it all and start from scratch.

She took another swig of beer. It had already started to go warm. The air had become heavy with humidity. She'd been in Perth enough years to become accustomed to a hot December. She liked it. Barbecue Christmases, sweltering New Year's Eves, days of sun and beach.

She liked the rain in Perth, too. None of that day-long drizzle stuff. No, the thunderstorms that rolled through in winter brought massive downpours that battered the roof and flooded the streets, then were gone five minutes later. It was cleansing.

She could use a cleansing thunderstorm right about now. But all the weather gave her was heat.

Someone knocked at the front door. She checked her phone. It was past nine. Either this was Mr bloody Wilcox coming to hammer another nail in her coffin or it was immigration. Neither option seemed appealing. She gulped at her beer and stared at the door, willing the person to go away.

They knocked again.

"Bri?"

Holy shit. It couldn't be.

A funny sound fell past Briony's lips. She set the beer down on a taped-up box and headed for the door.

She hadn't imagined the voice. It was really Kass on the other side.

"Sup," Kass said.

Briony stared at her blankly.

"This is where you say hey," Kass said.

"Where I…?" Briony trailed off. "What the *fuck*? Kass, what the actual fuck? You dump me out of nowhere, disappear, and show up two months later with a cheery 'Sup?'"

"Sure."

"Your phone was switched off. You weren't at home. Your family suddenly stopped talking to me–"

"Can I come in?" Kass pushed past Briony without waiting for an answer. She stopped in the living room when she saw the boxes. "You moving?"

"No shit. I didn't get your signature and my firm fired me. No job, no working visa. Back home to dear mummy." Briony slammed the front door and stalked after her.

Kass turned, and there was a moment when they just looked at each other, with Briony's vision focused on those three adorable freckles on Kass' nose —

Then Kass gave a wry half-smile. "Cute," she said. "The little rant. You're a helluva actor, ay."

"Actor? There's no acting."

"So Equinoxx didn't hire you to get close to me for Liv's signature?"

Briony's jaw dropped.

"Yeah, I know about that," Kass said. "I probs don't know everything, but I've got enough to know that you're a lying sack of shit."

Briony drew in a sharp, pained breath. "How did you…?"

"I have my ways. You weren't the only liar in this relationship, angelcakes." Kass perched on a pile of boxes. "You really got fired?"

"Yeah."

"Then you're no use to me."

An unwelcome tear dropped down Briony's cheek. She hastily swiped it away. She'd never seen Kass this kind of angry before; that slow-burning rage. Usually when Kass was revved up, she'd rant and pace and threaten violence in all kinds of creative ways.

"I really did love you."

There was the slightest flinch from Kass before she said, "Doesn't matter. Not unless I can use it against you now."

More tears slipped down Briony's cheeks. She hated feeling so vulnerable and weak. But this was her fault, all of it. She lowered her head. "If there's anything I can do…"

"Yeah, actually. I need you to get inside Equinoxx."

"What? Why?"

"A guy kicked it in the hub. Pravit Arya. Equinoxx is hiding the body, and you're gonna find out where."

Briony opened her mouth. Closed it. "Equinoxx would never do anything like that."

"I reckon if they're selling children for human testing, they'd sure as hell stash a corpse."

"If they're what?"

"C'mon," Kass said, with that awful, twisted smile. "You can't try that on."

"They're not selling children. They wouldn't. They're Equinoxx."

"Right, except they have the whole 'it's only a simulation' thing going for them."

"Simu…" Briony trailed off. "That's what the anomaly was. That's why they were trying to get Olivia's signature."

"No shit. What did you think it was for?"

"I don't know," Briony said, snatching her beer. "A castle? A waterfall in South America? I thought Olivia had mapped in some cool thing they were going to sell as a VR experience."

"You think Equinoxx paid you a shit ton of money to get a signature for a waterfall?"

"They're worried that any legal gray area will shut them down. They're keeping as strictly to the wording of the contracts as possible. If they get caught up in legal battles, they'll run out of time to prove their energy solutions work."

"You're not gonna get more of a gray area than a child that doesn't know she's a simulation."

"Say again?"

"Oh shit, you really don't know anything." Kass laughed, but it was a cruel laugh.

"I was the lowest dip in the lowest tier," she said. "Wilcox only told me what I needed to know. My job was to get a signature from Olivia without highlighting the fact she'd mapped in an anomaly." She hesitated. "And then to get a signature of reprogramming consent from you."

They looked at each other. Briony's chest felt like it was going to burst. "I'm scum," she said.

"Yeah, you are."

A painful pulse thrummed in Briony's skull. "I'm sorry." She massaged her forehead. "What's this you're saying about children who don't know they're simulations?"

Kass told her about levels of citizenship in Eidolon. About Olivia's daughter Bobbi. About how Equinoxx was selling children to pharmaceutical companies. Then she explained the real-life stuff, about a hitman, and Pravit Arya's death.

The beer wasn't sitting well in Briony's stomach. She sank to the floor, her back against the couch.

"I believed in them," she whispered. "They were going to save the world."

"Let me see the consent form again."

Briony's gaze snapped up. Kass had wandered while she talked, but she was back perched on the boxes, her face set with grim determination.

"Why?" Briony said.

"Because we'll be making a few amendments for you to negotiate with Equinoxx."

"You want to negotiate?"

"Hell no. But it'll get you back inside the hub."

"To do what?"

"We have a job for you, and it's a big one. You want to make it up to me? Find Pravit Arya's body."

To: jacobpwilcox@equinoxxtechnology.co
From: lakebroadsideprivateinvestigations@lakebroadside.
com
Subject: Reef Davidson

Dear Mr Wilcox,
Forrest Davidson has been in touch. We have an address for
AIDAN SMITH.

Current invoice is attached.

Regards,
Steven Saulsbury
Lake Broadside Private Investigators

EIDOLON

44

Even though it was four in the morning, the porch lights were on at the second safe house. Liv rolled the Land Cruiser to a stop at the end of the long driveway. A Hilux was parked in the patio. *Her* Hilux. But she'd left it at the charging station, at the mercy of the Equinoxx visitors.

"Whadya reckon?" Kazzy said. "Ambush or...?"

The front door opened. Reef stepped out.

"Oh my god." Liv unbuckled her seatbelt. "Oh my god, oh my god."

She stumbled out of the car and ran for him. He sprinted down the steps, meeting her halfway, colliding, hugging, kissing.

"Bobbi...?"

"She's fine. Safe." Reef's mouth journeyed across her jawline. "We got here about an hour ago."

She relished in the feel of him, still warm and alive and here.

"How did you get the car back?" Kazzy said.

Reef released Liv to hug her too. "Packed a go bag. When I

switched on my phone to check my messages, I prepped for Equinoxx."

"Without the gun?"

"I improvised." Reef looked between them. "What about you? What took you so long?"

"I knew the address, but I didn't know how to get here," Liv said. "We had to break into a few places before we found a road map. And we were traveling by night because they were looking out for our car."

Reef's questioning gaze fell on the Land Cruiser.

"Ran out of fuel, ditched the Monaro," Kazzy said. "Saddest fucking day of my life. My bro's going to straight up murder me."

Liv gazed at the cottage. "Are we safe here?"

"For now." Reef took her hand and gestured for Kazzy. "Come on."

Kazzy smiled, and the three of them headed inside.

OUTSIDE

To: jacobpwilcox@equinoxxtechnology.co
From: retrievalunit@basenxj451.com
Subject: Retrieval update

Address has been received. Will send retrieval
team to check it now.

45

The rain started overnight. It fell in bursts and gushes, flooding the city with persistent ferocity. Olivia woke to the whoosh and lay in bed, listening. It was warm beneath the covers, the light muted, the glow of the kitchen lamp haloing the door. When she finally rose, she padded to the shower and dressed before heading out to breakfast. Her hair was a tangle of knots. It was impossible to maintain it without the right products.

Valentina was reading a cookbook at the kitchen table. The windows were open to let in the fresh air.

"Morning," Olivia said. "Is Kass back?"

"She's still asleep in my room," Valentina said, looking over the top of her spectacles. "She was home late last night."

"Do you know if she had any luck with Briony?"

Valentina shook her head. Olivia picked up the kitchen scissors. She examined the blades, thoughtful. Her once-soft tresses were now ratty. It felt like she spent twenty minutes each day fighting a losing battle. How desperate was she to get rid of the knots? Enough to completely ruin her hair?

No, it was more than that. She thought of Liv in Eidolon – tank top, shorts, tufty ponytail. How easy it must be to live like that.

Olivia hacked at a fistful of hair before she had properly decided. It fell away from her head so easily. One second it was attached, a part of her. The next, it was a bundle to be tossed away.

"Oh," said Valentina. "Do you think you should buy some proper scissors for that?"

Olivia snipped another lock. And another. "No. I think I need to do this right now."

Her hair was starting to feel like clothes that were too tight, needing to be shed. With each snip she breathed easier.

It took a long time. There was so much of it – length that represented years of her life. They ended up on the floor around her feet. When at last she was done, each turn of her head was light and fresh.

"I'll bet that feels better," Valentina said.

"Much." Olivia scooped up the fallen hair and disposed of it. She ran her fingers through what remained, delighting in how quickly she found the ragged tips. It didn't matter that the job wasn't done properly. It was done, and that was a huge start.

"Wait until the others see. Kass will approve. Sophie won't. And where's–" Olivia cut off as the front door opened. Aidan stamped his muddy boots on the doormat before stepping in. He had the scrap bucket for the chickens. His hair and hooded jacket were drenched.

"Hey," he said, then stopped to stare at her.

Olivia's heart sputtered unexpectedly under his gaze. "Hi." She turned her head side to side. "Is it as bad as I think?"

He moved past her and set the eggs from the scrap bucket on the counter. "Not bad," he said carefully.

Olivia laughed, finding herself strangely nervous. She hadn't expected Aidan's opinion to have as much weight as this.

He turned, something new in his expression. "You look like Liv. Eidolon Liv."

"Is that...good?"

"Is it good that you think I look like Eidolon Reef?"

She bit her lip as that same teenager hormone from before surged through her. Yes, it was good. Not just the aesthetics, but the meaning behind them. Their Eidolon selves were together. They were friends, partners, lovers. Intimacy would be as natural to Liv and Reef as breathing. They got to succumb to desires whenever they wanted, no baggage, no anxiety. Just pure, unhindered passion.

Olivia wondered if it could ever be like that between her and Aidan. The way he was looking at her now, she liked to imagine the possibility was high.

"Can I make you breakfast?" he said, breaking the hot wave building inside her.

It took a moment to find her voice. "Sure. Thanks."

"Tea?"

"Okay."

He hesitated before turning to Valentina. "Tea, Val?"

Rather than answer, she licked her finger and turned the page of her cookbook.

"Val's not talking to me," he said to Olivia.

"Why not?"

"Because I'm weak."

"What do you mean?"

He filled up the kettle. "Just because she won't let me have alcohol in the house, doesn't mean the addiction's gone."

"You drank last night?"

"I need it to sleep."

"But we finished your vodka. There's nothing else in the house except…" She trailed off. "Oh no. The stuff Val uses for cleaning?"

He winced.

"You must've been desperate, to drink that rubbish." It was a joke, but he didn't smile. She touched his arm. "It's okay, Aidan. One step at a time, all right? We'll find you some help."

She didn't want to move away. In fact, she very much wanted to move forward, to reach up and kiss him. Despite the raindrops, his body radiated heat. It flooded into her, and again, she felt a rush.

A door opened from down the hallway and Kass finally shuffled out in the clothes she was wearing the night before. "Got any beer?"

"Kass," Olivia said, moving away from Aidan. "How did yesterday go with Briony? Did you convince her to help us?"

"Sure did." Kass opened the fridge and squinted in disappointment at the contents.

"You think we can trust her?" Aidan said.

"She knew bugger all. Was pretty devo to hear what Equinox are doing. Where's the booze in this house?"

"Non-existent," Olivia said firmly.

Kass made a sound of exasperation and shut the fridge.

"Is she going to be able to get into the hub?" Aidan said.

"Yup, she'll be heading in this morning. And if you wanted to know why Pravit was waiting until the new year, I figured it out. The pharmies are transferring the money by January. Pravit was holding out because he still wanted Equinoxx to be rich, I guess." She tsked. "I get that he ultimately believed in the company, but come on. It's better that they go under, amirite?"

"I suppose," Olivia said, but she had to wonder. Equinoxx were doing terrible things, and incredible things. She didn't want to see them fail to clean up the world, but at the same time…they'd sent a freaking assassin after her.

Aidan's phone rang before they could debate the ethics behind Pravit's choice. When he saw the caller ID, he tensed.

"Your dad?" Olivia guessed.

"Worse," he said, and walked towards the hallway to answer it.

Kass opened and closed cupboards now, probably searching for coffee. She was going to be disappointed again.

"What do you mean?"

Valentina looked up from her cookbook. Aidan had stilled in his spot. For a moment, there was no sound but the downpour outside. Then he rushed down the hallway. Olivia hurried after him as he threw open Sophie's door.

Sophie wasn't there.

"Where is she?" Olivia said.

"Call him," Aidan said to the person on the other end of the phone. "Tell him to turn around and take her back." To Olivia, Aidan said, "Forrest picked up Sophie this morning."

"What? Why?"

"I don't know, I don't – Indigo, no. I don't care what you say. We both gave up everything to get Sophie here in the first place. Don't be a coward on me now."

Val and Kass were standing by the hallway. Kass gave Olivia a puzzled look, but Val's expression was somber.

Aidan said nothing. He was listening hard to this Indigo, who Olivia suspected was Sophie's mother. The more Indigo spoke, the more unwell he looked.

"Okay," he said at last, much quieter, more subdued. "Thanks. I guess."

He hung up and turned to them.

"What?" Olivia said.

"It's over, isn't it?" Val said.

Olivia exchanged a glance with Kass. What the hell did that mean?

But Aidan seemed to understand, because he nodded slowly. "Forrest has screwed us all. We have to get out of here. Now."

To: jacobpwilcox@equinoxxtechnology.co
From: retrievalunit@basenxj451.com
Subject: Retrieval update

LEVEL FIVE CITIZEN (AUSTRALIAN POINT) SUCCESSFULLY
RETRIEVED

46

Sophie returned to Symbiosis a hero that morning. She rode into the muddy community square with her dad, their bikes pulling up to applause. There were at least thirty people milling about. Some of them she vaguely recognized. Some were new.

It was unnerving, being the center of attention. She was used to staying hidden, unnoticed. Even shopping with Val, she kept her head down, making herself small.

She received claps on the back, hugs, and handshakes. There were many comments on how much she'd grown. Her dad wrapped an arm around her shoulders and led her through, laughing. "All right, all right, let the poor girl breathe. Sweetpea, you doing dinner tonight?"

"Sure am," said Sweetpea from the porch of one of the houses. "Baked potatoes with goat's cheese and kidney beans was the order, right?"

Sophie's dad squeezed her tighter. "Your favorite."

"That was my favorite when I was twelve," Sophie said, laughing. "My tastes have changed, you know."

A strange expression crossed her dad's face, but she was already pulling free from him. She'd glimpsed the one person she'd been looking forward to seeing for a long time now.

"Wattle!"

It was a funny thing, puberty. She remembered him being short and skinny and fair. He was taller than her now, and he'd filled out. There was hair on his shirtless chest, fuzz on his upper lip. The only way she really recognized him was from the gap between his front teeth when he grinned.

"Hey, Joey." It had been years since anyone had called her that. He picked her up and swung her around with an ease that left her slightly breathless. "Long time, no see."

"The man of the hour," Sophie's dad said, joining them. His smile was back, broader than ever. "You little ripper. You saved our family, young man." To the crowd that was still hanging about in the drizzle, he said, "Wattle stumbled across Joey's YouTube channel in January. It's because of his patient communications with my daughter throughout the year that she realized she was being led astray. But now she's home, safe and sound again."

Another smattering of applause, this one slightly confused. Sophie wondered if they knew where she'd been all this time, and why she'd left in the first place.

She and Wattle had been besties before Aidan had taken her away. When Wattle had sent her a message after seeing her videos, it had only taken them a week of chatting before she'd relented and given him her address. He hadn't come for her, though. She'd hoped he'd sneak in and they could see each other in person. But he said he respected her privacy and would only see her again when she was ready to come home.

Instead they'd talked. A lot. He told her how much he missed her. There were hints that maybe there was something more than friendship between them, but it had been harder to message once Olivia had moved in. It felt like she was always in the way.

Not anymore.

"Joey?"

Sophie turned from Wattle to find her mum heading over from the main farmstead. Her hair had gone gray in the past five years, her cheeks sallow, her eyes lined. Sophie's next breath hurt. How much precious time had she missed?

Her mum stopped before her. "My girl," she said. "Look how you've grown."

And while Sophie had probably heard the sentiment, like,

twenty times in the past three minutes, it held weight when her mother said it.

They embraced. Her mum's body was bony and sharp. Sophie could feel her trembling. She smelled of lavender, like she always had.

"My girl. My little girl. I've missed you so much."

Sophie blinked back tears. "I missed you too."

But then her mum whispered, so low Sophie almost didn't hear it, "Why did you come back?"

"Now, aren't you blown away, Indi?" her dad said. He wrapped his arms around both of them. "I told you I'd bring her home. Forrest Davidson always keeps his word."

"Thank you, my love."

There was only warmth and joy in Indigo's voice as she pulled away from the hug. But now Sophie was looking closer, she could see the fear in her mother's eyes.

47

The shed's generator switched on and the lights flickered to life. Aidan fired up the computers.

They had driven all three cars in a funeral-like procession and trekked with their bags through the mud and rain to get inside. Olivia hadn't had breakfast. Valentina had scratches on her neck from the bush. But it was Aidan who appeared to struggle the most. Every action seemed to be laborious. Olivia wondered how he was handling Sophie's abandonment on top of what they had to do now.

While inputting coordinates for Valentina's house, he said quietly, "'I don't think I can face what's waiting for us."

Olivia released a shaky breath. "Me neither."

It had been a potentially fatal mistake. With Liv and Reef staying at Val's house in Eidolon, it meant that if one was caught, they were all caught. They should've planned better, should've factored in the opportunistic vengefulness of Aidan's father...

"I'll go in," Kass said.

"Are you sure?" Olivia said.

"Let me be useful. Besides, I want to see this other world for myself."

Aidan grimaced. "I'm afraid you might not like what you find."

"I can handle it."

Kass sat on the throne and Olivia set the crown on her head. Kass gave her what was perhaps supposed to be a reassuring smile, but it was small. Aidan switched on the NTD. The monitor flared to life.

It was sunny in Eidolon. Light streamed through the windows of a house that looked roughly like where they'd been staying, but not quite. It were as if someone had tried to design it based on what they'd seen years ago…which was probably exactly what had happened. Aidan was surely Equinoxx's only volunteer who could've mapped Valentina's house into the program.

"Holy…"

Through Kass' eyes, they watched a scan of the surroundings, taking in overturned chairs and smashed lamps, a broken window, blood on the corner of a wall.

Olivia thought Kass' astonishment had come from the scene, but Kass didn't take a closer look at the devastation. Instead, she held her hands to her face, stroked the dining table, picked up a tin of tea leaves to smell. She was experiencing the mindscape.

"I'm…here," Kass said breathily. "It's like I'm *here*." She crumbled the tea leaves between her fingertips. "I'm tripping balls. How did they do this?"

"Come on, Kass," Aidan muttered.

"Give her a minute," Olivia said.

"What the hell?" said a voice out of sight.

Kass turned to find the other version of herself. Kazzy was standing in the threshold of the kitchen, clutching a small, stuffed pig. There were red splotches on her cheeks and her eyes were puffy.

"No way," Kass said. She inched closer, but Kazzy backed away.

"Kassandra?" said a familiar voice, and from the corner of the monitor stood a version of Valentina.

In the shed, Valentina moved closer to the screen for a better view.

Eidolon's Valentina was still missing a hand, but her face was slightly thinner, her eyes a touch closer together, her skin browner than the outside Valentina.

"I forgot I wore my hair like that," Valentina said, eyeing the severe bun on top of her simulation's head.

"It's how I always remembered you," Aidan said. "Even when

I first saw you in the ship, starving and beaten, you had your hair up."

It occurred to Olivia that even after all this time, she had no idea how the two knew each other.

From inside the program, Kazzy said, "You're too late. They took her. They took Bobbi."

Her voice broke and she squeezed the pig to her chest.

Kass was quiet for a moment. "And the others? Livvie?"

"Gone," E-Valentina said. "Riot police came for them after dawn. They put up a fight, but were overcome, it seems."

Olivia reached out and Aidan grabbed her arm, steadying her. She could feel his tremors through the contact.

"Overcome how?" Kass said. "The riot police took them? Or are they...?"

"I have no idea. Liv and Reef told us to wait in the shed when they saw the vans pull up. After everything fell silent, we came out to..." She waved an arm over the mess. And the blood.

"Maybe they're okay," Kass said. "If there aren't any bodies—"

"I imagine Equinoxx wants to study the brains of level four citizens," E-Valentina said. "Through autopsies and such."

Kazzy shook visibly. She'd curled her body over the pig as if it were the last thing she had to protect.

"Where'd they take Bobbi?" Kass said.

"I don't know. Maybe the hub up north."

"We can get in there, ay. Even if the whistleblowing doesn't go to plan, we can pop in and get Bobbi back for you."

"A life on the run isn't easy," E-Valentina warned.

"S'better than being locked up for experiments."

"It won't last," Kazzy said. "They'll find us. They'll hunt us down. This world is theirs."

"We're just game pieces to them," E-Valentina said. "We'll never be free."

Olivia straightened from Aidan's hold. "Extract her."

Aidan returned to the computer and ended the program. The monitor went black. From the throne, Kass opened her eyes, blinking several times. She sucked in a breath as if returning from underwater.

"Fuckin' hell," she said. "That place…I don't know what it is, but it's not a computer program. And those people…" Her gaze fell on Aidan and Olivia, and Olivia realized she wasn't blinking rapidly from the change in scenery – she was tearing up. "I'm so sorry, ay. This sucks."

"We're going to end it," Olivia said.

Everyone looked at her.

"Even if the whistleblowing doesn't work, I know how we can stop Equinoxx from getting into Eidolon."

"How?" Kass said.

Olivia turned to Aidan. "We're going to blow up the transmission tower."

48

The couch seemed to be made of moss, but it didn't leave any stains on Briony's skirt. She ran her fingers along the softness and wondered how Nera Blake had done it this time.

Despite the rain and gloom outside, the lobby was bustling with workers. Briony had caught a StarShine bus from the city early in the morning. She hadn't had a good night's sleep. Somehow, by tomorrow, she had to infiltrate this place and find where they'd hidden a bloody body.

What if they'd just buried him outside somewhere in their acres and acres of property? What was Briony supposed to do then?

And would Kass ever forgive her if she didn't come through?

The receptionist, a redhead with eyeliner whose name Briony hadn't caught, was registering her details into the system. While he was busy, she eyed the elevators with their handprint security and large NO ACCESS signs. "What are on the other floors?"

"The laboratories are on the lower levels, and the top floor is closed for renovations. That's why there are so many extra staff down here today. It's not normally so busy, but we're all sharing space at the moment." The receptionist sounded cranky as he said it.

"That sucks," Briony said, and, hoping she sounded sympathetic rather than prying, added, "How long has that been going on?"

"Only a couple of days. Handprint here, please."

Briony stood and placed her hand on the touchscreen. Renovations sounded like a promising cover up to hide a body, right?

"Ms McKinney." Mr Wilcox came out of an elevator and strode towards her with a rare smile. "What a pleasant surprise. What can we do for you?"

"Good morning, Mr Wilcox."

"Jacob, please."

Jacob? Why was he in such a good mood?

He addressed the receptionist. "Killian, please make sure our guest has quenched her thirst. What would you like, Ms McKinney?"

"Nothing, please. I'm only here to speak to you about that contract."

"Why didn't you go through your firm?"

"I'm no longer working for them. I thought I'd come straight to you, since I have an amended version of that contract for you to look at." She held out her StarShine tablet.

He didn't take it. "I'm afraid you've come all this way for nothing. That signature is no longer required."

"Oh." Briony's chest tightened. What did *that* mean? "Are you sure...?"

"I'm sorry you wasted your time."

When he turned to leave, Briony said, "Is Nera Blake here?"

There was a beat of hesitation before he answered. "She's unwell, unfortunately. It was lovely to see you again, Ms McKinney."

He left, looking less cheerful than when he'd arrived. Briony steadied her breath. She would call Kass to find out what was going on as soon as she had the chance. First, though...

She turned and smiled sweetly at Killian. "May I use your bathroom?"

49

Olivia waited on a large rock. It was quiet save for the pattering of rain on the forest floor. Somewhere nearby, a magpie caroled.

A collection of boulders sloped behind her. Once upon a time, she would've been climbing those boulders just for the hell of it.

Her fingers returned to pluck at her short tufts of hair. She had dressed in cargo pants and a tank top today, which meant the tattoo of the infinity sign on her shoulder blade was visible. Kass had a matching one, done in Bali on a whim in their twenties. Olivia felt closer to being Liv than she had in a long time.

To think Liv and Reef might be dead. To think her other self had gone so far, found her strength again, only to be brutally cut down.

Boot steps squelched on the leaf litter, and she turned to find Aidan heading towards her. The backpack that had contained her emergency cash looked fuller now. Heavier. Her tension eased, at least until she saw his expression.

"What's wrong?"

"We don't have enough."

"What do you mean?"

"They couldn't pull what we needed together on such short notice." He patted the backpack. "This won't be enough for the base of the tower."

"So we can't do it?"

"It's going to be trickier than we'd hoped. There's not enough explosives to take down the *base* of the tower, but I can climb up and attach them to the antenna itself."

"It'll be slippery. And dangerous."

"I've worked on boats before."

"Yes, but it's much higher than a boat." Olivia chewed her lip. "If I hooked you up with a parachute, would you take it? Can you work a chute?"

"I've done jumps before. But is the tower even high enough for a chute to open?"

"I think so. A BASE chute, anyway. The tower's maybe a hundred and fifty feet?"

Aidan whistled and sat on the rock beside her. He set the backpack down, covering it with his jacket to protect it from the rain.

There was no sign of his contacts – or rather, Forrest's contacts. Whoever they were, they were quiet, and professional. This area was far from any official bushwalking trails. Near impossible to find. Easy to lose.

"We'll drop by the shed before we head up to Equinoxx," Aidan said. "It'll be dark in a couple of hours. Where are you getting this parachute from?"

"My old work. Aussie Adventures, on the way to Equinoxx."

"You used to work at an adventure place?"

"I would take people on tandem skydiving jumps. It feels like a lifetime ago." She curled her fingers in her lap. "Liv told me she'd been skydiving again. I can't even imagine how she got over her fear…"

She trailed off. She hadn't meant to bring up her simulated self.

When Aidan spoke again, his voice was rougher than usual. "Our biggest problem if we blow up the tower is that when Equinoxx is taken to court, we won't be able to prove the people in Eidolon are more than just coding. If judges and juries could meet the citizens for themselves, or if Pravit were still around to testify…"

Olivia's throat tightened. There had been too many sacrifices thanks to what Equinoxx had done. And if anything happened to Aidan on that tower…

Aidan must've sensed her rising panic. He tucked a newly shortened strand of her hair behind her ear and said, "Sometimes our risks are going to pay off, sometimes they won't. I've taken them too. It was a huge risk going to Val at first. That could've ended up being disastrous. I asked a lot of her, keeping me and Sophie hidden for all these years."

"How do you and Val know each other, anyway?"

Olivia wasn't sure whether he would answer – he still seemed to have a lot of secrets – but he surprised her.

"My team were chasing a whaling boat when we got a distress call. There was a vessel further north trafficking young girls. Val led a team for a private organization called Red Tooth that hunted human traffickers across parts of Asia, but they'd gotten caught. We boarded the ship, stopped the traffickers from killing her, and got the girls home safely. It's how she lost her hand – they'd already started torturing her when we arrived."

"Holy crap."

"She took me in because she said she owed me her life, but I've stepped too far."

"I can't believe…" Olivia thought of small Valentina. Stern, capable, quiet. Imagining her fighting on the high seas seemed impossible. She shook her head. "Every time I hear something new about you, I'm more in awe."

"Back at you." He smiled at her. "But, like you, it feels like another lifetime. Another person."

"Tell me more," she said. "Tell me everything."

And he did. He answered all her questions, no hesitations, no vague responses. She heard about his past activism, which had been focused on human and animal rights rather than climate change. He told her about his brief homelessness after running away from his grandparents.

They both knew they should be getting back, but out here, away from it all, it felt easier. Olivia wondered if Aidan was putting off the inevitable – returning to the shed to find Sophie still gone. To look at the throne and know they may have lost their other selves forever. There had been so many blows today.

It was only when they finally got up to leave that she looked again at the rocky slope behind them.

"I want to see," she said.

"See what?"

"I used to walk across fifty-foot clifftops without fear. I used to *jump* from them. Now even the thought of being up there terrifies me. What is it, twenty feet?" Taller than the jump at the back of Valentina's property. Nowhere near as tall as what she'd faced before.

Matt would've told her how slippery it was, warned her not to try. Parental, she remembered, fresh fury billowing in her chest.

She started for the rocks.

"Do you want me to come with you?" Aidan said.

"No. I can do it."

She started up the lowest boulder. It wasn't too steep, though rain made rivulets down the crevices. Her boots kept their grip. Looking down wasn't an option – at least, not until she got to the top. Instead, she kept her attention on her next step.

About halfway through, before a wide gap between rocks, she lost her nerve. Her feet stalled. Her gaze fell unwillingly downwards.

"Oh no."

"Olivia?"

"I want to get to the end. I do, but…" A groan. "I'm so tired of being afraid."

"One step at a time," Aidan said, echoing the words she'd said to him just this morning about his drinking. "For Liv. For Bobbi."

She thought of that little girl dressed in her pink swimsuit. Of her other self, sitting on the floor with her arms outstretched, patiently waiting while her daughter screamed. Of Reef cooking synthesized beef from a can, a tea towel thrown over his shoulder.

Equinoxx had to stop. Eidolon wasn't theirs anymore.

Olivia inhaled. Clean, fresh air swirled into her lungs. When she exhaled, she imagined expelling her fear in one long, hot breath, like her meditation instructor once taught her.

Then she reached out with a trembling foot, and took another step. And another. Her legs were shaking so hard she was worried she'd fall over. But she kept going. And going.

And suddenly, she was at the top.

"Oh," she said. Her heart hammered, somewhat with panic, but there was a touch of joy in there, too.

The bush spread out below her. It was hard to see far due to the drizzle, but the mist clung to the greenness in a way that reminded her vaguely of Borneo. She and Kass had been forced to sleep in hammocks over there because rain had flooded the jungle, making it impossible to set up tents. But later, clouds rolled across the mountains, thick and grey and cottony, like magic.

She missed traveling.

She moved to head back and…wow, the ground seemed further away than when she last looked. It was far. Really far.

Aidan must've correctly interpreted her hesitation, because he said, "One step at a time."

She searched for the courage she'd found on the way up. She tried to think again of Bobbi, of Reef, of Liv…

But there was nothing to hold onto up here. No railing, no higher rocks. And it was so slippery. What had she been thinking? She wasn't the Liv from Eidolon, or even the Liv from her past. Her legs didn't want to walk – they didn't even want to hold her up anymore.

"Um," she said. "I think I'm freaking out."

Dammit, dammit, dammit. She had done so well on the way up.

She expected Aidan to rescue her, but he didn't move. "Take the first step."

"I can't."

"Yes, you can. Move onto the next rock."

"It's too high."

"Don't focus on the whole journey. Just the next step."

Olivia didn't budge. She couldn't.

"Come on," Aidan said. "You fought off an assassin on your own. You can definitely do this."

A high-pitched laugh escaped her. "I'd take the hit man over this right now."

"I know you can get down on your own, Olivia. I want you to prove it to yourself."

He sounded so certain. How could he still believe in her, when she was acting like such a coward?

She shut her eyes. An image formed in her head, of her safely back on the ground.

Get it done, Livvie!

"Okay," she said, opening her eyes again. She concentrated on where she'd put her foot. She visualized herself doing it. Her boot would be stable, unslipping, and she'd be that much closer to the ground.

She took the step.

Her boot was indeed stable, unslipping.

"Good job," Aidan said. "Keep going."

She took another step. Carefully, balanced. She was still so high up.

"Fuck," she said.

"You're doing great."

"Why is it so hard? The way up, the way down. It's like I have to find my nerve all over again every time."

"It feels like that for me too," Aidan said. She heard the regret in his voice and imagined what it must be like to fight an alcohol addiction. Exhausting. Seemingly endless.

If she could do this, if she could show him it was possible...

Her boot slipped slightly. She stilled. Her breath turned short and sharp. Fuzzy dots appeared in her vision.

She hadn't fallen. She hadn't broken her spine. Her body was upright. She was still standing.

Slowly, even more carefully than before, she took another step. Tentative. Small. But it meant she was a few inches closer to the ground. And it was on this she focused – no matter how tiny the step, she was making progress. It could take her hours, all night even, but she was going to keep moving forward. Step by step by step–

She was so focused on each move, she almost didn't realize she had made it to the ground until her boots hit dirt.

"I did it," she said in surprise.

Aidan grinned. "Of course you did."

The feeling was so exhilarating, she gave a happy little jump. "I did it! I did it!"

"You're amazing, Olivia."

"Amazing? I'm *buzzing*. In your face, pile of rocks!" Giggles bubbled from her. She cupped her mouth, unable to control herself. "I'm so happy, Reef, I–"

His expression changed. She lowered her hands.

"Oh," she said. "I didn't mean to say that. It's just that you look like him, with your beard trimmed and…are you okay?"

He closed the gap between them. Maybe his expression hadn't been pain. When his fingers curled around her hips, she realized it had probably been a long time since anyone had called him by his real name. She wasn't the only one who'd lost herself along the way.

"Reef," she said again, just to let him hear it.

He responded by kissing her. Desire flared. Gone was her fear of him, her fear of risk. It felt as if she had been waiting for this for eternity. Every kiss was like a pulse of fire, and when his mouth found her neck, she melted against him.

The ache became unbearable. She peeled off her top, unbuckled his pants.

Outdoors? she'd asked Liv that day on the beach. *Really?*

At the time, adventurous sex had felt like a thing of her youth. But she couldn't wait any longer, and when she thought of what Liv had said – *You're missing out, you know. Especially on the sex* – she dropped to her knees right there, urgently needing to have him. The sounds he made nearly drove her out of her mind, and when he returned the favor, she came hard and quick.

They lay on the ground, naked and wet, tasting each other in their kisses. The only time he slowed was to admire her tattoos, one by one, before pressing his lips against the inked skin. And then finally, finally, finally, he was inside her. He moved as if he knew exactly which spots to hit – she had to bite his shoulder to keep from crying out. When she found herself straddling him, she rediscovered another part she'd thought lost. Her fantasies had always consisted of him on top; she'd forgotten the joy of taking control, which he gave to her willingly.

She'd also forgotten the box of condoms, so far away, tucked in a house to which they couldn't yet return. It was only when his fingernails dug into her hips and he gasped, "Can I–?" that she realized what this moment could mean.

The timing wasn't right, and the chances weren't high, but she still felt she had to say, "Yes – but only if you want – the possibility–"

Her words seemed to stir him more, and those final moments, as he reached his climax, she imagined that perhaps they were both thinking of the same result.

The same possibility.

50

Olivia and Aidan returned to the shed. Aidan took Olivia's hand as they trekked through the wet bush. They left the explosives in the car.

Valentina and Kass had been shopping while they were gone. They were setting up the bedding and gas cooker when Olivia and Aidan walked in.

"We have what we need," Aidan said. "More or less. Kass, see if you can get into Eidolon and take Bobbi out of the hub so the other Kass can take her away. Maybe go to the other Kass first and arrange a meeting point? Valentina can be your anchor – why are there five sleeping bags?"

Kass busied herself at the computers. Valentina, connecting the gas pipe to the cooker, said casually, "Just in case Sophie decides to come back."

Aidan released Olivia's hand. "Oh."

Any joy she had seen in him since their time in the forest drained away. He sank onto the throne.

"I'm sure she'll be okay," Kass said. "He's still her dad, right?"

A breathy, bitter laugh convulsed across his chest. "She has no idea what he's capable of. Why would she? I never told her."

Olivia thought again of his story – of how Forrest had smothered him and let his mother die. She couldn't begin to imagine what Aidan was feeling. All that time and effort and pain and sacrifice to keep Sophie safe from her father, and she'd still ended up back there.

"I thought she trusted me," he said. He leaned forward, elbows on knees, his fingers laced together as if in prayer. "I know I haven't been the best recently, but before that…I took care of her. Didn't I?" His gaze fell pleadingly to Valentina.

"She was very happy," Valentina said, then added, "Until this year."

A helpless sound escaped him and he dropped his forehead to his knuckles.

Olivia edged towards him. "Aidan…"

"I fucked up."

"You did your best in the circumstances."

"I should've done better. I should've talked to her. I should've stopped drinking–"

"You can't be so hard on yourself."

Aidan stared at the floor. "What if he kills her?"

"Who's killing what now?" Kass said in alarm.

"He's not going to kill her," Valentina said firmly. "If he's gotten into her ear, it means he's worked hard to get her back. She's a commodity to him; someone useful to his cause."

"You think he's not furious she left? That she spent the last five years with me? She doesn't know what sets him off. She'll run her mouth – you know what she's like."

"But she'll run her mouth on the right things. She agrees with all his stances on environmental issues, no matter how twisted they are."

Aidan was shaking his head. "She's going to say something wrong. She'll hit one of his triggers, he'll remember that she slipped from his control, and then he'll get angry."

Olivia could see where his thoughts were going. He was no longer inscrutable, impenetrable. When he stood and turned to her, she'd already anticipated what he was going to say. "I have to go."

"Aidan."

"I can't do nothing. I have to talk to her."

"Aidan–"

"If you must go, wait until tomorrow," Valentina said. "You have work to do tonight."

"I can't risk leaving her with him for that long. I shouldn't have waited so long in the first place."

"Can't you pick her up and go to Equinoxx after?" Kass said.

"It's hours of driving in the opposite direction to Equinoxx," Valentina said.

"You don't have a huge window," Kass said to Aidan. "All eyes will be on Equinoxx as soon as we release the files. Hell, Bri's in there now trying to find a body. You think you're gonna be able to sneak in and blow shit up with coppers swarming the place? It's now or never."

"You want to keep Bobbi safe, don't you?" Valentina said.

"Obviously, but…" Aidan turned to Olivia, his brow creased. "You were the one who told me my family is here, with Sophie and Val. I can't just leave Sophie–"

"Reef," Olivia said, and finally, Aidan stopped. She drew a breath. "I'll do it."

"You'll do what?"

"I'll plant the explosives."

Aidan stared at her blankly.

"I'll sneak onto the property and climb the tower." Already, bile rose in her throat at the thought. "As long as you teach me how to set the timer."

"You–" Aidan stopped and tried again. "You said the tower was a hundred and fifty feet."

"I know."

"You barely made a twenty-foot climb today."

"I know."

"I'll go," Kass said.

"No," Olivia said. "You need to be here, where you can make Pravit's dossier public as soon as the transactions go through. And you have to help get Bobbi out of the hub. Valentina can be your anchor."

Aidan stepped to her, lowering his voice. "Are you sure about this?"

Olivia wasn't sure about anything anymore.

But she smiled and turned to Kass, saying, "We gonna live forever, Kass?"

Kass gave a strained smile in return. "We gonna live forever, Livvie."

"Right then," Olivia said. "I guess that settles it."

Eidolon

51

It had been hours and hours since Liv had seen anyone but Doctor Nowak. As well as being a citizen of Eidolon, he was also an expert in his field, which was the only reason she hadn't attacked him. She was relying on the good doctor to keep Reef alive.

They were locked in a row of empty offices somewhere on Equinoxx property. The windows had been boarded up. Liv had scoured every corner for a letter opener, a pen – hell, a drawing pin would do. But word about her must've travelled, because the folk of Equinoxx had been extra careful to clear the place of potential weapons.

Reef had been placed on a low camping cot in one of the offices, his head bandaged to stem the bleeding. Liv alternated between sitting beside him and prowling the corridors, searching for an escape. The sun went down. Automatic lights switched on. Still, no one came for them.

Liv stood against the wall opposite Reef's cot, chewing her thumbnail and staring at the carpet. Doctor Nowak had said if Reef wasn't awake by nightfall, they would have to transport him to the hospital. That would be her chance to escape…but could she? Could she leave Reef behind?

Equinoxx probably knew she wouldn't. They had only managed to take her alive because of what the soldiers did to Reef. Every time her gaze fell on his bloodied shirt, she heard the crack of his skull hitting the wall. A part of her soul had left her body at that moment. She barely remembered being dragged into the van.

If he died, she would burn this place to the–

"Liv?"

Reef's eyes were open; his face turned towards her.

"Oh my god," she said, diving to her knees beside him. "Oh my god, oh my god." She cupped his bearded cheeks. "Are you okay? Is your head okay?"

"Funny you should ask. It feels like someone hit it with an anvil. Like in the cartoons. But real."

Liv laugh-sobbed and kissed him.

"Where's Bobbi?" he said.

"Somewhere here, I think, in the Equinoxx hub. Reef, we're in trouble. They knew we were at Val's house. Someone must've betrayed us–"

The door opened. "Ah, good, you're awake."

Reef jerked back.

"It's all right," Liv said. "This is Doctor Nowak. He's been keeping an eye on you."

She moved out of the way so the doctor could carry in his equipment and examine Reef. He tested his cognitive memory and movement, which seemed fine. Working. Perfect.

"But he's going to need rest," the doctor said, looking at Liv. "Lots of rest. No trying to barge your way out of here, okay?"

"Doc, you know–"

"Yes, I know. And I feel for you, I do. Your story is…unfair. But if you want Reef to recover safely, you need to take it slow."

"Is he one of us?" Reef said.

Liv nodded. "Level three citizen."

Doctor Nowak pointed down the hallway. "There are showers and toilets that way. Equinoxx have left you a towel and a change of clothes. Don't get your bandages wet."

"Why?" Reef said.

"The wound–"

"No, why did they leave me a change of clothes? Why are we still alive at all?"

Doctor Nowak shrugged. "I imagine level four citizens are rare, and valuable to Equinoxx. Perhaps they're still hoping to find use for you."

They helped Reef to his feet and he made his way unsteadily down the hall.

"Doc," Liv said as soon as he was out of earshot.

"No," Doctor Nowak said.

"You can't even bring me a pen?"

"This is a 100% green workplace. They don't have pens."

"We have to get out of here. I have to find my daughter."

"I understand, but like I told you the last dozen times, I'm not here to get involved. I'm here to help Reef. Be careful. If you push your luck, you might find even your value isn't worth the effort to keep you alive."

"Has Equinoxx reprogrammed you?"

"No. Now. I have something to help ease Reef's pain–" He folded it into Liv's palm as the door opened again, and a man Liv didn't recognize walked into the office.

"Olivia Sharp," he said. "Jacob Wilcox. It's an honor."

Liv ignored his outstretched hand. He dropped it.

"I've heard it's not a good idea to let you get too close, anyway." He looked to Doctor Nowak. "Reef's awake, then?"

Nowak nodded.

"Where's my daughter?" Liv said.

"Safe. That's why I've come to talk to you. I think we've suffered from a grave misunderstanding. Your little girl isn't in the terrible danger you think she is. Neither are you, as a matter of fact. You and Reef are level four citizens, as precious and miraculous as Bobbi. None of our scientists could've predicted the life that's sprung from this program. Because that's what you are. *Life*."

Liv gestured to the spots of blood on the cot. "Is this how you treat life?"

"Perhaps we went about it the wrong way. But I'm here to make it right."

Liv snorted.

"Olivia, I don't think you appreciate the opportunity I'm offering. Your whole family is incredibly valuable to us. You'll be fully compensated – property, stock portfolios, more money than you could ever–"

"Are you listening to yourself? I don't want *money*. You're going to use my child for human testing!"

"Let me finish. I've made it clear how important you all are. We won't let pharmaceutical companies throw whatever they like into Bobbi and the others. There'll be rigorous trials before it even gets to that stage, and even then it'll be vaccines and bone strengthening – things that shouldn't harm them in the long run. Is it so terrible to have a child vaccinated against cancer before the rest of the population gets the same thing?"

Liv caught sight of Doctor Nowak pursing his lips. He wasn't buying Jacob Wilcox's spiel.

"How do I know you won't give Bobbi those diseases in the first place, to see if the cure works?" Liv said.

"You'll have to trust me."

"Er, right. Excuse me if I'm not jumping at that option."

Jacob Wilcox spread his hands helplessly. "We're all making sacrifices. The world – the *real* world – is hurtling towards climate catastrophe. Everyone's babies are in danger if we can't prove we can change our trajectory. We need to harvest data from Eidolon–"

"Let me see her," Liv said.

Jacob Wilcox dropped his hands. "In time, I will. But trust goes both ways, does it not?"

"Not when you lie, batter, and kidnap people. Where is she?"

"On the grounds. In a nursery, being cared for. Pampered, even. She's happy and unhurt. I promise."

Liv had asked for answers, but his words were tearing a hole in her. All day she had tried not to think about what was happening, to concentrate on the task rather than what it meant. But Bobbi had been gone from her protection for sixteen hours, and now Reef was out of the worst danger, her thoughts couldn't help but obsess over torturous ideas.

She was empty, aching without Bobbi. Those little giggles, that endless chatter, the grumpy pout when she first woke up. The smell of her mango shampoo.

She imagined her small voice – *Where's mummy?*

"Let me see her," she said again. This time, her voice cracked.

"Perhaps, if we can come to some sort of arrangement, you'll be able to spend most of your time with her. Does that sound fair to you?"

"You're a liar, a kidnapper, and a thief. None of it sounds fair."

Reef came into the room, freshly cleaned, with new clothes on. He regarded Jacob Wilcox warily.

"Reef Davidson," Jacob said. "Yes, I know your name. Olivia had tried to file a missing persons report for you months ago. The officer that day kept the records, and passed it to us when we got involved." He stroked his chin. "I don't know much else about you, though. Your past is…quite the mystery."

Liv met Reef's eye. "Hold him."

Reef wouldn't have had any idea what her plan was, but he lunged without question, grabbing Jacob's wrists while Liv kicked the fancy suit right in the crotch. He fell to his knees. She unclenched her fist, which still had the needle Doctor Nowak had given her, and jammed it into Jacob Wilcox's neck.

"I don't know what this is," she said, "but I have a feeling you'd better extract yourself."

Jacob wheezed and vanished from Reef's grip.

Liv turned to Doctor Nowak. "Thank you."

"Don't thank me. I shouldn't have done it. I don't know how you think you're getting out of here without anyone stopping you–"

"My plan is to keep fighting until we win."

"Reef's head injury–"

"Isn't a priority," Reef said. "Let's go."

The doctor had access to get them out of the row of offices, but the door didn't lead outside. Instead, it led to more dark corridors, more offices.

"Where are we?" Liv said.

"I can show you the way out, but I don't know where they're keeping your daughter."

An emergency light began to flash, and a blaring siren rang through the facility.

"You make a run for the exit," Liv said to the doctor. "They'll come after us, and hopefully leave you alone."

"Are you sure–"

"Yes, go!"

They watched Doctor Nowak hasten to the left. Liv flexed her fingers, which had started to cramp while she was holding the needle. "He was the proof I needed."

"Proof of what?" Reef said.

"That Equinoxx doesn't own this place, or the people here. They may have created it, but Eidolon is our world now."

Outside

52

Olivia took Kass' car north. The country roads were slick from the rain, red taillights few and far between. Her high beams scoured for roos in the twilight. In her pocket was the burner phone Kass had bought. Beside her lay the backpack, holding enough explosives to blow a hole in the top of the transmission tower.

She breathed, and accelerated to a hundred and ten. The sooner they finished this, the better.

Starfish Steve had left the lights on for her at Aussie Adventures. She pulled up in the car park and climbed out, her body stiff from the journey. The air was heavy and warm.

"Liv-ee-ahhhhh!" The voice boomed like an announcer at a wrestling match, and Starfish Steve sauntered towards her, pointing with both hands. "She. Is. *Back!*"

He'd put on a touch of weight since she'd last seen him a decade ago, and his goatee had become a full, bushy beard, peppered gray against his black skin. Olivia let him pick her up and swing her around. He cackled.

"How you going, girl? Tell me I have my best jumper back."

"It's good to see you, Starfish. How've you been?"

"Ah, you know." He shrugged as if modest, but his grin was broad. "Got a couple of ankle-biters now."

"No! You? A dad? Heaven help us all."

He playfully punched her arm. "Hey now, be nice. How about you? What are you needing a chute for?"

She passed him the cash that had been left over from the explosives transaction. "Does this cover it? I can't promise I'll bring it back, but I'll do what I can."

He was silent as he sifted through the notes.

"I could use some gloves, too. Like climbing gloves, if you've got them. And some rope."

"Livvie." He stared at her in the glow coming from the building. "What's this about?"

"I'm helping a friend."

His brow crinkled.

"Tell you what," she said. "Put me down for a couple of shifts next week. No jumping – I'm nowhere near ready for that. Ground work only. Admin. Rigger. Something like that."

"For real?"

"Yeah. Believe me, I'm going to be needing the cash."

He held the money out. "Then take this back."

"Consider it a security bond."

"You sure?"

"Yeah."

"All right," Starfish Steve said, sounding slightly appeased. "Come and choose your chute."

"You get them. I'll wait here. By the car."

Again, he gave her a worried look, but he left and brought back what she needed.

"BASE chute," he said. "State-of-the-art. You remember how to use one?"

"Like riding a bike, right?"

He didn't laugh.

She tossed the pack, gloves, and rope in the passenger seat, over the backpack. "I won't need it anyway. It's just a precaution."

"You sure there's nothing else I can do?"

"You've done more than enough. Especially if you give me those shifts next week." She hugged him again. "Be seeing you soon, all right?"

"You're still my best jumper," he said.

"Don't you forget it."

He knocked her in the shoulder one last time before she got in the car and drove away. Towards Equinoxx.

53

Briony's body was cramped from being in a cubicle for so long. People did this all the time in spy movies. She'd thought it would be a cinch. Turns out, being trapped in a tiny space for approximately a billion hours was a nightmarish way to spend time. She couldn't even play games on her phone because she wanted to conserve battery.

Would it even be worth it? Would she be caught the second she walked out? And was there even anything to see upstairs? It had only occurred to her in the last hour that they probably didn't have to close the entire level for one body.

So what were they hiding up there?

Briony's phone buzzed.

Any luck?

She let out a long whoosh of air and typed her answer to Kass.

Don't think this place ever closes.

It was late, and there was no sign of people packing it in. She could still hear the hustle and bustle outside.

Another buzz.

Can I call?

Always, thought Briony, texting back a simple **yes**. What a sappy thought. Maybe being imprisoned in here was making her emotional. She picked up as soon as her phone vibrated.

"Hey," said Kass. "No luck, then?"

"I peeked out about half an hour ago and the receptionist is still there! Does he ever go home?"

"You need to make your move soon. Liv's got a plan to keep Equinoxx out of Eidolon. They're gonna blow the transmission tower. Hopefully, when the coppers show up, they'll find the body at the same time."

"If they find Pravit before I do, does that mean I've failed?"

Kass was silent.

Briony crisscrossed her legs on the toilet seat. "Are you ever going to forgive me, Kass? I'm trying, you know. I – I want to make it up to you. I want you to know how sorry I am."

After a beat, Kass said, "We'll talk. You and me. When this is over."

"Really?"

"Yeah. But don't get too excited. It's just a talk."

Talking was more than Briony had ever expected. Hope buoyed her enough to find her drive again. "If I wait until the front receptionist leaves his desk, I might have a chance to get into his computer and get access to upstairs. Um. If you don't mind walking me through it? I'm not exactly hacker-competent."

"Leave it with me."

Kass disconnected before Briony could ask what she was planning to do. It was less than half an hour before she called back.

"He should be going now," was her greeting.

Briony peeked out of the loo doors, trying to see through all the native trees planted across the lobby. It was quieter than before – night technicians and janitors mostly. Killian was still there. He tapped away at the screen that covered his desk. After a moment, he paused and frowned. A few taps later, and an almost comical expression of horror crossed his face. He glanced around surreptitiously before scampering off through the front doors.

"What on earth did you do to the poor bloke?" Briony whispered.

"I have dirt on him."

"Dirt?"

"I hacked his emails, ay. We've got a connection to the Equinoxx network here. It's this wicked spider web antenna – anyway.

He's feeding data they've gathered from Eidolon to SInation, a competitor. And he's using his work email to do it. What a dud."

"So you sent him a threat?"

"Anon email, *I Know What You Did Last Summer* style, with attached screenshots. Told him to meet me at the front entrance on the main road. That should give us enough time. Now get to the desk."

Briony dashed across the lobby, which was blissfully empty after the busyness of today. But when she reached Killian's desk, she swore. "He locked access – oh."

The system had unlocked itself.

"You think I didn't put a Trojan horse in the attachment? What am I, a noob?"

"Kass," Briony said. "Who *are* you?"

"After. We'll talk. Find the settings. I want you to allow me access to your screen. Then I can do all the work, and you can watch and marvel."

It took Briony a painfully long time to find the permissions she needed to give Kass access, but as soon as Kass took over, things happened fast. Screens opened and closed, passwords were typed, commands changed.

"This is incredible," Briony breathed.

"What are you talking about? This is humiliating. I'm normally much better than this. I'm not used to Equinoxx programs."

She pulled up Briony's guest registration and spent some time fiddling with the settings. Briony glanced at the entrance. How long would it take Killian to drive to the main road, hang around anxiously, then rush back when he realized he'd been had?

"All good," Kass said, logging out. "You've got access to everywhere. Get to where you need to go."

"Will you stay on the line?"

"Can't," Kass said. "Got other stuff to do."

"Oh. Well…er. Thank you."

"S'what I'm for. Be careful in there, babe."

Briony's heart lurched as the line disconnected. Had Kass meant to call her babe, or was that a slip of the tongue?

She steadied her breath and hurried to the elevator. No one paid her a lick of attention. There was a moment of truth as the scanner registered her handprint, but it flashed green and opened up. Briony spent the elevator ride wondering who exactly she'd fallen in love with.

When she reached the next floor, she was unsurprised to find it empty of construction, but was unnerved that some of the lights were on. This company wasn't known for wasting energy…so who else was up here?

She moved stealthily along the corridor. There were open work spaces up here, and doors to enclosed offices. It was eerily quiet.

Her handprint gave her access to each locked room. They were all empty. No dead – or living – bodies to be found.

She slowed when she reached the regional director's office at the far end of the building. This had been Pravit's. If she were going to find any clues to what happened to him, they would be in here.

She scanned her handprint. Nothing happened. She tried it again. The screen flashed green, but the door didn't open.

It was then she realized there was a giant magnet holding it closed. Briony touched it, and the exterior lit up. She had the option to lower the magnetism or switch it off completely. She swiped her finger to switch it off. The magnet fell to the carpet with a dull thud.

Too late, she realized that if the magnet was on this side, it was surely to keep something in rather than out.

"Bollocks," she whispered, stumbling back as the door slid open.

The last person she expected to see burst from the room. Briony recognized her, even though she didn't look much like her pictures from the articles. Her clothes and hair were crumpled as if she had been trapped for days.

"Where is he?" roared an infuriated Nera Blake.

"W-who?"

"Jacob Wilcox, that two-timing, double-crossing cretin." Nera stormed towards the elevator. "He is absolutely fired. As soon as I stop the business deals going through, I'm going to–"

"You're too late."

"I'm – what?" Nera swung to Briony, who had been hurrying after her.

"You mean the pharmaceutical deals, right? They're already happening." Briony hesitated. "You didn't want them happening?"

"I was trying to stop them when Jake *imprisoned me in my own building!* I was trapped in there with no computer, no phone, no way out. I screamed myself hoarse–"

"The upper levels have been closed to everyone."

Nera snarled and continued stalking down the hall. "He's lucky there's a restroom in there, or I'd have to hurt him in unpleasant ways."

"Listen, don't worry about the deals. We have a plan."

"Sorry, who are you?"

"Briony McKinney."

Nera squinted at her through what seemed like a haze of exhaustion. "The lawyer?"

"You've heard of me?" Briony couldn't help the lurch of pleasure at the thought Nera Blake knew who she was.

"You were the plant."

"Oh. Right. That."

"What are you doing here?"

"I'm looking for Pravit Arya's body."

Nera shut her eyes with a long sigh. "Pravit."

"You know where he is?"

"In my nightmares."

Briony grimaced. "I more meant in a physical sense."

"I heard Jake say he was going to bury him in the wetlands – the sewerage treatment area."

"Oh."

"He died to save those children. He took his life rather than let us access his thoughts. He – he made me realize…" She trailed off and looked at Briony. "You said you had a plan?"

"Okay, I know it might sound over-the-top, but we have someone who's about to blow up the transmission tower."

"You what?"

"It was the only way to make sure the pharmaceutical companies won't have access to Eidolon–"

"But then *none* of us will have access to Eidolon!"

"So?"

"So! It's my world. My people! You say they're heading there now?"

"Yeah, but–"

Nera didn't wait for Briony to continue. She took off at a sprint, running as if there were wolves at her heels. No – as if she were trying to retain access to an entire world.

And Briony wasn't entirely sure that she should.

54

On rainy days, the Symbiosis community didn't have their usual campfire, but took turns hosting dinners inside. Sweetpea's cottage had a woodfire pit where she baked the potatoes in a cast iron pot. The place was already crammed with people, chatting and drinking organic wine.

Sophie snagged a bottle sitting on a barrel that had been repurposed as a table.

"Can I get you a drink?" she said to her parents.

"Oh, you don't have to…" her mum started, but Sophie said, "It was my job to get the drinks when I lived with Aidan. I don't mind."

Her dad grimaced. "Let's not use that name here, eh? But sure, grab a glass, fill me up. We should be celebrating."

Sophie poured him a drink. Her mum declined. She didn't seem that interested in what Sophie had been up to the past five years. She barely asked a single question. Considering Sophie had cried every night for weeks after Aidan had first taken her away, she thought things would be sunshine and apples now she was home. Instead, it was strange between her and her mother. Strained.

But she was in a social gathering, with food and friends, just like on TV. It was awesome. And a little overwhelming. She kept swinging between joy and a need to run outside and hide in the dark.

She continued to top up her dad's glass through dinner. Her mum gave a minuscule shake of her head that became more pronounced with each pour, but Sophie shrugged and mouthed, *Celebration!*

A dark red stained the tips of her dad's bushy gray moustache. He laughed a lot. People seemed to want to be near him. Sophie remembered the way those from the community milled to him, asked for his advice, came over day in, day out for a chat. He was always so cheerful with them.

"No worries," he'd say. "Any time, mate. Door's open. Want a cuppa?"

He's a beacon in this dark world, Sophie had overheard Sweetpea say to her mum once.

Sophie, in the middle of topping up her dad's glass, stifled a yawn.

"Tired already?" he said. "Suppose it's been an emotional day."

Sophie blushed. She'd cried on the drive home. Being in her dad's car again, smelling distinctly of home, had brought up a lot of feelings.

Her dad got up. "I'll walk you back."

Her mum, who had been chatting to someone Sophie didn't recognize, turned. "I'll come with you."

"Nonsense, Indigo, enjoy yourself."

"But—"

"Stay, love. I'll be right back." To Sophie, he said, "Your room's still exactly how we left it."

Wattle looked disappointed as they headed to the door. "Are you going? It's still early."

"I'll see you tomorrow," Sophie said with a smile. "And the day after that."

"And the day after that," Wattle said, returning the smile.

The clouds were starting to clear as they headed across the square to the main farmstead. Her dad sucked in a deep breath. "Beautiful rain, wasn't it? Filled our tanks. We desperately needed it. I remember when summer was a time of ice creams and drinking from hoses. Catastrophic bushfires doesn't have the same ring to it, does it?"

"No."

"I'm sorry, kid. I'm sorry we did this to your generation. Your old man's doing everything he can to make it right."

"I know, Dad." Sophie pulled her phone from her jacket pocket. No messages or missed calls. She fiddled around with the settings. "Just putting it on Do Not Disturb," she said when her dad glanced at her. "In case Aidan tries to bug me in the middle of the night."

"That boy." He shook his head. "I don't know what happened to him, honestly. He fell off the path after his mother died. There was nothing I could do. Breaks my heart, every day."

"I thought he was all right at first," Sophie admitted. "But he's just mean. He doesn't care about anything. You know?"

"I can imagine."

"He still buys food in plastic sometimes. Even when I tell him there are alternatives. And he doesn't recycle as much as he should."

"He didn't grow up in Symbiosis like you did. A lot of people need educating."

"I tried to educate him! He never listens to me." Sophie climbed the porch steps. "Anyway, I guess he's doing *some* good. You know he's with the Guardians?"

Her dad's hand stilled on the doorknob. "Beg your pardon?"

"That activist group. He thinks I don't know, but he underestimated me, every hour of every day."

Her dad glanced over his shoulder at the four houses lit up and overflowing with people. The other houses were quiet, as was the surrounding bushland. It was dark out there, past the warm glow of Symbiosis.

"Let's talk inside," he said.

They headed in, her dad swaying slightly as he closed the door behind them. Sophie switched on the lights.

"I'd call the cops on him if I didn't agree with his technique," she said. "He's bringing down loggers, coal mines, chicken factories. And not with protests or petitions, which do nothing. He's making proper change. People are going to pay attention. I wanted to help him, but of course he'd never bring me into his inner circle."

"You're into that stuff, are you?" her dad said, sitting on the couch to pull off his muddy boots.

"For sure."

"You don't think it's overboard? They killed someone earlier this year. And they could've killed that train driver."

"They should've."

"You think so?"

"He's working for a coal factory. He's part of the problem." A wicked smile crossed her face. "Imagine if people like that train driver were afraid to go to work. They know they're doing the wrong thing, destroying the planet, and they still show up day after day. But if there were Guardians out there planting bombs, taking down oil rigs, blowing up planes taking miners to quarries – well. They wouldn't show up to work anymore, would they?"

"That's some radical thinking, my girl. Where's it coming from?"

"I've been following the Guardians for ages. I reckon the only thing they're doing wrong is not thinking big enough."

"Maybe they don't have the resources yet."

"They need to figure out how to crowdsource under a front."

"Yeah?"

"If only Aidan had just asked me to help. He missed out on a good opportunity."

Her dad regarded her. His red-stained mouth twitched. "You really are my daughter, aren't you?"

"You agree with me?"

"More than you know." He got up and padded to their kitchen, pouring himself yet another glass of wine. He swirled it, sniffed it, and watched Sophie over the rim. After a swig, he said, "What if I told you there were ways you could help the Guardians?"

"Sign me up," Sophie said. "Anything. Do you have a contact with a Guardian? Someone besides Aidan, I mean."

With a chuckle, her dad said, "Reef is a pawn. He had skills that were useful to me, so I utilized them."

"You?"

"Yes indeed." He drank deeply, draining the glass. "I always planned to get you involved. I just had to be certain you were up to the challenge. Mentally, I mean. I wasn't sure whether those five years away had made you complicit to the system."

"I was never in any system," Sophie said. "I was trapped in a house. No school to brainwash me, no capitalist bullshit to deal with. I made up my own mind."

"That's good, Jo-Jo. That's very, very good." He wiped his mouth with the back of his hand. "Smart girl."

"So you're...you're part of the Guardians?"

"I *am* the Guardians."

"What! No!"

"It's my brainchild, my passion. But from the sounds of it, I'm not thinking big enough."

"Sorry," Sophie said, flinching.

"No, don't apologize. Let's go bigger. You have a fire I haven't seen in my other people."

"That is so freaking amazing. My dad is the head of the Guardians."

"Let's talk about the kind of big things you were thinking."

"You want my opinion?"

"Of course."

Sophie beamed. "You started strong this year. Well, Aidan did. Spiking the trees and not putting up signs was brilliant. Logging companies won't be quick to take down old growth forests if they don't know which trees are spiked. I don't know why he took the coward's way out with the train."

"Reef's always been a coward," her dad said with a snort. "You think he didn't put up signs when he spiked the trees? Of course he did. I had to go in later and take them down."

"Seriously? Why does he bother being a part of the Guardians if he's not going to do it right?"

"Because," her dad said, advancing on her with fresh intensity, "he doesn't understand that fixing this planet requires sacrifice. The government is never going to move fast enough to save us. We have to act swiftly and violently, which is something Reef doesn't have the nerve to do. Just because he has the skills, doesn't mean he's worthy of our cause."

"Then why…?"

"He may have had incentive to do what I asked of him."

"What kind of incentive?"

Her dad gave a secretive smile.

"What, you blackmailed him or something? You're shrugging. What does that mean? C'mon, what could you possibly have on him? You hadn't seen him in years."

"I'm sure you can figure it out on your own."

Sophie stared at him blankly. He gestured to her.

"Me?" she said. "What do I have to do with it?"

"You said yourself how protective he was of you. He wanted to keep you from my 'bad influence.' Doesn't matter that you can make up your own mind, does it?"

"So he was doing jobs that were meant for me? But wait, how could you use me as…oh. I told Wattle my address." Hurt crept into her voice. "If he'd told you where I was, why didn't you come get me?"

"Like I said, I didn't know whether you were up to the challenge. And I had to utilize Reef's skills while I could." Her dad clapped his hands on her shoulders. His eyes were hazy. "But now he's no use to me. You're stepping up to take his place. My girl. My Joey, home again."

Sophie's phone rang. They both jumped, the buzzing loud in the silence. Sophie dug it from her jacket.

"It's Wattle," she said, answering it. "Hey."

But her mum's voice came through, cheerful and loud. "Just checking on you. Your father said he'd be right back."

"Oh. We were just talking."

"You had hours to talk in the car!"

"Give it here," her dad said, beckoning for the phone.

"Mum, I'm going to bed. Dad will – oh."

Her dad had snatched the phone from her hand. "Indigo, it's

fair dinkum, love. I'm coming right back. Just wanted to chat with the daughter I haven't seen in half a decade, you know? All right. Love you too."

Sophie's heart pounded as he hung up. She tried to grab her phone back.

Her dad stared down at the screen. "What's this?" When she grabbed for it again, he shoved her away. "Why is the voice recording open?" He lifted his gaze to her. "Were you recording me, Jo-Jo?" Rather than angry, he sounded curious.

"I was recording myself singing earlier," she said, talking so fast she stumbled over her words. "The app's still open because I haven't used my phone since—"

"But you said you put it on Do Not Disturb."

"I—"

"Your phone shouldn't have rung just then."

"You can change the settings—"

"Look, it has the time and date of the recording. You were recording our conversation." His words came out mildly amused, which is why, when he raised his arm, Sophie wasn't ready.

His knuckles crunched against her nose and cheek. The impact was enough to send her flying to the floor. The world whirled in sparks and colors. Blood dripped from her nose onto the boards.

He tossed the phone away and stood over her. "Did Reef set you up to this?"

"No, id's nod whad you—"

He grabbed her arm, yanking it behind her back to near breaking point.

She gasped. "Waid—"

There was a sickening crack and pain roared like fire up her arm. She screamed.

Her dad spun her onto her back and bent over her. "Shh, now." He covered her mouth with his hand, his fingers clawing into her bruised cheek. Blood pooled beneath her nostrils. It was getting harder to breathe.

She couldn't see through her tears. The pain in her arm was

unbearable. It flopped, broken and useless beside her. She used her other arm to try to push him away. All that training with Aidan, and she couldn't come up with a single move, a single way to escape. Agony had overridden any other thought.

Her dad pinched her nose closed. "What a waste," he said as she began to suffocate. He spoke as if she were expired food. "I've bred two defects. What happened to your passion, Jo-Jo? Don't you want to save the planet? Or did Reef corrupt you?"

Her head was getting floaty. The lights grew fuzzy, like fairies.

There was a distant thump, and movement behind her dad. His hand lifted from her face. She sucked air into her desperate lungs. Every breath was knives. Blood streamed into her mouth, but she couldn't stop gasping, and began to choke on it.

There were sounds near her. Thuds. Smashing. Breaking glass. She could hear her mother's voice shouting, and–

She rolled onto her undamaged side and hacked between wheezes. She couldn't get in the breaths she wanted.

Someone crouched behind her. "Sophie?"

Aidan. It was Aidan.

He tried to scoop her up, but the movement jolted her broken arm and she wrenched away with a cry, too weak to scream.

"What–?" Aidan started. He must've seen the way her arm hung, though, because he swore and tugged her, gentler, towards him.

The side of her face felt like it had ballooned. She could no longer see out of one eye.

Aidan wrapped her good arm around his waist and he and Indigo hauled her to her feet. She didn't have the strength to resist, even though it hurt, it all hurt. They half-dragged her towards the door.

"Waid," she said. "My phod. My phod!"

He scooped up her phone on the way past. People were crowding outside. When Aidan and Sophie emerged onto the porch, there was a roar of outrage.

"What have you done to her?" someone cried.

Sophie felt her mother's hand fall away, as Aidan pushed through them. "Move!" she shouted. "Let him take her to the hospital." The car was in the main square, near the bikes Sophie and her dad had left earlier.

The crowd parted to reveal her dad groaning in the garden bed, beneath a broken window. He was bleeding, but Symbiotes were tending to him.

Wattle stood between Aidan and the car. "Let her go."

"Get out of the way, kid."

"We've called the police."

"Good."

Aidan advanced, but Wattle held his ground. "We're not going to let you leave. You expect to come in here and attack us—"

"That's not what happened," Indigo hissed.

"How can you say that?" Wattle demanded, gesturing to Sophie. "Look what he did to her!"

"Fud off, Waddle, id wad my dad."

Wattle's righteous hand weakened in the air.

"Ged oudda de way. We gon to the hoddible."

Aidan guided Sophie forward again. This time, no one stopped them. He helped her into the car and pulled on her seatbelt, careful of her arm.

"I sobdy, Ai'n."

"It's okay."

She waited for him to get around to his side and start the car. Some people half-heartedly stood in front of them, but when Aidan revved the engine, they got out of the way. Sophie's mum watched them leave.

Aidan left the property without any more issues. "We've got a bit of a distance to the nearest hospital," he said, opening a maps app.

"Id hurds."

"The doctors will have painkillers for you."

"Do you hab my phod?"

"Yeah." He pulled it from his jacket pocket and passed it to her.

She held it gratefully to her chest. "I recodd im."

"Didn't catch that one."

"I re-cod-ded im. He sed ebberding."

"Sorry, Soph, I can't understand you."

Sophie huffed and played the recording. Aidan's face changed the more they listened. It was all there. The confession about being in charge of the Guardians. The blackmail. Removing the signs for the tree spiking. They had everything they needed to go to the police.

Aidan was looking more emotional than she'd ever seen him. "You – you did this for me?"

She nodded.

"You went back to Forrest to clear my name?"

She nodded again. She wanted to explain how she had been there that day, sulking in the cubby house rather than doing lessons, when Aidan had told Olivia and Kass how he'd been forced to work for the Guardians. Sophie hadn't really betrayed him, but she knew he'd never let her go through with her plan. Now she understood why. Their dad was a freaking psycho. Aidan was right. He'd always been right.

But she couldn't tell him any of this, because her face hurt, her arm hurt, her lungs hurt. She would have to explain later.

Her forehead fell against the cool window as she stared out into the darkness. It only occurred to her later that Aidan had completely fallen for her play. He'd believed the whole time that she'd abandoned him.

And he'd come for her anyway.

EIDOLON

55

"I think we've been here."

Liv groaned and turned back the way they'd come, squinting past the solar-powered streetlights. "I think you're right."

After searching through the offices where they'd been held, she and Reef had decided to investigate outside. Only, outside was a maze. They were in a compound filled with impressive buildings and soft, mossy streets that all looked the same. Research laboratories, from what Liv had seen. No sign of any nursery.

No sign of any *person*.

Where was everyone? Even at night, she'd expected to see a guard at least. And considering they were escapees, with lights still flashing and sirens still blaring, she thought they'd come across more obstacles.

"This is so frustrating," she said as they rounded the corner of a building. "It feels like we're–"

Something moved from the shadows. It snatched at Liv, giving her no time to defend herself. An arm locked around her neck. She flailed her legs, trying to stamp on her captor's foot. He seemed unperturbed by her attempts.

Reef started forward, but the man's grip on Liv's neck tightened until it blocked the air from her lungs.

"Uh uh," he said, and Reef stopped.

She clawed at the arm. Even drawing blood, her captor didn't mind, or even notice. His breath was hot against her ear as he said, almost lovingly, "I'm going to break your spine."

The voice was familiar. Her memory flashed to gold teeth in a face that had been smashed with a meat tenderizer.

Her struggles turned to desperate wrenches as she tried to get away. This guy was unstoppable, a complete maniac–

There was a horrific crack. Together they lurched forward, and the man's grip loosened. She staggered away, gasping. The man fell on his face to reveal Kazzy behind him, holding the butt of a shotgun aloft.

Reef's shotgun.

"Shit," said Kazzy. "Never used a gun before."

"I'd say you still haven't," Liv wheezed, grabbing the gun from her.

Reef joined them. "You okay?"

"I hate this guy." Liv kicked her attacker's prone body.

"You're alive," Kazzy said, a slow smile growing. "You're alive. You're fucking *alive!*" She clapped and laughed to the starry sky. "Olivia-fucking-Sharp is invincible!"

Liv rubbed her neck sourly. "Not invincible. Lucky. And that luck's going to run out if I'm not careful. What happened? Where did you get the gun?"

"Found it when I arrived. Cool, ay. It just happened to be in the room I popped up in. Spare ammo and everything. Thought I should probably snag–"

Liv pointed the shotgun at her.

"Oi!" she cried, raising her hands. "What the fuck?"

"Liv," Reef said.

"This isn't Kazzy," Liv said. "This is the outside one. Friend or foe?"

"Friend, obviously!"

Reef rested a hand on Liv's shoulder. "Liv."

"We don't know who we can trust."

"Didn't my Liv tell you I was good quality?"

Liv took aim. "Someone betrayed us. We still don't know who it was."

"Aidan's dad on our side," Kass said. When Liv lowered the gun in surprise, she added quickly, "I'm sorry, all right? But we're fixing everything. Eidolon me is driving here to meet us. And the other you is climbing the transmission tower in the outside world to blow it up. We'll be able to stop anyone from getting into Eidolon – hey, what?" Her attention fell on the empty space where the attacker's body had been.

"That's what they do," Liv said. "They appear, screw with us, then disappear."

"Not for much longer, if my Livvie gets those explosives on the tower. Look," Kass said, staring nervously at the shotgun, "I've been running all over the place trying to find where they're keeping Bobbi."

"Do you know where the nursery is?"

"No, but there were a bunch of people standing outside a building three blocks away. I reckon we try there."

Liv considered her for a moment before lowering the gun.

Kass sagged and dropped her hands. "Holy fuck, you're terrifying."

Liv turned to find Reef leaning heavily against the wall, eyes closed. Fear gripped her. "Reef?"

"I'm fine," he said. He opened his eyes and shoved off the wall. "Let's get Bobbi. You want me to take the gun?"

"No!" Kass and Liv said together.

"That's fair."

Kass led them left, away from where they'd come.

"What is this place?" Liv whispered as they moved along the sides of buildings.

"Dunno," Kass whispered back. "My Liv said something about a crystal forest in this area – that's where I thought I'd pop in. I guess, since the crystals are servers for Eidolon, they didn't need that here."

"They've repurposed the area?" Reef said.

"Yeah, looks like."

Kass held up a hand to stop their progress. Beyond was a squat unit. She'd been right – there were at least thirty people standing outside it. Some were slightly relaxed and chatting, others were glancing nervously into the darkness.

"Guess we know where everyone is," Liv said, her grip tightening on the gun. "Guarding the nursery."

Through those people, through those doors, was her baby.

"They don't look armed or anything," Kass said.

"They're probably just research scientists," Reef said. "Repurposed." He pointed out a frizzy-haired woman standing at the side of the crowd. "She has a gun."

It was a solid piece, like from cop shows.

"Is she the only one?" Liv said.

"From what I can see–"

"Wait a second. She's the piece of shit who snatched Bobbi from the charging station!"

"Uh…Liv–" Kass said, but Liv was already stepping out into the open. The crowd swung towards her. The frizzy haired woman raised her gun. Liv lifted hers too.

"Stop there," said the frizzy haired woman.

Liv advanced.

"I've been ordered to shoot you if you approach."

Liv didn't slow.

"This is your last warning."

"No," Liv said. "This is *your* last warning. If anyone here is a citizen of Eidolon, run. No matter what Equinoxx is paying you, it's not worth your life."

The frizzy haired woman sneered. "I doubt you've got enough rounds for all of us."

"I don't need that many."

She shot the woman in the face. Her frizzy head disappeared

mid-explosion. The cloud of blood vanished before it could land.

Liv pumped the shotgun. Several people at the edge of the crowd made a run for it. The frizzy haired woman's partner lunged for the gun that had dropped to the ground, and Liv shot him too. More people ran. Some ran for her.

Reef and Kass joined the fray, much stronger and faster than these people who weren't trained to fight. Kass hadn't been trained, exactly, but Liv recognized that gleeful expression from their teenage years, when they occasionally got into bar brawls.

A woman moved to club Reef's bandaged head and Liv shot her in the side. While she was distracted, someone else grabbed the loose gun. There was resounding thunder as it went off. Lead hit flesh.

Kass looked down at her stomach, which had started to bleed.

"Ah, fuck."

She vanished.

Liv used her last round to destroy the person who had shot her best friend. Then she smashed the butt of the gun into the nearest person's nose.

"Well, my love," she called. "Guess it's just you and me."

She turned in time to see Reef drop to the ground. He lay facedown on the mossy street, unmoving.

Liv looked to the person he was fighting off – a smaller man with ears that stuck out. The man saw Liv's expression and lifted his hands in panic. "It wasn't me! It wasn't me! He just fell over, I swear!"

Liv picked up the loose gun and fired. The shot missed. The man turned on his heels and sprinted away.

In the soft light of the solar lamps, blood began to stain across Reef's bandages.

OUTSIDE

56

The transmission tower was hard to miss. It loomed above the crystal forest, its antenna a giant spider web in the starlit sky. It was much taller than she'd remembered – closer to two hundred feet.

Olivia had left Kass' car parked off the road, in the bush. She wasn't sure whether she could drive into the property, but she thought she remembered seeing some red-lit scanner when her automated StarShine car had gone through, and she didn't want to risk detection. So she'd trekked her way through the bush, the chute on her back and the bag with the dynamite tied around her waist with the rope she'd borrowed from Starfish Steve. When she reached the large purple crystals, the ground was clear enough to break into a jog.

It was a surreal experience. The full moon shone onto the crystals, turning them almost silver. Occasionally, something sparked through them, like heartbeats, or magic. She tried to tell herself it was just data, that these were only computer servers, but part of her felt like she was on another planet.

When she reached the tower, she was coated in sweat and out of breath. She mopped her forehead with her shirt. Thank god for her recent training.

On the other side of the tower was a river, much bigger than the one on Valentina's property. It gushed and roared, full from the rain.

There was a service ladder on the tower that started about twenty feet up, but she had to climb the latticed legs first. She stretched her arms, pulled on her climbing gloves. Checked the bag was secure on the rope. Double checked her chute.

Now she was just stalling.

"Come on, Liv," she said. "Just like riding a bike."

She stepped up onto the steel. Her boots gripped nicely, even though everything was still wet.

"There. See? Easy."

She hauled herself to the next level. It took a lot of arm strength. She was going to be sore tomorrow.

That was okay. As long as she lived to see it.

Climbing the lattice was less scary than climbing the rocks. Here, she had to concentrate on where her hands went. She was looking for the next handhold, her attention away from the ground.

To think, three months ago, she had been lounging in bed with mimosas, booking facials, and attending painting classes. What would Matt say if he saw her now?

That's much too dangerous, Olivia. Let's call someone to do it for you.

The man was incapable of doing anything himself. And she'd let him turn her into the same helpless being.

The thought fired her upwards, adrenaline surging in a way it hadn't for too long. She reached the ladder and started the long vertical climb.

Damn Matt, and his damn anxious voice in her ear, and his damn lies, and his damn affair.

Wear something sexy underneath, okay?

"Fuck you!" she screamed into the night.

She was feeling herself again, high on the rush, flames in her blood. She had forgotten how to live.

Not anymore. No turning back. She would take a job with

Starfish Steve, go up in the plane a few times, find the courage to do another jump. She would book an overseas trip with Kass. She would properly move in with Aidan and fuck him every goddamn night.

The angry fire turned into a different kind of fire as she thought of that afternoon. Her heart thrummed at the promise of more. More Aidan. More *Reef.*

She thought of how happy their other selves were in Eidolon, an assurance that they belonged together in this world, too.

How happy their other selves *had* been.

Olivia's boot slipped. Her heart leapt to her throat as she grabbed the rungs to steady herself. And she looked down.

"Oh shit."

The ground was forever away.

Her limbs locked up.

"No."

She tried to move her hands, her legs.

"No."

Panic extinguished the fire. She was so high. Impossibly high. It was no longer adrenaline in her limbs, but fear, heavy and insurmountable. She clung to the ladder. There was no going up. No going down. She couldn't move.

She shut her wet eyes. "Come on. Come on. Please."

The wind picked up, buffeting at her. She held onto the ladder so tight her arms ached.

Again, her gaze was drawn downwards. The river's roar had become a dull rumble. The crystal forest glinted behind her. Somewhere in there, Bobbi was trapped, imprisoned by Equinoxx for sale to the highest soulless bidder. There was no one left to help her. No one except Olivia.

"Come *on*, Livvie."

What did she used to say to people who freaked out before a jump? She couldn't remember. She couldn't think of anything but how afraid she was.

"Then go down. Just climb down. One step at a time. Please, Livvie, please."

She pictured her feet stepping down the ladder. Then she tried to do the action.

Nothing happened.

"Come *on*, dammit!"

The burner phone rang in her pocket. She let out a sob. There was no way she could answer it.

The phone rang out.

Olivia dropped her head against the steel rung. "Help me," she said to no one. "I can't do it. I can't do it. I can't–"

The phone rang again.

She had to answer it. She couldn't stay here forever.

Shaking, she used her teeth to pull off her glove and clung hard to the ladder while fumbling for the phone. She almost dropped it before answering.

"Livvie!" Kass screamed from the other end. "They're alive! Reef and Liv are still in Eidolon!"

"What?"

"Your other version is so cool! And terrifying!"

"Kass–"

"And the pharmies' money's gone through. I'm sending the dossier to a bunch of places now. It's happening, bay-bee. We did it! How's the climb going? Sounds windy."

"Um. It's not so good."

"Well hurry up. Your other self needs you to cut Equinoxx's access, like, yesterday."

"I can't do it."

"What d'you mean?"

"I'm stuck halfway up the tower. I can't climb."

"Course you can climb. You're Olivia-fucking-Sharp."

"I'm so scared, Kass. Please help me."

"Look, I wasn't kidding about your other self needing you to blow the tower. I don't know how much longer she can hold Equinoxx off. Get your ass up there."

"I can't."

"You can't let her die now! Bobbi can't grow up without her mum."

"But—"

"And if Equinoxx finds a way around this, they're going to let those pharmies experiment on your daughter. Is that what you want?"

"I—"

"Is that what you want, Livvie?"

"No."

"Then *climb*, biatch."

"I can't while I'm holding the phone."

"So stop holding the phone! Do I have to solve every problem? Drop it, shove it down your top, I don't fucking care. Get it done, Livvie!"

"Okay." Olivia put it on speaker and secured it in her top. "Can you hear me? You're in my bra."

"Hot. You climbing yet?"

"Hang on."

Olivia stared at the next rung. Intensely. She remembered her fear on the rocks, of Aidan talking her through each step. She visualized one hand wrapping around the rung, safely, securely. Then, since her hand had already been free to hold the phone, she raised it and grabbed the rung, gloveless. Her arms were weak, her legs shaky, but she pulled herself up.

"I'm climbing."

"Yeah you fucking are. One step at a time."

Olivia dragged herself to the next rung. And the next.

"Keep going, Livvie," Kass shouted over the line. "You are Olivia-fucking-Sharp. Say it."

"I'm Olivia-fucking-Sharp."

"You are *Olivia-fucking-Sharp*."

"I'm Olivia-fucking-Sharp!"

"Don't you forget it!"

Olivia was crying, but she found her pace, step by step by step. Kass kept screaming at her. It was just like rehab, when Olivia was learning to walk again.

Get it done, Livvie!

Kass had yelled that to her daily, pushing her past the pain, forcing her to do what the physio had instructed, forcing her to take those precious steps.

And they were so very precious. She was here, alive, breathing, moving, something she had promised herself to never take for granted again after the accident. More than that – she was using this second chance to fight for something good. Something right.

When she reached the top, it felt like she had made it to a new plane of existence.

"Holy fuck," she said, heaving herself onto the platform. "I did it. I'm here."

"Yeeessss!"

"My arms are going to fall off."

"Not yet, they aren't. You need to plant the explosives."

"Wait." Olivia took a few moments to catch her breath. Standing up felt like too much. She was still shaking. Still terrified. So she crawled on her belly to the antennae and opened the bag. They were magnetic, attaching easily to the steel. Aidan had shown her how to set the timers. She gave herself ten minutes. No choice of freaking out on the way down.

She crawled to each side of the platform, planting more explosives. Her fingers were almost numb from fear. The ground and the river were so far down. But she had to make sure the whole top would blow, buying them plenty of time before Equinoxx could get it repaired.

"Olivia."

Olivia jumped at the voice, almost dropping the last bomb. Nera Blake climbed onto the platform with her.

"What the hell are you doing here?" Olivia cried.

"What's wrong?" Kass said on the phone. "Who are you talking to?"

Nera Blake clung to the railing. Her black curls wobbled in the breeze. She looked like she hadn't slept in days. "Please don't do this."

"Climb down. These bombs are going off."

"Don't cut off Eidolon."

"It's over, Nera. My friend's released all the documents Pravit gathered."

"I know my company's done wrong. I'm going to make it right. Jacob Wilcox will take the fall. I'll testify that the people in there are human – I'll do whatever you ask. Just please don't take Eidolon away from me."

"You can't be trusted with it."

Nera's face changed. She looked as if she were in pain. "I – I wanted to protect them."

"They don't need your protection. Not anymore."

"But they're my people."

"You sold their babies for human testing."

"It wasn't me!"

"You consented, Nera! By turning your back, by ignoring it, you're as much to blame as anyone."

"I'll do anything. I'll give you anything–"

"You created life, then made them live at your mercy. The only reason I'm not bringing down your entire company is because I know you're capable of saving the world."

"I need that data to prove our energy solutions work."

"You'll have to use the data you've already gathered."

"*Please–*"

"You want to protect the people in Eidolon? Then let me do this." Olivia set the timer for the last bomb. "Climb down. I'm not switching them off."

"I–" A happy tune jingled from Nera's pocket. She swore, the tension broken. "Hang on. It's Jake. Jacob." She kept one arm wrapped around the railing as she tugged her phone out. "Jake, you need to convince – Hello? Who is this?" A strange expression crossed Nera's face as she listened to the person on the other end. Her gaze lifted to Olivia. Then, with a shaking hand, she held her phone out. "It's for you."

EIDOLON

57

It took all of Liv's strength to drag Reef's body into the building. She swapped her attention between where she was going and his breaths, which were alarmingly shallow.

She'd tried to use the other gun to keep away the mob, but missed each time. In the end it hadn't mattered – they'd turned tail and run shortly after Reef had fallen. Liv wasn't sure why they'd decided to flee all at once. It couldn't be good.

The only shot she hadn't missed was the one aimed for the door scanner. The screen broke in a crackle of electricity, and the door slid open for her. Automatic lights flickered on. There was the sound of infants crying.

Liv set Reef gently on the ground and straightened to inspect the room. It was bright and colorful, with toys, games, rugs, and baby mobiles hanging from the ceiling. Cots had been set up against the walls. A boy of about one was standing, peering curiously at Liv through the bars.

There were no carers in sight, though there were adult camping cots like the one they'd put Reef on.

"Mummy?"

Bobbi sat on a princess-style bed in the corner, with a canopy and pink sheets. Her face lit up in delight when she saw Liv.

"Mummy!"

She climbed out of bed and ran forward. Liv sank to her knees. Her arms enfolded around Bobbi; her nose buried in curls that smelled of unfamiliar wash, but were still Bobbi's, still her baby's.

"Mummy, I saw a cow! Moooooo. Cows go mooooo. Mummy? Moooo. And then I saw sheep, baaa. And then I saw possum. No? Horse. Mummy, I missed you. Where did you go? Mummy, why you crying?"

Bobbi patted Liv's wet face.

"I'm so sorry," Liv burbled. "I'm so sorry, baby. I'll never let anyone take you away again. I love you so much."

Bobbi beamed. "I love you, Mummy!"

Liv sobbed and pulled her into another hug.

"Mummy, all the babies are crying. Why they crying?" Bobbi let out a loud gasp. "Daddy!" She left Liv's embrace and ran to Reef, still on the floor. "Daddy sleeping? What's on Daddy head?" She reached for the bloodied bandages.

"No, don't touch," Liv said breathlessly, scooping Bobbi up. "Daddy's sleeping, yes. Mummy and Daddy had a big day trying to find you. Daddy's pooped!"

"Pooped!" Bobbi said, then cackled.

Liv clung to her. Reef would be okay. He had just overdone it. He needed rest and recuperation. Maybe if she could find Doctor Nowak again…and someone to help with everything else. She glanced at the other children. How was she supposed to get six kids out of here?

It was only when she heard the boots that she realized they were no longer alone. The soldiers in riot gear who had taken them from Valentina's were lined up outside the door, and in front of them, at the threshold, was Jacob Wilcox.

Liv bit down a curse. She'd left both guns outside to drag Reef in. She backed away, holding Bobbi tighter.

"You've said your goodbyes," Jacob Wilcox said. "We've been kind enough to give you that."

Liv ignored him, instead addressing the soldiers. "You don't have to listen to him. This is our world, not his!"

"Oh, they're not citizens," Jacob Wilcox said, waving dismissively. "I needed people I could trust for this particular job."

Bobbi wrapped her arms around Liv's neck and hid her face. Liv didn't realize she was still retreating until her back hit the wall. "Please."

"The time for negotiations is over." Jacob stepped aside. The soldiers came in. Liv couldn't see their faces behind the tinted face shields. One pointed a gun at Reef.

"No!" Liv cried.

"You're going to come with us," Jacob said. His voice was terribly calm. "Outside. Where the children can't see."

"No."

A soldier walked forward and pressed a gun against her temple.

"No." Liv held a protective hand against the back of Bobbi's head. "No. No."

"Please don't make us shoot you in front of your daughter."

"No."

"Because we will, if you don't cooperate."

"No."

Another soldier put their gun down and walked over. They placed their hands on Bobbi's shaking body.

"No," Liv said as the soldier pulled Bobbi from her grip. "No. No. No!"

"Mummy!"

"Do *not* make us shoot you here, Olivia."

"No! NO!"

Soldiers dragged Liv past Reef's body, to the door. Bobbi was screaming. The other babies were screaming.

Liv wasn't strong enough to fight her way free. But she tried. God, she tried.

OUTSIDE

58

Olivia stood up and took the phone from Nera. "Hello?"

"Hello, Mrs Alexander."

Cold sweat beaded across Olivia's skin. She'd heard that voice in her nightmares.

"It's over, Winken," she said, hoping she sounded braver than she felt. "Equinoxx is ruined. They're not going to pay you for killing me."

"They can take this one as a freebie. It'll be my pleasure." He was panting slightly. Olivia didn't dare imagine what he was doing.

To Nera, she said, "Call off your assassin."

"A-assassin?"

"Yes, assassin! Why do you think I'm so pissed at you?"

"I didn't have anything to do with that! It would've been Jake–"

"No one's going to be calling me off," Winken said. "Wilcox is busy killing your other version. So I'm coming for you."

Goosebumps needled across Olivia's arms. She gripped the railing beside Nera and slowly edged forward.

Winken was scaling the latticed legs of the tower.

"Oh my god."

"Close enough," said Winken, laughing. He used both hands to climb – he must've had an earpiece.

"Nera's right here," Olivia said. "You're not going to murder me with a witness."

"I'm done letting things come between us. Witnesses will be dealt with."

"You're going to kill Nera Blake?"

Nera's eyes widened.

"No," Winken said. "You are. You came here to blow up the tower, and she tried to stop you. The tussle was short and sweet, before you both fell to your deaths."

"How did you know–?"

"Your freckle-nosed friend has a loud mouth."

Dammit, Kass.

"The timers are already set, Winken."

"You'll switch them off." He sounded arrogantly certain.

"No, I won't."

"Hmm, I'm calling your bluff. The last time we were together, you begged me not to shoot you. You're a coward, Mrs Alexander."

Olivia hung up on him. "He's going to kill us both."

"He wouldn't – what are you doing?"

Olivia was unstrapping her chute. "Have you ever been BASE jumping?"

"I've skydived. Once. Years ago. In a tandem. Is that a parachute? Don't give that to me."

"I don't want you to die."

"I don't know how to use it!"

"I'll walk you through it."

"What about you?"

"We can't go together, not with our combined weight and the height of the tower." Olivia started strapping the chute to Nera. "I'm going to hold the parachute and release it when you jump. It's the safest way to get you down." She explained the technique of jumping, how to use the steering lines, how to flare before landing so she wouldn't break both her legs.

Nera was trembling. "I can't do this."

"It's this, or let Winken push you off."

"If we can just talk to him–"

"Trust me, he can't be reasoned with."

"But what about you?" Nera said again.

"I'm going to jump too."

"Without a parachute?"

"I'll jump into the river."

"From this height?"

"I used to cliff jump on the reg. I'll be fine. Now–" Olivia checked the timers, and Winken's progress. Two minutes, twelve seconds. "Do you remember what to do? Run me through the process."

Nera rapidly listed off everything Olivia had said, word for word.

"You *are* a genius," Olivia said, impressed. "Ready? On three–"

"I can't do this!"

"If you don't jump on three, I'll shove you off."

"Please."

"One."

"Olivia, don't!"

"Two."

"Pleasepleasepleasepleaseplease–"

"Three."

Nera jumped. Olivia released the parachute, along with the pilot chute, and watched them catch the wind. Nera's scream echoed across the crystal forest.

Winken was about forty feet from the top.

Olivia began unlacing her boots. "Hey, Kass?"

"I'm still here," said Kass' voice from her bra.

Olivia released a long breath. Thank god.

"How high are you?" Kass said.

"Two hundred feet, I'd say."

"Oh, fuck." Kass' voice broke, but she caught herself and said, "New world record, ay?"

Olivia kicked off her boots and socks, the grating sharp on her bare feet. "It's gonna be amazing."

"Doesn't count if you don't do a flip."

Winken was almost at the top. Olivia stared at the starlit river. It was beautiful. Everything was beautiful. Night, rain, fresh air, the moon, the crystal forest that held a whole other world.

Life. Life was beautiful.

Hope buoyed her heart. Olivia Sharp was a survivor, no matter what version.

Nera Blake was a survivor, too. She would save this world, like she was always meant to. People would rally behind her when they saw what she could do. They would fight with her. Fight *for* her. Olivia found she believed it, fiercely. She believed there would be change. There was hope for this world. Always hope.

Over the phone, Kass was crying. "Livvie–"

"Hey, it might be okay. If the water's deep enough, and I land properly–"

"Livvie!"

"I'm not afraid," Olivia said.

And she wasn't. She'd been standing, talking, and walking on this platform without thinking much of the drop. She was shaking, but it wasn't fear. Not exactly. Her body was anticipating the freefall.

She was going to fly again.

"We gonna live forever, Kass?"

Kass sobbed.

"We gonna live forever, Kass?" Olivia said again, louder.

Winken hauled himself onto the platform. The moonlight glinted off his gold teeth, his grin maniacal. There were fifteen seconds left on the timer.

"We gonna live forever, Livvie," Kass croaked.

Olivia Sharp smiled. Then she sprinted towards the edge. And jumped.

EIDOLON

59

The soldiers threw Liv to the mossy ground outside the nursery. Wilcox wavered for a mere moment. "I truly am sorry. But you've given me no other choice." Then he nodded to the soldier training the gun on her. "Fire."

OUTSIDE

60

The tower exploded.

61

The bedroom door was ajar, and through it came deep, even breathing. Briony poked her head in, knocking gently.

The man sitting on a chair next to the bed stirred. He blinked hazily at her.

"Hi, Aidan," she whispered. "I'm Briony McKinney. Valentina let me in."

He straightened at her name, but then his gaze fell to the teenager sleeping on the bed. The poor girl looked battered, her arm bound in a cast, her face bruised and swollen.

"Is she all right?" Briony said.

"I hope so. They gave her a lot of painkillers." Aidan swiped a hand across his eyes. "Sorry. We spent most of the night at the hospital, and then we had to deal with the police."

"I understand. If you want me to come back–"

"No." He got up. "No, stay." They left the room and he closed the door, not quite all the way. "Any word from Olivia?"

They walked to the kitchen.

"Not yet. Nera Blake's all right, though. I hear she's telling the police everything. And they found remnants of that assassin bloke, only they won't be able to identity him."

"Do they even know to look for Olivia?"

"I'm not sure Nera's said anything about her involvement. Kass is searching the beach now. She'll call me if she finds anything."

"Olivia will be okay," Aidan said. He sounded certain.

The older woman, Valentina, was boiling the kettle. When Aidan sank down at the table, she squeezed his shoulder. He covered her hand with his own in a familial gesture.

"I've listened to your sister's recording," Briony said. "It's pretty damming for Forrest Davidson. I have friends who can help you. You've got a solid case, Aidan."

"Reef," he said.

"Sorry?"

"That's my name. Reef Davidson. It's over now. Might as well take it back."

Briony glimpsed Valentina wiping her eyes with a tea towel.

"All right," Briony said, feeling slightly wrong-footed.

"I'm not registered with any system," Reef said. "The government doesn't know I exist. I suppose I'm going to have to do something about that, if I'm testifying against Forrest."

"I imagine so. I'm sure it involves a lot of paperwork and sitting on hold."

Reef groaned and dropped his forehead to the table. "I picked a hell of a day to quit drinking."

Valentina set a cup of tea in front of Briony. "What about Equinoxx?"

"The dossier's only just been released. It's still circulating, but from the looks of social media, it's gaining traction quickly. The process will be complicated, because Equinoxx is a global corporation and every government will have a different way of dealing with it. It helps that Pravit saved Wilcox's memos ordering the hit on Olivia and another woman in the US. That means the police can act against Wilcox immediately. As for Eidolon, there'll be hearings and ethics committees and it will go on and on and on." Briony sipped her tea. "Mmm, thank you. I needed that."

Reef lifted his head. "Will they rebuild the tower?"

"I hope not. Nera seemed hell-bent on keeping access to Eidolon open when I saw her last, but she let Olivia plant those bombs, so maybe she changed her mind."

Briony's phone rang, making them all jump. She pulled it out and checked the caller ID.

"Is it Kass?" Reef said.

"Yes. But Reef—"

"She'll be fine."

"The river—"

"Liv's a survivor," Reef said, staring desperately at the ringing phone. "Now please…"

"Okay. Sorry. Here we go." Briony dragged in a steadying breath. And answered.

EIDOLON

62

On a long stretch of country road, a StarShine bus rode in a southerly direction. Kazzy had figured out how to switch off the autopilot and was enjoying her time behind the wheel. The babies had been strapped into carriers on the seats. It wasn't the safest way to transport them, but they'd made do with what they had.

Liv sat next to Bobbi, who was clinging to a toy she'd picked up in the nursery. Liv listened to her babbles, stroking her curls and occasionally glancing to the back of the bus where Reef lay. He was being overseen by the vigilant Doctor Nowak. Just as Liv had predicted, he would be fine with some rest.

And then...

They had a job to do. Liv scanned the five other children whose homes were in different parts of the world. She wasn't intimidated by the task. It was, after all, a brand new world out there. Not perfect, but neither was the outside one. And this one had yet to be fully explored.

Liv turned back to the window and smiled. "Look, baby."

Together, she and Bobbi watched as to the east, beyond the hills, the sun began to rise in a clean, summer sky.

OUTSIDE

63

Kass flopped onto the sandy beach, next to her best friend's body.

"Fuck." She wiped the tears from face. "Just...fuck."

Olivia tucked her hands behind her head, gazing up at the sunshine. "I did it."

"No shit."

"It was incredible."

"Did you do a flip?"

"Nah."

"Doesn't count then."

Olivia turned to face her. "You reckon? Might have to do it again."

"Not from the transmission tower." Kass laughed through her tears. "I hear it sort of exploded."

Olivia grinned and stretched her fingers to the endless blue sky. "I guess I'll just have to find another one, ay."

64

"*On the count of five, we jump."*

"*Holy shit, what am I doing?"*

"*Kass, got the GoPro ready?"*

"*It's on."*

The three voices have to shout over the roar of the wind. The footage flashes to patchwork fields and bright blue ocean some 8,000 feet below. Then it lifts to show tandem skydivers — a tall instructor strapped to a teenager — waiting at the plane door.

"*One," says the tall skydiver.*

The teenager flinches.

"*Two—"*

The skydiver jumps. The teenager's shriek is cut off almost immediately. Kass, with the GoPro attached to her helmet, jumps after them.

There's a lot of screaming. A thumbs' up selfie. A whoosh of the parachute. More screaming. Silence as they take in the beautiful scene below. In the distance is a crystal forest, a demolished tower and a bustling hub.

An older woman and a man with a close-shaven beard are waiting on the beach as they land. The moment she's unstrapped, the teenager bounds to them, high on adrenaline as she explains the jump in detail.

The tall instructor takes off her parachute. She joins the bearded man, who pulls her into an embrace. They kiss, blissful in each other's presence, unaware they're being recorded. There's laughter in the kiss. Happiness. Even when the teenager interrupts to hug them both.

The camera swings away from the family as another woman arrives, this one with gray eyes and a Yorkshire accent as she welcomes Kass back to Earth. She comes closer with a sly smile.

The video fades to black.

Author Acknowledgements

Enormous thanks to Atlin Merrick, an extraordinary publisher, editor, and human in general, who not only read several of my manuscripts before finding one that suited Improbable Press, but actively encouraged me to keep submitting after each rejection. Who does that? I'm so lucky to have you in my corner.

Thank you to Narrelle Harris, who steered me to Improbable Press in the first place.

Thanks so much to Bo Starsky, for your careful eyes and thoughtful comments.

This story required expertise in many areas, so thank you to the following people for their time and willingness to share knowledge: Jennifer Liu for the psychology behind trauma, Chris at Skydive Jurien Bay for the parachute information, Rachel Pitt for the personal experience of a broken back, Andi Potts for the sustainability books, David Klup for the lawyer stuff, Rachel Kirk for all things Leeds, and Chris Potts for patiently explaining guns and cars to my clueless self. While all these people contributed to my general understanding, any errors in this manuscript are my own.

Marissa Meyer, thank you as always for the beta read and for bouncing ideas. I'm so glad we're still crit partners after all these years.

Thanks to my best friend Marguerite and my mother Sue for being early readers (and thanks, Mum, for getting me into crime and thriller books well before an "appropriate age" – this book wouldn't have been written without those weekly trips to the library).

Thanks to Scout, who didn't exist when this book was written, but may read it one day and notice the publication year and feel left out. Love you, my little one.

Finally, to Chris Potts. You've already been thanked earlier but you need to be thanked again. You come home from work eager for the next chapter of all my drafts (even the shitty first ones scrawled in notebooks!). You make sacrifices to ensure I always have time to write. You talk plot points and character arcs and worldbuilding with me late into the evening. You drink celebratory rum with me at midnight when I get acceptances and commiserate with me when I get rejections. I don't know what I did to deserve you, but know that I'm grateful each and every day that I have you in my life.

www.ingramcontent.com/pod-product-compliance
Lightning Source LLC
Chambersburg PA
CBHW020508020726
47493CB00001B/243